LOOK AFTER HER

a novel by
Hannah Brown

inanna poetry & fiction series

INANNA PUBLICATIONS AND EDUCATION INC.
TORONTO, CANADA

We gratefully acknowledge the support of the Canada Council for the Arts and the Ontario Arts Council for our publishing program. We also acknowledge the financial support of the Government of Canada.

Cover design: Val Fullard

Look After Her is a work of fiction. All the characters portrayed in this book are fictitious and any resemblance to persons living or dead, is purely coincidental.

Library and Archives Canada Cataloguing in Publication

Title: Look after her : a novel / Hannah Brown.
Names: Brown, Hannah, 1946- author.
Series: Inanna poetry & fiction series.
Description: Series statement: Inanna poetry & fiction series
Identifiers: Canadiana (print) 20190147830 | Canadiana (ebook) 20190147849 | ISBN 9781771336734 (softcover) | ISBN 9781771336741 (epub) | ISBN 9781771336758 (Kindle) | ISBN 9781771336765 (pdf)
Classification: LCC PS8603.R6837 L66 2019 | DDC C813/.6—dc23

Printed and bound in Canada

MIX
Paper from
responsible sources
FSC® C004071

Inanna Publications and Education Inc.
210 Founders College, York University
4700 Keele Street, Toronto, Ontario, Canada M3J 1P3
Telephone: (416) 736-5356 Fax: (416) 736-5765
Email: inanna.publications@inanna.ca   Website: www.inanna.ca

For the original Hedy and her sister whose story inspired mine, for the young sex workers who confided in me, and, most of all, for my late first cousin and first best friend, Ruthie Casselman. We never knew whose idea it was.

1.

W̲E HAVE BEEN FORBIDDEN to come here. This path by
the canal is hidden from view by river willows, and our
mother is convinced it provides cover for the worst of Vienna,
at least the worst of those who travel on foot. But it's the only
place to find what we're looking for.

The light of the day has gone, the sky has fallen to the ground,
and all around us the air is a thick deep blue. We are running
now, and I can feel the tug of my dress flying out behind me.
All I can hear is the sound of my own breathing. I stop to get
a better grip on the empty lantern. My sister doesn't stop.

We lie where we have fallen, on grass that is cold and wet
from evening dew. When we look up, there, at last, sparking
and darting, the reason we are here—the last of the midsummer
fireflies. I stand up, but my sister doesn't move. She's staring
at her dress. And then she repeats what the milkman said this
morning. A new swear word for her.

"Susannah. Do not."

"But look. My dress is torn all along the waist."

She must have stepped on the hem. I tell her to get up, to
go past the fireflies and chase them back towards me and the
lantern.

"Why don't you go and I stay?" She is still on the grass, her
dress tenting around her.

"I have to hold the lantern steady. If you run over to me, as
soon as one flies in, the others will follow." I brace myself and

1

hold the lantern high above my head with both hands.

She lurches to her feet. I watch her walk carefully below the bright net of fireflies. At the bend in the path, she stops. "This is ruining my shoes, Hedy."

And then she is gone from view. I begin to worry, but she reappears, flinging up her arms, a stage comedienne. The fireflies instantly move together, like a lady's skirt gathered to step into a carriage, and when she runs, they flee from her and fly towards me and the open lantern.

~

We crouch in our usual spot on the stair landing, where we can see everyone in the dining room. Susannah sighs. She is a year younger than me, but taller. Just before she stretches out one long leg, I move the lantern to safety. What my sister is going to do, I can usually anticipate. What she is going to say, no one ever knows.

"Mama is going to be so angry." Susannah's eyes dance.

"No, she isn't. She bought these dresses to show us off, and they're even better now. We look amazing. Her guests will tell all their friends about us."

Susannah snorts. "She didn't invite them to look at us."

Our mother is a connection between those who paint and those who have money, and we can see exactly that combination around our dining room table tonight. Egon Schiele painted our portrait four years ago for not very much money, and now that he has become a little famous, the new fellow to watch, our mother is thrilled. Yesterday she reminded us that this dinner was for him, so he could meet people who could further his reputation.

"And yours!" Susannah had widened her eyes, trying to make her remark seem innocent.

After a moment, Mama had said, "Do not." Nothing more. Just, "Do not." Susannah knows to retreat into a better-behaved version of herself whenever Mama says those two words.

People who appreciate the arts, especially painting, and are free in the afternoon to call on one another are often invited to our home. Mama chooses our dresses for these afternoons, and then we're free to wander among the guests. We have learned to approve of the Expressionists and to register doubt about the Jugendstil. Of course, we abhor Makart. So sentimental.

Paintings hang in every room. We are among those who know when someone has acquired a new patron, or what the reviewer in the feuilleton section of the paper is likely to say. But in the evenings, when formal dinner parties are held, we only make a brief appearance before we are shuffled back upstairs. As if we were children.

Tonight will be different. I watch my mother toy with her wine glass. Her topaz ring catches the light. I covet that ring, dark and brilliant. Her dress imitates the striped caftans worn by the eastern Jews here in Vienna, but it is narrower and the tailoring is exquisite. Her friends will be guaranteed to follow her lead, and they will all look like Galicians who have come into money. No one is likely to copy what Herr Schiele is wearing—an odd white suit of his own design. Herr Moser keeps stealing glances at it.

Our neighbour, Herr Mischlinger, shifts in his seat. Susannah and I refer to him as "the Old Dear," as our parents do. But not within his hearing. He has been very nice to our mother, escorting her to art studios in not very nice parts of the city. When she proposed last year that we come along on these excursions, the Old Dear acted as if he were delighted. "Lovely, lovely," he said, and patted first me and then Susannah on the head. He owns four of the best hotels in the city, and Papa says it shows. Now the Old Dear is grousing about the rigors of Werkstätte furniture design and shifts in his chair again.

My mother jumps up, startling everyone. She knows how to make use of the element of surprise. "Do you know what we must have, we humans, more than anything? What we cannot live without?" She looks at each guest, as if sharing a naughty secret. "Air!" She flings open the nearest casement window with a flourish that makes them all laugh.

Fraulein Lowin closes her eyes and tilts her head back. Her soft collar flutters in the breeze. Her opinion, always delivered in a compelling voice, low and husky, is the one Mama seeks at every art show opening. We adore her. When she asks a question, she pays close attention to the answer, first drawing on her cigarette, then holding it out of the way while she listens. Susannah and I often mimic her gestures and offer critiques of each other's imitations. *No, not like that, we say. Like this.*

To us, it is normal to have adult friends like her. We have no friends our own age. No cousins, either, as Papa is an only child and our mother considers our Tante Freyda, her unmarried sister, a Vile Philistine. So do we. They do not speak to each other, not after what happened when we stayed with her.

We do not have any school friends. At our last school, the headmistress dared to chide our mother about Susannah. "Your daughter's vulgarities suggest a familiarity, perhaps, with the talk of ill-trained or poorly supervised servants." Mama repeated this, word for burning word, when she told Papa that it was our last day at any school. It was also the last day for all our servants but our housekeeper, Marta, our least favourite.

No governess ever lasted. Susannah's vocabulary drove them away. So now Papa teaches us mathematics, which Susannah likes and I abhor. Mama teaches us everything else, from the newspapers or from whatever she is reading. Sometimes she reads aloud to us and forgets we're there, reading on in silence. Susannah leans against her, in dreamy collapse.

I sometimes wish I could be like other young girls. I see them at the end of the school day in their uniforms and hats, waving to each other from family carriages or automobiles. Calling to each other.

Herr Mischlinger is complaining about Vienna's crowded streets. "Quite impossible to move with so many foreigners here." He raises his chin as if to avoid a smell.

"But that is our Vienna now, Herr Mischlinger." Fraulein Lowin is very willing to correct opinions she does not share. Susannah and I love this about her.

Mama comes to his rescue. "To succeed in Vienna guarantees your fame, so—the world comes here!" That is how she talks: a pause—and then, delight. The guests beam back at her.

"That, my dear sister..." whispers Susannah.

"Shh! They're talking about art."

"What else do they ever talk about?" She waves away the comment, and cracks the back of her hand on a bannister. And swears. That same word that Victor the milkman said.

"Susannah, do you want them to hear you? You promised."

"I did not." But she covers her mouth with her hand.

"Hedy and Susannah? Would you come down, please, and greet our guests?"

Now. Here we go. "Papa, turn off the electric chandelier first. Please? We have a surprise."

He pulls his mouth down and widens his dark eyes at his guests. "Oh, a surprise." He sips from his glass, and puts it down. "Excuse me. One moment." He makes a little drama out of moving to the ball switch on the wall. Mama smiles at him uneasily. "I install electricity, but if young ladies wish to surprise us...."

We each hold an end of a shawl threaded through the top ring of the lantern and enter the darkened room with our arms raised above our heads. Inside the swaying lantern and inside our knotted dresses, fireflies dart, quick as thoughts. The room falls quiet. Then Herr Schiele's deep voice. "Two small galaxies approach."

Susannah stumbles, but the Old Dear jumps up to steady her. Together, the three of us lower the lantern onto the centre of the table, where it pulses with light. The Old Dear laughs and waggles his fingers. They have a phosphorescent glow. He leads the applause for us. Susannah and I cross our arms and sink down into curtsies. Like prima ballerinas, we gaze kindly, as if from a great distance, at the mortals in the dining room. This has gone very well. I steal a glance at Mama.

Her smile does not match the look in her eyes. "Thank you, darlings. If you can say your good nights, please."

We have not pleased her. The one person who matters.

Everyone stands, glad for the chance to stretch. Herr Mischlinger turns to Susannah. "Tell me, dear child, do you know this song? '*When the night falls silently, the night falls silently, on forests dreaming...*'"

Susannah joins in, off-key as usual, "*Lovers wander forth to see, they wander forth to see...*"

"Perhaps we won't sing for our guests, darlings." Mama has included me to soften the decision. We often exist as a duo when she needs to control Susannah. We move, smiling, from guest to guest. I can do this without thinking, which is good because I am devastated. Our entrance did not impress her. Not at all.

"Fraulein Lowin, what event this week compels your attendance?" Papa is so good at steering the conversation.

"The Klimt opening. You will come, of course."

As if it has just occurred to her, my mother says, "You know our companion this evening, dear Herr Schiele, has been called 'the silver Klimt.' He painted this portrait of our Hedy and Susannah." She flicks on the electric chandelier.

They all turn to the portrait of us hanging on the wall, where our younger selves gaze directly at the viewer as if we are waiting for a turn.

Herr Mischlinger takes a step forward. "Lovely, lovely. Perhaps, Herr Schiele, I might impose upon you? Would you permit a visit to your studio?"

"Please, you are welcome to visit my studio. Any Tuesday." Herr Schiele hands Herr Mischlinger his card. "But, I must warn you." He stands taller and grasps the back of his chair. "Klimt is very good, but you will find I am not he. I share his devotion to the portrait, yes. But what I do, no one else has done. No one. My subjects are not third-person symbols; they do not disappear into decorative pattern in the foreground as they do in Klimt's portraits. No. No, I free them from any background. I paint young people, yearning and, frankly, too often, hungry or cold. I paint in the first person, raw and specific, real human energy confronting you directly..." He stops abruptly.

Silence. Everyone stares at him.

Papa slaps the table. "Passionate and outspoken, sir! Bravo!"

"Passion, like truth, should not be hidden."

When we sat for him, Herr Schiele often made pronouncements in that deep voice. We chanted his "desserts should be doubled for all those who sit still" for two weeks, but Marta never relented, no matter how manly we made our voices.

"I might counter, sir, both as a hotelier and a fellow somewhat familiar with this city, that in Vienna, we do sometimes veil the truth. In what other city is the art of the charming lie so appreciated?" Herr Mischlinger looks around for approval, a nod of endorsement. A smile.

Nothing. No one says a thing, not even our mother. It's embarrassing, that tired old saying about Vienna. It is precisely the opposite of what is championed all the time in our home: that art should be frank and true. He tries a different tack, smiling as though he hadn't noticed the silence. "Do you collect art, Frau Moser?"

"I'm a Jew, aren't I?"

Herr Mischlinger explodes, a very loud laugh. No one else joins him.

This time Papa comes to his rescue. "Oh, I am remiss!" Everyone turns to him. "I almost forgot to thank my darlings for their wonderful gift to this evening."

"Yes." Fraulein Lowin draws upon her cigarette and smiles. "Actually, Hedy and Susannah, my compliments on your *coup de théâtre*. Very eloquent, visually."

Susannah beams at her, and I thank her for being so very kind. I avoid looking at Mama, focusing on Herr Schiele's suit instead. It has strange wide lapels meeting at a single button below the waist, where I suddenly realize I shouldn't look.

"And now, my darlings." Papa extends a hand in the direction of the staircase. "It's time to return from whence you came." He begins to sing more of "Glow-worm." He has a baritone voice with a catch in it. The catch makes all the difference. Papa has impeccable taste for what goes with what, and the song's hesitations are perfect for us to go up the dark stairs one step at a time, swishing our skirts like coquettes. The grown-ups join in, lingering on "*glimmer, glimmer*," half-laughing at the fact that they know the words to such a sentimental song. "*Light the path below, above, and lead us on....*"

Herr Mischlinger knows all the words. We are around the corner of the stairs and out of sight before the song ends, but we can hear Herr Mischlinger sing the last two words, the *to* swooping down the scale, and the last word, *love*, sung meaningfully, softly. A little applause, a little laughter, a little talking all at once. We return to the landing to eavesdrop, to hear what else they will say about us.

Nothing. We're going to be abandoned. Left at home, again.

Susannah takes my hand. "Wait, Hedy. We still have a chance when Mama pretends to be inspired."

"What would you think...?" Mama begins. "The evening is so lovely—oh, let's go to Sachers, for torte! We can return for the savouries, if we wish, later,"

A happy buzz of agreement. An occasion for everyone to be seen together, those with money and those with talent. Mama's proposal sound spontaneous, but earlier in the week we had heard her reserve a table at Sacher's. Susannah pulls me to my feet as the guests fill the hallway with buoyant chatter and, hand in hand, we rush down the stairs, costumes still blinking.

"You know—we're in the mood for torte, too!" I imitate my mother as best I can. Susannah donates a bright smile.

My mother turns to me. "Hedy. Dear child. You and your sister are not old enough to accompany adults in the evening."

I beckon for her to come closer, and whisper, "But we are! According to you, we both are!"

"When? When did I say that?"

Her beautiful face so close. Her perfume, *Inconnu*. I lower my voice. "When ... you know ... what happened to Susannah last month?"

She straightens, flushing. I continue to assemble and present my evidence.

"You slapped her face to bring the roses back in her cheeks, you said. Like when it happened to me. You slapped my face, remember, Mama, last year? Susannah asked you if you were going to do that every month, remember? You laughed and you said no, that we were now young adults, young ladies, and you said..."

"*Hedvig!* Stop. You are not going." When she says the formal version of my name, like that, drawn out—*Ehhhd-vidj!*—like a wind-up and a slap, she is not to be crossed.

"What is it, Esther?"

"Actually, Papa, we had hoped that we might join you."

Mama gives him a fierce, fast glance but turns to smile at her guests. "Young girls are always in such a hurry to grow up."

The adults look indulgently at us. Susannah's smile has disappeared. Slack shoulders, sulky mouth. I don't feel like smiling either.

Herr Mischlinger tips his head to one side. "I'll escort you to Sacher's myself, ladies, if your parents will permit, some afternoon? We'll go in my Daimler? I keep it in perfect running order." He touches a finger to his eyebrow.

Papa has confided that the Old Dear says those exact words, 'in perfect running order,' whenever he talks about his automobile. I catch Papa's glance. I touch my finger to my eyebrow and he smiles. My conspirator. I touch his arm.

"Do let us go with you tonight, Papa."

"Hedy, my darling, you are charming, but your dresses look like you could signal for Marconi!"

Laughter. He will never go against our mother.

Herr Schiele makes a bow towards us. "Your daughters have a sophisticated sense of what is beautiful, Frau Edelstein." I have a sudden hot feeling in my nose, and my eyes sting. He understands. I concentrate on how he has brushed and waxed his short hair to stand straight up.

The Old Dear continues. "Tomorrow, or the next day—what do you say, my dear Esther? If you permit, I'll let them sit up front with me."

His automobile does cause heads to turn; it's dark red with a spoked spare wheel on the passenger door. When you sit inside, the sound of the engine is like listening to a waterfall of tin, drowning out anything we say from the back seat. The front seat could be a pleasant change.

His perfect manners are persuasive. Mama nods.

"Till then." He bows and kisses the air over my hand. I lower my eyes and turn my head to one side, perfectly Viennese.

Frau Moser clasps her hands to her large bosom. "They are darling girls, Esther, truly."

"Yes, they are. Here's the splendid Marta with our wraps and hats."

Marta holds the door open for the adults who gather in the lobby. As the warm night air rushes in, Susannah and I rush out, waving goodbye from the stone step, our dresses still sparking. The conversation floats back on the night air.

"If this weather continues, we are going to escape to Baden bei Wein for a few days."

"Too many people. I prefer Bad Ragaz."

The dark blue wallpaper chosen for our bedroom is not childish. Nor are the stained glass lamps on either side of the bed. Where we live, Mama has pointed out more than once, is one of the best addresses in the city. But tonight I wanted Mama to see that we could contribute to an evening's pleasure, that we could leave the background for the foreground, where the adults live. Where my mother lives.

"Hedy, do you think our dresses would have caused a sensation in Sacher's?"

"Or a scandal." I point to the two large phosphorescent handprints on her dress where Herr Mischlinger had steadied her. "But I suspect Mama realized Sacher's is too well-lit to show off these dresses. They only look wonderful if the room is dark."

"Ha. She just doesn't want our company. Fine. I don't want hers."

"Yes, you do. I do."

"Why did Papa make that comment about Marconi? Did he think I looked stupid? You said they would be amazed, and that we would get to join them."

"He thought you looked Italian. They *were* amazed."

"And yet." Susannah looks around our bedroom. "Here we are."

"For now."

When it becomes obvious that our parents and their guests will not be returning any time soon, we open the bedroom windows wide and undo the knots holding our skirts to our underslips. Anyone outside who happens to look up will see a small constellation of fireflies escaping into the night air.

2.

WE WERE GOING NOWHERE. Our parents were sick. Everyone we knew had escaped the August heat of Vienna to vacation at their usual holiday spas. Susannah had been looking forward to Baden-Baden, and had told Papa that with her height and a little lip rouge she was sure she could enter the baccarat lounge. She explained that she had figured out a system. He had laughed and teased, "In that case, with your winnings, I will stay home with your mother and let you take my place at the stock exchange."

But on the morning after the party, he had crawled from his bedroom to one of the guest bedrooms, and by the end of the day, Mama had staggered to the other one. They had never slept apart, but their own bedding was ruined and the opened transom windows over the doors of the guest bedrooms would at least allow them to hear one another. By nightfall, they had each asked that the doctor be called for the other.

When the doctor was about to leave, we blocked his passage down the stairs and asked when our parents would be well again.

"They will get better when they get better," he said, and brushed past us, moving us out of the way with his brand-new doctor's satchel.

Our usual doctor was on holiday himself, which may have been why, when the young doctor told Marta to burn the soiled bed linens and towels, she didn't. Instead, she poured boiling water into the laundry tubs and scrubbed. The smell of carbolic soap filled all the rooms, even ours on the third floor. When I asked Marta why she wasn't using the incinerator, she said she had no time to go out and purchase fresh bed linens and towels and besides, she had to guard against me and my sister sneaking in to see our parents, which we might have done if not for the fierce reaction of the young doctor.

He had scolded us comprehensively when he saw us trying to slip some playing cards under the door to tempt Papa to get up. Our father had taught us how to pick a card, any card, and how to turn the deck around and say *"Sim, salabim!"* before plucking the correct card and holding it up. I was quick with my hands, and I practised. Susannah was astonishingly good at distracting Mama, our usual audience.

Marta's hands became so raw her knuckles bled. Groceries continued to be delivered to the service entrance leading into the kitchen, and we were told to get cheese, bread, milk, and apples out of the icebox ourselves. The broth and ginger tea were for our parents. We were not to light the stove. We were not to.... Marta couldn't think of anything else, but it was obvious she thought we might do what we shouldn't. She glared. We were to amuse ourselves, wash our hands, and, above all, we were to do everything quietly.

The morning of that first day, when only our father was sick, Marta, as instructed, had gone outside with us for half an hour so we might practise riding our new bicycles—Sterns, the latest and the best, like the British Stanleys, with their high handlebars and leather seats.

Outside on the Schottenring, Susannah didn't care if she crashed into the curbs, and she did. I was methodical, and didn't. The heat was oppressive. Even the lindens drooped, and Marta wanted us to come in. We argued with her, but it was not true that we had mocked her, which is what she told our mother. "Do what Marta asks." Mama held onto the doorframe, her eyes glassy. "And if you care nothing for me, you could at least give your father a little peace."

It was awful that she thought we didn't care about her. And as for Papa, we were so worried. Susannah stood near his door, reading the newspaper aloud. It was a report of the mayor's speeches, and she emphasized the word 'Jews' every time it occurred. Usually this prompted him to leap up, grab the paper, and say, "Here, let me see that."

But this time there was no response. We went to our room and didn't talk for a long time. The curtains were closed against the heat, and the room was stifling. We flipped through our mother's art books. The air felt heavy, slow. We soaked our hair in the bathtub and wrapped damp towels around ourselves. There was nothing to do.

Susannah tiptoed down the hallway to our parents' ruined bedroom and returned with Italian scarves and delicate georgette nightgowns. It was thrilling to pull Mama's things over our bodies. It was a way to climb into who she was. Like everyone else, like our father, we adored her. *Esther.* But our mother was a mystery, not to be hugged, not to be kissed. And not to be crossed, either.

We tied her scarves around our chests. We bent our arms in postures of anguish, eyes beseeching the heavens.

"Rescue me!" Susannah cried.

"Oh, my love!" I murmured.

Susannah produced a stick of Mama's lip rouge. I felt a rush of heat to my cheeks. I remembered another afternoon when we had been bored.

"Susannah, do you think Mama ever told Papa about us playing doctor?"

"Why would she?" Susannah dabbed the rouge onto her lips, and then onto my already burning cheeks.

A year ago, we closed our bedroom door. Lie down, Miss. This will take a moment.

Yes, Herr Doctor.

One of us lies on the bed, obedient, clothes pulled up, while the other touches.

Now be still, no giggling.

A stick of lip rouge pressed down and turned to make a bright red dot above a cleft: a Spanish exclamation mark.

The doctor becomes the patient and lies down for her turn.

Eyelashes drawn firmly around nipples. A rosebud mouth around the navel. Lie still.

Herr Doctor, it tickles.

Yes, it seems your belly-button wishes to speak.

We had both burst out laughing, and the spell was broken. We were still laughing, still half-naked, when Mama had walked in on us. "Do not," was all she said, and left. We pulled up our clothing in silence that day and went downstairs to bother Marta.

I piled my hair on top of my head. I looked at least sixteen, I thought. We gazed over our shoulders and pouted at what we saw in the mirror. I tied a silk scarf tighter around my chest, and pressed my elbows together.

Susannah jumped up to stand beside me and arched her back. She tipped her head to one side and draped one hand over the opposite shoulder. She jerked her striped scarf up, and the effort made her stumble backwards onto the bed. "Oh, to hell with this. I'm going to read the paper for something to do."

There was no point telling her not to swear. She thumped downstairs to the drawing room and stayed until it grew dark, poring over the newspapers Marta had bought for Mama, who said she would read them when she got better.

I followed Susannah to the drawing room. She ignored me. I grabbed one of the newspapers and pair of library scissors and took both back to our room. I spread out pages from the *Neue Freie Presse* and drew stems, each with a leaf, and cut them out. I glued these along a length of stiff card and tied the ends of the card together with a ribbon. I painted everything green. When I put the crown on, the leafy stems bobbed and waved on my head, like the top of a tree in the wind. It needed something: I drew a small dog on the front of the crown. Its collar read *From Esther*. This was to remind Mama of how much I longed for a dog.

I approached Marta carefully. She finally agreed to deliver the crown and when she came back, she delivered our mother's message, loud enough for her employer to hear, that she had been told to say that the hat was beautiful, and it was just what was needed for headaches. "When your mother is better, she will make a hat for Hedy. Also with a dog. And kisses, she sends kisses." Marta finished with an exhalation of breath and hurried away.

"Mama sends kisses."

"But only," Susannah said, "to you."

The next morning, we flattened ourselves against the hallway mirror when Marta hurried past with another packet from the chemist. Susannah showed me what she had written beside the mouths of all those lucky enough to appear in photographs in the morning paper. She thought it was funny, all those important people cursing with abandon. She drew moustaches on the women. This gave me an idea for a ruse so we could keep riding our bicycles.

We had never stolen anything of Papa's before. There had been no need. He wasn't mysterious or distant. He hugged us and played with us. I wondered aloud what Papa would do if he caught us.

"He only threatened to beat us once, when we set fire to Tante Freyda's curtains, Hedy."

"When *you* set fire to the curtains."

Susannah ignored the correction. "Let's do it tonight. I can't stand listening to Marta. *Ennn hanh, ennnnn, hanh,* like a donkey, all night long. No wonder she can't get the milkman to marry her. And if Papa catches us, *good*—it will mean he is better."

That night, once Marta's snoring became steady as a metronome, we slipped out of the house, each wearing one of Papa's full-body wool bathing suits. They were too big for us, but belted, they looked like the clothing of the racing champions in Mama's newspapers. We pulled his socks up to our knees, and tucked our hair into watch caps to tilt over our foreheads. We opened the front door and left it unlocked.

One o'clock in the morning. The street was empty. We sat on the stone step to put on our shoes and strutted down the narrow laneway to the drive shed, our shoulders held back like men in the moonlight. When we walked the bicycles out into the cool night air, we could hear geese on the canal, calling.

We rode down our street to the bourse, wheeled around, and pedalled hard past the gesturing statues until we arrived back to our home, exhilarated with the exercise and with our own daring. There was nothing like riding a bicycle, the smoothing *now* of it.

"One more time!" Susannah called over her shoulder.

I had to follow. What if she talked to someone?

Marta noticed how late we slept in. She made the doctor examine us, but we did not suffer from diarrhea, only from embarrassing questions about diarrhea. Our voices were not hoarse, just heard too often, in Marta's opinion.

"These are healthy young things," the doctor said. "The mother and the father, on the other hand…" He took his glasses off and beckoned for Marta to follow him into the hallway. "Be good, girls," he said as he left.

"Be good and bored, girls, you mean," Susannah warbled loudly at the closing door. "Hedy, what do you say? Shall we visit someone? Maybe the Moser brothers would like to chase you around."

I had rather liked being chased at the Moser house by those two older boys after the Purim play, and it was a point of contention between us. "The Mosers are like everyone else we know, gone to Bad Ragaz. Or Baden bei Wein."

We heard our father moan. We were still, listening. Then Marta came pounding back up the stairs.

"We don't even like the Mosers, Susannah. Any of them."

"I know."

We listened. Nothing.

"Did you see the flowers the Old Dear left for Mama? He told Marta he would call again on his way back from Herr Schiele's studio."

We listened. Only Marta, going back down the stairs.

"Why don't we go there?"

"To the studio? We don't have any money for a fiacre."

"We could sneak some from Papa's desk."

"Susannah, no!"

"Then let's ride our bicycles. I'm going to, even if you won't."

3.

THE WOMAN WHO OPENED THE DOOR had an abundance of red hair and sorrowful blue eyes. When we introduced ourselves, she made a little bow with her hand on her chest. "*Gruss Gott*. Fraulein Wally Neuzil." I saw her cast a worried glance at Herr Schiele.

"Your mother knows you're here?" he asked.

We had never been inside his studio. He had painted our portrait in our drawing room, with canvas under his easel to protect Papa's pale wool carpet.

"No, Herr Schiele, but we're donating quiet to the house today. Please don't worry." I was distracted by the sight of an older girl sitting on a padded bench in the middle of the room. "The doctor says we're fine." The girl had thick blonde hair, but a *schnabel*, a beak, for a nose. "They're keeping us separate," I said. *Black grit in the corners of her eyes. A lurid green skirt in some shiny material.*

Susannah walked up to her. "Are you the maid?"

"No." She had a black blouse with a high collar around a dirty neck. "The model."

I remembered my manners. "Gruss Gott, Fraulein."

She nodded and extended her hand to me. Every single one of her fingernails was bordered in black. "Margarete Gaboncz."

I took her hand, but so gingerly Susannah laughed.

"Hedvig Edelstein. My sister and I have also been models for Herr Schiele."

She gave us and our clothing an imperious appraisal and said, "I don't think so. You wouldn't be allowed by your parents."

"The painting hangs in our dining room."

She looked skeptical. "Is that true, Egon?"

"Yes." He removed a paintbrush from his mouth and examined the improved shape of the bristles. "It is well placed, actually, between those windows."

The look of shock on the older girl's face delighted Susannah. Anyone familiar with the life of the arts in Vienna—our mother's favourite phrase—knew that Herr Schiele painted very frank nudes of himself and of others. These were not at all shocking to me, nor to my sister. But no need to spoil Susannah's fun by admitting to this Philistine of a girl that we were nine and ten years old in the painting and fully clothed.

"Girls, I think, perhaps..." Fraulein Neuzil hesitated. "Do you think, Egon, it would be best if I escorted them home?"

An alarming offer. We thanked her, said it wasn't necessary, and explained that we knew the way.

"Yes, we ride our Sterns everywhere," said Susannah. "All over the city."

"Perhaps a quick note, then, to take back to your mother. Please, girls, do sit down."

I did immediately. Herr Schiele was making short, rhythmic brush strokes in blue-white gouache around a figure. I was interested in the *work* of art, how an artist worked, unlike my sister, who flopped down on the settee to stare at the Gaboncz girl. Fraulein Neuzil pulled out a chair at a small writing desk and sat.

Another surprise. Right by her feet, a boy. One hand with large, long, flat fingers rested on the side of his sleeping face. His other hand clutched the handle of a canvas school bag with a school insignia on its flap, *Akademisches Gymnasium*. That school was attended by the offspring of the very rich, like the Moser brothers. My admirers. This boy would never be allowed inside its doors.

Margarete Gaboncz had followed my gaze. "That's Kaspar. Egon and Wally allow us to stay here any time we want. They don't kick us out like they do the others. We don't do nothing—we're quiet and we just sit. Or sleep."

I knew that as soon as Fraulein Neuzil finished scribbling her note, she would suggest we return home. But it was agony to be in our home, to hear Mama or Papa moan, and to be unable to do anything but keep quiet.

Susannah was not interested in doing nothing. Not at home, and not here, either. "Fraulein Margarete, would you like to try riding a Stern?"

"Susannah, we have only just arrived."

This was the second time in one day that my younger sister had proposed an activity instead of waiting for my lead. What was she thinking? Besides, she knew it was not done, to arrive and immediately leave as if the company were not interesting. To me, the company of Herr Schiele was intensely interesting—that focus, that relentless patience.

The girl looked at Susannah and then back at me. If she hoped for drama, she was out of luck. We never fought in front of others. Susannah came over to sit down beside me. I continued to watch Herr Schiele. He painted as if no one else were there: his face slack, his dark eyes seeing only what was in front of him, or within him.

Kaspar woke up and immediately tucked himself under Fraulein Neuzil's arm. Susannah asked how old he was, and he hesitated. Margarete answered for him. "He just looks small for twelve. Right, Wally? Except for those big hands. And I look older than fifteen. Much older. Where do you live, Hedvig?" She jerked a thumb at Susannah. "And why is her hair so blonde when yours is so dark?"

"You don't have to tell her anything, Hedvig."

Kaspar sat up. "But why are you still in the city in August? All the other rich people have gone away. And those Sterns! How much did those bicycles cost?"

This intense interest was flabbergasting. Stimulating. A distraction from what was filling me with dread. I didn't want to go home. I had a wild hope that if we stayed away long enough, Papa would be smoking by the open casement window when we returned. Mama would be ridiculing the reviews in the newspaper supplement. They would be laughing.

I don't care if they take away our bicycles or scold us. I need them to be well.

"You two are my first rich friends." Kaspar beamed. How likeable he was! He and Margarete called Herr Schiele and Fraulein Neuzil by their first names. Egon, we knew, of course, but we had never addressed him that way. Fraulein Neuzil—Wally—didn't seem to mind their lack of manners, and was solicitous of Kaspar, insisting that he take a slice of cake that we had declined. And she joked with Margarete as if she were an adult. Is this how poor people behave, like pirates, no one deferential to anyone else? Pirates, Papa had told me, only obeyed laws they had made up amongst themselves.

Herr Schiele stood back from the easel.

"Please come outside, Hedy," said Kaspar. "I can drive an automobile. And I have driven a pair of fiacre horses, more than once. But, please, I need you to show me how to ride a bicycle."

Who could refuse that smile?

Kaspar was quick to balance and sped about in figure eights. As for Margarete, she turned out to be as terrible a cyclist as Susannah—worse, as she not only crashed into curbs, she swore in public as well. I pretended not to hear what was making my sister explode with laughter, her eyes full of tears. Margarete's crude inventions delighted Susannah. She didn't care that her bicycle was getting damaged. Margarete did and tried to straighten the bicycle seat.

Kaspar said, "Here." He was surprisingly strong. He gripped the seat, grimaced, and it was once again aligned perfectly.

"You're hired!" said Susannah. "You can be in charge of all my bicycles, and all of my automobiles."

He grinned, tucking his cheek into his shoulder. He was much nicer-looking than either of the Moser brothers. Susannah apparently thought so, too.

"Unfortunately, at the moment, I don't happen to have any horses." Susannah shrugged.

Kaspar hopped on my bicycle again, and announced, "I do! To the bourse!"

I was aghast. He was going to ride my bicycle to the stock exchange, to my father's place of work. Margarete tipped over on Susannah's bicycle trying to catch up to him. Although the bourse wasn't far away from the studio, just several blocks south, this destination was alarming. The Vienna stock exchange was so close to our home that on rainy days we could see Papa's umbrella almost as soon as he left the building. We barely got wet at all when we ran to join him.

We can't let these two near our home. Our parents will be appalled that we have even talked to them, never mind spent most of today in their company. And they are riding our new bicycles.

Susannah ran after them, laughing her head off. I walked as quickly as I could.

She surely won't tell them where we live.

By the time I caught up to them, all three were sprawled on the steps of the bourse with the bicycles in a heap. I collapsed beside them, out of breath. And almost immediately got to my feet. If Papa knew I was sitting on the entrance steps of the Vienna bourse, his place of work, he would be horrified. I moved away to lean against the entrance pillar.

"If you stand here, friends," said Kaspar, "you will see my horses." We craned our necks. "Neptune's chariot and team in marble," he announced, as if he himself were Neptune, or a connoisseur of heroic statuary.

"I don't see any damn horses," said Margarete.

"Move over here, Margarete," said Susannah. "You can see their front hooves. They look like they're about to run off the roof of the building."

But Margarete wasn't looking up at the roof of the stock exchange. She was fluttering her fingers by her head, waving at someone down the street. I turned to look, and ducked behind the pillar. Susannah instantly did the same. I didn't have to say anything, thankfully. She was far too used to doing everything I did.

Heading east towards his home—which was immediately beside ours—was the Old Dear, in that dark red Daimler. He had said he would call at the house again. If he saw us, he would certainly tell Marta that we were loitering, like street children, on the steps of the bourse, with actual street children. And Marta would tell Mama.

"Margarete!" Mischlinger leaned out from his automobile to talk. "What, dear child, are you doing here on my street?"

"Hoping to see you, of course." She swished her ugly green skirt back and forth. "Could you give me a ride back to Egon's studio? And," she added, hauling Susannah forward from her hiding place, "may I introduce my friend, Fraulein Susannah Edelstein?"

He was startled. "Your friend?"

"And your neighbour, Herr Mischlinger." Susannah drew herself up to her full height.

"Can we come with you?" Margarete smiled. Her teeth were so white in that dirty face.

"Fraulein Edelstein. Does your mother know you are out with this one, with Fraulein Gaboncz?"

Susannah lied. "Of course she does."

"And your sister?"

She shrugged. And like that, without a backward glance, she followed Margarete to the car, climbed into the front seat and away they went, past his home and past ours. They turned north. I was astonished.

Kaspar joined me. "So, where exactly is your place on this street?" He picked up Susannah's bicycle and straddled the cross bar. Despite a broken front tooth, he had a sweet, happy smile, like the rat who got away from the ship. He wouldn't alarm Mama the way someone like Margarete would.

I wanted to tell Mama about being at the bourse with those two before anyone else did. The Old Dear was always doing that, telling her things that we did. He always said we were 'lovely, lovely,' even though he must have known what he said would get us in trouble.

We stowed the bicycles in our drive shed, and Kaspar put his shoulders back and walked with his head held as high as he could toward the service entrance. It was open, but the door leading to our kitchen was locked.

Please, please, don't still be sick.

"My parents aren't well. We will have to be very quiet."

We slipped around to the front. At the door to our building, we saw the young doctor talking to Marta. Kaspar didn't need to be told to crouch down. We watched the doctor shake his head and climb into the waiting fiacre. Marta wiped her eyes with the corner of her apron, leaving red marks from her cracked and bloody knuckles.

"My God in Heaven," she said. "Now what?" She crossed herself, and used the doorframe to haul herself inside.

Kaspar moved up the outside steps immediately and peeked into the lobby. He beckoned and whispered, "Come on!"

The door to our apartment was ajar. Beside a reeking laundry basket at the bottom of the stairs sat my suitcase and Susannah's. Marta was talking on Papa's new telephone. "But Fraulein Freyda, you must! Your sister is so ill!"

Tante Freyda. Surely we were not being sent to her. Not after what happened the last time. My sister and I had never seen an adult so angry.

Kaspar nudged my arm. We stepped over the threshold into the apartment. Kaspar closed the door carefully, not all the way, and darted directly up the stairs, spraddle-legged. I couldn't make my feet move properly. He came back and took my hand. "Walk on the outside of the steps," he whispered. "Then they won't creak."

When we got to the landing, Kaspar hung back. I went ahead and listened outside Papa's room. No sound. I was too frightened to knock on his door. I opened the door to my mother's room instead. "Mama?" *Please, please be well.*

She turned, her head soaked in sweat. She looked confused. "Hedvig?" I must have been in silhouette from the bright afternoon sun streaming through the window blinds. "No! Stop. Don't come any closer. Do not. My Hedy, you can't be here. You have to go away."

"To Tante Freyda? How can you even think to send us to her? You said you were never going to talk to her again."

"Darling, please. You must be with … where the air is fresh. The lake. Where you can be healthy. Freyda is your only aunt. Where is Marta?"

I walked towards my mother. "I want you to pay attention to getting better."

My mother's gaze was awful. "I will. No closer, Hedy."

"Do you give your word?"

"Of course." She beamed at me, smiling with all she had. I felt the whole room light up. It was very bright in there. My knees felt funny.

"My Hedy. Take my ring from the box on the dressing table." *What was she saying?*

"I'm perspiring so much, it won't stay on." I stared at her. "You will give it back when I am better."

Oh. When she is better. I pried open the yellow leather box that had always held the ring. My leaves-and-dog hat sat by the mirror.

My mother kept smiling. "Hedy, my darling, you know I love you and your sister. Look after her. Promise me." Her voice was so hoarse.

"I promise."

She blew a kiss and turned her face to the wall. I stood still, who knows for how long, looking. *I love you, too.*

Kaspar was in the hallway, a cigar stuck behind his ear. I couldn't move. He adjusted his flat cap and smiled. His broken tooth. His shirt front, bulging. I could hear Marta downstairs on the telephone, frantic this time, talking to her love, Viktor the milkman. Kaspar took my hand. His rough fingers. He led me down the staircase, past the waiting suitcases.

Once we were on the bicycles, he lit the cigar. I felt for the ring in my pocket. *Yes.* We headed north. Schools and trade institutes had dismissed for the day, and nuns moved in relentless lines to four o'clock services. Evening shift workers rolled their shoulders in anticipation of that night's demand on their bodies. Vienna was inclined to ignore any untoward thing and was in a hurry to get to work, to prayers, to the pub, or to dinner at home. No one paid any attention to us.

The traffic became heavy. Kaspar tucked the cigar back behind his ear and darted Susannah's bicycle through the traffic. I followed. He knew the city. We lurched between cars and carriages, avoided the trolley cars and, even worse, their tracks. On the Ringstrasse, its diagonally-laid bricks were going to toss us, so we rode on the wide sidewalk until we got to the first statue, the man holding onto the wild horse. We pedalled up the empty ramp. Kaspar careened on an angle so he could slap the sandalled toe of Herodotus.

"For luck!" he shouted back to me, but I was past the statue, past luck, already down the ramp, past the marble men with leaves in their hair. The sound of the slick glicking of the gears was soothing. The hissing of fine gravel underneath the tires where there had been construction calmed me. I let all thoughts run through my head without judging them, except this one: *I have to talk to Susannah before we go home.*

4.

HERR SCHIELE WAS HELPING Fraulein Neuzil into the front seat of the Daimler. When he saw me and Kaspar, he grabbed his head with both hands. "Wally, what now? There are four of them!"

Fraulein Neuzil patted his arm and hopped out. "They can wait here for us, Egon." She let us into the studio and told us not to allow anyone else in. "Touch nothing that isn't yours. Take your shoes off. We're going to a restaurant in one of his hotels. We'll be back soon, no more than a couple of hours."

From the doorway, Margarete called out, "I like the cut of your suit, Egon." He was dressed in another odd suit, ochre in colour this time, with cuffs on the pants.

"Tell Werkstätte! Maybe they'll take my clothing designs!" He hopped in the back seat where we usually sat when we went on excursions with our mother and the Old Dear.

Initially, Susannah had found those excursions boring, but once she knew he couldn't hear her over the engine, she called out terrible things, like "I hope we kill a pedestrian!" or "Your hair pomade smells like eau de underarm!"

Every time, he called back, "Lovely, lovely." We guffawed into the cushions, trying not to give her game away. Some of the best afternoons had been spent muffling our laughter in the back seat of that car.

We all crowded to the window and watched them drive away. As soon as they were out of sight, Kaspar picked up the school

briefcase and hurried into the water closet. Margarete turned
to me. "Want to see something?"

"You aren't supposed to touch anything."

"Nothing that isn't mine." She took Susannah to the water
closet. "Kaspar, don't worry, we won't look! Susannah and
me have to get something."

They dragged a wicker basket out by its leather handles,
and Kaspar slammed the door behind them. Margarete pulled
a folded sheet off the top of the basket and turned it upside
down. Dirty knives, forks with food crusted on them, and
two silver teapots clattered to the floor. "I have to wash these
before Wally gets back. Go pump some water in the basin,
Susannah."

"What are you going to do with this cutlery?"

"Cutlery." She smiled at Susannah. "I'm going to sell this
cutlery, my rich friend, to the same fellow my father sells his
stuff to." She dumped everything into the basin, and handed
one end of the sheet to Susannah. "Dry these, fast." She plunged
her hands in the water. "Hedy, want to help?"

"No, thank you. Where did you get those things?"

"Me and Kaspar sneak into houses and take whatever we
can in the first five minutes. We carry the laundry basket with
a clean sheet on top. We look like we're delivering laundry."

Susannah stopped drying a fork. "Wait, how do you know
which houses to go into?"

"You just go right up like you're supposed to be there. Once
you're in, you grab whatever you can, throw it in the basket,
and go. The folded sheet goes back on top to hide what you
take. If you get stopped on the way in, you just say, 'Isn't this...'
and then you say the wrong address. And then you say, 'Oh.
Sorry, Ma'am.' And get the hell out of there."

"Did you bring the sheet from home?"

"No, from a clothesline behind a brothel. They always have
lots of sheets out on the line. Kaspar hopped the wall and got it."

Susannah balanced a fork on a finger. "But, Margarete.

How much money will you get for this? Hell, it's not even good quality."

"Oh, no? You want to come with me? The guy will be in an alley not far from here with his wagon soon. And you just swore."

"So?"

"Susannah!" I had to step in. "What if you were to be caught? Mama would be so embarrassed! And I need to talk to you."

"Oh, please." Margarete dumped the water out of the basin and hung it on its nail. "Look, big sister, they aren't going to arrest someone who's dressed like her and talks like you. As long as she doesn't say 'hell' in front of them. Or shit. Or piss. Or…" She continued with other possibilities, some quite disgustingly impossible. Susannah was collapsing with laughter. "Glad this work makes you so happy. Put the forks with the forks, and the knives with the knives. Teapots on the bottom. Are you coming, Kaspar, or do you want to sit and wait for Wally and Egon?"

"I don't want to leave Fraulein Hedy here by herself."

"I'm coming." Susannah grabbed a handle of the basket and shoved her feet into her shoes without doing them up. Margarete had never taken her shoes off.

"If I let you come with me, you can't tell anyone."

"I promise."

"*Kazeet choke alohma*, as we say at home. I kiss your hand, Susannah." She lowered her dirty, pretty face over Susannah's hand. "Now you kiss mine." Susannah did. They looked at me.

"I'm not kissing anything. Susannah, I have to tell you something."

"She'll listen to you when we come back. We have to get this out of here before Wally and Egon return. If the Galician isn't in the alley, we'll come right back."

Before I could tie my shoes, they were out the door and gone. The last thing my mother had told me to do was to look after my sister, and already I didn't know where she was.

Kaspar patted my arm. "Don't worry, Fraulein Hedy. We'll find them."

We rode the bicycles around the alleys until we were back at the studio. We had seen no one. I could hear sparrows arguing in the bushes. For the second time in my life, I sat down like a beggar on the outdoor steps. *I can't keep arguing with Mama, she's too sick. But I can't force Susannah to go to Fuschl, to Tante Freyda, either. Not that I want to go. We have to make Mama understand.*

Kaspar opened the door and swept his hand towards the open room. His interpretation of a perfect host. "Do come in, my dear friend." One of Papa's cigars was still tucked behind his ear. Theft, but to say so would have been embarrassing. I had also noticed that his shirt was no longer bulging, and his canvas school bag was.

I knew. Money from Papa's desk. I could feel myself blushing. I was angry, but I didn't want to be rude and let him know what I suspected, especially when he was making such an effort to be formal and gracious. I tried not to look at him directly.

"Oh, thank you, but you know," I said, as casually as I could, "I think I would like to wait outside, if you don't mind."

"Of course, dear Fraulein Hedy." He followed me out and sat beside me, folding those big hands neatly in his lap. "It is lovely to sit on the steps with you."

And somehow, I liked sitting with him, too. He put his arm around my shoulder, and kept it there until Wally and Egon returned in a hotel fiacre. Kaspar was smiling, completely at ease. I felt in my pocket. The ring was still there. But no sign of my sister or her new friend.

A brush rattled against the side of a jar and I could smell the turpentine, even with the tall window open. The studio was in disarray. Rolls of canvas, a large painter's easel, and, curled up on a flourish of blue cloth, Wally. Her back was to Herr Schiele and to me, but still, I was shocked. I had seen lots of nudes, but I hadn't ever been in the same room with someone who was naked, other than my sister. Herr Schiele wore a muslin caftan like the ones in the Galician market, and had paint on his stocking feet. I watched as, brush stroke by brush stroke, an unforgettable Wally emerged on the canvas, a Wally coiled into herself with the intensity of a small centrifuge, the red of her hair balancing the demand of the blue.

"We're back! Let us in, Wally!"

Wally turned her head and smiled. Her eyes remained anxious, which made her smile sweeter. In a single motion, she rose, covered herself with the blue cloth, and unlatched the door.

Margarete flopped down on the desk chair facing me and fanned herself with Susannah's hat.

"Egon! Don't you have something to drink? Or eat?"

He kept painting.

Susannah winked at me, and flashed some banknotes that she pulled part way out of her shirtwaist pocket.

"Egon," Wally said, "some of us do need to eat." She had dressed quickly behind a screen. "Come with me, Margarete," she said.

"No, I'm too hot, and anyway, you won't buy me a beer. Which is what I want."

Wally ignored her. After she had pinned on her hat and tugged on her gloves, she kissed Herr Schiele, who continued to paint.

Margarete peered over the back of the desk chair and watched her leave. I watched Herr Schiele's precise brush strokes build a pale cream background that made Wally's image float in space. Or rather, it made nothing exist but Wally.

Margarete stood. "You could paint me," she said and posed, one stiff arm behind her head and a leg splayed to the side. She was dirty and beautiful. "I know how to pose nude."

"When Wally gets back, perhaps."

Susannah sat down beside me. Kaspar was once again asleep, letting out a small asthmatic wheeze with every second breath.

"Who gave you that money?" I whispered. "I have to talk to you."

"I can't tell you."

She had always told me everything. I had been waiting to tell her about the ring. To talk to her about how Mama was still really ill, and how she was going to send us to our aunt. How Papa was silent. How we would have to make Mama understand that we could not go to Fuschl. Not after what had happened the last time:

My sister was locked in a front room for calling our aunt a bad word. She begged to be let out. "I want my Hedy," she cried. I had begged to be locked in with her. Then the smell of smoke. My sister had calculated that setting the curtains on fire would force Tante Freyda to unlock the door, and it did. Once she had put out the fire, however, she stood us on chairs in front of the window, framed by the soaked and charred remnants of the curtains. She hung signs around our necks. Mine said, Arsonist from Vienna, Age 6, *and Susannah's said* Arsonist, Age 5. *If we moved, Aunt Freyda said, she would call the police. As soon as she left, Susannah hopped down from her chair, grabbed a pen and made the signs say 36 and 35. When passersby pointed and laughed, Susannah grinned and took a bow.*

She had told Papa that he would never see her again if he tried to make her go back to that woman, or to that town, Fuschl. Susannah could say Fuschl like a swear word, and did. She also said that it was no wonder Mama hated the town she came from.

"Fine," Papa had said, "but the agreement is, no more burning things, or I will thrash you. And your sister."

Margarete was bargaining. "You paint other women, Egon. My price is only fifteen *pfennigs*. I want to buy a beer."

"That would buy three beers. Maybe a sketch, later." He

continued to paint. Half an hour went by before Wally entered with some parcels, a newspaper, and a bottle of limewater.

"It's awful out there. The canal really smells on days like this."

"Wally! I'm going to pose, too!" Margarete pulled down a sleeve, revealing a scratched shoulder.

"Stay still!"

Margarete froze. Herr Schiele pulled out a wooden box and stepped up on it. He pinned a sheet of paper to a tall easel.

"Why do you stand on that? You're not so short."

"It gives me the perspective from above that I need. I said, stay still." He looked at her, pencil in hand. Once the pencil touched the paper, he kept the line moving.

Wally put bread and sausages on a plate. She poured water from a carafe into glasses for us. She pried the cork from a bottle of limewater, dribbled a little into each glass, and then sat down with her drink to read *Die Zeit*. Herr Schiele continued to draw without looking at the paper. He looked only at Margarete, his pencil never leaving the page.

"The announcement is here about your association with the Werkstätte," said Wally.

"They didn't want my postcards. They didn't want my suits. But good. An announcement might bring buyers to the studio. Be still, Margarete."

"I am still. And hungry." He kept drawing. She didn't move. After a while, Margarete said, "It's so hot, Egon."

He didn't reply. The continuous line racing along the borders of Margarete's shape finished, finally, out of breath. He stepped down, stood back—and surfaced.

"Aren't you hot, Egon? How can you stand this heat with all those clothes on?"

He tore off his caftan. He was now in his drawers and black socks. He grabbed the blue cloth and wrapped himself in it. He wiggled his shoulders. Wally looked at him, love in her eyes. And then she looked at me. "Fraulein Hedvig. And you, Fraulein Susannah. You must go home, girls. Now." She rolled her stockings back up. "At the restaurant, Herr Mischlinger mentioned more than once that your parents aren't well."

No. We can't go home yet. The later we return, the more likely they will be better. And then there will be no need to argue about going to Fuschl, to Tante Freyda. And whatever the Old Dear says about seeing us with these two vagabonds, these new friends, that will be forgotten. All that is needed is a little more time.

"Draw me," I said. I put my hand on my hip and tipped my chin up. I looked directly at Herr Schiele. "Egon, please, a little drawing." I don't know if calling him by his first name helped persuade him, or if it was my pose, but he leapt to pin a pale yellow sheet of paper to an easel.

"Put your arm out more so it forms a triangle. And keep looking at me."

I did both of those things. After a while, I said, "Egon, my arm is getting tired."

"Think of something else, for a few minutes more."

So I thought about getting a dog. It would have its own basket to sleep in, and its own bowls. If it were a girl dog, I would call it Schatz. I would train her to run without a leash, beside me.

A knock at the door. This time, Wally didn't move. Egon shrugged into his long caftan and pulled on his trousers.

It was Marta, grey-faced and out of breath. She looked past Egon, to us. "I was told I would find you girls here," she barked. "Put your hats on! You are going to your Tante Freyda on the next train. Your bags are in the fiacre waiting outside and your tickets..." She clutched her waist and gasped. "Sir, your water closet?" Egon had backed away from her. Wally pointed to the back room.

Susannah kicked the table. Her eyes were fierce. "I'm not going to Tante Freyda. Hedy, we have to talk to Mama."

Margarete put on a winning smile. "If you're going away, can I look after your bicycle?"

"No." I dragged my sister out the door. I made her get on

her bicycle. We pedaled past the fiacre with its patient horse and driver, and by the time we were on the Schottenring, she had stopped crying and I had figured out what I had to do.

When I emerged from the *Die Zeit* telegraph office, I brushed my hands together. "Done. We don't have to go. I sent a telegram saying we are not coming after all. To hell with you, Tante Freyda!" We were so startled at my swearing, and in public, that we both burst out in laughter. Then we both said it. "To hell with you, Tante Freyda!" Another cascade of laughter. The next time we only managed to say "To hell" before shrieking.

A woman huffed at us as she entered the telegraph office. That was funny, too. We leaned against each other, my arm around Susannah's waist, her arm around my shoulder, bending over, tears in our eyes, trying to catch our breath. Our bicycles teetered and then collapsed on top of each other, provoking another stanza of laughing. Finally—were we? Yes, finally, we were released from the spell. Now we had to go home and tell our mother why I had sent that telegram.

Harsh late afternoon light glared on the side of our building. The leaves of the copper beeches tossed in a gust of wind, and we shivered. Susannah reached for my hand, or maybe I reached for hers. She said, or I said, or maybe we both thought, *Please let them be better.* We went by the service entrance into the kitchen, so full of hope we dared not talk.

Men's voices.

"Susannah! Quick, the drive shed." She bolted. I wasn't fast enough and hid under the zinc-topped worktable. Through the door I could see two men wearing cotton masks and gloves carrying a stretcher down the stairs. A body nearly covered by a sheet. The top of someone's shaved head.

Papa has thick blond curls. There was a cloth knotted on top of the head, as if for a toothache.

*A long-lost relative who had come to take us to his house.
And then got sick. Or, someone who tried to rob us, and Marta
hit him. Hard.*

I think I wasn't breathing. Marta held the door open for the
men. She groaned, one arm over her belly. "What should I do?
I've already let the fiacre driver go."

I knew.

"You don't have to do anything. We're Jews. We know what
to do," said the taller one.

I stayed down. *I knew.*

After a few long minutes, they came back in and went up
the stairs. I shifted to a crouch.

"Hedy?" Susannah was at the kitchen door. I jumped up and
dragged her out of the kitchen, out of the service entrance, into
the lane. Into the drive shed.

"What are you doing?" I hissed. "I told you to wait."

"I did wait. You were in there for a long time. Who were
those men?"

"Officials from the Department of Public Health and Safety.
Where did that lie came from? "Be quiet until we hear them go."

It was dark in the drive shed. I held her hand. *I knew.* They
were the *chevra kadisha*, who care for the dead. *What would
we do without Papa?* I told myself not to cry. *Don't cry, no
crying, not in front of Susannah.*

"You're crushing my hand. What does it matter if those
men see us?"

"I told Mama about the telegram." *Distract her.*

"Was she angry? Is that why you're crying?"

*Susannah was Papa's favourite. She will be wild, unman-
ageable.*

"I'm not crying. No, she said we were to go—not to Fuschl.
To Baden bei Wein. Stop asking questions, those men will
hear you."

"But who is going to look after us?" Susannah whispered.

"Fraulein Lowin." That was so unlikely, but attractive. Lies work if they are what someone would like to hear. I had to get her out of there.

"Thank you, Hedy. I couldn't have gone to Tante Freyda." She heaved a sigh and hugged me, her sister. *Her sister, the liar.*

I could hear the clonking of hooves going west on the Schottenring. The sound of cars and carriages, fiacres, going west. Or east toward the Donaukanal, going away. Away.

"I have to thank Mama. And go in and see Papa."

"No." In the breeze, the late afternoon sun cast moving shadows on the side of the building. "Look, there they are, at the dining room window. Don't you see them waving to us?" I waved at the window. *The glare on the glass.*

"I don't see them."

"Do you think you are going to need eyeglasses?" I kept waving. I felt like I was drowning.

"I don't need anything." She waved.

There was no one there.

"We have to go back to the studio and get your hat, for the train." *And I have to make Kaspar give me that money.*

"Hedy. What about our tickets?"

"Hop on your bicycle. Mama gave me money for the tickets. I have it in my pocket." Or I would, as soon as I got my hands on Kaspar, that thief. *Is this what parents do when things are terrible?*

5.

AFTER SEVEN-THIRTY THE TRAINS left every hour, on the hour. It was the holiday season, and we could hide in the crowds. As soon as we walked to a main street, we could flag a fiacre. I counted the banknotes I had taken back from Kaspar.

When I had beckoned for him to follow me outside Schiele's home, he had kept his long fingers on the side of his head while I talked. I told him that I would say nothing, if he said nothing. Otherwise, I would report him for theft. He looked at me and said, "No, you won't. You wouldn't hurt me, Hedy."

I told him not to say anything to Susannah. He patted my hand. "Of course. But me and Margarete need your bicycles, please, just to borrow, just for a little while."

Margarete said they would return in a few minutes and they rode off. I didn't believe her, but I didn't care. I was too tired. It was exhausting to lie, to keep secrets. I was appalled at what I was doing, and I still had to do the next thing: get Susannah on that train. I couldn't tell her about Papa until we were on our way. I could figure out later how to return.

There was no sign of Wally and Egon. I went to the window. No one. On the street, a man was walking a dog. The man stopped and held his arms out, and the terrier leaped into them. "Oh, my honey doggie," he said.

I needed to sit down. I moved Susannah over as if she were a sack of root vegetables. Mama always said, "Susannah can sleep through anything." Unlike me. I was exhausted but wide awake.

I could feel someone looking at me. A quick look through my eyelashes, less than a second. Herr Mischlinger. When I saw his eyes shift away from me, I sat up.

"Oh, dear child, you're waking up. You know, I never would have guessed your mother would permit you to come here and model for Herr Schiele. Egon looked alarmed. He drew Herr Mischlinger over to another painting, a nude, a young woman gazing up with baleful eyes. "You haven't seen this one," he said. "I have to finish it, but do you see the challenge in her eyes? You know, Hedy and her sister have only been here today to raid my extensive pantry holdings. That sketch was just tossed off, a quick drawing of a pretty child. Look, here are the canvases you chose."

Herr Mischlinger didn't turn away. "I see, Hedvig, why Herr Schiele might recognize your appeal." He moved towards me, avuncular, and reached out to tousle my hair. I drew back. I had been all over the streets today, outside on my bicycle. Sitting on public steps. I needed a brush for my hair. A bath. Even my hands were dirty.

He pouted, a comic face. "I thought you could sit very still." He walked back to watch Egon wrapping three canvases on the worktable in doubled paper. I nudged Susannah hard. When she sat up, her hair sprang up from her head like leafy branches on a tree. Like the hat I made for Mama. Like Papa's hair.

"Don't say anything about Baden bei Wein."

Susannah nodded.

Wally brought a tray with three glasses and a bottle from one of the city vineyards. "Egon, they can't stay here. It's very late. We have to get them home."

I gave Susannah a warning look.

Wally poured wine into the little glasses. "That maid, Marta, will be looking for them. She was quite upset—irritable, in fact—when she was here earlier."

"Marta?" said Herr Mischlinger. He put his glass of wine down carefully. "I can handle Marta. I talked to her about the girls. She's in a different mood. Much different." He raised his glass. "To art, and our continued association."

Wally took a sip from her glass. Egon tossed his back.

"You know, I am their parents' nearest neighbour. I'm happy to take them. Help me get them into the Daimler."

Wally looked at Egon.

"I don't mind. It will save Marta another trip. Come along, too, if you like. Oh, and why don't I buy that little drawing of Fraulein Hedvig for her to keep?"

Wally and Egon hesitated.

"The Daimler will accommodate all of us, and the paintings." He brightened, as if a sudden sunny thought had occurred. "The English royal family finds it roomy enough. Their king has a Daimler just like mine!"

Wally smiled, but her eyes remained sad.

This was clearly not the response he'd hoped for. "I especially like driving along the river at night—the lanterns on the bridges are pretty. Have you seen them, Susannah?"

"Yes. They're lovely, lovely." Her tone was sarcastic. I elbowed her again.

He regarded her for a moment and then handed an envelope to Egon, who handed it to Wally. "With my admiration. Oh, and there is no need, Egon, to apologize for the girls being here—their mother and I—Esther and I—have been very close for a long time. I saw Marta holding the door for her today as I was driving by." An odd smile. He looked pointedly at Wally. "Daughters and the things they do—what can you do but shrug?"

Wally looked down.

Our mother is able to go downstairs. I could feel my shoulders relax. Mama would need me. Together, we would tell Susannah

41

about Papa. *Stop. No crying. Don't cry.* Mama was better. She would know how to tell Susannah. She would want us to be with her. The telegram to Tante Freyda wasn't important now. We would have to comfort each other.

"Don't cry, Hedvig." Herr Mischlinger patted my hand. "Everything will be forgiven."

He helped me get Susannah on her feet. "You two girls should be in bed." He clucked his tongue. Then he lowered his voice and said to Egon and Wally, "Do come along. No one there may be able to speak to you—cholera does take its toll—but I'm sure it's understood that of course you didn't entice the girls here."

Wally looked at Egon.

"Do come. Hedvig, dear child, where is Susannah's hat?"

It was gone. A pert little straw boater. No doubt with Margarete, along with the bicycle. Egon carried the paintings to the Daimler and placed them in the back seat. We climbed into the front.

Herr Mischlinger dawdled, talking to Wally. "You've seen what the papers are saying about the possibility of an epidemic? We really need to attend to our water supply in Vienna. We know it's not in the air; it's in the water. We have lovely buildings and filthy water."

I hugged Susannah. "Mama is better," I said. She pressed my hand and leaned her head against me. *No one can smile like my sister. How wild will she be when she finds out about Papa? I will have to help Mama.*

Herr Mischlinger waved as he drove away, calm and smiling, with the two of us beside him, Susannah once again half-asleep. Once we turned onto the Alserbach, he pulled over, wrenched the brake into place, and left the engine puttering. "So, Hedvig. You've joined that little band of gypsies that camps at Herr Schiele's studio." That soft voice. "Between us, now, do you and your sister pose for him?"

"No, Herr Mischlinger."

He looked at me, up and down. "I didn't think so."

I was insulted. "Herr Mischlinger, you don't understand. Only I posed for him, by myself, today. I was a good model."

"That isn't what he said." Mischlinger smiled at me, shaking his head.

"What did he say?" I was hurt. Papa would have been proud of how still I was when Herr Schiele was drawing me. *Papa. It was Papa the chevra kadisha carried down the stairs.*

"There, there. Don't be upset." He patted my knee. "But, dear child, what would your mother say if she saw you like this?" He pointed. The straps to keep my shirtwaist in place were hanging outside, like reins, over my skirt. "Come here, Hedvig. I'll fix those for you."

"They're fine."

"No, they are not. If you are coming with me, you must look decent. Get up. Lean forward. Don't make a fuss, you're not a little girl."

I did as I was told. I wanted to go home. He shoved my shirtwaist back into the waistband of my skirt, jerking me about. "There you go. Now you look like someone I would take with me, Hedvig." He shifted back behind the wheel, and released the brake.

We will be home soon, I thought, my hands clasped together tight.

He drove across the bridge. "Herr Mischlinger, you've driven past our street! The Schottenring is back there. You'll have to go back over the Augartenbruke."

"Such knowledge of our city! Have you seen the lights on the bridge?"

"Yes, but we have to go the other way!"

He ignored me.

I didn't recognize any of the streets he was turning onto. "Where are we going?"

"To a good house, Hedvig. Don't cry. I think it will suit you and little Susannah."

"I don't think it will! Take us home!"

"That's not possible."

"Then take us back to Egon and Wally."

"Stop this. They don't want you there. No one wants you, or your sister. Where I'm leaving you, there are others like you, other little girls who do not behave like young ladies. No one knows or cares about them, either."

Look after her. That's what Mama had said.

"Herr Mischlinger. I just remembered. We are supposed to get the late train to Fuschl. Our aunt is expecting us." *Keep this lie alive. Don't stop.* I elbowed Susannah.

"Leave me alone! I'm sleeping," grumbled Susannah. "A few more minutes."

"We already have the money for our tickets." I held up a fan of banknotes. *If I smile at him, maybe he will think it impolite not to go along with my lie.* "Marta is meeting us with our suitcases."

"Marta? Marta can hardly stand up. Her brother had to help her walk. She showed me a telegram from your aunt. I know you're not going to Fuschl."

"Yes, we are!"

"Don't worry, Hedvig. Haven't I always been your friend? I told Marta I would take care of you." He lifted the money out of my hand. "And I'll take care of that too."

"You told Mama you would take care of us?"

"No, I told Marta."

He's lying. Only our mother would make such a decision. "Oh, Herr Mischlinger. I forgot! I meant to say Baden bei Wein! Mama changed the plan. We're to meet Fraulein Lowin there." *This might work. He's a little afraid of her.* "You will have to take us the other way, Herr Mischlinger, to the train station."

"You're not meeting anyone," he snorted. He switched on the headlamps. "And I'm not taking you to any train station."

"Turn around! Please turn around! Please, Herr Mischlinger! Take us back to our street!" I grabbed his hand on the steering wheel. He hit me hard on the side of my head, knocking me into Susannah. She muttered in her sleep, "Leave me alone."

A giant of a man in an odd white homburg, the brim folded up on both sides, stood behind a blonde woman. The beads on her black dress glinted in the light from the car's headlamps. She signalled, and Herr Mischlinger turned off the engine.

Darkness surrounded us. We were in an empty side street with no streetlamps.

"Wake up your sister, Hedvig, and get out," said Mischlinger.

I couldn't move.

The giant in the white hat jerked the car door open and hauled Susannah out by her arm. Like an animal, she leapt out of sleep, hitting him with her fist. He grabbed her wrists and wrestled her around until her back was to him. He picked her up around her waist, clamping her against his torso. Her eyes were wild. She called to me, and he covered her mouth with his huge hand, grinning.

"Susannah!" I scrambled out of the front seat and ran to him. The woman in black and Herr Mischlinger caught me in a coarse blanket. "Susannah!"

My mouth was covered with the blanket. I tried to bite. I couldn't move. I watched my sister drum her heels back into the man's shins. He paid no attention and walked straddle-legged around the corner.

My arms were pinned at my sides. I could hear the door of the Daimler slam and the engine start.

"We will join your sister as soon as you behave." A cooing voice, a woman's. I stopped struggling. She pulled the blanket away from my face, and we moved around the corner to the entrance. The door had been left open.

"Move your feet. You don't want to trip and fall." She spoke calmly and held me against her body. I was shaking. "There, there," she said. "Shh." She kept her arms around me. "Shh. You will be fine. Your sister is waiting for you."

Nothing felt real. My heart was pounding. We waited on a landing for a long time, and then she steered me, still wrapped in the blanket, up the stairs, into a dark room, and onto a bed. She lay down beside me.

Susannah was already there, sleeping again. There was an odd smudge above her upper lip, like a white moustache. The lady stayed there, holding me, patting my back. Her breath was like cinnamon. After a while, she stood up. Her black dress rustled as she backed away from the bed, and in the long slit of light just before the door closed, she smiled at me. "You will call me Frau Kreutzel."

My eyes adjusted to the dark. Susannah was on the other side of the high bed. My rolled-up Schiele drawing was crushed in her belt. On the bedside table was a glass with a white smear. A hanging lamp. A shuttered window. Dark red flocked wallpaper. A washstand with a pitcher, a washbowl, and a crumpled linen towel. And over by the door, on a chair, Herr Mischlinger.

He walked to the bed and turned on the lamp. He held me down with one arm and knee. "I need to see you. You are lovely. Lovely. No wonder Schiele felt you up."

"He didn't." Tears rolled into my ears.

"Shh, Hedvig." He peeled away the blanket and pulled up my skirt. He pulled down my drawers.

I could hear myself crying.

"Shh." He put a finger to my lips.

I grabbed at his hand. He hit me, the back of his hand, the front of his hand. His knee shoved between my legs. His awful groaning.

It hurt.

"Please don't wake my sister."

"Don't you."

6.

OH, MY MOTHER, if you are still alive, come and get me, get me out of here, get Susannah and me out of here.

Why did they think I would be the right girl for this?

It's my fault we are here. I was the one who sent the telegram.

As soon as Susannah woke up, she raced to the door and started pounding on it. "How dare you lock us in! Open this door!"

I sat on a chair beside the door. Stunned. It hurt so much down there. I was in my clothes from the day before and so was she. I checked my pocket for the ring. *Yes.*

"How can you just sit there? Does the Old Dear think Mama would tolerate us staying here? How dare he? It's not even a proper hotel." She stopped kicking the door long enough to yell, "We are expected in Baden bei Wein!"

There was no response. Somewhere in the house a gramophone began playing. Susannah went over to the window and rattled the shutters. They were locked.

"Hedy, help me smash these shutters. Bring me that chair. Fraulein Lowin must be beside herself with worry about us. If Papa weren't so sick, this would never have happened. Hedy, please help me!"

I couldn't move. She shoved me off the chair. The shutters were made of painted metal, not wood, and the noise of the

47

chair smashing against them made it impossible to understand what she was yelling. She stopped, breathless and furious. "Papa will kill him." She sat down on the chair and cried. Everything about her was slack, her arms dangling.

I took her hands. "Susannah, I have to tell you something."

She glared at me.

"I was hoping Mama would tell you. I thought the Old Dear was taking us home, and then Mama would tell you."

She pushed me away.

"Susannah, listen. Yesterday, sometime before we went home, something terrible happened." *Was it only yesterday?* Every part of my sister was alert, tensed. "Susannah, I'm so sorry. Our Papa died yesterday."

She launched herself at me, wild, crying, pummeling me with her fists. I raised my arms up to protect myself, but she spun around and picked up the chair, throwing it against the door. She didn't look at me. She stood there panting. "Why didn't you tell me?"

"Because I was afraid. I was afraid of what I had seen and afraid of what would happen next. I didn't know what to do, and I was afraid of what you might do. And Marta was still there, and those men were there. I wanted to get you away so I could tell you."

"You said Mama and Papa were waving at us. You were lying. Did Mama tell you to go to Baden bei Wein?"

I couldn't answer.

"You're a liar, Hedy. Cry all you want. Stay away from me." She began kicking the door again methodically, until the woman from last night opened it. Susannah landed a flurry of punches on her shoulders, her head, her arms.

The woman caught her and held her. *Frau Kreutzel.* "Shh, shh, I understand, little one. I lost my father very young, too. Shh, shh."

She must have been listening at the door.

She pulled Susannah closer and wouldn't let go. She kept

talking to her. She glanced at the new indentations in the shutters and said nothing. Susannah went slack again.

Frau Kreutzel stepped away from her, and Susannah was still. But when she went to pat Susannah on her back, Susannah told her to get her whore hands off her, that this was a whorehouse.

The sympathy in Frau Kreutzel's face disappeared. A hard smile, but still, that calm voice. "That's right. This is one of the best specialty houses in Vienna." She looked at me. "If your madwoman of a sister does not stop, she'll be taken to a very different house, not anywhere near as nice. Away from you." And she left.

Susannah grabbed me by the shoulders immediately. At least she was looking at me. "Did you talk to Papa before he died?"

"No, the *chevra kadisha* were carrying him away. His body."

"Are you sure it was him?"

"It was him. Yes. His head was shaved, but it was him."

"Why would anyone do that to Papa?" She was crying and holding onto me, and then, just like that, she stopped. "He was so proud of his hair."

"Maybe his fever was so high..."

"I cannot believe Mama would let the doctor do that to him." And then she pushed me away from her again. "Does she know we're here?"

"No."

"This is her fault. She decided to send us away. I was right about what I told you before: she doesn't care about us." Her face twisted. "Mama and her dinner parties and her wonderful artists." She rattled the door handle again and then collapsed on the thick carpet. I sat down beside her.

And she said, or I said, or we both thought the same unbearable possibility. But I reserved a sturdy space in my mind that Mama might be alive. That she would do whatever it took to stay alive. And in the meantime, I would do what she said.

"Susannah, Mama doesn't know about this place. I'm sure." *Or about the Old Dear.* We were holding each other. "This is what we'll do: when that woman opens the door again, pretend to be nice. But when I give you a half-wink, yell, run down the stairs, and get out."

Frau Kreutzel knocked, asked to enter, and unlocked the door. We waited. She carried in a tray and set it on the small table. Hot soup in covered bowls. She smiled and bent to take the covers off. I half-winked. Susannah flipped the tray, and we were already over the threshold and down the stairs before she yelled, "Hans!"

And suddenly the huge man from the night before emerged right in front of us, out of a doorway at the bottom of the stairs. He lunged and missed. We ran back up the stairs, but he caught us, looping his long arms around us. He hauled us up the stairs, with me pedaling with my heels against the steps, and Susannah kicking and yelling, "Ass! Pile of shit! Shit ass!"

He dragged us down the hallway and threw me all the way from the doorway onto the bed. He hung onto Susannah. "Jewish brats," he said before he shut the door.

Frau Kreutzel had soup all down her black dress. "Are you going to stop this?"

I looked at her, killing her with my eyes.

She picked up a towel and tied a knot in it. She smiled at me and said, "Come, Hans."

He entered, his huge hand over my sister's mouth. Without another word, she began hitting Susannah with the knotted towel. Susannah cried out. I ran and put myself between them, facing Frau Kreutzel. Hans laughed and pulled me away. Susannah was on the floor, crying, asking her to please stop. Please stop. Hedy, make her stop.

I insisted I wouldn't try to leave. Neither of us would try to leave. Frau Kreutzel tossed the towel on the bed and raised her eyebrows at me. A curt command from her and Hans released Susannah, his fun over. On her way out, Frau

Kreutzel pinched me, hard, underneath my upper arm. "It's up to you," she said.

Susannah got her second wind. I tried to stop her, but she ignored me and rocked the headboard of the bed back and forth, yelling and swearing. Frau Kreutzel opened the door for Hans, who took Susannah out of the room, his horrible hand once again over her mouth.

Immediately afterward, a man with a small black valise followed Frau Kreutzel into the room. "This is Doctor Bloch," she said, and quickly left the room.

He pointed to the bed. I was to get up on it. "Pull them down." It was hard to know how to look at him. He turned his head so I could only see his mangled ear. *This is why he's here,* I thought. No one is sure how to look at him. He pushed my knees apart, grunted, and plastered cold ointment all over down there. He flattened a towel against the ointment, and told me to pull up my drawers, and not to touch the towel. He shut the clasp on his bag and left as quickly as he had come.

When Hans carried Susannah back in the room, she was sound asleep. She had that white moustache again. Frau Kreutzel tucked a blanket over her. Then she gently removed my drawers, followed by the towel.

Susannah didn't wake up when Mischlinger shoved her away from me.

Oh, my mother. Please be alive. Please come and get us out of here.

The bells of Vienna rang at four o'clock. Frau Kreutzel unlocked the door and came in with a crystal goblet on a tray. "Did you enjoy the luncheon I sent up to you?"

I had devoured it, and now I felt sick. Susannah had eaten nothing and was silent.

"Your friend will be here soon. Here is a special drink for

you, Susannah." She lowered the tray towards my sister. No response.

"This is for you, Susannah," she said again. She put the tray down and held out the goblet. "Drink."

Susannah's face was a mask. She took a very small sip and spat it out. She put the goblet down precisely and stood. She held Frau Kreutzel's gaze without wavering, reaching back to hold my hand at the same time.

"Hans!" Within seconds, he was pounding up the stairs. Frau Kreutzel opened the door. "Make her sit down."

When Hans stepped towards her, Susannah swore at him. "Shit bag."

I pulled on Frau Kreutzel's arm. "Don't make her drink that. Please. She doesn't want to!" Before I could get to Susannah, Hans had spun her around and imprisoned her hands within his. Susannah plunged forward.

"She bit me!" He let go of her to stare at the back of his hand. "Look, she broke the skin!" Blood dripped down his wrist. "Little Jewish bitch!"

The two of them trapped her against the wall. I pulled on Frau Kreutzel's arm again with all my strength. "Please, Frau Kreutzel. Don't!"

Then suddenly I was on the floor. She must have hit me with the back of her hand. My sister was also on the floor, her back against the wall, kicking at them. "Bag of shit! Whore ass! Leave Hedy alone!"

"Stay where you are, Fraulein Hedy," said Frau Kreutzel, keeping her eyes on Susannah. "Your sister is out of control. Look at her. If she doesn't drink, she will be sent away."

I froze. Susannah made herself go limp. Hans pulled her up and pinched her cheeks together to force her mouth open as Frau Kreutzel tipped the goblet. Susannah could only drink or choke. She did choke, the liquid dribbling out of her mouth. And then she drank.

"There you are, dear."

"Whoremonger," Susannah said. They lifted her up onto the bed, and Frau Kreutzel climbed up beside her, holding her in an iron grip.

"Go, Hans," she said.

Over her shoulder, Susannah said, "Yes, go, you bag of shit." By the time she fell asleep, her tears had dried into stripes on her cheeks.

Frau Kreutzel got up and covered her with a light blanket. "She will be calm now. And you, Hedy dear, stop crying. As long as your sister does not cause any more problems, she can stay here with you. Get up on the bed. Your caller will be here soon."

My caller. My mother's friend. *I am so ashamed.*

As soon as I woke up, I looked immediately to see if Susannah was beside me. She was, frowning in her sleep. The sky above the shutters was still dark. Frau Kreutzel was there. She whispered for me to sit up and drink a cup of tea with her. Then she brought cold compresses for my eyes, and told me to go back to sleep. Mid-afternoon, she unlocked the door and took a tray from a maidservant with broth, bread, and cheese. I was hungry, but Susannah only had a few spoonfuls of broth and then lay back on the pillows, glaring at me.

Just after four o'clock, there was another knock. This time it was Hans. Susannah drank all of what was in the goblet, looking steadily at Frau Kreutzel. A cold, blank look. Then a defiant look at me. She said nothing. But she was still with me.

Oh, my mother. Please come.

Frau Kreutzel was cheerful and ran a bath for me, checking the water temperature. I felt limp as she washed me. Powder on my body. Creams on my hands and face. My legs felt wobbly. She dressed me in a shirtwaist that didn't come down far enough. She shoved her hands under my breasts and pulled them up to the edge of the neckline. "You have such nice little legs!" she said, pulling up a pair of white stockings. There was no skirt, nothing to cover down there. She patted my shoulder. "How pretty you are, Hedy."

She moved Susannah into the armchair.

This is all my fault. Please, my mother, come soon.

Herr Mischlinger was on top of me, grabbing at me. I looked at Susannah in the chair and heard myself speak. Not about what he was doing. Not about myself. "My sister's head is at an uncomfortable angle."

"Don't look at her. Look at me. I want to see your face when I do this."

Each time he left, Frau Kreutzel gave me ointment and a towel for down there. She patted my hand.

I am too young for this. Oh, my mother, please. Please find us.

It was a Thursday evening, as far as I could calculate. I watched from the chair as Frau Kreutzel arranged Susannah's floppy body on the bed. She spread her hair out on the pillow and undid the top of her dress. She moved my sister's arms up by her head, hands upturned. Open.

"Nothing is going to happen, Hedy dear. Keep your mouth shut."

I tried to be invisible. I was wearing the awful clothes she had given me. Still no skirt. Frau Kreutzel opened the door. "Shh. Our princess is sleeping."

Three men slipped in. They glanced at me, and then stared at Susannah. One stepped closer to the bed. Frau Kreutzel wagged her finger. "Only looking." Then she moved my sister's feet together a little, watching the men's reaction. Her spitty smile.

7.

"**B**UT I BROUGHT SUSANNAH to you. I could have taken them both someplace else." Frau Kreutzel and Herr Mischlinger were arguing, just outside the door.

"Yes, but not to any place as safe as mine. I am discreet. Whatever your particular desires, that information stays within this house. It will not be disclosed that you, Herr Mischlinger, owner of the Hotel Vienna, the Hotel Donau, the Hotel Austria, such a well-known person in this city, you brought them to me."

"And the Hotel Royal. You received goods from me, for my use."

"But the younger girl? A girl like that, untouched? Some very nice goods, yes. Why shouldn't I have the others bid? You will have to compensate me. Meet the best offer. I have already spent a great deal on their medical care. Their room and board. Security. Bribes. And these little Jewesses break things and bite. Look at this bruise."

Two men were let in to see Susannah the next evening. I had to sit there in those stockings with a babyish bow in my hair. Susannah's clothing was more undone. At the hem of her skirt, you could see her drawers around her ankles.

"An angel with her knickers down," one of them said.

"Lovely thing," the other said. "Costly."

When Frau Kreutzel turned to open the door, one of them pinched my breast as he walked out.

Oh, my mother, are you alive, maybe you are alive, oh, if you are alive, please come and get us. You have to come and get us.

Herr Mischlinger must have made his deal with Frau Kreutzel. Half an hour after Susannah drained her goblet, she was collapsed, floppy. But this time, Frau Kreutzel took Susannah's drawers off and told me to sit in the chair.

"She won't know what happens, unless you tell her."

I wished I didn't know what would happen. I wished I could drink whatever it was they gave to my sister. I had to think of something, a plan.

When he came in, I said, "Leave her alone. Just me, just do it to me."

He smiled. "Stay in the chair then, Hedvig, and stay still." He pulled those stupid stockings she made us wear down to my ankles and wound the tops of the stockings around the front legs of the chair, as if he had done it a thousand times. I couldn't press my legs together.

He was touching me, watching me. "There you go, there you go," he crooned, holding me tight against the chair with his other hand, until I couldn't help it—a sudden flood of pleasure and then, within moments, a flood of shame.

And for nothing. He cupped my face with his hand, smiling. He said, "Be quiet, and it will go better for her. She may take to it even quicker than you. Don't raise your head. Don't look."

But I could hear.

Before he left, he took my hands inside both of his and held them. "Shhh, Hedvig, no tears. We are old friends. You and your sister will be fine."

I was sure Susannah hadn't woken up while he was on the bed with her. But for several days afterward, her face would suddenly screw up as if she were about to cry. She never did, but she couldn't keep anything down. She threw up every time she tried to eat. The smell would make me gag and then I would throw up, too.

The room reeked. Frau Kreutzel made us sit together in the chair while Brigita, who worked there, cleaned up the mess. Frau Kreutzel ran warm water in the tub and poured in lavender scent. Over tea, she patted us and told us that we were sweet.

I couldn't help it. Another round of gagging.

No one, not even Brigita, talked to us.

I kept the ring safe. Susannah didn't know I had it. I hid it, sometimes in the pocket of her shirtwaist when she was becalmed. And no one knew the drawing was under the mattress. Brigita the Romanian had found it that first day and handed it to me while the Kreutzel woman was busy bathing Susannah.

As soon as Brigita left with an armload of sheets, I had lifted up one corner of the mattress and held it up with my shoulder so I could lay the drawing flat before letting the mattress fall back down. Even with Brigita changing the bed linens, it was safe—that drawing of the girl I had been that day when my mother had said she loved me. *Hedy, my darling.*

Mischlinger asked Frau Kreutzel about the drawing, but she told him to look in his Daimler. While they were on the subject, she told him to take a fiacre next time. His automobile attracted too much attention. She also made sure Susannah's clothing remained on for the duration of his visit. "Let's delay the questions," she said.

I shared that desire to delay questions from Susannah. I dreaded my sister asking what Herr Mischlinger did, or about what had happened to our mother, but I needn't have. She refused to look at me or to talk to me. She focused on the narrow section of the window above the shutters, the sky framed by the wrought iron supports for the balcony above.

What he did to me on the bed had stopped hurting. He talked to me as though he hadn't touched me everywhere, as though he hadn't smiled at my humiliation when I responded to his fondling. As if he were still the kindly neighbour who shared an interest in art with a younger person, and enjoyed hearing her opinions. One day he unfurled two drawings and asked which I thought was most like Klimt's work.

I was astonished at how eager I was to talk about painting, about art, that I had so much to say to this awful man who made me feel helpless with pleasure and sick with shame. *Even a bad person needs conversation.*

Every time he visited, my sister was in a deep sleep. For a long time, I was sure that she didn't know what he did to her. He would place her on the bed so he could look at me, sitting like that, with my ankles tied to the chair, while he took a turn with her. That's what he called it, a turn. I didn't try to stop him. I had decided that I didn't want that drink they gave her. Someone had to know what was happening and be ready.

I wanted to run away, to take Susannah's hand and run, but the door was locked. Outside on the staircase, I could hear men's voices, their footsteps, their coughs. No one talked to me except Mischlinger. He was the only person who sought my company. Once, when he had finished with me, he gave me a blank look, as though he didn't know where he was. He stood up, naked, staring into space. I stood up, too, and then he noticed me. "You could be a dancer, Hedvig," he said.

He was the only person who used my real name. I don't know what else he said, but hearing my name reminded me that I did once belong to the real world, that there was a real world.

"I know Mama's dead." Susannah looked out the window. She didn't look at me. "I knew she had to be, when he shoved himself into me. When she didn't come for us. Don't hug me. Don't say anything."

The look on her face was what I felt, too.

"Mama's friend. Even the milkman knew! I heard Viktor tell Marta that Mischlinger was a shithouse rat. He's a degenerate! Someone should kill him. If Papa had known!"

"Neither of them knew, Susannah. Don't cry. How could they? They trusted him."

"Like I trusted you. Baden bei Wein, ha. Don't talk."

I didn't.

She wiped her face. "Swearing and the truth. My best gifts from living on the Schottenring. From the servants."

We both watched a cloud form and re-form in that part of the sky we could see above the shutters.

"I always thought Mama would like me better as an adult. She laughed at my jokes sometimes, Hedy, even when she told me not to say such things. Get away from me! I told you I don't want to be hugged."

"Not everyone liked those jokes."

"I did. I liked the way people were shocked, and then laughed, like they forgave me everything. Stop talking to me. I told you not to talk to me. I don't deserve to be here, Hedy."

Maybe I do, I thought.

When I was younger, I thought all the time about what I would do when I was a grown-up. How I would be acclaimed for my art, even though I wasn't sure what that art would be. When I travelled, crowds would assemble to welcome my arrival. Nicely dressed men played a role in those fantasies, escorts for me and my sister. I chose and changed my mind about locations, about what my sister and I wore. Susannah was always with me in those elaborate daydreams. Now she was with me here in this nightmare where I got to choose nothing. If I didn't do what Frau Kreutzel said, Susannah would be sent away. I had no choice but to please Mischlinger. I hated him, and I longed to see him. Not just because he talked to me. I knew that was pathetic, but it was not as shameful, not as disgusting as the truth. I liked the feeling in my body when he touched me.

He hasn't been to see me for three weeks, and I wish he would call.

I am a terrible person.

The next time he visited, he was distracted and didn't answer when I talked to him. Finally I asked him if he still liked us. "Of course I like you." He pinched my nipple. "But it is the fall season, and my hotels are keeping me very busy."

December snow was blowing against the windows when Susannah finally talked to me. She put her hands, palm to palm, by her cheek and warbled like a bad actress, "Do you still like us?" in a high, bleating voice, and then laughed. She was mocking me, but she was also trying to make Herr Mischlinger into a joke. I mustered a half-smile. I had a plan. If we had seen the last of him, this sojourn in our lives might be over. I asked to speak to Frau Kreutzel, alone.

"Do you think we could leave, since Herr Mischlinger isn't coming to see us anymore?"

She leaned back in her chair and laughed at me. It was my day to be mocked. "With what? And to where?" She called to Hans and told him to bring Susannah down to her office. She opened a long green book and showed us a page with our names on it and what we owed her. Lodging, meals, laundry, clothing, medical care, dental care, sundries. It even listed "protection," which she said was Hans, barring riff-raff from the door. She said that we could easily go once we had paid off our debt. All we had to do was be nice to a couple of gentlemen, with very nice manners, she said, who paid well. Susannah said she didn't care, that she didn't notice if a man was in her room or in her. She didn't care.

Frau Kreutzel smiled as though she liked her response, its vulgarity. Susannah didn't respond. Instead she looked directly at Frau Kreutzel, her eyes dead, and then left me with her in the vestibule office.

"What if we were to leave but paid all we owed a week or so after we left?"

We could leave here, and say nothing about being here. We could tell people we had been overcome with grief, lost, taken

*in by a woodsman and his wife, succoured by wolves, any-
thing, and even if Mama and Papa's finances were in terrible
shape, there would be some money, surely, and we could pay
Frau Kreutzel, and be free. But we couldn't tell anyone where
we had been.*

I didn't tell Susannah what Frau Kreutzel said, so calmly,
as if she had said the same thing a dozen times before. She
would report us as thieves to the police, she said, if we tried
to leave. She yawned. We would be shamed, jailed, and have
our hair cut off. We would be beaten by the prison guards who
would hire us out for the pleasure of their friends, or worse.
And, she said, shooing me out the door, without medication,
Susannah could die.

8.

ZEHRA THE TURK MADE SURE we knew of her status as the house favourite when she brought us into her rooms to demonstrate how to use prophylactics. It was embarrassing to meet her caller, who was paying extra to have us watch. She showed us how to make sure the wash water was warm, what a healthy man should look like down there, how to safely do what the callers wanted. She promised to show us more later.

The first time a caller heard Susannah swear, he was taken aback. She smiled dreamily at him as if she didn't know what she had said. Whether he liked it or not, she only ever did it once, in case the fellow was hoping to hear it the next time.

We had begun to have regular callers, like the others. The others visited back and forth in each other's rooms. We could hear them, but we were not invited. We overheard what they called us, "those little Schottenring snobs." God knows what part of the city or the Empire they were from. Some weren't even Austrian.

The only one who talked to me was Brigita the Romanian. She did household tasks for Frau Kreutzel, and one day when she had brought in fresh linen and was fitting the arms of her wire-rim spectacles over her ears to read the laundry marks, I took a chance. Susannah was in our bathroom. There was no one else around.

I told her what Frau Kreutzel had said. I said it so fast, I was out of breath. "Is it true?"

Without even looking up from the folded sheet in her hand she said, "Yes, it is. I don't take medication, but everything else is true. About the medication, perhaps that's true as well." She watched the door. "When I tried to run away two years ago, Frau Kreutzel said I had stolen money. I had a sentence of three months. The guards are paid very low wages, so they make deals with really bad people to make money." She picked up the linen basket. "There are people worse than Kreutzel. Be careful."

Later that winter, when the Sicilian came around to sell his boots, Brigita ordered red slippers with pointed toes and no backs on the heels, and boots in oxblood leather that went above the knee. And shoes, open-toed gilt and pink. Feathers. Like a small rooster. Her feet were very small and beautiful. It was obvious what her specialty was.

9.

SUSANNAH AND I HAD ALWAYS told each other our dreams, first thing upon waking, when we lived on the Schottenring. Sometimes we dreamed the same thing. In the brothel on Verstektstrasse, I didn't remember my dreams, if I had any. I had circles under my eyes from being awakened every night by Susannah. Before I could remove the arm she flung across me, she had already sunk back into her lagoon of sleep.

Frau Kreutzel told me my circles were unattractive and said it was the Jewess in me coming out. She preferred Susannah to me, and my sister let her think the feeling was reciprocal. Susannah reassured me she was lying. "Now you know what it was like for me," she said, "when Mama preferred you to me."

When we were alone, Susannah leaned her head against mine on the pillow and read aloud from the newspapers that kept coming long after Mischlinger had stopped calling on us. We did this instead of talking about how we were, our thoughts, our feelings. She commented on politicians, or fashions, or scandals about people she didn't know. Italians, if possible.

"Hedy, get out of the bath. Frau Kreutzel wants us all downstairs, right now."

I hurried to follow Susannah and the others who rushed ahead of us down to the parlour office by the front door. Frau Kreutzel introduced us to the others as "the Schottenring girls." Stiff nods. I couldn't bear it if, even in this place, we were to be the outcasts again, not invited, not talked to, as if we were still in school. I took a chance.

"I'm Hedy, and this is my sister, Susannah."

Frau Kreutzel took off the little half-glasses she wore and said, "That's not necessary."

But tall Katerina had already begun to say her name. She told us she was from Martinique. Then a tiny little person scampered down the stairs. When she apologized for being late, her voice was so high and squeaky that Susannah laughed.

Frau Kreutzel changed her mind and introduced Bebe Raton, or Little Mousie, from Argentina. They smiled at us, a little wary. Susannah, however, had found the perfect audience. Frau Kreutzel wanted to prepare us: several English callers were about to arrive, and we were to make sure that, if we knew English, we were to pretend not to.

Susannah said, "Well, that will be easy. I only know 'bloody expensive coozie.'" They all burst out laughing. The shock of my sister's dead-on perfect English accent, the vulgarity emerging from that calm, upper-class Schottenring face. Even Frau Kreutzel laughed.

Back in our room, I ventured that she would soon have Frau Kreutzel in the palm of her hand.

Susannah stopped polishing her shoes, held up her hand, and then squeezed it into a clenched fist. Her nature, always ready to fight.

"Hedy, do you know how those Englishmen found us?"

"No. I hope no one in the street knows what this place is."

"No, only very rich men. Listen, Zehra, the Turk told me. She said rich men, no matter where they are from, gossip to each other about specialty houses. A caller has to be recommended to get in."

"Our family was rich."

"A lot of good that did. I don't think anyone from our old life ever looked for us."

"They wouldn't have looked for us here. We arrived here

when everyone was out of the city on holiday. No one would have known what happened to Mama and Papa until later. As for us, they would have assumed we had gone to relatives."

"To stinking Fuschl. No one cared about us, Hedy."

I had nothing to say. That was what Herr Mischlinger had told me, too, in the Daimler that awful first night.

Six months had passed when Frau Kreutzel told us we looked pale. "Herr Emil complained that you, Suzi, look unwell." Frau Kreutzel was the only person who had ever dared to shorten Susannah's name to the affectionate diminutive. My mother would have been appalled.

We had been summoned downstairs. Hans leaned against the wall, rocking a tooth in his mouth back and forth until she gave him a look. He folded his arms and knuckled his jaw from the outside.

She tapped a pen on a ledger. "You have been behaving very well. Laundry out on time. You keep yourselves looking very pretty, if a little pale. And your accounts are correct. You, Suzi, are cheerful. It wouldn't hurt, you, Hedy, to be merry, as Suzi is. She understands. Callers like giggling. You should practise. Experiment." The smile she put on her face would have been winsome but for the spit in the corners of her mouth. She produced a little cascade of laughter.

Susannah looked delighted. "Oh, Frau Kreutzel, that is so adorable. Oh, sorry, it's not my place to comment, my apologies."

One day, I thought, she is going to overdo it.

"Sit outside with Zehra any time you can. You need to get some colour. Both of you."

Once we were back in our room, Susannah said, "She thinks I like her."

"She likes your flattery."

"I'm good at it. If I could get my hands on her money, we

could get out of here. Hedy, listen: when she invites me to visit, I act impressed and ask about her art objects."

"The tin stags?"

"I know. They're terrible. But if I win her confidence, she'll tell me about the mementoes, and then I'll find out where she hides her money."

"How do you know she hides money?"

"Everyone with money hides it."

Frau Kreutzel decided to buy us new clothing, new under-garments, new stockings. A stage version of the clothing a wealthy, well-brought-up girl might wear, tailored a little tight for modesty or decency. But no coats to keep us warm in the Vienna winter.

It was an icy cold spring, but on the twenty-first of March, there was a big rainstorm, "an equinoxial rainstorm," Papa would have said, and you couldn't see the middle of the street from the window. Frau Kreutzel had gone out very early with her usual driver, and this time she took Hans with her. The others in the house were still sleeping.

"Hedy, let's leave, right now." Susannah got down from the chair. She had been peering over the shutters.

"With what? We don't have enough money or proper coats. Where would we go?"

"I don't care. We could go back home, to the Schottenring. We could sell some of the silver, and then we could go to Baden bei Wein."

"How would we get in?" *Anything to keep her talking.*

"I'd smash the back entrance window with my shoe, and then I'd break the lock on the kitchen door. And then we'd be in."

"What if someone new has moved in? We don't even know whether Mama's and Papa's things are still there."

"But those things belong to us! Somebody from Papa's work will help us."

"Susannah, he wasn't close to the other men of the bourse. His interests were different. Name one person he worked with."

She couldn't. I did not want to go to the Schottenring. What if one of our parents' friends saw us, and everyone found out what happened to us?

There was another reason. I didn't want to take a chance on seeing Mischlinger. I couldn't face seeing someone who didn't want me. At least the other callers wanted me, or the version of me they imagined.

I am not a good person.

"What if we went to Fraulein Lowin?" Susannah asked.

"You really would like to ask her for help? You want her to know what we are?"

"No."

"Can you imagine anyone who knew us then who'd want to know us now? We're whores, Susannah."

"I know we are." Susannah's face was crumpling. I could feel my eyes stinging. We sat down on the bed together.

"I hate having to look at their cocks, Hedy. I can wash them without looking at them."

"But Frau Kreutzel says we have to look at them ourselves. She says it's better if we do it ourselves. She says she wants us to be safe."

"Lifting those things up and looking underneath. I hate her."

"She likes you. She doesn't like me."

"That's because you don't tip your head and smile at her." She went back to standing on the chair. "What if we ask someone out there who doesn't know us?" She pointed to the street. "Someone who looks nice, like that woman."

"To do what? Adopt us? Who would want two half-educated girls? And you might not look Jewish, but I do."

"I do so look Jewish." She sat down on the chair.

I put my arm around her and patted her hand. "How will we live? What will we do? We don't know how to do anything. And how could we explain what we have been doing, if we were seen by one of Mama's old friends? At least here, no one knows who we are. Or were. Haven't you noticed that our callers are either foreigners or old government men?"

The rain pounded against the windows. Susannah stood back up on the chair. "What about accounting? I'm good with numbers."

"I'm not. And you don't have a certificate of graduation from anywhere. Where would you say you lived? At 13, Verstektstrasse? What about references?"

She looked out the window. "That's why we should go to Baden bei Wein. We could make up where we lived, and you could write a fake letter. We could be assistants to people with art galleries. There are people there who support the arts. Baden bei Wein has lots of people like the ones who used to visit our house."

"Not *like* the ones. They *are* the ones. You'd want them to see us, as we are now?" I couldn't bear to talk about our house. Our parents. The life of the arts in Vienna. I missed our home and the intellectual talk that happened in it. I missed wondering what would happen next, instead of knowing what would happen next. All of that Schottenring life, I missed it, and I couldn't have it. I didn't want to think about it.

"Hedy! Maybe we could be dancers. Or actresses. Maybe we—Hedy, listen! I can ignore those old men pushing my legs apart, but I can't stand them trying to kiss me."

"I think we both hate Emil. What's that?"

She held up a key. "Nothing anyone will miss. It's double-sided. It works from either side of the door."

Our door had a narrow ornate plate of metal with a long curving handle, and in a little metal cabbage of leaves at the top, a slit for a key. It was exactly like the handle and lock on the other side of the door.

"How long have you had it?"

"Weeks. I've been waiting for a chance like this. The old gutbag doesn't know it's missing from her desk." Susannah jumped up. "You know what, Hedy? If you like it here, you can stay. I don't care what happens when I leave. I know what happens here, and I don't like any of it."

I grabbed at her, but she told me to get out of her way. I couldn't stop her. I had to go with her.

To step into the street without Hans as a minder was a shock. Without an umbrella, so was the rain, even the surprisingly warm spring rain. Our dresses were soaked before we reached the corner where Verstektstrasse opens onto the square. Susannah had a fixed look on her face and walked right into the street. I pulled her over to the sidewalk.

Two women in high-crowned hats and well-tailored dark coats emerged from the confectioner's, chatting happily under the store's awning. Susannah headed directly over to them. They stopped dead and looked at us like no one ever had. As if we were what we were. Whores who looked like whores.

"Excuse me, Frauleins," Susannah talked as though she didn't notice their contempt. "We are young ladies whose home is on the Schottenring, and we are a bit lost."

The stouter woman pulled her friend away, clucking her tongue.

"Girls." Frau Kreutzel was right behind us, under a black umbrella. She gave an upward nod of her head, and Hans scooped me up, and then Susannah, one under each arm. He was so tall that our toes never touched the ground enough to give us purchase, although Susannah tried. He galumphed back to the house, catching rain in his open mouth.

Once he was in the vestibule, he mocked us. "Now you'll see. No one can trust you Jews."

"Upstairs, Hans."

He clomped up the stairs ahead of her. Then he dropped Susannah outside on the floor and kicked the door closed. My head pressed against his vest. My feet were off the floor. My skirt was pulled up. Her hands were on my leg, peeling my stocking down. Not a sound from Susannah. Over the top of my head, his breath, putrid from those teeth, black and rotten.

I screamed. She had pinched the skin in the back of my knee with something small, metal. I felt as though all my blood had fled to my hands, my fingertips, my toes, trying to get away. I had wet myself. Susannah pounded on the door, swearing. Hans dropped me on the floor, complaining about his boots. Frau Kreutzel handed me a towel to clean up the floor and told Hans to get out of the way.

When she unlocked the door, Susannah flew in, took one look at me, and then went after Hans. "You reek of dog. No wonder you smell like dog shit. You get your pleasure from a dog's ass, don't you?" She spat.

Frau Kreutzel motioned for Hans to leave. "Next time, be more careful locking their door. There, there, Suzi. Shh."

Susannah collapsed on the bed. Frau Kreutzel turned to me, her old face inches from mine, so close I could see the long blonde hairs on her chin. "You didn't like that, did you? Try to run out on me again, and it will be her turn. Wash yourself." She closed the door. I could hear the lock click. Susannah scrambled over to me.

"Did she let Hans do anything to you?"

"No."

"She doesn't like him. She smiled when I insulted him. I saw it, just for a second, a smile."

"Look at the back of my knee."

"Oh, Hedy. There are two deep red marks, like blood vessels have burst. Let me get a cold cloth."

How odd, to have my sister looking after me.

She whispered, "We can try again, later, once it's dark. I still have the key. They will never think we'd try again right away."

It was still raining by the time night fell. Susannah was in agony, clutching her stomach and shivering. She said the cramps were terrible and she kept running to the commode.

"Hedy, what if it's pneumonia? I'm so cold!" Her feet kicked out from under the blanket. "Please, get Frau Kreutzel to come."

I pounded on the door and called for help. "Please, my sister is sick! Please, Frau Kreutzel!"

No answer. After a while the door opened.

"Zehra the Turk! It's you!" Susannah called from the bed. "Please, ask Frau Kreutzel to send for a doctor."

Zehra shook her head.

"Don't go! Tell Frau Kreutzel I've caught pneumonia!" Susannah was shivering like someone was shaking her even though I had wrapped her in all the bedclothes, even the bedcover.

"First, I'm not a Turk. That's just what I look like."

"You mean the ever-growing Pasha moustache?" My sister, even in pain, had to crack a joke. It was ignored.

"The doctor is on his way. But I can tell you, it's not pneumonia. It's because you need your medicine. When you don't get it, this is what happens. Frau Kreutzel needs to know that you won't do this again."

"I'm sorry, I promise." Susannah stumbled to the bathroom. "I promise!"

Zehra pulled me close. Listen," she whispered, "it's the morphine. That's what she gets mixed in water and has to drink before callers come. People keep taking morphine because it's so awful when they don't. And it keeps girls like your sister looking like girls, not women."

Susannah was moaning.

I grabbed Zehra's sleeve. "Please, Zehra, ask Frau Kreutzel if I can talk to her."

Her desk was set back from the window. Glittering, pointed Turkish oil lamps hung from delicate black chains behind her. She had a rope of skin hanging down the middle of her neck from her chin to her collar. Her neckline was low, so my eyes were drawn to her plump bosom, the ropey skin becoming part of the landscape of flesh. She made Hans leave. "So we can talk," she said.

She was the one who talked. "You are not a Schottenring princess. You are a little whore in debt to me. Do you think you can live here, eat here, be clothed, be seen by a doctor for free? You pay me by being kind to the few gentlemen I provide to you. Are they rough with you?"

Not like you are. "No, Frau Kreutzel."

"I provide protection, with Hans. Do you think he is free?"

I am not free. "No, Frau Kreutzel."

"I have shown you kindness, taking you in when you had nowhere to go. I was once in your situation. Your sister reminds me very much of myself at her age. When I was young, I had nowhere to go, no parents, no family, and the woman who used to run this place took me in. I did whatever she asked. I was grateful." She looked at me and raised her eyebrows.

"Yes, Frau Kreutzel."

"I cannot pay the cost of your sister's medical bills. This, you must do. The way she talks, she needs medication. Your callers want an innocent girl, and if she says 'shit' or 'arsehole' the illusion is spoiled. Creating that illusion is an art. Do you see?"

"Yes, Frau Kreutzel." *An unexpected aspect of "the life of the arts" in Vienna.*

"Why are you smiling? Are you listening? Look at me. If you ever try to leave without my permission again, I promise you I will call the police. You aren't registered as prostitutes, but I will tell them you are thieves, and I will say you stole money from me. Which, in effect, you would be doing. Don't think about leaving. Jail guards do what they like with prisoners."

Brigita.

"Especially the pretty ones. I know." Frau Kreutzel was silent and then her eyes brimmed with tears. "I don't want to think about that happening to Suzi. It's too awful to think about."

She was in love with how kind she was, with how much she,

Frau Kreutzel, could feel for others, or at least, for others in whom she saw herself. Like my sister.

"And you had better hand over that key you made your sister steal."

After a while, the doctor who came to the house, Bloch, arrived and showed Susannah how to inject morphine and how to keep the syringe clean. He told her to eat plums and prunes. He said her dosage wouldn't affect her logic or her memory, but her body would delay in maturing. "You will seem young for a long time," he said.

When I told Susannah the next day that Kreutzel had complained about her vulgarity with callers, she shrugged. She was not going to surrender anything she didn't have to. I told her she made me promise to not run away. I didn't tell her I had promised to make sure she didn't, either.

"Kreutzel is a good businesswoman." That was what Zehra the Turk said. When it was sunny, and not too cold, we were encouraged to sit outside for an hour among the drying sheets, with Zehra to watch us. It was a chance for her to smoke those little brown cigarettes of hers. There was nothing to see, no grass, no trees. The yard was small and the brick wall around it was high. The air smelled like bleach. And tobacco.

10.

BY SUMMER, KREUTZEL WAS ALLOWING us excursions again, escorted by Hans. I saw the Mischlinger's dark red Daimler in the square once, and to my shame, I watched for him. But I knew he didn't want us. We were too old for what he liked.

Over the next year, we saw more automobiles all over the city—parked anywhere, half on the curb, on the sidewalk—so many that when Hans escorted us out, Susannah liked to alarm him by saying, "That one? Shall I steal that one?"

In the evening, the square at the end of the street was jumbled with cars parked by men going to nearby cabarets. Loud and happy from drinking, the men would come back to wheel their cars out of the square, lurching over curbs and honking their horns. We often heard them speaking French or English, and sometimes, according to Susannah, Hungarian.

Whenever Susannah thought she heard calls from the street in Hungarian, she seized my hand and kissed it, saying, "*Kazeet choke alohma.*" Then she would hang onto my hand and recall again how well she had bargained over spoons with the Galician on behalf of her friend, Margarete.

On rare occasions, our callers were Italian, wealthy commercial travellers from Milan or Venice. Susannah did not treat these callers with her usual caprice. She told Kreutzel she wished she had a picture of Italy, and the next day she was presented with a lithograph. We hung it over the bed. The first time a caller pressed banknotes into our hands, saying "Shh, a little extra something for my little rich girls," I waited until he was gone before hiding the notes under the canals of Venice.

I hid Egon Schiele's drawing there too, so I could keep the connection to that sudden moment when I had delayed going home, when I had convinced myself that my parents would be better if we didn't go home right away. I looked at that image of myself every time I slipped the banknotes under the back paper. There I was, with my elbow out, a girl who thought she could influence what happened to her. She should have gone home.

We had almost enough money from callers now that I began to hope. We could get to a spa. They had doctors at spas and, our callers said, whores. At a spa, I could earn money to hire the help needed for Susannah to be weaned off morphine. Her habit was exhausting. For the first few minutes after her injection, she was a little drunken goat, frolicky and clumsy. She threw things at me—pillows, or her slippers, or if I ignored her, plums. By the time I was provoked enough to retaliate, she would be moments away from a deep torpor. At night, however, I was often wakened by an arm thrown across me, as if preventing me from a collision. I had turned sixteen and I craved sleep, all the time.

At a spa, I knew I might need skills that Kreutzel told Susannah didn't suit our current appeal of being well-born girls, only recently "ruined," and therefore still innocent, still capable of being exquisitely embarrassed. Actually, I was embarrassed. Susannah acted as though each caller had never happened.

I listened very carefully to Bebe Raton squeaking about special things to do with callers, and paid attention to Zehra the Turk, who spoke awkward German on purpose, but was very good at demonstrating.

"This is called the lazy man," she said, and flopped on her side, pretending to lift an imaginary leg so she could slide one of hers under it, and put her other leg on top. She showed me "the Italian sign of approval" and a few others. When she had callers, we could hear her laughing. Susannah only raised an eyebrow and went back to her newspaper.

I was at ease with the physical side of what I did. Most of the men were old, and Mischlinger had been old, and he was where I had started, so I was used to it. Old skin is wrinkled but very soft, like thin tissue leather, especially where it creases—near the armpit, or at any joining part, really. But their conversation was another matter. They often gave us pet names.

They said I was their little sweetie or—Susannah cackled over this one, so pompous, as if the fellow were Adam in Eden—"I think I shall call you Kitty."

We tried variations. "I think I shall call you Horsie," I told her.

"And you," Susannah said, "I think I shall call you 'Hairbrush.'"

I couldn't stand it when a caller said he loved me. Or warned me that he loved his wife. I told Susannah, love is nothing.

Our callers visited both of us at once. That was what made us unique. We were a novelty, never apart, always with each other. I paid close attention to our callers. I saw who had bitten his fingernails, and who was always a little drunk.

One didn't want any talking at all. He wanted me with my clothes on, so he could slide his hand around. And he didn't like it when Susannah rattled her newspaper. He asked if she could leave the room and Kreutzel told him, no, we were a twosome, period. For commercial purposes, we were. Sometimes a caller wanted us both to lie down with him at the same time, but we didn't like it and Kreutzel didn't either, as it complicated her bookkeeping.

Susannah didn't like any of it. "I don't pay attention. I say the same thing, 'Oh my darling.' And, 'rescue me.' And laugh. I do what they want, and then when they leave, it's as if they were never here."

And of course, she had her medicine.

She also had that section of blue sky that we could see above the shutters. It was like she was having an ongoing conversation with it. When I asked what she was thinking about, all she said was, "Hmm?" I was very lonesome for someone to be interested in what I was thinking about, and no one was.

Not since Mischlinger.

Susannah and I did not talk about our childhood, nor about anything else that mattered. Only the immediate present: our callers, the other girls in the house, Kreutzel. Maybe it was lonesome for Susannah as well. She was on her own when she flattered Kreutzel. I couldn't do it. Some days, everything around me seemed not quite real. I pressed my hand against the corner of the dressing table to make it real, so its sharp edge would keep me in the world.

Kreutzel began to insist we call her "Tante." As if we were a jolly family, one that, as it happened, provided a unique variety of sexual services. Now we were not only acting roles for our callers, we were acting for her as well. She had no idea of the level of scorn we all had for this.

She liked to recount her past successes with English callers. One Monday night, she walked into our room unexpectedly and to our horror, sat on our bed. To get rid of her, Susannah mentioned, on purpose, the increasing number of English callers we entertained. As expected, she launched into her prize story of how English royalty once sought her out.

"Some say that the old king of England actually died in a certain bed in Vienna and that the body had to be shipped back to Whitehall quickly. In secret." She lifted her eyebrows and composed her mouth into a miniature smile when she told this story.

We were supposed to believe it, and to believe that the bed was hers. At this point in the story, she usually put on a look, as though she were taken aback at having revealed so much. Then she would make a coy exit. We anticipated that all we had to do was look impressed, and our room would be ours again.

But this time she had a surprise. It seemed one of our callers, Emil of the Weak Chin, had again complained about our pallor, and had added that we were dull to talk to.

"So, tomorrow, Suzi, I would like you and your sister to enjoy a few hours out, on your own, without Hans, whenever the house is quiet. Tuesdays. A few hours, two or three. I don't want you to be seen in the square. There are too many little street tramps, angling for the men who drive those motor cars. The Augarten has a better quality of air. And people. You have to be out in the fresh air more to keep your youthful look. Even the most innocent young girls must have up-to-date manners, and do things the way wealthy people do. I can't let you become bumpkins. Go to cafés, but be careful about talking to people. My driver Hermann will take you and wait until it's time to come back." That triumphant, spitty smile. "You will have to pay for his services yourselves, of course."

"Oh, thank you, Tante." Susannah could sound so sincere.

Kreutzel left, buoyed by her sense of her own generosity. Whatever she had touched, we pulled off the bed, and asked Brigita for fresh bed linen. After our bed was made, I told Susannah I thought Kreutzel was softening.

"You can think that if you want," she smirked.

11.

"WAKE UP, SUSANNAH. when the body moves, the mind must follow."

"I can think without moving," she said. "Unlike you."

But like dance partners, we made the bed: the bottom sheet, the top sheet, the feather comforter, the two pillows punched until they were plump and placed on the counterpane like hens on nests. There, and there. Coats, hats, gloves, handbags; smiles at each other in the mirror, arm in arm through the door; down the stairs, out the door, down the steps, up into the waiting carriage. We were going to be out in the city for hours, on our own.

Fog was rising from the Donaukanal that morning. It was chilly. I could tell exactly when we crossed over the river on the Augartenbruke by the sound of the horses' hooves on the pavement. I peered out, but all I could see were the pillars. The bronze figures standing on them were lost in the fog. I didn't care. It was so good to be out on our own in the city.

"What?"

"You're smiling, Hedy."

Our driver pulled into the line of carriages for hire on the boulevard. Every carriage had two black horses. Every horse hung its head. It would snow later, by late afternoon. We walked to a bench in the open part of the Augarten. The fog lifted, and we turned our faces up to the bright morning sun. Our mother used to bring us to this park. It was calm at this hour, quiet. We sat, side by side. "We could take off, you know," Susannah said.

"No, we couldn't. We have to know where we're going," I replied."

"And have enough money, Hedy, to get us there."

"Before she knows we're gone."

Children's voices. A ball bounced towards a dark-eyed young man on a bench further up the path. He caught the ball and tossed it in one fluid motion back to the boy who had thrown it. The boy caught the ball, but pretended it had been thrown with such force that he had to stagger about. The young man laughed and looked over at us to share the moment. He had slight gaps between his teeth, and his eyes were hooded. His hair was a little long, parted in the middle. No hat. I returned his smile with a polite half smile of my own.

"I'm sorry," Susannah blurted without looking at me. "I don't want to take morphine, but it hurts so much if I don't."

I didn't turn to look at her. "I know."

"Everything is just a little softer after I take it. My thoughts swish, and I feel like all the things I have to do are everyday nothing kind of things."

"Don't be hard on yourself." I just wanted to enjoy the sunshine, even though I could feel Susannah staring at me. "What?"

"I want it to feel like it once did, being with you, just the two of us having fun. You look so exhausted."

She stuck her hand out in front of her and waggled it. One of Papa's hand games. She threaded an invisible needle, rolled a knot and pulled it tight. Then she inserted the 'needle' through her baby finger, and with perfectly timed winces, 'pierced' through her ring finger, pulling the thread so that the baby finger was pulled tightly against the ring finger, and so on with the other fingers. Then she 'punctured' her palm, pulling the fingers in. I grinned. I knew what was next. A fist. She punched herself in the jaw and pretended to be knocked out. Our old game. I pretended to cry.

"Don't cry for me, Hedy," she begged theatrically. She threw an arm out, a pointing finger, stage melodrama. "You must leave me."

"I shall, after I have wept copious tears. But first my eyes must be clean." I pretended to take out my eyeball, and squinting, pop it in my mouth. I poked my cheeks with my tongue to make it look like it was rolling around, first one cheek plumping up, and then the other. Then I spit into my hand and carefully inserted the eyeball back into its socket.

When I turned to look at her, I was cross-eyed. I gave myself a smack on the head and the eye righted itself. We sat peacefully, leaning against each other, smiling, as though nothing had happened.

The young man on the bench up the path laughed out loud. He didn't move towards us, but he applauded silently. We smiled at each other openly. No one could see us. No one cared. He pulled out a cigarette case, and raised his eyebrows enquiringly.

This was an invitation, and I shrunk back. I put a hand out, as if to protect Susannah from a sudden aggressor. We both shook our heads "no," so he held the cigarette in his mouth and took out his match case. He attempted to light his cigarette, unsuccessfully. Others might have been able to ignore this dilemma. Not my firebug sister.

The Augarten was designed for movement across its lawns; its wide paths were perfect for running. She strode smoothly over to him and in a deep manly voice said, "Allow me."

He proffered a match, and held up the match case so she could use its square of sandpaper. Instead, with a flick of her thumbnail, she lit the match and held it steady, just so. She had learned that trick a long time ago, with only one or two mishaps over the years. That fire in the drive shed when she was ten years old had been nothing. A few foot stomps and it was out. Marta had made such a fuss.

The fellow seemed impressed. He cupped his hand and drew on the cigarette. She bowed. Holding the lit cigarette out to the side, he stood, a true Viennese ingénue, knees locked, eyes closed, head tilted to one side, one arm extended, and a drooping hand for her to kiss.

"Kind sir," he said, in a high delicate voice.

She was with him on this. In her deepest voice, she said, "Your little hand, so..."

Helpfully, he supplied, "Furry."

I laughed out loud. They were so pleased with themselves. They strutted back to the bench where I sat. Susannah sat down and leaned away from him. He stepped back to a formal and courteous distance.

He had a broad chest, an easy stance. He flung both hands out, fingers spread. "May I comment? You are young ladies, yet you play like young girls such as I see in the park. Only better. Pardon me, Herr Doctor Jacob Moreno. Or almost. My studies are almost complete."

"But, Doctor, we aren't young girls." Susannah beamed at him. "Are you Italian, may I ask?"

"I was Romanian, but we are all Austrians, now, yes?"

"You may call me Fraulein Susannah Edel..."

"And I'm Hedy," I interrupted, and pulled her up from the bench.

"Be more careful," I whispered to Susannah. "Nothing has changed. We still belong to the brothel. No one needs to know our last name."

The fellow kept his voice neutral, soft. "What are two young ladies doing in the Augarten so early?" His dark eyes were kinder than I could bear.

"Early for whores, you mean?"

He stepped back at my response, arms opening backwards. I grabbed my sister's hand and we walked arm in arm to the line of carriages. As our carriage moved away, I leaned forward just enough to see that the Moreno fellow was still watching us. It had begun to snow. He pulled a bright blue scarf out of his sleeve and wrapped it around his head.

12.

ONE LATE JUNE MORNING, it was intermittently sunny with the rain likely to hold off, and all along the boulevards the linden trees were in bloom. Small boys hid in their branches to toss the white flowers down into their mothers' aprons. On our way to the Augarten, we leaned out of the fiacre to breathe in the intoxicating scent that spilled into the air.

The other whores had leaned over the stair railing and clapped when we left. A chance to safely annoy Kreutzel about her favourites, although I was hardly her favourite. Susannah was her favourite.

I was not sure what I thought about Moreno, but I had watched for him whenever we went to the Augarten. And now, just as we strolled past the fountain, there he was. He was walking with one arm above his head, his hand brushing against the hanging linden blossoms.

Susannah tugged on my arm. "Who are you pretending not to look at?"

"Moreno."

"That doctor from a couple of months ago?"

He saw us. I kept Susannah moving, but I nodded, a curt acknowledgement, a cover for the delight I felt. I walked faster, forcing Susannah to pick up her pace as well. He doffed his hat as he came closer.

"Ah, the Frauleins Hedy and Susannah!" He had covered a lot of ground without looking like he was in a hurry. He was almost in front of us. He swivelled neatly and now began to walk backwards alongside us on the grass beside the path. Susannah looked off into the distance. I made myself as tall as I could.

"You move very quickly, sir."

"I can think better when I am moving." He drifted to beyond arm's reach, still moving backwards, not tripping, his hat doffed again. "*Gruss Gott*. Jacob Moreno."

"Doctor Almost," said Susannah.

"You know..." he was smiling, completely at ease, "I haven't been able to stop thinking about you."

Susannah smirked. "I've heard that before."

Why is she so bold? I have to decide so much for both of us, all the time, and this situation calls for caution.

"Do you want to know what I was thinking? May I tell you as we walk?"

"You are already talking, and we are already walking." I couldn't believe I had said that. Now I was the one being bold.

Susannah laughed at my rudeness. It was fun, to talk to a man this way, the way she usually did. I felt lighter, as if I suddenly weighed less. He smiled at my sauciness, as if he liked it, too. Still, was he getting us to let down our defenses before he pounced? With a handkerchief, maybe, loaded with chloroform? He was a doctor, or said he was.

I reached for the long hat pin I kept in my purse. I looked to see where his hand was. We rounded a corner where the path was wider. I held the pin ready in case he tried to insinuate himself between me and my sister.

But he maintained the same easy distance from us, still walking backwards. His eyes were merry. What a show-off. I stuck the pin into my hat.

"Go ahead, sir, please continue."

"Thank you, then, with your permission." He began to walk forward alongside us. "When I saw you the last time, I thought that you were both so full of tension, there was going to be a big argument, or even better, a fight. Fraulein Susannah, you sewed a fist!" He was smiling, his eyebrows raised, his eyes dancing.

"I'm surprised you remember my name."

"I'm surprised you would think anyone could forget it. And you, Fraulein Hedy," he turned and smiled at me, "you washed your eyeball. You, I thought, wanted to see clearly."

I couldn't help it, I was smiling back.

"Oh, sentence algorithms!" Susannah leaned around me again to see him. "Did you really think I wanted to hit someone?"

"At first, at first! But then..." he paused.

"But then what?"

"I saw you leaning against each other afterward like a couple of baby seals in the Tiergarten. Aaah." He shrunk his head onto his own shoulder and closed his eyes. "You were so relaxed and unselfconscious." He opened his eyes and straightened his hat. Pearl grey, a doctor's hat. New. "As though the uneasy feelings—uneasy, yes?—as though they were released in the safety of the hand games."

"Our father taught us a lot of hand games."

"Do you think it stimulates the imagination?

"How do you mean?" This was exciting. We were talking, simply talking. He was asking my opinion. And then he extended both his elbows and waited. What kind eyes he had. I took his arm first, and then we were each holding onto one of his arms, escorted like proper young *frauleins* under the protection of an uncle. A brother. Someone like that.

"Let me tell you what I've been thinking about. What you, Fraulein Hedy, and you, Fraulein Susannah, caused me to remember."

We were walking comfortably with him. He had shortened his stride to walk with us at our pace. That kind of adjustment of pace was something I had become very good at as a whore. That, and asking questions to keep the caller talking.

"When I was a child," he said, "games of the imagination were all I cared about, all the time, every day. Sometimes at night! Ah, there was another spring, a long time ago, and there was a ladder, the tallest one my brother William and I could find." He paused.

"Why did you need a ladder?"

"So that I, Jakob—eight years old, mind you—could stand on the top and be God." He shrugged and shook his head. "I was a confident child."

"We used to be very confident. When we were little, we would run outside and order hansom cabs for ourselves to go to Prater Park."

"Ah, you understand. I thought you would." He beamed. "So I told the little ones on the street to be joyous. 'Be joyous!' I shouted. And guess what they did." He paused again. He was very good at that, those pauses.

"What?"

"They all stood there. William held the ladder steady. 'Listen to my little brother!' he said. And what do you think they said?"

"Something rude?"

"They said, 'We don't have to listen to you, William.' But from the top of the ladder, in my most manly voice—like yours, Susannah, the other day—I said, 'No, you don't have to listen to William. But you have to listen to me. I am God! You are the first cats and dogs in the world.' And they asked..."

"What? What?" Susannah and I asked in unison.

"They asked, 'What about goats?' Moreno was laughing. "And God flung his arm out, and said, 'No goats!'" A grand sweep of his arm. "'Now, be joyous, dogs and cats!' And then they started pouncing and sniffing. Rolling around!"

Susannah and I were laughing.

"What a wonderful start it was to that summer!"

Susannah pulled up short. There was a vagrant in front of us, a ragged man in pants stiff with dirt, a hat with a broken brim. "Happy Belly Boy!"

He was shouting at Moreno, who smiled and raised his eyebrows, enquiring.

"Yes, you! Happy Belly Boy!" He clutched his belly and shook it at Moreno.

Susannah and I stayed still, but Moreno continued forward. He clutched his own belly and shook it. He and the ragged man laughed, delighted with each other. Then the ragged man disappeared into the shrubbery, and Moreno turned back to us.

"Don't be afraid, Frauleins. I would never let anyone hurt you."

We recommenced walking with him. He was quiet. So were we. Just walking this way felt so good. And then, looking straight ahead, he said, "How honest people are when they have nothing to lose! The mad beggars of the street make painful observations about those who pass them by, even the ones with kind smiles. They shout at the ill-fitting trouser, the disapproving mouth. They make a theatre on the street. They make others afraid, so that everyone is equal: afraid, just like they are."

As I walked alongside him, I did not have to look at him, and he couldn't see my immediate reaction. I felt safe, at ease. "We all need company in our fear."

"A trenchant observation, Fraulein Hedy." We were nearing the fountain again. "They were going to put a fountain in the hospital where I work, but this is Vienna, so instead of a fountain, it will be another marble statue." Moreno's smile was rueful. "I know I am very close to figuring out—something—that will heal the sorrow I see around me. I've learned how to do basic medicine, but I'm interested in the mind, in the soul. The *psyche,* as my colleagues say who learned Greek at an earlier age, and in better schools. But I can feel a kind of radiance within myself, a beneficence, and if I wasn't so sure of my own goodness, I might be a pain in the ass."

He looked to see if we were shocked at his vulgarity. He had no idea what we had listened to at 13, Verstektstrasse. I sat down on the ledge of the fountain. Susannah sat on the other side of me.

"You, young ladies. I feel I can talk to you two about what's on my mind, for some reason."

"That's what a lot of ... people ...of our acquaintance say." Susannah smirked. She was always at a distance from what happened. It helped her be funny.

He looked at us, and then looked into the fountain, or beyond it, flicking the water with his hand. "We are human because of our human bodies. Some people can think their bodies into sickness, and need the mind to heal the body. But I am convinced that the body can heal the mind. It's one human, one soul, one total being. It's all meant to work together." He paused, and then jumped up. I looked quickly, but there was no handkerchief, no chloroform.

"I smell the beginning of summer! Come! It's not just the scent of the linden blossoms that calls this city outside. In Vienna, it's also the smell of coffee! Shh!"

He looked left and then right, his dark eyes widening. "Everywhere, especially on this side of the Augarten, if one listens, one can hear the sound of tables and chairs being dragged outside. Wherever you look, there are waiters, their arms raised up like dancers, holding trays and moving around each other. Vienna likes to collaborate, to work together, closely."

His left arm was folded in front of his waist, and his right was extended in the air, the hand bent flat as if holding a tray. With more grace and dignity than I had ever seen, even at the Vienna State Opera, he performed a waltzing pirouette precisely, once, and returned to a calm walk, as if nothing had happened.

"Frauleins, I wish to alleviate human suffering, as a doctor should, and my thesis, if you will, is that in order to do so, we need to communicate about our feelings."

Susannah rolled her eyes. "That's not new. Especially in Vienna."

"Yes, Fraulein, but it is very hard. It's difficult to feel safe, to feel calm enough to be honest."

"Which is why they say that in Vienna," I reminded him, "we love the pretty lie."

Susannah groaned. He looked at her, registering her impatience.

"My approach is different. Everyone thinks it's just a matter of talking. It isn't. We are not statues. Vienna has enough of those. We move! We humans were meant to move; we were always on the move—we hunted, we gathered, we moved. When we move, we feel safe, and it lets us be spontaneous in our actions. If we are spontaneous, we are not pre-meditating, we are not manipulating, we are not fearful, and so, I believe, we speak what is on our minds." He stopped and looked at me. "In our hearts, Fraulein Hedy."

Herr Schiele used to talk like that. Make pronouncements. But this Moreno has such kindness in his dark eyes.

We were walking again. "May I make a personal comment, Frauleins?"

What an experience this is. "Please, go ahead," I said.

"I think, if I may say so, you, Fraulein Hedy, are a brave person, protective. I notice how you always stand ahead of your companion."

"She's my sister."

"So you are the perfect older sister."

I looked at him. *Papa had said that to me.*

He was saying something. "Perhaps she also, in her own way, is protective of you. Or willing to be."

"Oh, no!" Susannah's newspaper had come apart. War and fashion, criminals and royalty, all floated up together in the breeze. We ran, all three of us, to catch the sheets of newsprint. And then, like soldiers on furlough, we linked arms and laughed and were on the move again.

"Now, please," he said, "I cannot bear another minute without my first outdoor coffee of the season. Will you join me?"

We were beside a boxwood hedge surrounding a bustling outdoor café. The Arundel. Susannah let go of his arm and stepped back.

"Fraulein Susannah, there are dozens of people in that courtyard. I do not want to harm you. I need the advice of a normal woman, like you, who does normal things, like read the daily newspaper."

She tightened her grip on her reassembled *Die Welt*.

"You can feel safe. Look about. There are many people around, all of them able to see every person—the tables are set up so that people can see and be seen."

This was a man being nice to us. *What did he want?* I understood Susannah's reluctance. I shared it, a little. But he was young. And, like her, he was funny.

"We'll talk to you, Herr Doctor," I said, "for the length of time it takes to have a chocolate. We will order it, wait for it to cool down, sip it, and when we are finished, you must get up, tip your hat, and walk away."

Look after her. Our mother had been clever—if I looked after my sister, I was also looking after myself.

"You are very gracious." He touched the brim of his hat and bent forward in a little bow. His eyes were merry. "Thank you, Frauleins. Now, this way." He steered us gracefully to a table that was half in sunlight, half in shade. Once we were seated, Moreno walked over to the café's rattan rack to get a newspaper of his own.

"Hedy!" Susannah whispered. "I can't believe that we're here. We spend enough time with men who want something."

"He's not on the prowl. If you spent less time reading your newspapers, you'd have seen that. You'd think you'd never watched men, and you're in the same business as me."

It had turned cool, so on the next Tuesday we sat indoors at the Café Arundel, with me beside Moreno this time. Susannah looked directly at him, not up at the sky through the window, as she usually did when she had to talk to men. She could produce a charming giggle every few minutes regardless of what a man said to her, or was in the middle of doing to her. But Moreno had a good face. His whole face listened.

The three of us were at ease, talking and reading, our umbrellas parked by our chairs. I watched Susannah as she talked to him. She had been so wary the last time. But an item in the paper had caught her attention, and she talked enthusiastically about how the Mona Lisa was back in Florence. She admired the thief, Perugia. An Italian patriot, a man of principles. And a thief.

Moreno leaned back, smiling under those hooded eyes and nodding. Waiters in long white aprons bustled by the small marble-topped table, carrying trays, dramatically avoiding the violin-shaped wire backs of the chairs. A waiter must be noticed for what he does; he can't make it look too easy. A little flourish will encourage tips. The working world is not so different from a whorehouse.

By the door, newspapers, a complete variety, were organized in rattan racks, free for customers who wished to read while they sipped their coffee. Or chocolate. The place was full of conversation, but the high ceilings and the sound-absorbing palm plants let us hear each other perfectly.

"How do you assess a caller? You are very intelligent girls, but you are young, and people don't always want to say directly what they desire."

He was very diplomatic. He never said "customer," and he never asked about the actual sex. He was a gentleman, discreet, and truly interested in the part of our work that was not sex, but theatre.

"When a caller has everything buttoned up," Susannah said, "then we know we have to be shy. We raise one shoulder up, like this, and keep our eyes looking down, like this, and then look up like this, worried, but with a little smile."

Moreno grinned, applauding silently.

"If he's well-dressed, but somewhat dashing—like Max Linder, you know—we can be slightly bolder. Hedy can do the Arabian dancer look!"

They both turned to look at me, and I accommodated, lowering my eyelids and resting my chin on the back of an arched hand. I let my eyes look left and right. Then I lifted both elbows up behind my head for a brief moment, as if I were adjusting hatpins. This, I knew, moved my bosom up and forward. Hatpins and Arabian fantasies have their uses.

"Brava, Fraulein Hedy." Moreno turned his hand out in my direction, as if to say, 'here is what we have been waiting for.'

Susannah said, "Here's the school mistress; we can both do that really well!"

I kicked her foot and put my head down.

She looked at Moreno, annoyed. "If you don't want to see that one, just say so." Moreno straightened and looked blankly at her.

"It was me," I whispered. "Not him. I kicked you, Susannah. Be quiet. Don't let them see you."

But, of course, she turned to look, and then turned back quickly.

It was Fraulein Lowin, in an elegant violet coat, a duster meant for motorcar travel. Her unmistakable tobacco voice greeting Frau Moser on the other side of the room. She swept past, not noticing us, not seeing Moreno. We had become invisible. I heard the double front doors of the café open, a little outdoor noise.

"Who were those ladies who passed us?"

"No one. Friends of our mother's. Still alive. Still part of the life of the arts in Vienna."

Unlike us. We drank our chocolate *mit schlag* in silence.

"I'm thinking, Frauleins, of going to a spa. Which one would you recommend?"

"Don't ask us. We make bad choices." Susannah had a chocolate moustache.

"The last time Susannah and I had planned to go to a spa, we ended up under the care of Frau Kreutzel. Our family used to go to Bad Ragaz. We aren't likely to go anywhere, now, not while morphine rules our lives, and Kreutzel has our papers."

Moreno leaned forward, opening his arms. "But really, you are actresses, you are young women, and you can be the monarchs of your lives. Your life is like a kingdom, and you must find a way to rule it."

Susannah brightened. This was the spirited conversation she craved. Loud, grand, earnest. "Are you sure you're not Italian?"

"He's Jewish, Susannah. Aren't you? Jakob Moreno?"

"I am, and more. I was born Jakob Levy in Romania, more or less, in a boat on the Black Sea, but I am now... I have become Jacob Levy Moreno." He beamed. "Who is due at the hospital for his turn in the emergency in an hour. And tonight, I'm going to hear a lecture given by Doctor Freud. No doubt you ladies also have a busy schedule." He blushed, and then regained his aplomb within seconds. "May I offer you a ride?"

We insisted on using Kreutzel's Hermann, who was waiting for us in his ancient fiacre.

Moreno insisted, before we parted ways, that he had an idea of how to help us.

13.

I SHOOK SUSANNAH, who mumbled, "No! I want sleep, we don't have any callers, it's Tuesday." She pulled a pillow over her head.

"We have two."

Susannah sat bolt upright. "Oh, no. Not those kinky twins, the Kronenbergs again. I want my day off. I don't care if they pay double. Anyway, they want theatre, not sex. Which takes much more effort. What is it this time, the rolling down of one stocking?" She started to rustle through a drawer in the bedside table.

"No, it's..."

"Oh, the peeling of the glove. You have them, in the cupboard. Kid, pale green."

"Susannah. It's not the twins. It's two doctors. Well, a real one, Dr. Gruen, and Moreno."

"Doctor Almost. I told him I didn't want to express my true feelings. Vienna is crazy for feelings."

"Vienna is crazy for sex."

"No, Vienna is crazy for crazy."

This was clever, maybe insightful, but before I could talk to her about what she might have meant, she stumbled against the slipper chair.

"Oh, shit." She kept her head down and rubbed her ankle. "Is Dr. Gruen licensed?"

"Yes, he will examine us and give us our own medical

certificates to keep for ourselves. Kreutzel won't know. And without charge. Free."

"Free. Please. While Moreno watches, I bet."

I opened the door. Moreno and Dr. Gruen took off their hats and bowed. Dr. Gruen was stiff, ill at ease. Moreno gave him a little push.

"Relax. We've paid for their time," Moreno said, and introduced us.

Gruen nodded and immediately gazed around the room, his smile cement. I could tell he was curious, and appalled to find that he was. I'd seen this reaction before with first-time callers.

"Dr. Gruen will be able to give you your medical papers."

"Good! Doctor Bloch smells, and he always gives the documents to Frau Kreutzel. You, Herr Doctor Gruen," I said for my own amusement and that of Moreno, "smell nice."

Somehow, in Moreno's presence, I felt playful. The young doctor blushed to the roots of his wavy hair and opened his case. Quick. Professional.

"Please, if we may begin, Fraulein?"

Susannah leaped out of bed.

He backed up, his hands palm up. She tugged the three-panelled screen closer to the bed, and even though she had done this many times before, she nearly knocked it over. Nothing like a little emergency to get the adrenalin flowing in a caller. Doctor Gruen steadied the screen and had to duck as a flouncy dressing gown flew past his head. She peeked around the edge of the screen at him before she hopped back onto the bed wearing nothing but an underslip.

"I'm ready, Doctor."

She had no mercy. She pulled up a sheet, rested her chin on the back of outstretched fingers, and batted her eyelashes.

Moreno was delighted with her performance. He mouthed to me, "The Arabian Dancer!"

I quite like him.

Doctor Gruen picked up his satchel and stepped towards

Susannah. Moreno and I sat down with our backs to them on the cream-coloured leather bench.

"I want to thank you for helping us. If we get a chance to travel, to escape, we will need to have our own papers."

"And if it takes a little while to organize this escape, Dr. Gruen can renew them. He's quite respectable. He already has a burgeoning practice." He stretched his legs. "Fraulein Hedy, there is something else I want."

"Told you!" Susannah's voice was merry.

Moreno smiled and shook his head. His eyes sparkled with laughter held in.

I ignored her. "Wait, first, can you write a prescription for Susannah's morphine?"

"No. But I can help you! I like the way you can pretend. You know." He hit himself with his fist in the jaw by way of demonstration.

"You forgot the sewing part."

He shrugged. "Are you happy?"

"We're the youngest and most expensive whores in this house."

Moreno was quiet at my answer and then touched my hand. "I need both of you."

"Told you," said Susannah again.

"Excuse me." Gruen poked his head out from behind the screen. His face was fiery red, but his voice was steady. "Look, Jacob..."

"I only need them to talk, Gruen."

"To talk dirty?" Susannah poked her head out from behind the screen. "I can do that."

He smiled and said, no, he needed us to talk to other whores.

Gruen poked his head out again, "You mean fallen angels."

"No, Doctor Gruen," said Moreno," they're not. They're whores. I've talked to so many. They are so young, they experience such shame, and they cover this shame up with such bravado."

Doctor Gruen emerged from behind the screen, and stood, listening.

"Many of them are orphans." I felt myself go very still. We don't talk to callers or other whores in our brothel about our families. Or the lack of them. We usually don't even tell anyone what our real names are.

"I do what I can as a doctor," said Gruen. "But Moreno, what are you suggesting?"

"You, sir, are like everyone else, like Fraulein Hedy, or me, or Fraulein Susannah. You must see yourself as you are, if you are to change what surrounds you as it is." He tossed a hand towards me. "Hedy, you and your sister are both intelligent, creative people, who are not under any illusions. Please, I need your help."

I knew I had to bargain for what I wanted, and I also knew I was not very good at bargaining. "I've got expenses," I said, and I doffed my hand towards Susannah who had appeared from behind the screen, dressed and solemn-faced. "And there they are."

"I'm afraid what I propose to do is voluntary—but very interesting. It is a new approach. My own. One I'm developing. I think it will help those who suffer, who've been made fearful. In fact, I'm convinced."

"I have to say, I'm convinced it will, too," said Gruen as he washed his hands in the small basin. "What you said about Freud to one of his acolytes, well, he was non-plussed." He looked at Moreno with frank admiration, even though he was addressing Susannah and me. "Imagine saying to an older man, a man who is a doctor already, published in the top journals and written up in the newspapers, 'Well, I think it is no good to meet people in an office. Do we go to an office to fall in love? Do we go to the Office of Grief to mourn? Our conflicts happen in our homes, on the streets. To look back, to look inward is all well and good, but talk alone? We are not just mouths. We are bodies! We moved once through our conflicts; we must move through them again.' Well, the man didn't know what to say!"

"I am not sure that's what I said, but you imitate me very well. I do fling out my arm like that, don't I?"

Gruen smiled back at Moreno, full of undisguised admiration. He turned to me. "You're next, Fraulein."

Once we were behind the screen, he asked, "Tell me, why not simply leave?"

"Kreutzel gets Susannah's morphine from Doctor Bloch."

The young doctor signed and stamped our medical papers, and tucked them into an envelope.

It would be hidden with other treasured papers behind the gondolas in Venice within the hour. Moreno also had envelopes for us. "The invitations to the meeting," he said. "Next week."

14.

THE CANVAS BLIND ON THE DOOR was pulled down, and a large "For Rent" sign had been papered over the display window of the store. It was raining. We stood under a shared umbrella and listened to the women around us begin to chat. It was Tuesday, the city's traditional day off for prostitutes.

Waiting had made the women tense. They sighed and shifted their weight from one foot to the other. They cast quick glances at each other's hats and clothing. It was daytime, so the city by-laws were respected: no bright colours, especially red. But the cheapness of the materials easily identified them as whores, and they looked at me and my sister with suspicion.

We had been allowed, thanks to Susannah's wiles, to choose our own fabrics and the cut of our skirts and jackets. As long as everything could easily be undone—no double fasteners or eyehooks—Kreutzel saw how the contrast between modesty in clothing and vulgarity in behaviour could work to her establishment's advantage. We were her "Schottenring girls," after all. When Susannah objected to the pretense that it was a happy accident—*oops!*—that a forefinger and a thumb encircled a cock struggling to be upright, Kreutzel said she was surprised that she had to remind her that nothing pays as well as the chance to sully the young and inexperienced, or the proud.

"An upper-class girl is more of a draw than a whore with sexual prowess," Kreutzel had said.

So, we were to know what we were doing, but to pretend that we didn't.

We listened to the others gathered there who agreed on two things: they had met with Moreno a second time because they trusted him, and they liked shy Dr. Gruen. They had apparently come from all over the city: from brothels in the Spittelberg, from streets near the Prater, and from the avenue by the Canal. The longer they waited, the less wary they became. They began to lean against the building, or hang off each other's shoulders. This was, they agreed, the right address. Something going wrong was nothing new, and actually made them more at ease, they said, laughing under their large hats. And just as it seemed that they had forgotten why they were there, Moreno opened the door. One whore after another scurried in. Susannah and I waited and went in last.

There were seven of us all together. The others were our age or a little older. A roomful of young women. Inside, the space was small, with chairs set in a circle. After shaking Moreno's hand, I took the chair nearest the door as Susannah struggled to close her umbrella. She handed it to Moreno, and it dripped onto his hand. He caught on to her game and made a show of looking about, confused. A little laughter. He wiped his hand quickly on his front before shaking hers, making her newspaper fall to the ground. There was more chuckling around us, and then outright guffaws when she sat in the chair I already occupied.

"Oh, shit!" Susannah moved and nestled into the chair beside me. I held myself erect, formal, head high, and looked only at Moreno. I knew what we were doing. We were the distraction, to put others at ease. Susannah needed me to be very proper, which suited me. She made a fuss about deciding to imitate how I sat and acted as though she had never heard anyone, ever, including herself, utter the word 'shit'.

Moreno pulled the faded red curtains closed. The room was washed in pink light. He had arranged a long white cloth on the former sales counter and had set out plates of pastries, tall chocolate pots, cups on trays, and cloth napkins arranged in chevrons.

"Now..."

Someone knocked on the door. We all froze.

"Ah. *Not* now!" Moreno held up a hand, and opened the door to the tiny tiled vestibule.

It was Margarete Gaboncz. She entered in a rush, a bruise on her cheek, and the sleeve of her green jacket torn away at the shoulder seam. Two of the other young women immediately clutched their handbags. Susannah touched my arm with hers, a flexing of an arm muscle. I didn't say anything.

Nor did Margarete, though her face brightened for a moment, I think, when she saw Susannah. We had agreed instinctively, without a word, not to acknowledge that we had once been children who had lounged about in Schiele's studio. Or that she and Kaspar had stolen our bicycles. Or that we all knew about Mischlinger. Moreno offered her a chair.

"Now, everyone, stay where you are. I've brought you something for a chilly day." Moreno handed each of us a brimming cup of chocolate. We sipped and warmed our hands on the cups. Moreno released a contented sigh, and stretched. He sat down.

"Well, *Liebchen*. Tell me how things are with you." He was looking at Margarete.

"My savings were stolen by a customer, and this is what the police did to me when I complained!" She showed us a red mark on her arm and another on her neck. "They laughed at me. But it was my money!"

Moreno nodded. He asked what Margarete and the police should have done, and there were several suggestions: they should have arrested the thief; she should get a pimp to make arrangements so she would not be bothered by the police again; she should carry a knife.

"Or a gun." Everyone laughed at Susannah's suggestion. This led to complaints about being stopped and questioned when all they wanted was a walk in the Prater, or coffee at Sacher's. A small volley of comments. They were street walkers, all-weather whores, forced to continue their work by poverty, abandonment, illness. My sister and I were trapped by her morphine addiction and my desire to hide from those who knew us. We soon learned that we were not the only orphans here, not the only ones who had been kidnapped. It made me feel, to my surprise, some relief. Others had been tricked, beaten, betrayed. We were not alone in our experience. We were just like those around us—only somewhat safer, and less likely to be stopped on the street.

Moreno went about the room and eased the cups from the women. It might have seemed an accident that he was touching their hands or wrists. But not to me, nor to Susannah. This was how one made contact with a nervous caller. "How would you describe yourself?" he asked.

"I'll go first. My customers like Dirty Slut."

"For me, Jolly Wench." A hand placed delicately on her shirtfront.

"I thought it was Fat Fuck." Some half-laughter.

Moreno's head stayed down as he put the last of the cups on the counter. We did this with callers, too—we ignored negative comments so things didn't get derailed.

He looked back up. "And when you were younger, what was your favourite sweet?"

Their response was like bird song.

How had he learned to do this? I wondered. This was the topic guaranteed to set callers at ease.

Moreno tipped his head to one side. "When you were a little girl?"

Yes, we know about tipping the head to one side, too.

"Greedy Girl. My father called me that. He was a baker, before he went to jail. He used to cut me such a slice of cake that I needed both hands to hold it."

Moreno's attention was calm, fully on this baker's daughter.

"Show me how you would eat it."

She did, looking around at first, then back to the anchor of Jakob Moreno's steady dark eyes.

I recognized that slow nodding; that was the permission we gave to first timers.

He mimicked what she did, acting it out, pretending to have difficulty balancing an imaginary cake and cutting a slice. This was exactly how we mirrored a nervous client: if he cleared his throat, we made a little cough, a modest variation on the sound, so he had company.

Susannah jumped up. She took the imaginary knife from Moreno and cut big slices with a flourish—*Sim, salabim!*—for everyone, in less than a minute. While some sat with their imaginary cake in their hand, others devoured theirs in a gulp. After Susannah 'ate' hers, she licked her thumb. "More anyone?"

"Thanks, I'm stuffed," said Margarete.

Those two childhood conspirators cackled, and then all the others laughed with the giddy relief that laughter is for young women. The real pastries went quickly, and then they all slipped away into the sleepy afternoon, a constellation of whores who would appear later on their usual transits through the city's night.

We were the last to leave. Once outside, Susannah turned to me. "So. Margarete has become a professional, too."

"I think she might have already been on the game when we met her at Schiele's."

"Two years ago."

It seemed as distant as the Napoleonic Wars. For a few moments, to hang onto the buoyant feeling of that room, Susannah and I were quiet. We walked quickly to the back entrance of the Café Arundel where Susannah convinced the bare-armed dishwasher to let us in, then through the café and out the front door. We walked casually towards Hermann's fiacre.

Susannah stopped. "Did you notice how he touched their wrists?"

"Yes! The way we do with callers."

"Yes! It's odd, what he had us do in there, but I liked it."

"I did, too. But then, I'm pretty odd."

"No, Hedy, you are oddly pretty. You have that little waist. I wish I had hips to sway around the room like you do."

"I don't sway my hips around the room."

"Oh, yes, you do." Susannah nodded. "To great effect. Dramatic, like your eyes."

"They're hooded."

"Like Mama's, like you know a secret. Mama's used to brighten like yours. You have her pale skin, too."

She is talking about our mother. We never talk about her.

"So I look Jewish. Unlike you."

"I do so look Jewish." She opened the door to the fiacre. "There are lots of blonde Jews, Hedy." She stumbled on the step, righted herself, and pulled me up after her.

"Not all of them make ridiculous compliments, I hope."

"I'm not finished. I know my sister, and I say her mouth is lovely. We are more than what we do. Talk to me."

"I am."

She settled into the cushioned seat. "Let's keep talking."

And we did, my sister and I, arm in arm, inside the quiet of the fiacre on our way back to the brothel, and then on into the night's small waking hours.

The meetings with Moreno were held during the day, as it was understood that some of the women would begin to work their favourite street corners at the day's close. For us, it became a habit when we came back in the late afternoon to ask for hot tea from the kitchen on our way up the stairs. It would arrive in no time, almost before we'd taken our hats off. When we unlaced our shoes, Susannah would leave hers in a heap that she would trip over, every time. And then we would sit together, talking, the old sun sinking down on his elbows below the window.

"Margarete complains every meeting about how someone has stolen something from her. I have to suppress the urge to ask her if she still has your bicycle, Susannah. Or your hat."

"But you have to agree she's entertaining. That old stuff doesn't matter. And those hours I spent with her were eye-opening. Wonderful. I remember thinking I would like to become a master thief."

"And steal what?"

She sipped her tea. "Anything I could. It was the idea of sneaking around, no one knowing what I was doing. Speaking of which, I'm going downstairs."

"You're spending so much time with Kreutzel!"

"I am finding out all I can about her finances. And it's nice being someplace other than in here."

"In this room with me."

"Hedy, please. That's not what I meant."

"As long as you are only pretending to be Kreutzel's best little friend in all the world."

She hugged me. "How can you be jealous, Hedy? I don't trust her. Or Margarete, for that matter. But Margarete is fun. Like you used to be. If you want to ask Margarete about that old Stern, oh, and the hat, go ahead." She stumbled over her shoes, slipped them on, and slammed the door. Which we weren't supposed to do at 13, Verstektstrasse. I didn't remember ever being fun.

15.

ONE MORNING, I WOKE to a clatter on the stairs and sudden street noise. When I went to the window, I saw Susannah talking over her shoulder to Kreutzel in her office. My sister was so happy with her latest way to bother the old girl. The day before, a very young man, an adolescent, had waited for Susannah to come out and buy the afternoon edition of a newspaper. He told her that the only thing that made his life bearable at his high school across the street, *Real Gymnasium,* was watching from a classroom window to see her descend the brothel steps to buy a morning newspaper.

So this morning, she put on her lip rouge, her high-heeled silk mules, and my shawl-collared wrap to buy the morning paper. I could tell Kreutzel was watching. The casement window always squawked when she opened it. She kept an eye on the entrance to her house from behind a curtain, which blocked her from the view of anyone on the street.

Kreutzel hardly ever heaved herself upstairs anymore. Tuesday was now the only day she left the premises, and she had to be helped into Hermann's deteriorating fiacre so that she could do her banking and pay bribes to the authorities, to the police and the local councillor. Hermann had been with her for years. We called him "the Hound," a nickname he loved—he relished being a spy for Kreutzel. She relied on him to be discreet about regular callers and to haul away the few who caused problems.

The way her spine was forcing her over, bending her into submission, was impressive. She was irritable. Her spine pained her, but she was still able to see over her half glasses because her chair now sat on a flat wooden platform. This was the second one she had Hans build, higher than the first one. Susannah said that eventually she would be as high as a Jewish bride in that chair. Hans had half-finished painting the platform. He half-did a lot of things. When they argued about his various tasks, we all eavesdropped at the top of the stairs and laughed when he talked back.

This morning, as she talked to Kreutzel, Susannah pretended to struggle to grasp the coin out of her pocket, the better to part the wrap and expose one long bare leg. She waved the coin at the newsboy, and she made sure that her breasts bounced when she tripped down the steps. She had an audience of four: the newsboy, Kreutzel in her chair by the curtain, me, and, guaranteed, the high school student watching from his classroom window. To make the show last longer, she refused the top papers, one by one, on the newsboy's pile and finally took one from the middle. She stretched one arm and yawned a little girl's yawn. Then she sashayed up the steps, reading the paper as she went, and closed the door with a kick of her foot.

Back in our room, she flopped into the chair with her paper. "What a show."

"There should be an award, Hedy, or at least applause."

"I don't know why you waste your time teasing that boy."

"If I am to rule my life as if I were the monarch of a kingdom, that kingdom had better be fun."

The sessions with Moreno were having an effect. Her relationship with Kreutzel had changed: now they argued and made up all the time. I was torn between a jealousy I didn't want to admit to, and an anxiety that Susannah would go too far and jeopardize my plans for our escape. I was sure we had almost enough money to leave.

"You have to stop tormenting that boy. Stop drawing attention to yourself and making her worry."

"That's the idea. If she is worried about me and a boy, the last thing she'll worry about is us leaving. I am going to flirt with him every afternoon, and put on a show every morning. It drives Kreutzel crazy. And besides, Billy's sweet." She grinned. "I love bothering her. Every day I walk a little further down the front steps, and I can hear that old chair of hers creaking. One day she's going to fall flat on her face."

16.

I YELPED AND FELL BACK on the bed. I thought I was hallu-
cinating. Susannah had left our closet door open again, and
I could see our matching floral dresses begin to move apart,
separating from each other, wider and wider.

Susannah's young man stepped out, holding a dead mouse
suspended by its tail. He turned to gaze at the creature. "You
can't be afraid of him." He turned his head back to beam
at me. "He's dead. But I'm not. I'm young, with impeccable
manners." He had an elfin face, merry, and a slightly drooping bottom lip. "May I introduce myself? Herr Billy Wilder,
here to visit with Fraulein Susannah." He bowed, the mouse
swinging behind him.

Susannah emerged from the bathroom, grabbed the mouse,
and threw it in the commode. Our guest washed his hands
and dried them, completely at ease, but when he went to bow
once again over my hand, he staggered as if he had lost his
balance. "Ballast," he explained mournfully. "My little friend
was ballast."

I couldn't help laughing at him as he strolled around the
room, his hands in his pockets. He paused and looked at my
Schiele portrait. Kreutzel hadn't been up to this floor for six
months, so we had hung it on the wall right beside the canals
of Venice.

"I've seen other drawings by Schiele. Naughty ones. The way
his people look out of his paintings at you!"

"We knew him." Susannah linked her arm into his. "He painted our portrait when we were children. Very bourgeois, completely clothed."

"Oh, I know you couldn't possibly be street girls, the kind they say hung around his studio. I can tell by the way you talk. You were rich girls." He shook his head, looking around our room and laughing. "With very bad luck."

Nothing was tragic; nothing made him angry. He said he was bullied at school for being a rich Jew, and it didn't matter if he told them he wasn't. "In fact, that makes it worse. You are supposed to be what they think you are. You know how it is."

I didn't. And Susannah didn't care. She adored him. Billy slipped up the stairs every time Kreutzel was out. He and my sister argued happily, laughing at the extravagance of each other's insults, and practised their questionable English. Both devoured newspapers. I regularly agreed to an urgent suggestion that I myself might want to read a newspaper. News of the art world and fashion were punctuated by their sighs and muffled laughter.

We had, I was sure, enough money. This would be our last night here. A brown cardboard tube moved up and down on Billy's sleeping chest. The Schiele drawing was carefully rolled inside, and the canals of Venice were on the floor. They were no longer needed to hide banknotes. That first night at 13, Verstektstrasse, I had been younger than the boy who was now asleep on our bed.

He was like my sister, able to fall asleep easily, undisturbed by the usual racket in the house on Tuesday that began as soon as the old girl left with Hermann. Phonographs played competing waltzes, and young women called to each other and scampered across hallways.

Susannah and I were changing as fast as we could into the men's clothing that Billy had brought.

"This is perfect. No one will pay attention to young men leaving a brothel."

I pulled on black socks and attached them to gaiters. "Billy is not the man I would have picked for this," I grumbled.

"Oh, who cares? He's my little Jewish boyfriend." Susannah was having trouble buttoning a starched shirt—the buttons were small, and the buttonholes apparently smaller. "And he's very sweet in bed."

"He's not one of us. Our kind of people, that is."

"Please. We aren't, either, not anymore." Susannah buttoned her suspenders to her trousers. "We're whores, Hedy." She stretched the suspenders, testing them.

"He's also shorter than you."

"I find that adorable in a man. Younger, shorter, stupider—the kind I like."

"He won't always be short. And what kind of a name is 'Billy'?"

"His mother was keen on the Wild West. Buffalo Bill. Oh, shit!" The suspenders sprang back. "Ouch!" Susannah laughed, her automatic response to anything difficult. She had her hands over her breasts. "Ow."

I looked at myself in the mirror. "Do you think that Schiele would mind that I'm going to sell the drawing?"

"No. It's your drawing. The one thing Mischlinger never got."

This startled both of us. I had never known what she might say, and neither did she.

"You never take this much time getting dressed, Susannah."

"But I'm not Susannah. I'm Horst, and he's very careful."

"Horst is a good name. I'm Reiner."

"Billy's going to be a journalist." She kept looking at him. "Maybe in America. Maybe I should go with him." She looked at me quickly in the mirror. "I mean, maybe we should. They have spas there, too." She lay down on the bed, looking at Billy.

We had heard from an American caller that one could acquire false papers in the spa town of Baden bei Wein. He us to "skip town" with him, but after our experience with Mischlinger, we decided we would never go anywhere with a man ever again. Billy didn't count. He wasn't really a man, not yet. Susannah said he had to return to Vienna on the next train back or his parents would go mad looking for him.

"Susannah, did Billy make sure the carriage knows to pick us up at the side of the house?"

"My Billy does everything right." She snuggled up to him. "Did you pack my medicine?"

I flipped my hat so she could see the crown lined with small packets. "There's enough to last until we can start the cure. Susannah, I'm worried. I think Kreutzel is getting suspicious."

"Only because you've been smiling. Hedy, do Italians ever go to Baden bei Wein?"

"We'll find out. Get up. *Mustachios, bella!*"

We dabbed fixative on our upper lips, one sweep to the right, one sweep to the left, and then pressed on our moustaches. We shrugged into our jackets. We shoved our hair into tight nets, and put on our hats—mine, pale grey, Susannah's, black.

"Wait." I put a rolled up stocking down the front of Susannah's trousers, and its mate down my own. We turned in tandem to get a side view in the mirror.

"What's that rustling noise?"

"I've got money in my underwear." I snapped my fingers twice. "And a very good plan." I was buoyant. The small leather suitcases were at the closet door.

"What are we going to do until it's time to go?"

Billy opened his eyes and grinned. Susannah was crazy for that boy. I decided to fold my arms and tip my hat down over my eyes. Susannah's moustache was apparently a problem. I didn't look up. I had lots of practice in not looking up.

It was a soft, foggy Vienna evening. We were three young men: Horst, Reiner, and Willem, carefully dishevelled. We had successfully slipped down the front stairs and out the front door—just like that, with no one noticing. No doubt because we were in our stocking feet. We took a moment to slip on our shoes around the corner, with "Willem" carrying both our suitcases under one arm. The sidestreet was empty. No carriage.

"Where is it?"

Billy was bewildered. "Where is what?"

Susannah clung to his tie in order to stand. "Doesn't the air smell nice?"

I knew what had happened in an instant. Morphine. She'd given the money to Bloch, not to Billy. My plan was a remnant of plan. But it was better than no plan at all.

"Come on, there are always carriages at the back." I pushed Billy, who half-dragged Susannah around the corner. I was right: there were two fiacres. Vienna likes uniformity. City carriages are all supposed to look the same: two black horses and a black-hatted driver. A motorcar honked and drove by. I got the attention of the fiacre driver closest to us in the deepest voice I could manage.

"The train station, my good fellow, the Aspangbahnhof."

The driver looked at me suspiciously. "Aren't you in the wrong part of town?"

"Yes," said Susannah, in a voice more hoarse, more believable than mine. "We are, since there are no trains here. Will you take us, please, to the train station?"

The driver stared at her.

"I'm in charge of these two, sir. Hop in, boys." Billy also tried to speak in his deepest voice. I climbed up, and Susannah clambered in after me.

"Not so fast. I don't know what you young nancy boys think you're up to, but you're not going to do it in my fiacre. Get out!"

We did, Susannah falling into Billy's arms. I pulled out some banknotes, tucked my head down, and ran to the second carriage. I blocked the driver's view of my face by pulling on the brim of my hat. I held up a fan of banknotes. Fiacre drivers were used to men not wanting to be recognized on this street.

"Aspangbahnhof, in fifteen minutes," I barked. The driver grabbed my money, just like that. I stepped back quickly and opened the door. We piled in.

We're off! My smile must have been stretching my moustache—the left side was coming loose. *Here we go!* The train. The spa. The cure. We rounded the corner at a fast trot and were in front of the brothel, about to bid it goodbye.

"Hermann!" It was Hans, lurching down the front steps and calling to our driver. "Where are you going? Hermann!"

Hermann. With a new fiacre. With us in it.

The moment Hermann reined the horses to a stop, Billy and Susannah were out the far side of the carriage and tiptoeing so fast around the corner, I had to run to catch up. Susannah's hair hung out of its net over her face. We could hear Hermann talking.

"Hans, Hans, don't get those old balls of yours in a twist."

"You are supposed to pick up a guest here in twenty minutes."

"That guy is always late leaving. Slow to get started, am I right? Not everyone has a ready prick like you and me, Hans. Don't worry, I'll be back in time."

We waited until the fiacre sped away. Billy and I moved Susannah in the other direction toward the back of the house.

"Stop." An out-of-breath Hans appeared in front of us at the end of the alley. He began to stroll over to us, rolling his shoulders. "Did you think Hermann wouldn't tip off his old buddy?"

He rubbed his thumb against his first two fingers. "Pay me, or I tell Old Crustypants," he barked.

"How much to let us go?" Susannah surged upright, her feet apart, a little unsteady. Billy stuffed our bags into the silver lace vine climbing the wall.

"Who said anything about letting you go?"

I yelled, "Run!"

Billy sped off, dragging Susannah along. They were quickly

far ahead of me. Hans clouted me on the back of my head. I leaped sideways, and the rolled stocking tumbled out of my pant leg. I nearly fell over, scuttling in the other direction. I could see Billy and Susannah running back towards me.

Hans bent over and unrolled the stocking, grinning, until he realized there was no money in it. Suddenly his expression changed from anger to shock: Susannah had kicked him in the crotch. He clutched himself.

"Men's shoes," explained Susannah to Billy, pleased with herself. She gazed into his eyes. "Billy. Run."

He didn't. He put up his fists instead. Susannah shoved Billy, and he ricocheted off the wall. He raised his fists again. Hans was still bent over, but he was hitching himself closer.

"Hedy!" Susannah and Billy yelled at the same time. Too late. Hermann had grabbed me from behind. *This is how it began for me at this address*. I felt a terrible panic, even as I kicked him as hard as I could.

Susannah glared at Billy. "Run!" She pulled her foot back, as if to kick him. "Billy, leave now!"

"You!" Kreutzel came chugging up the alley, her feet churning on the cobblestones. She stopped, heaving, and crooked her head to the side to see us. "You young brats have no respect!"

"And you're so perfect?" Billy shouted over his shoulder, finally running towards the square, clutching in his hand a drawing of a girl who didn't wanted to go home one afternoon, and had stalled for time.

17.

SUSANNAH MANAGED TO PERSUADE Kreutzel that we were only trying to make some extra money by going to the latest thing, a party where young women dressed as men. A specialty. She proffered a bundle of banknotes that she said was the deposit.

The old girl couldn't resist and snatched them. "We are *not* that kind of a specialty house!" she shouted. "You are playing with my reputation! Who was that young woman who took off on me?"

"The one I was ready to kick? Wilhelmina."

Afterwards, Susannah said she wanted more than anything to see Billy and tell him that Kreutzel thought he was a woman. But at the time, she made a huge sacrifice and threw her arms around the old girl's bulk. "Oh, dear Tante, I only did it because I wanted to buy you something nice for your birthday. Hedy didn't want to, but I had seen a cape, with vines of silver lace that would show off your hair."

Clever. If *I* didn't want Susannah to do something, then to Kreutzel, it was an understandable thing to do. And she did still have lovely blonde hair. She sighed. "I will give you a bigger allowance. Suzi, you are never, ever, to offer yourself to anyone who has not made arrangements with me. It isn't safe. You could end up in the hands of those who would not protect you."

"But Tante, Hans..."

"Hans has proven himself to be unreliable. Incompetent. I may have to find a replacement."

Back in our room, Susannah was in tears, but not because our attempt had failed. She was going to miss Billy, and we were not likely to see him again. The money from my underwear returned to the care of the canals of Venice.

We retrieved our bags from the vines the next day. We were afraid the Kreutzel would limit our freedom to go out on our own, but she didn't. She was uneasy and suspicious, but we were her highest earners. Even if we could no longer pretend to be innocent ingénues, we were still upper class and young, and the idea of two girls in one room continued to appeal to Vienna's voyeurs and exhibitionists.

Spring sunshine revealed which windows in the city needed to be washed, and which doorsteps needed sweeping. The air was fresh, but the same young whores gathered at Moreno's premises, each claiming her chair, the one she had had last time. Susannah and I sat by the door. Margarete, as usual, arrived late.

"Ah, good," said Moreno. "We may begin." He turned to the others. "We need to warm up the body."

"There were so many demonstrators at city hall." Margarete was still talking. "I could hardly get out of the Spittelberg."

"Ah yes, May Day, Margarete. Perhaps we will march together in the parades, next year."

We each stood facing a partner, as we had been doing at every meeting for these last few months. We mirrored gestures, we arched and bent our torsos—*contraposto,* our mother would have said. Moreno moved among us, imitating this movement or that, echoing our choices. It was quiet. We were all soon glowing from the exertion.

"Ah, let"s talk, too," said Moreno.

"Some water first," said Margarete. He poured a glass and handed it to her.

"Yes. Margarete, tell us something you think about."

She looked at her water. Nothing. Light spilled in through the papered-over windows and threadbare curtains. A large chandelier with pressed teardrops hung over us.

And then in a matter-of-fact voice, Effi spoke. "My son died six months ago."

We were all still. She was very young to have been a mother. *How old had our Mama been when she died?*

"He asked for a drink of water. 'Please, Mama,' he said."

Had Mama been thirsty? Had she needed someone to give her a glass?

Effi had nothing more to say. Some of the others were in tears. The one with two children, Magdalena, walked over and climbed into the chair. "There, there. Move over. Here I am."

I pressed my nails into my hand until I felt their sharp edges.

The air was sweet with the smell of warm earth. Summer had discovered itself again. Susannah and I waited outside, watching the others go up the steps to Moreno's door. I looked over at my sister, and placed a hand on her sleeve. "Susannah, this is..."

"Fun. Both more than, and less than. Remember Papa's arrows in algebra?" She hurried up the steps, more eager than I was, less affected than I was.

Moreno walked around the room, shaking hands, looking directly at each of us, enquiring after our health. We were last. He had already closed the old curtains to keep out the bright sunlight. He always did the same thing, in the same order. It made me feel safe. In these stories we re-lived for each other, the roles we took on had rules that helped us to feel safe when we revisited our memories. Some memories were awful, and some so awful they were funny.

From the centre of the room, his usual calm invitation: "Ah. When you are ready."

And we began, mirroring our partner's movements until it felt like there was a rolling energy underneath all of us, a deep current. Moreno asked his questions in the troughs of the waves, and listened to the answers. Susannah and I were often quiet, but we had become anchored to each other again.

Kreutzel didn't like this change in our relationship. We didn't expect her to burst into our room. We hadn't heard her struggle up the stairs. But she was alive with energy, slamming the door against the wall. "What exactly, Suzi, do you do when you go out?"

My sister was never at a loss for an answer. "We go to cafés and hat shops."

"Why don't you come home with hats, then?"

"Hedy is too fussy. She points out faults. I see them and then I don't want the hat anymore."

Astounding. My sister had come up with the perfect excuse in an instant: a great cover story for what we were doing, and another opportunity for Kreutzel to see herself as a champion for her "Suzi."

"We also read newspapers and drink hot chocolate, Tante."

"Don't Tante me, Hedy."

"But," Susannah let her mouth wobble, "don't you want us to call you Tante? Do we have to call you 'Frau' like before? Would you like to go with us?" She was not actually going to cry. Neither of us had cried for a long time. There was no point.

"No." Kreutzel patted her hand. "Just be back in good time, Suzi. With a hat."

After she left, I looked at Susannah. "You had to make it my fault."

"The old girl likes to think she has come between us. Which will never happen. The more she trusts me, the closer I am to finding out where she hides her money."

"You haven't found it yet. In over two years."

"I can only look a little at a time. She has to feel like my presence isn't threatening. Don't be upset, Hedy. I'm better than you at lying."

Two years ago, when she discovered I had lied to her about our parents, about money, about where we were going, she was angry. Now lying was an accomplishment. I shoved away thoughts of my mother and what she would think.

Moreno moved to the centre of the room, and we adjusted the position of our chairs, like iron filings in response to a magnet. "Now, just breathe," he said, and fell silent for a few minutes. Then he said softly, "When you are ready."

This was the signal. It was quiet, the afternoon light dim, golden. At an almost sleepy pace, partners mirroring a hand covering an ear. A foot lifted up and moved back. A kind of listening to the other's body, readying us to listen to our own, and to words said aloud, even if we were the ones saying them.

"Why should anyone pity us?" I heard myself say aloud. We all continued to move. "We do what we do. Some of us like the work."

Susannah murmured, "Some of us don't." Everyone was still moving, crossing arms, stretching backward, listening. Their motions were calm, unhurried.

"Lots of women do things they don't like." Margarete swished her skirt with both hands. Her partner did the same, and then Margarete followed her partner as she turned slowly around.

"This is a roomful of women," my partner Effi cupped her breasts, "who know more about bodies than most people in Vienna." Slow smiles, and everyone mirrored gestures until like a kaleidoscope, some arms raised and waved, some arms cast backward and forward, swaying. Cheeks on shoulders. Big heaving breaths of air. I followed Effi's gestures as she fanned herself with one hand, then the other.

"And rest," said Moreno quietly.

We eased into our chairs, leaning against each other. I sighed. I think I was tired. I pressed the heel of my hand into the edge of my chair. I wanted it to be real, to be separate from me.

"What is on your mind, Hedy?" Moreno's soft encouragement.

I knew the others were there, but they seemed far away. "Nothing is on my mind. It's too slippery. I only trust what I can touch." I looked around, not at anything, not at anyone. Eventually, I looked at Moreno, who gazed back and then eased closer, then was on one knee beside me, his open arms surrounding but not touching me, sheltering. Things stopped being blurred. He sat back on his heels and took my hand. He kept looking at my hand, so I did, too.

"This," he said, "is the mind." And then in a big gesture, he gave me back my hand.

This physical world, this real, physical world. I rose to my feet. Susannah stood, too, and leaned her shoulder against mine. Lightly, she touched first the back of my hand and then the palm, and then the others got up and repeated her gesture. We were like small boats tied together, rising and falling on the waves. Until one pulled free.

"I cannot stand to be alone." Margarete's voice was loud, as usual. "I am always in hotel lobbies, I am always with someone, I have to be with someone, even if I don't like him, or even if I have enough money for the next day or so, I still go with him. I'm not alone here," she paused. "I know I'm with all you other whores, so what the hell, but I feel like I belong to myself here, and I can let myself be alone."

Moreno waited, nodded, and asked, "When you are alone, what do you think about?"

"My mother." Her face crumpled. We were quiet.

"Do you want us to make the scene for you?" Moreno spoke softly. "You are alone..."

"My mother died, and no one told me." Margarete spoke softly, too.

Susannah tucked her hand into mine.

In that first week at Verstektstrasse I had half-pretended to myself that Mama was alive. Logic's thin thread suggested that she could still be alive, and Mischlinger hadn't yet assaulted my sister, though I knew it was a matter of time. I knew.

That second week in the brothel, while Susannah lay sleeping, I had approached Kreutzel. She was sitting at the table in our room with a stack of envelopes. "Our mother will be happy to pay all that is owed to you for our care, and more."

She frowned and made an impatient gesture, brushing my words away, as if I were stupid. "Your mother? She's gone. Dead. Dead from cholera."

Like that, it had became become a fact.

"Let us go, and I promise I will pay you back myself."

She smirked, tamping banknotes on the table. "And where will you go?" As if the news of my mother's death were nothing more than a winning hand at cards, a minor triumph. She swept out of the room and locked the door.

I hid myself in the bedclothes beside my sister. I cried without making a sound. The terrible news within me, like frightening and valuable treasure.

Moreno's voice was soft. He suggested to Margarete that she was the seeker, the protagonist. He prompted her to choose someone to play the role of her inner self. He said it should be someone who understood her, who knew how she felt. Of course she chose Susannah.

Moreno had been refining, little by little, what we did in the studio. Susannah knew what to do. She moved a small footstool to sit beside Margarete. She didn't look back at me.

"And, to play Mother?" Moreno kept the momentum steady.

Margarete pointed to me. Moreno set a chair for me opposite Margarete. I sat with my head down. I was Mother, and death was coming for me.

Moreno nodded. "Yes. The Silent One."

"Nobody told me. I didn't know." Margarete's voice, rough and low, directed at Mother. "Why didn't you send someone?"

Head still down. *My daughter cannot see me like this. I cannot bear to see her reaction to how sick I am.*

"It's wrong to leave me!" Margarete's voice rose.

I was once again in that bedroom, filled with sun and shadow, in the house on the Schottenring. "Do you promise to get healthy?" I had demanded. How lonely my own mother must have been, how desperate. Oh, to love someone, and have to leave them, and have them not be afraid. *My poor mother. My mother.* I raised my eyes, full of tears.

In the role of Margarete, Susannah looked directly at Mother, at me. Her soft voice. "Don't leave," she said, being Margarete, feeling all that she felt. "If you love me, stay."

Margarete's mouth made the word *Mutti*. Mommy. No sound came out, and her face crumpled, her mouth open, turned down.

Susannah's arms around me, my arms around Margarete, around them both. Susannah's eyes glistening.

I didn't notice when we began talking out loud—if it was on the way home in the fiacre, or once we were in our room. Now we were facing each other, our heads on our pillows. We had asked for tea, but it sat on the tray, untouched.

"I didn't think that when Mama said she loved us, it would be the last time, Susannah. I thought *of course* she would live."

"I know. To think someone that strong-willed could die. Do you know the last thing I said to Mama, Hedy? *Sorry.* Marta had claimed we mocked her when she told us to stop riding our bicycles. Remember? And it wasn't true."

"Not that time." I did not want to cry. I pulled the covers up over Susannah's shoulder.

"Hedy, do you ever think about how you were the one who pleased Mama when we lived on the Schottenring, but here, in this brothel, I'm the one who is favoured? Even though I'm the one who hates what we do with men. Even though you like what we do."

"Only the sex." *My shame.* "I don't like being here."

"I didn't get the kisses I needed to become older. Mama was so focused on her precious life of the arts in Vienna."

"I know. She left Fuschl behind when she married Papa. But she loved you, Susannah. You are like Papa, and you know how much she loved him." The streetlights had come on. The tea had grown cold.

"That last awful day. She told Marta she was sending you kisses. So I went off with Margarete and the Old Dear."

"That's why you took off with her? You were jealous of me?"

"I was angry. Yes." She sat up, clenched hands on her knees. "I sounded so angry, the old Galician man gave us almost all his money for that second-rate silver. Margarete said she wished she had a crabby rich girl with her all the time. She kept hugging me." She fell back onto her pillow. "It was thrilling for me, to be liked, so intensely and so quickly. No one at any of the schools we went to ever wanted to be my friend. Margarete did."

"You also were impressed with her swearing. So much more creative than anything you had ever said."

"I should never have abandoned you to go with her."

"Kaspar was with me, Susannah. It might not have made any difference." I didn't see how it could have. "We're never alone now."

"And Kreutzel profits. A caller takes a turn with one of us while having a good look at the other, at what he's going to take next."

18.

WE GAVE BRIGITA MONEY to buy hats for herself and for us, so we could pretend to be shopping for hats instead of attending Moreno's group. But Susannah didn't care about hats at all. Jam them on and go was her method, and Zehra knew it. She was jealous of Susannah's emergence as a favourite, and tried to pry out of Brigita how she could afford so many hats.

"I told her you gave me some money." Brigita flushed. "I didn't know what else to say. I can't do it anymore."

"Of course, Brigita, don't worry. It's been fun to improve hats we might not ever have picked ourselves."

I had taken great care with the last hat Brigita bought. I had rolled and pinned up one side of the black straw so Brigita looked jaunty, and then attached a Turk—an eight-sided knot with two flowing tails—out of dark red grosgrain ribbon, so she looked sweet.

"Perfect," said Brigita, looking in the mirror. "And I won't tell, I promise."

"Why would you?" Susannah stood closer. "You get the hats for free and then my sister makes them suit you. Leave the hatbox there, and our receipt. What good would it do to tell Kreutzel that you bought hats for us?"

"None." She looked at my sister to see if she was about to lose her temper. "A slip of the tongue."

Susannah had learned a long time ago that it worked to her

advantage when people were unsure if she was about to lose her temper. She leaned back in the chair and put her feet up on the slipper chair, her legs flopped open. A whore doesn't have to sit modestly. She looked out the window.

After a while, Brigita said, "Hedy, may I ask, if you don't mind," her eyes darted away from the mirror to look at Susannah, "when you go out, what are you actually doing?"

"Just following Susannah around. Making sure she doesn't fall on her bottom."

This was too good not to use. Susannah fell off her perch. "Oh, hell! My ass! Shit!"

"Lie on the bed, Susannah." I helped her up. Her eyes were full of mischief.

"I think," Brigita was being sweet again, her actual temperament, "it's the medication she takes, Hedy. So terrible." Spying for Kreutzel was not her forte.

"I have to really keep an eye on her, Brigita. Lift your chin up, please."

Frau Kreutzel was still to be feared. We froze when we heard her gasping for air as she staggered up the stairs and into our room one day, wearing a navy felt hat. She lifted up the bedspread.

"Oh, I thought I caught my foot on something, Suzi." Tripping on things on purpose in order to confuse and distract was Susannah's trick, and Kreutzel did it badly.

"Nothing under there, Tante," said Susannah from the bed. "Not even dust."

"If you have improved hats for Brigita, Hedy, perhaps you can re-work this one for me." She lifted up a pillow. It was enough that we had to share our little space in this world with callers who climbed into our bed and our bodies. That pillow, and everything on the bed, would have to go into the laundry basket as soon as she left. "This is a good mattress. I only buy the best for you." She bounced on the bed, laughing. She tried to pull us toward her, one hand on each of our shoulders, as if we were all girls, all together. We both pulled away. She may have seen my look of repugnance. Susannah's expression was innocently enthusiastic, something she had practised since she was a toddler.

"What can you do with this *chapeau*, Hedy? A certain friend, an admirer, brought it to me from Paris, years ago. It's a very expensive hat."

I tipped the brim up at the back to show off the Kreutzel's thick French-braided blonde hair. I could have made it look terrible, but I could not bear to make anything look terrible. How something looked, this was what I could not compromise on. I did justice to how things looked.

Kreutzel thanked me, in a voice that had become scratchy, like a needle that wasn't straight in the groove of the record. But she never wore the hat. The others said it was flattering, but every time she put it on, she hesitated and took it off. She may have thought that my sister liked her, but she knew I didn't. She was cautious around me. Even though she nosed into everything, she never dared to ask about the ring on a ribbon around my neck. I half-wished she would. Maybe she sensed that locked-up treasure, my anger. I would have liked to open it, just once.

Despite her distaste, Susannah had become as good at whoring as I was, and I was very good. I knew how to make it pleasant, even if the callers had no stamina. In response to their efforts, I made little helpless sounds. What I pretended for them became honest cues for me: a signal that I myself would experience pleasure.

My favourite perfume, Jicky, smelled like new-mown hay. Since some men used it as cologne, when I dabbed some on their trousers—not too much, of course—it didn't incriminate them when they went home. But every time they buttoned their flies, they were reminded of being with me. Susannah didn't like sex at all, but she seemed relaxed and silly, as long as she had her medicine. She said, 'rescue me' in a variety of ways, apparently all pleasing, and giggled. Or looked out the window and said, "Hmm." I sounded upper class and seemed shy, so we both did very well and had callers who preferred us. Regulars.

~

It was July 27, 1914, and there were great crowds in the city, again. The weather was impossibly hot. People didn't go to bed, they stayed up and gathered in the streets. There was a giddy feeling of everyone together, *Alle, alle zusammen.*

On July 28, war was declared. We knew from the sound of the crowds cheering and singing in the streets. They said our old Franz Joseph stood on a balcony and waved, the black feathers on his military hat fluttering. Old cock.

Frau Kreutzel said that soldiers are the reason establishments like hers flourish. She bustled about, singing to herself. She kept ice in sawdust in the cold room, so that we never ran out of the house specialty, a drink of chilled raspberry and vinegar. She hired another laundress. The local vintner came every two weeks, and every week, a large bouquet of lilies and roses was delivered to the vestibule where the callers entered.

Susannah and I tried to take turns going out, but that changed when canny old Kreutzel opened an additional establishment on the western edge of the city. She was so busy that she had to trust us to take the money and settle up every Tuesday. Each whore had to report on her callers and to account for the money handed over. She preferred that Susannah do this, not me, so I had to be the one who carried out our plan.

My sister's constant newspaper reading had paid off. The reports on war profiteering were like instruction guides, and little by little we had been converting the banknotes under the image of Venice's canals to gold at the exchange office. For a small fee, they kept our gold in their vault. The only gold out in the open was on a ribbon around my neck, the topaz ring I wore even when I was naked, which I often was.

Callers liked such evidence of sentiment. Some of them, when they undid their stiff collars, had charms or lockets around their necks. War increased the interest in talismans and signs, in reading cards or coffee grounds, hoping for luck. The business in brothels increased, too, and munitions factories ran round the clock. Death and maidens.

Despite the rise in the cost of everything, frothy operettas always sold out. Kreutzel attended matinées and then demanded that we learn the songs. "War makes people very sentimental," she pronounced as she handed us sheet music with a rose on the front. "Especially men. You girls should learn this one." She began to croak, "*It must be a waltz...*"

"Do we have to dance with them?"

The question took the old girl aback. She was always surprised when Susannah said anything negative to her.

"No, Suzi, dear, just sing a little as they approach the bed. It will be adorable. Hedy, you help her learn the song."

There were terrible battles, and many dead, but not immediately near Vienna, so someone still made sheet music, and we were still adorable.

As we had only the highest-ranking officers here, Herr Doctor Bloch had no trouble getting morphine for Susannah. They were using it for the army's maimed and wounded. I wondered what they thought would happen when the war was over and the army wasn't supplying young men with morphine. Maybe they thought they would mostly be dead. I wondered how weary a person had to become to wish she were dead.

A street photographer had taken our picture in the park, just as I was biting into an apple. My arm had been around Susannah, supporting her as she turned away from him. He had promised he would be there a week later with the print, and he was.

I paid him and pored over it to see how I looked. My hat had a wide brim, as wide as my shoulders. I had circles under my eyes, but I looked lively. A lace collar spread out over the lapels of my fitted jacket. On the side seam, my narrow grey skirt had three exaggerated buttonholes, bound by darker velvet. The emphasis on what could be undone.

Susannah's image, however, was blurred. She had moved at the last moment, and her face was distorted. She looked at the photograph and told me to rip off her side of it.

"Why?" This felt like a terrible thing, to tear apart an image of us together.

"So no one will see me looking like that."

She wrenched away from me and staggered along the fine gravel path. Late afternoon sunshine cast long shadows across the manicured green lawns. Susannah was weeping, her shoulders shaking. People hurried, as they did in Vienna when the day was waning.

"Look at the photograph. I look stupid, like a drug addict."

"You look like my sister," I said.

"Yes, whom you are stuck with, and who you think is disgusting!"

I stood still. Susannah's face was blotchy, tear-streaked. Her short jacket was undone, and long loops of blonde hair escaped her rolled-up pompadour. Her hand squashed the hat in her hand.

"Susannah, your hat."

"To hell with the hat!" Susannah flung it on the grass. I hurried to bring it back to her. Susannah slapped my arm away. She kept turning so that I couldn't look her in the face.

"Leave me alone!"

"Susannah!" I kept my voice low. I looked around to see if there were any busybodies who might think they needed to interfere. No one. "Please come with me. It's true—you're an addict, but I have to look after you."

Susannah stepped off the path, and staggered to a halt on the grass. "You have to look after me? Well, stop! You're doing a terrible job."

I watched her careen away from me. I couldn't remember why I did anything.

By evening, each street lamp along the paths created its own island of light, surrounded by the fathomless dark of the Augarten. There was a rumour, likely true, that a soldier on leave had been killed there only a week before in Vienna's beloved park. *How could I have left her there?* I ignored the paths and made my way diagonally across the lawn to where I had last seen her. *Oh, my sister, be safe.*

Hans followed me carrying that old scarf, a Roman stripe of our mother's that Susannah was wearing that first night of our arrival and refused to wash. When Kreutzel told me to bring it, I wondered how safe our other secrets were. The grass was wet with evening dew, and Hans hesitated at the lawn's edge. He was wearing his indoor, patent leather shoes. But he had his instructions and stepped doggedly after me across the lawn.

I stopped. Hans did, too. We were near the fountain, and its cascades almost drowned out all other sounds. I motioned for Hans to stay back. I could hear something inside the sound of all that water falling. A song, but off-key.

My sister had not disappeared, had not been killed. She was sitting on the stone bench that circled the fountain. The pale water was illuminated by the streetlights. "*Shine, little glow worm, glimmer, glimmer.*" She sang the same words again.

I walked steadily over to her.

"*Glimmer, glimmer…*"

I knew this dream, its anxious plot. I sang the next line, "*Lead us lest too far we wander.*" Susannah rose and walked towards me. She was shivering. "Six hours without my medication," she said.

I took the scarf from Hans, who had caught up to us, and

wrapped it around Susannah's shoulders. She let me. Hans and I half-carried her to Hermann's fiacre. When the horses moved, Susannah began singing again, looking out the side of the carriage.

The carriage lights were on. Hans patted his foot to her tune as he looked out the other side. "*Light the path, below, above, and lead us on to love*" trailed behind us into the humid night.

One Monday afternoon, two field marshals in full uniform arrived and ordered oysters on the half shell, champagne in magnum bottles, quails en croute, and us in frilly undergarments. A meal in our room required quadruple the usual fee. And then they left us with a pile of banknotes "'to get a little something for yourselves.'"

I was awake. I couldn't sleep. This money. All the things we could do with it. Train tickets. Booking a hotel. I thought about how, once the war was over—everyone knew it was winding down—the "little something" our callers gave us would get us out of Vienna, and keep us for a month at a spa. Susannah was asleep almost immediately, and for once did not flop her arm over me in the middle of the night.

On Tuesday morning, she flopped her newspaper on our little table. "I need a holiday from this war and from this place."

"This guarantees both." I fanned myself with the field marshals' banknotes.

"Nice to see you smile, Hedy."

But that morning held a surprise. Susannah and I linked arms to go down the stairs. The old girl always preferred to go over our account book with Susannah, so I was going to put our little something in the bank. We were no longer those daughters who, a long time ago, had descended a staircase in clothing filled with sparkling insects. We were whores, whores descending from our whoring bedroom. In a few minutes I would be on my way to the exchange, my purse bursting with what would mean never having to whore again.

I was about to go out the door when Hans whistled and jerked his thumb for me to follow Susannah into the old girl's office. Kreutzel put a protective arm around my sister.

"Why do you make Suzi do all the work while you go out? Let your sister have a turn for once."

Susannah quickly slipped my purse strap over her shoulder. I took off my hat. Susannah grabbed it and was out the door. *Why does the old girl suddenly want me here?* Through the window I could see my sister jamming hatpins into her hair, not exactly elegant. She had our money. She would take it to the exchange.

Only she didn't. At one o'clock, Kreutzel called me down to her office. By four o'clock, she started to make threats, all accompanied by little drumrolls of her nails on her desk, all starting with "If Suzi doesn't come back..."

At five o'clock, Susannah walked in the door. Kreutzel looked relieved, and struggled to her feet. "There you are! Next time, let Hermann take you."

"Oh, Tante," Susannah burst into in tears. "Tante, you are so kind. There was an accident in front of my carriage, so I got stuck right in front of the Vienna bourse. The driver couldn't go backward or forward, and I was afraid. The crowds are so volatile in Vienna these days."

That part was true. The war had filled the streets with people, some homeless and harmless, others desperate from hunger and not entirely sane. Kreutzel believed every word: that the driver yelled at Susannah when she had complained, and that when she asked him to give her a hand to step down into the street, he jerked the door away from her hand and she fell. That the traffic had suddenly moved. That she looked for the carriage but couldn't find it and had to walk so many blocks to find another. That she knew dear Frau Kreutzel would be worried, and she got a little lost....

"You're back here, now, Suzi, you're safe."

Susannah whipped her hands up to her face so her elbows

were out to ward off the hug waddling its way towards her. As a last resort, she stumbled over a footstool. "Oh, shit. Sorry. Sorry, I have to lie down." And up the stairs she dashed, leaving me with Kreutzel.

"You had better always go with her from now on. She means a great deal to me, and she should to you, as well."

Yes, I thought, she brings in a lot of money into this house, so she should mean a great deal to you. She is also taking money out of this house as fast as she can, and so am I.

I marvelled at how I felt slighted by the Kreutzel's lack of appreciation of me as a source of profit. If Susannah weren't my sister, I could have walked away. But how we worked was unique in Vienna. It was a specialty house, after all. If I were gone, Susannah would have had to continue with a substitute for me. Some other young woman would have to take turns sitting on the chair half-naked and lying on the bed. To do that with me was terrible enough. With someone else, it might have broken her altogether, no matter how much morphine they dosed her with.

She had always counted on me. When she was little, her whimpering only stopped when her eyes lit upon me, on my face. And me, I didn't want to be in the world with no one to love. Thinking about her meant I could avoid thinking about myself. My life. I wondered what it might be like to have sex with someone I chose, instead of the many I hadn't.

What Susannah told Kreutzel was obviously not what happened. What she told me was this: she fell getting out of the carriage in front of the exchange, and didn't realize the envelope had fallen in the carriage. Or in the street. She was shocked when she couldn't find it in the purse as she approached the exchange clerk.

"I'm so sorry, Hedy. It was your purse, the way it does up. But there will be other field marshals. This war isn't over yet." She looked at me so boldly that I knew there was something she hadn't told me, and didn't intend to, either.

We once again had a little money, not glorious funds. Susannah apparently couldn't think under stress. I couldn't think if there wasn't any. I missed the sessions with Moreno. They had made me feel like I could do the next thing, whatever it was. But he was busy with war refugees from Tyrol in that camp just north of the city. I wished I could talk to him. Once again, Susannah abandoned talking to me and went back to staring out the window.

19.

A CRY. *I RISE UP on one elbow. Susanna is asleep beside*
me, on top of the bedcovers. She frowns, still inside her
dream. I move the dead weight of her arm and cover her as
best I can. It's very early in the morning. Four o'clock. The
light is gliding further and further across the ceiling. I would
like, just once, to sleep the whole night through.

The city turned like a weather vane. One March day, the wind
seemed to bring everyone together. *Alle, alle zusammen.* They
had put up a statue of a soldier in the Schwartzenbergplatz,
and when the new whore, the little Hungarian Kislany insisted
on making a donation like the others, we watched under our
umbrellas as she flailed away with the hammer they gave her,
pounding a nail into his wooden body. The *Wehrmann* was
bristling with nails, even some gold ones.

Kislany listened with me when Susannah read out the names
of the wounded and the missing in her newspapers. We knew
we had only been parting gifts from their senior officers, but
some of the soldiers had held us and cried, and we dreaded
hearing their names among those of the dead.

The senior officers made little Kislany very popular. She was
moody—fiery and sweet, then something else, they never knew
what. Hiring her was like playing a game of chance. The war
made all the soldiers interested in chance, in luck.

In the newspapers, soldiers smiled and posed beside war

machinery so enormous that the images seemed like those trick photographs of rabbits the size of houses. Their size was incomprehensible. I said they didn't look real.

"What is quite real are the profits made because we want to read these lists," said Susannah, crushing her newspaper and tossing it in the grate.

"They profit from the sacrifice of young men's flesh," said Kislany, her curls trembling.

"You are determined to cry," said Susannah. "What about our flesh? Brothels profit from war, too."

"But only," I argued, "because our flesh is forgettable. Not like that of soldiers. They say the nation will never forget their sacrifice."

"We won't!" Kislany stormed out of our room. "Never!" she cried, and slammed the door. Her callers that night would be in for a passionate experience, as long as they didn't bring up anything they read in the newspapers.

The headlines were about riots over food in Vienna's suburbs, according to the front page of the *Arbeiter-Zeitung*. The report said a "corpulent" man, a Jew, had both his arms broken by a mob shouting, "Now try to eat everything." In another report, a small band of people from the south end of the city had decided local farmers were hoarding food and deserved to be beaten.

Susannah and I saw two men, their arms full of dirty wizened cucumbers, bartering with the little street whores when we went out to make a deposit at the exchange. Two respectable women—sisters, I think—with glittering green eyes under their worn hats challenged us when we walked towards the same fiacre they had chosen. One turned to look at us, pawing her chin, and said, "You two don't look like you're suffering from the war. It's good to be careful on outdoor streets."

Susannah wondered where the indoor streets were. I tried to shush her. "Be more circumspect. People are looking to blame someone, and we're not only whores, we're Jewish whores."

Young Austrians were being blown up or captured. One of the Moser boys who chased me so long ago was on the list of the missing. So many young men were simply missing, and all I could think about was this: if getting food from the farms just outside Vienna was beyond the ability of the authorities to organize, it was no wonder that they could not organize this war. Thousands, the papers said, had been killed on the border. That was the true scandal, not that other one that sold newspapers, about traitors in Vienna.

Susannah and I knew the truth about that scandal, but we would never tell anyone what we knew. By now, we knew how to keep secrets. We were told so many. The truth was that one day, when a breeze picked up in the evening after hours of sunshine and heat, we had been walking just up to the Donau-kanal and back, not far, when someone suddenly appeared at our side and grinned. Clamped between his teeth were four gold nails, gleaming in the light from the street lamp. It was Kaspar, tall and handsome, and not in uniform. He took off, climbing up and over a wall. And just like that, he was gone.

The newspapers were full of the scandal. Politicians promised to track down the traitors and hang them, claiming that these thieves who pulled the gold nails out of the warrior statue could not be true Viennese. That scandal only lasted three days in the papers. No one was paying to hammer nails into him anymore.

20.

A CRY. *WHO IS HURTING my sister?* I sat up, my heart pounding, ready—but there she was, asleep on the bed beside me, that arm flung across me. We were in this familiar bed, in this room, and once more I had woken up in alarm, sure she was being attacked. Not for the first time, I shook her awake.

"What's wrong?"

Susannah kept her eyes closed and kicked off her high-heeled shoes. "Leave me alone," she muttered. She was on top of the covers, her silk chemise twisted up around her waist. Everything naked below. I tugged the top quilt out from under her and covered her. She frowned, once more inside her dream. I was wide awake. I shivered, and moved closer to Susannah. The morning light glided across the ceiling. I could hear canal geese calling—they were leaving. Winter would soon arrive in Vienna.

~

After Armistice, Austria shrunk. Vienna continued to turn inward, into itself. There were many wounded veterans on the streets, and Kreutzel was very careful about the locks on the doors, and about bribes to the police.

She had shrunk as well; she was smaller, even more bent over than before the war. She piled her braids higher, and had her old chair rebuilt with thicker, longer legs so she didn't have to look up at people. The house had always been quite warm to ease the transition out of clothes, but now she shivered under her shawl and turned the heat up so much that the rooms felt tropical.

Envy at how she favoured us had collapsed. The others loved how Susannah laughed at their dirty jokes, and how she told her own in an upper class accent, delicately patting her blonde curls out of the way, while saying *asshole, prick, piss, shit.* Me, they only came to me to get help with their hats.

The war was over, and the city of Vienna staggered, but it was also awake. In Susannah's newspapers and in the street, there was talk about why we lost: outsiders and Jews were blamed, of course, but more frequently, with greater energy and derision, blame was laid at the doors of the cowering old regime, the manufacturers, the wealthy. I used to think that Mama and Papa were wealthy, but perhaps they had lived as if they were, so that we could have wonderful new things, wonderful art.

The city adopted a new self: "Red Vienna." Change was hovering, wanting to tell us something—it didn't care what. Moreno was once again doing his work, not just with whores, and not just with émigrés. Some of us were one or the other, or both, but many were like Mama and Papa's friends, deeply curious people, artistic, enthusiastic about change.

Kreutzel wanted to be up-to-date herself about life in Vienna cafés or in the little kinos showing motion pictures. She thought that was where we were, when in fact we were attending Moreno's group. Once a week, we listened to what the others, especially Margarete, told us, so we could report back to the old thing.

I also listened to what people said about themselves before we began a session. Some of them talked about themselves as if they had been watching strangers whom they owned. It made me anxious. I no longer belonged on the Schottenring. I lived where I worked, on Verstektstrasse and I didn't want to tell people what I did. I was a whore, an orphan, and my sister's guardian. I had chosen none of those things. I felt like a lost and found bureau—many things, none of them mine.

One day, Billy and Susannah both reached for the same paper in the Café Arundel. They hugged, kissed, and picked up their arguments from where they had left off. She supported the programs of Red Vienna, its plans for housing the poor. He countered that the reason everyone voted for the socialists was the secret pleasure of knowing that, if the rich paid taxes according to the number of servants they had, Jews like the Rothschilds would have to pay a bundle. He said he was off for Berlin, first, and Hollywood as soon as he could after that. I didn't ask him about my Schiele drawing.

We wondered how much longer Kreutzel was going to keep Brigita, and we knew old Hans was in trouble, too. He was always showing up late for work and arguing with everyone. Kreutzel had kept him on, even though she had said she was going to get rid of him. At the time he knew too much, but after the war, what he knew didn't matter.

She wanted him to bathe more often, and to wear different clothes, to look more like a young man about town, instead of the brute that he had always been in a stiff collar and that hunter's homburg. Her plan was doomed. Hans was more like a not-so-young Golem about town, glowering and lurching into doorframes, frightening the new whores.

As often as possible, Susannah flattered Kreutzel. I tried, but she knew I didn't mean it. She was sure Susannah did. My sister became very good at fleecing the old girl: after a visit downstairs, she always returned to our room to fan small paper bundles of pink *kronen* at me.

I liked Brigita, and I wanted to help her. I wanted her to speak to Moreno, but I knew she would tell Kreutzel where we went in exchange for the old girl's protection. We could offer her nothing. Where we went, the place on Maysedergasse, didn't matter as much as what we were doing there, and it had nothing to do with what we usually did, whoring. It mattered to me, at twenty-one years of age, that there was one thing that I did that had nothing to do with callers.

Going upstairs with Susannah to see everyone at Moreno's rehearsal hall was wonderful. Our only genuine social life, once a week. Everyone leaning on something, a foot up on a chair, chatting. Doctor Gruen threw back his head and laughed at joke made by Effi, one of the whores in the original group. She rode on that laughter over to an actor with round black eyeglasses and an intense gaze. He called himself Lazzy Lowenstein. He was not yet ready, he told me, to try 'Peter Lorre', the stage name that Moreno had suggested because it sounded "more international."

"More international," Lazzy said, "means less Jewish." He had a feminine face, mobile and delicate, with liquid dark eyes and creamy pale skin. But he was jumpy. Abandoned by Effi, he rounded on the table, took a pastry, ate it, walked away—and came back immediately and took another. He was small and compact. I told Susannah he had a beautiful look. Haunted.

"That's because he looks like you, but in a suit."

I must have looked shocked.

She shrugged. "He carries himself well. He would make a lovely woman."

Still, after all these years, still, I could not predict what she was going to say. I wanted to look at myself in the mirror. My mother's friends had said I was beautiful, and so did my callers. But my mother's friends were very conscious of what my mother valued, and my callers needed to think they were ravishing a beauty.

A very young actress, Elisabeth, was watching me as I watched Lazzy, so I stopped. Maybe sixteen, she was blonde with large gestures and a heart-shaped face. Then someone pulled up a chair beside me, a new fellow, a fair-skinned man with high cheekbones. I decided to gaze at him instead. He sat, notebook in hand, one leg crossed over another. Moreno looked over his shoulder.

"You're taking notes in English! Ladies and gentlemen, we are more international than we thought!"

There were murmurs of welcome.

The man pulled his mouth down in an apologetic smile. "I can speak German, but I can't write it. Sorry."

Effi's voice rose above the others with the confidence of someone new to the authority of socialist politics. "Why not a syndicate for actors? The glaziers have one; every trade does. I know an oboe player, Daniel...."

"Don't we all!" laughed Margarete.

Effi blushed, but braved it out, continuing to hawk collective action. I understood the notion, but it was only good for those who intended to continue in their current occupation. I didn't.

Margarete still remembered the one long day she had spent with Susannah, so many years ago. She was sentimental about what she and my sister had done together, selling silverware, riding bicycles—a golden memory, a perfect day. "My Schottenring friend," she would say, mystifying the others. Even though I thought Susannah shouldn't rely on her, that her memory was false gilt, easily chipped, there was a thread of understanding between the four of us from the original group of whores. We all said we were actresses if anyone asked. No one was surprised if an actress wasn't working, and it was acceptable to be vague about plans and residence.

Moreno went about the room, introducing everyone, even if they had been coming from the beginning, as if he had just discovered them and was delighted. "And here, not a glazier, not an oboe player, but an actor—Lazzy Lowenstein!" He applauded Lazzy, who swallowed the last morsel of the pastries, wiped his mouth, and bowed.

"*Gruss Gott*, Lazlo. Lazzy Lazlo," he said, smiling, not

smiling, and then smiling again. He had a pretty mouth.

I puzzled over whether or not I looked like him, and then over whether he thought he looked like me. He had told me how he tried out the new name by going out in the dead of the night to city kiosks and printing it on posters for plays in the middle of their run. I told him that "Lazzy Lazlo" might seem more cheerful than the parts he was likely to get with those eyes of his. I wondered if my eyes were that sad.

"And this young man is not an oboe player, nor an actor, but a journalist, very interested in how people learn with their bodies—George Andrew." The man beside me tucked his notebook under his arm, stood, and bowed to Moreno.

"I could learn him a thing or two with my body," said Margarete.

"Yes, you could," said Moreno, smiling, making it funny and warm. George Andrew blushed but eased back down into his seat, head up, a gallant.

Why do I like it when others blush? I never do.

Susannah's arm was around my waist. "Margarete says she comes here so she can have a heart still open. She says she likes herself when she's in love."

"But she's a thief. She's ruthless," I whispered.

"Yes, but she says she only has to be like that for work. Don't be jealous."

"Of a thief, of course, of course I am extremely jealous. Who is the young man lucky enough to be in love with her?"

"She didn't want to say. I think he is much, much younger."

"She blabs about everything else."

Susannah whispered that she didn't care. I whispered back that she had stolen her bicycle.

"I know, I know. For all we know she still has it. What I also know is who I can count on." She hugged me. "Don't worry, Hedy. I'm just gathering information."

"Susannah, the Mata Hari of the Maysedergasse."

"You're hilarious. Margarete says people who want to hide

money invest in property."

"We are not giving her a single banknote. I mean it."

The room was suddenly silent. I was glad we had been whispering. We were about to begin.

Moreno walked to the centre of the room. He moved with a fluid grace and he stepped up onto a low platform with the ease of the sun rising in the morning.

"So," Moreno said, beaming. It was the signal. We all stood and began to move, watching each other, touching head to shoulder, hands to elbows, actions spontaneous and stately. At intervals, sighs of released tension. "Now," said Moreno, and we all completed our gestures and sat, relaxed. Most of us returned to where we began. "Can you tell how someone feels by how he moves or gestures?"

George Andrew was beside me again. He looked at his notes and muttered, "Or how he thinks?"

Moreno looked around.

"I have a gentleman caller who smooths his hair with his hand whenever he boasts." I had volunteered before I knew I was going to. Not everyone knew "caller" was a euphemism.

Margarete said, "Herr Prahler!"

Susannah looked at her and grinned.

"What does he feel?" Moreno asked.

It was Margarete's turn to grin at Susannah. "As much of me as he can."

Moreno suggested we smooth a hand over our partner's hair. I was partnered with the journalist. He stroked my hair confidently, as if I were a pet. I couldn't identify the feeling. My face was warm.

"I think you are supposed to smooth my hair as well," he said.

21.

T HINKING ABOUT GEORGE ANDREW became a pleasant distraction from what loomed. I had asked to be the protagonist in the next session with Moreno. His method had developed so that when an event was acted out, some of us took on the roles of whoever had been there, and others acted out different aspects of the protagonist. Even though I knew that as the protagonist, I was in control of the event, I was frightened. Frightened and ready. We would act out the story of what happened, of how I came to be a whore. It sounded like melodrama, except there would be no vicarious thrills, no afternoon matinées.

I couldn't sleep. Susannah slept through the night—no arm flopping over on top of me. I thought about the first night in the brothel. Or about George. Or escape. Or one of the three. I knew what was going to happen, but I didn't know what else was going to happen.

The rehearsal hall was well heated, which may have helped the warm-up exercises. The windows were all above eye level, and the early afternoon light filtered in on the diagonal. The hall had been renovated for a dance troupe by a wealthy patron, so not only was there a sprung wooden floor, smooth and polished, but there were also mirrors along one wall and a barre. In front of the mirror, a heavy velvet curtain hung from hundreds of small hooks attached to rings that slid on a rod. Before the exercises, some people watched themselves as they talked to the others.

The mirror was covered when the curtain was pulled, creating a delectable metallic shushing sound. This, along with "when you are ready" from Moreno, was the signal to begin our own movements, to match each other's simple gestures. The warm-up went on for about half an hour. Afterwards, everyone was flushed, at ease, collapsed on the floor, or leaning against the wall, smoking. Moreno chatted with everyone, rolling through the room like an amiable planet.

He spent a few quiet minutes with Susannah and me, and then he climbed onto the small platform. There was a feeling in the room as if everyone knew that this would be memorable, as if everyone felt a deep excitement, a pleasurable anxiety.

"So, Hedy. Today, you are the Protagonist. You are unhappy with your current circumstance." His fingers were spread, and his arms were open, including everyone.

"I never chose it."

"You would like us to help you act out the particular event that led to your situation. This is a demanding choice."

The room breathes. His voice was quiet. "Remember…"

Those dark warm eyes were looking only at me, but talking to everyone. *The part in his hair is getting wider. He's young to be losing his hair.* I felt at a distance, as if the world were blurred. He was still talking.

"…who models an idea, an action, or an emotion for the Protagonist is a 'Double'. Is this desired, Hedy?"

"Yes," I said, feeling very tired. *This life is exhausting.*

"Would you accept Elisabeth as a Double?"

I took a breath and nodded. *I feel like I have no borders.* "Who else do you need?" He kept the momentum going.

"Someone to play our neighbour."

"Would Lazzy be acceptable in this role?"

"Yes." *How calm my voice is.*

Lazzy sat on the edge of the platform, his eyes darting about.

There was a collective settling in the room.

"Who else is there?"

"My sister. She's sleeping."

Moreno turned and met Susannah's gaze. "Susannah, you may want us to use our method for your own experience of this event."

"Maybe. I mean, I might."

"Hedy, we need an Auxiliary to play your sister."

"Margarete."

I was ready to do this. There was a tightness in the muscles of my chest, my shoulders, like a cat's tension before it leaps.

"Susannah, is this acceptable to you?" Susannah nodded. "Hedy, where are we?"

"In a strange bedroom. I'm here." I pointed to a green-striped pallet on the platform. "My sister is there on the bed." *It's cold in here. The blurred feeling has gone away.*

Margarete moved with Susannah's syncopated, gawky walk to the platform. Years of paying attention to what was coming her way had taught her to be observant. The skills fear teaches.

I caught Susannah's eye. *I'm ready.* She smiled.

Margarete lay down, resting her head on a pillow with green and black lilies. She adjusted herself into a sleeping position on her side.

"Where should I be?" Elisabeth asked.

Moreno placed a well-worn footstool by the pallet. Elisabeth swayed towards it, pushing from the ball of the foot outward as she moved.

So that's what I look like. We have all watched each other. She sat, listening, her head hanging down. *Open.*

I sat on the edge of the pallet.

Moreno prompted. "Soliloquy. When you're ready."

"That night." I trembled, but my voice was firm. "That night I was left on the bed."

Breathe.

The room was quiet. I dropped down to the pallet. "I can

see Susannah, there. Asleep. The room is dark. Mischlinger is there in the dark, waiting. He turns on the light."

Lazzy stepped forward, reached out his hand, moving his thumb and forefinger in a tight turn, and then flung his hands open.

"Susannah is asleep…"

There was a delayed ripple in the room. *Mischlinger.* The owner of the best hotels in the city, and the worst politicians. Moreno lifted his hands, the movement of his arms widening, keeping the momentum, keeping my drama focused.

Susannah's Auxiliary, Margarete, said, "I can't know."

It's beginning.

"You've been drugged, though I don't know it. I'm glad you're asleep."

I took a ragged breath.

Elisabeth, my Double, voicing my feelings, said, "I'm afraid."

I nodded. "What is he going to do to me?"

Moreno looked with infinite kindness at me, with those steady eyes. "Where is he?"

"Above me," I croaked. *This is my fault.* I looked quickly into the audience, directly to my sister, whose eyes were riveted to the drama on the platform.

"Here," Moreno said to me, bringing me back to the moment. His hand lowered soft, soft to the side of my face. "Here," he said, indicating Margarete. "Here is Susannah, your sleeping sister."

I turned towards her. Moreno nodded to Lazzy, who positioned himself above me. His head shrunk down into his shoulders, and he tilted forward, his arms braced, his hands on either side of me.

Cold. I can feel the room. They are inside my terror, they are breathing with me.

"Role reversal," said Moreno.

Everyone stood. No one talked.

"Lazzy, you are Hedy. Hedy, you are Mischlinger. Margarete,

you continue to be Susannah, and Elisabeth, you continue as Hedy's Double."

We returned to the low platform. On the pallet, as Mischlinger, I propped myself on my hands and knees above Lazzy, who was playing me.

Mischlinger's thoughts arrive in a rush. *Look at me.*

A girl's voice, underneath me: "Why are you doing this?"

Shivering. To be Mischlinger, to be him.

Suddenly Moreno was moving towards me on all fours, like a cat, hunting. Holding my gaze.

Elisabeth's hand, soft on my shoulder, then steady.

Breathe.

Mischlinger's thoughts raced in my head. *This girl should be quiet.* And then, rasping from me, Mischlinger's voice: "What do you know about it? Who are you anyway? No one cares about you, Hedvig. You never do what you're supposed to do, anyway. Everyone knows that."

A high trembling voice from below me: "Why do you hurt me?"

Mischlinger's voice emerging from my lips, slow, and full of self-pity: "I can't help myself. I have no control over this. It's there all the time. I want to escape from myself. But I can't, except when someone else, a girl, cries. If I make her cry…"

A cry of pain.

The same cry that woke me nearly every night.

I was the one making that sound. Not Susannah.

I realized I was crouching as if I were coming out of a cave. I shivered and yawned. I had always known in my mind what had happened to my body. Now I knew, body and mind, what had happened to me.

I looked to see where Lazzy had gone. He had moved back from being underneath me, from being me. Elbows out, hands covering his face. I stood up to go to him. The room was unsteady. Someone holding my hand. George Andrew, his jacket around me. My sister's arms around me. Susannah holding me. Holding me and holding me. Over her shoulder, I could see Lazzy in tears and Elisabeth with her arms around him, and then I saw the others, a cascade, seeking to hold and to be held.

22.

AFTER THAT SESSION, I began to sleep all through the night. The circles under my eyes disappeared. And even though Kreutzel's rota of renovation had arrived back to our quarters, with elegant grey and white striped wallpaper, curtains instead of shutters, and smart casement windows to open for fresh air, it remained 13, Verstektstrasse. We had to leave. We had to be open to the world. We had to make friends, and no respectable person thinks, 'If only I had a former whore for a friend.'

Unless you were Moreno. But therapy had moved to the suburbs as Moreno had taken a bride and his practice to Bad Voslau. That was too far for us to travel and still have a good excuse. I missed the focus on physical movement and the companionable talk with the others afterwards. I saw a photo of him in the newspaper. He was sitting in front of a wall covered in ivy. A good suit, but the trousers needed lengthening. You could see the top of his boots.

Our clothing had changed, too. Susannah and I had been converting banknotes directly into gold coins, and I was sewing them into the linings of our coats. The day we tried them out, we met the journalist from Moreno's sessions, George Andrew, coming towards us over the Augartenbruke.

The newly planted Lombardy poplars made the sunlight reflect off the water intermittently—sun, shade, sun—not unlike George Andrew's mood, though he was obviously pleased to be our guest for lunch. As we said our goodbyes, despite the fresh wind sweeping up the Donau, the hems of our lightweight coats stayed still and we walked away as if we were mobile statuary, unassailable, impervious to the elements.

Susannah flung an arm across me, stopping me in my tracks. I hadn't seen the automobile that had lurched over the sidewalk and nearly hit us. I couldn't stop shivering, and oddly, yawning. Susannah was very tender towards me, holding me and patting my face until I could breathe normally. "I could shoot him."

"The driver?" I asked, although I knew who she meant. She often said things that seemed to have no connection to her surroundings, but this time I knew, before she answered.

"No. The Old Dear."

We would never be entirely free of him. Mischlinger was mentioned occasionally in her newspapers, but otherwise he, too, seemed to have disappeared. We never saw that old Daimler in the neighbourhood again, which was no surprise. After the Great War, there were so many girls, young and desperate, to choose from.

23.

"YOU DIDN'T MENTION THIS to me." Susannah rattled her newspaper straight and turned a page, ignoring George Andrew, who had taken off his hat. I had, of course, talked to her about inviting him here, and she was pretending to be indignant. Convincingly.

He rotated his hat by the brim as he looked around the room. "Swank," he said, in English. I didn't know what he meant at the time, but it *was* swank: flowers, china swans on pedestals. It was in good taste, really, a little over the top, but a little over the top was Vienna. He held his dark grey coat folded over his arm.

"Please, Herr Andrew."

I indicated a well-upholstered slipper chair, low enough that he would come up to my bosom, if I were to stand closer. He sat and crossed his legs protectively, one ankle on the opposite knee. He was a little anxious. *Good. This will work.* I stood closer.

"Your madam seemed impressed when I asked for you, specifically. Thank God I was able to make up an English name as a reference. A Lord Highstone, who doesn't exist."

I took his coat, and moved away to hang it up. The space around him was his again, briefly.

"Don't worry, we'll pay you what you paid her."

"Thank you." His shoulders dropped. "I had no idea how much... I'm glad to know I can hang onto my flat for another month." He glanced over at Susannah, who had remained behind a copy of the *Neue Freie Presse*. "The madam suggested the house has always favoured English gentlemen, and in her case, vice versa." He shuddered comically. "She has the most awful grin. Really, quite splendidly awful."

At that, Susannah put down her paper and offered her hand, arm straight out. He jumped up, bowed slightly, and shook her hand. Her arm remained stiff.

We do work so well together, I thought. *She knows it's important that first, he should feel awkward, and second, that I should rescue him.*

He was confused and looked at me. *Perfect.*

"If you grew up, as we did," I smiled, all forgiving, "on the Schottenring, your manners would be formal. So when a young lady extends her arm, like this, you kiss her hand. That is how it is done traditionally in Vienna."

George kissed Susannah's hand. And then he surprised me, and kissed mine, looking up at me. That was not how it was done in Vienna. Not at all.

"The first time we were at Moreno's, I got the impression you were from a level of society—that you were well-born, basically."

"But whatever made you think that?" Susannah sounded very impressed.

He was caught off guard. He couldn't tell if she was being sarcastic. I gestured towards him. "He read your body." No one would think for a moment that I was anything but gracious. Susannah and I can work on instinct.

It is one thing to pay attention to another's body in a group with a director, in a quasi-theatre setting, but George Andrew acted as though he was suddenly and clearly conscious of being in the bedroom of two whores, in a brothel. He wouldn't have felt alarm coming up the steps of the place. It looked like an ordinary dwelling. Hundreds of men walked up the front steps each week, and no one turned a head. Vienna and its discretion.

He sat tentatively, no doubt wondering how long he had to stay. He played with his hat, turning it round and round by its brim. I took it and hung it up. I felt like this was a scene I'd acted a hundred times. *What a good plan this is.*

"And you didn't try to escape?"

Susannah slapped both hands down on the bed. He jumped. She was naturally good at this. "We planned to, with a little Hungarian, Kislany. But I fell asleep, and Hedy couldn't wake me. Kislany was arrested before she got to the station, as a thief. Old Kreutzel waited until the police had cut off all that Hungarian hair before she paid the fine. She looked so pretty with short hair that I cut mine, too. Then Kislany got away with an Italian after the war."

What an elaborate lie that was! My sister could have written novels.

"Your shorter hair does flatter your face." He brushed at nothing on his trouser leg and then looked up. "But, forgive me for asking, did no one from your family...?"

I touched his arm. "Everyone, you see, thought we were with someone else. Our parents were dead. A neighbour who had his eye on us brought us here."

"Mischlinger was your neighbour? I heard his name in your session, but I didn't realize he was your neighbour! He owns several of the large hotels, Hotel Vienna..."

"Yes, so lucky for us to have been very rich girls, and to have a well-known hotelier as a neighbour."

Now he knew she was being sarcastic. It made him relax, which I hadn't counted on. "Rich girls, then. With very bad luck."

Susannah shot me a look, and mouthed, *Billy.* She needn't have. I remembered. But George Andrew's tone was different, calm and sympathetic.

"I have heard that Herr Mischlinger collects more than art. That he also collects politicians. At least that's the current café gossip." He stretched. "As a journalist, I need to measure what's being said in the papers against the local gossip. I can make out the headlines, but I need someone to read the articles to me. My ear for German is good, but my eye, not so much."

"Perhaps we can help you. But we need you to help us too."

"Of course. "

I could tell he was wondering what has he got himself into. *Perfect.* "Herr Andrew, teach us English, real English, everything. Gestures, taboos."

"Frauleins, please. You flatter me. I am very interested in the emotional sciences. They are new, ground-breaking, really. The methods are ... well, no one has done this before! I am working on an idea that might, perhaps, be useful to diplomacy. To nations in conflict."

I nodded all through this, not taking my eyes away from his. He was still on the hook. An idealist. I moved closer and rested my hand lightly on the calf of the leg he'd crossed over his knee, as if I didn't know I had.

He continued, trying to keep his poise. "Right now, individuals are helped with what might seem contradictory methods—not alone, but in groups, like ours. Some of us are interested in the science, some of us are interested in expanding the art of theatre, some of us have sorrows that go deep. I understand, you have told me, that you wish to leave this place. But, may I suggest, there is a syndicate for your kind developing. Perhaps..."

Susannah jumped up. "*Our kind*—do you mean whores, or Jews?" Her tone wasn't playful at all. It was flat, like that of a good interrogator.

He was dumbfounded. I knew what to do. I knelt. "Help us learn English. Please." I took his hand and rested my cheek on it. And he let me.

We were now the only ones still in the house, other than Brigita, who had been here before the war. I was so tired of all of it. The closer one is to leaving a terrible situation, the harder it is to bear. My sister and I were rapidly becoming fluent in English. Susannah did mention she would have preferred American English, the kind she and Billy used to practise. "That would suit me just fine," she muttered. But we paid George and took him out for lunch, and while we ate, we listened to him carp. In English.

One Tuesday after he left, Susannah looked annoyed. "Hedy, you should see your face. It's all dreamy. You're smiling. You're not talking."

"No, but…"

"But you're always talking, Hedy. You like him."

"Of course. We both do." I sat on the bed and looked in the mirror. George Andrew had left hours ago.

Susannah talked to my reflection. "I thought you wanted us to be able to move through the world as we once did, welcome in the best homes. George Andrew doesn't come from money. Did you look at his shoes?"

"I was looking at his face, his eyes."

"Oh, his eyes. Do you want him to teach you English, or," she fluttered her eyelashes and clasped her hands, "the language of love?"

"Stop. I want to learn English, so that we can get out of this terrible city and never come back. I'd like to choose how we live. He's a *mensch*, and he's willing to teach us, both of us. Don't worry! Other than Moreno, he seems to be the only man who has ever been perfectly interested in talking to us with our clothes on."

Susannah picked up a brush and started in on my hair, her conciliatory gesture from when she was quite small. "It's funny when you use the old words, Hedy. I think Papa was a *mensch*."

"He was. When I think back, though, I can see that he wasn't a good money manager. He was often in a jam over debts. I think old Mischlinger helped him out several times."

"Yes! I remember that he was always embarrassed about

getting those envelopes! Papa had to have the latest thing, the best."

"But he did love us. Remember him buying us the bicycles? Whatever we wanted."

"Hedy." Susannah paused, brush in hand. "Do you think Mischlinger has their things?"

"Who knows? I simply want to get out of Vienna. I want to see you get better. The swiftest, the most effective cure for morphine addiction is in Bath. In England. So we have to learn English. I'm under no illusions, Susannah."

That's what I told her. But I was thinking about George Andrew's hands, which were so nicely shaped. I was thinking about the small, infinitely small curls at the back of his neck. I told myself I liked him because, clearly, he was ambitious and practical, the kind of fellow who nosed out useful friends. Like ones who could get us false British passports. I hadn't given up my desire to escape.

Without Moreno's group, we were lonely again. We went out for fresh air, for coffee, but always unfashionably early. If we wanted to see the latest Ivor Novello picture, we slipped in the kino's doors at the last minute. In the winter months, in hired cars, we went past doorways where young girls shivered and stepped out into the light of the street lamps to offer themselves if a slow-moving car drove by. We lived in an alternate Vienna, safe from harm, but parallel to the city we had once known and could no longer dare to enter. Art galleries, where I most craved to be, were impossible.

24.

WE WATCHED HIM HURRY over to us, holding his hat on his head with one hand. His thin coat was plastered to his legs in the wind. He hadn't yet seen us, and his handsome face was full of worry. I recognized that look. I had seen it on my own face in the mirror when I was worrying about our finances.

He caught sight of us and brightened. I knew he liked my company, our company, but I also knew that he was relieved that I always insisted on paying for his meal. I was in charge of finances, because even though Susannah was wonderful with numbers, she was not wonderful with a purse.

"*Gruss gott!*" I called out to him.

He waved and caught up to us. And immediately began telling us how much he hated the fakery of Vienna, all its borrowed buildings from other cities, other times. I agreed, and said I knew how he felt. I was glad to see him, even when he was upset. I was thrilled about his quick glances towards me when he said something sharply critical, his eyes flashing.

Susannah said she didn't like Vienna, either. "I'd like to be in Italy. San Remo, specifically."

I wasn't sure where that was, but it didn't matter. I didn't respond to her. We had to go to England. One of our regular English callers, Nigel, a very voluble fellow, had enthusiastically confirmed what I had read about successful treatment of addicts, morphine and otherwise, in the city of Bath. The

Austrian army hadn't been alone in administering morphine to its wounded.

George didn't respond to her either. I wasn't sure if he had heard her. He declared that everyone knew that Paris was the best city to live in. "They do not openly discriminate against those who are willing to fit in, to live like Parisiens."

Susannah leaned against a lamppost, one foot up on the metal column. "So Jews are allowed if they don't act too Jewish."

George was embarrassed. Susannah's solution to this was to fall into her usual comedienne routine: to stagger and stumble and swear.

"Oh, shit!" And away she went, backwards, crouching, her arms out wide for balance, which she regained just before George and I reached her. She smiled as if she were delighted at this new method of locomotion, continuing backwards until she plunked down on a bench and crossed her legs neatly in one movement.

What would my life have been like without her making me laugh? Susannah patted the seat of the bench beside her. George remained standing, laughing, still hanging onto his hat. It was a fedora, he had told us, made in Paris, and he did not want to lose it in the wind.

"I wonder," Susannah patted her blonde bob, "how Parisiens would find out we were Jewish."

I interrupted. "They won't. Because we're going to England. To Bath."

"Well said, Hedy, well said." George was laughing. "You present your side of an argument so well, in spite of..."

"In spite of what? My occupation? My lack of education?"

He covered fast. "Your lack of height. You're like a little sturdy statue, Hedy. One that thinks."

"A statue? So, you think I have a heart of stone?"

"I wish I had your focus. If I did, I would probably be in Paris already, with Hemingway. Callaghan said he'd introduce us. Did I mention that?"

"A few times." He didn't notice what I had said about my heart. He was hardly without focus. "You've been in Vienna so long, George Andrew, you're already thinking that it needs another statue."

"Yes. I can see you in a garden, carved in stone, surrounded by ivy. In the style of the Sumerian, I think, given your…"

"Shape?"

"Bearing." He wasn't biting.

"So not surrounded by ivy, surrounded by, I think…"

"George Andrew!" interrupted Susannah. "Whatever you are thinking about my sister is no doubt pleasant. Horticultural." Our flirting had made her tense.

"Yes, I am smiling, aren't I?" I joined Susannah on the bench and looked up at him. This was one of my ploys, just as stumbling was for Susannah. Our ploys had become integrated into everything we did.

"You know, we want to fit in when we get to Bath."

"I assure you, the pools are quite large enough to accommodate the two of you."

Susannah laughed. She knew how laughing at men's jokes put them at ease. "Oh, Herr Andrew! We have a proposition for you." She paused. Mama's old trick. Moreno's, too. "Old Kreutzel approves of us learning proper English because she thinks it will enhance her profits. So you don't have to pretend that you have a need for specialty whores anymore."

He blushed, exactly as we intended. We needed for him to be to be uncomfortable, so that he would agree to our proposition in order to be at ease again.

"Could you come more often? A few times a week? We need to practise as often as possible with a real Englishman. Intensively."

"Oh, I'm sorry, I'm not sure if I can be available. And I'm not actually English." He sat down between us. "Sorry. I'm Canadian."

"You're a sorry Canadian?" said Susannah.

I gave her a look that meant, "stop." That meant, "Do not." I liked this man with the pretty mouth. He was proper, even formal, in his behaviour, yet so frank when he talked. Even though he never tried to touch me, he always tried to sit so he could look directly at me. I had a surging feeling, of being as alive as I once had been, when I was a girl and the Moser brothers had fancied me.

"You sound English."

"I was educated in Edinburgh, and I lived in London for a few years."

"We can certainly make it worth your while." *Oh no. He thinks I mean whoring.* "I mean, you will be well compensated. I mean, *paid.*"

"It's a tempting project, but right now I'm not sure if I can afford the time. I'm working on an article, an essay, and I expect to sell it. It's about the changes in the world, how the world sees itself. Not just Austria. It occupies nearly all my waking hours, and some of the hours when I should be sleeping. It will be my calling card." He shrugged. "I'm not sure I can be of much help."

Susannah watched my reaction to this and then waved a hand dismissively. "Oh, George, it's easy, you lovely man. I'll read the daily papers to you in German, and you teach us English! We'll all take notes!" Susannah grabbed both of his hands and wrinkled her nose. "It will be fun!" She hung on to his left hand, lightly, as if she didn't realize what she was doing. She was good at this.

"Well. I really do want to write an article about Moreno, about the new politics. I suppose, perhaps..."

I didn't want to lose this chance. "She'll read. I'll pay." I smiled my best smile. I extended my hand. George took it and then sat, his hands crossed in front of him, holding the hands of two of the loveliest young whores in all Vienna.

Susannah read the articles in George's newspapers as they were written—no mocking accents, no drawling some words out longer to make fun of the writer as she used to do with Papa. When he came, George would bring two or three newspapers. He wanted Susannah to read articles on the same topic. He would take many notes.

As did Susannah, who called our meetings her "classes." This was the only time she ever seemed to revel in organization. She lined up her things neatly—her notebooks, her pens, and her dictionaries. At George's request, she underlined sentences, which he copied, along with a translation, in his tight and energetic handwriting, before taking the newspapers with him. We gave him money for Kreutzel, and money for himself.

Susannah was sprawled on the bed. "Hedy, listen: school girls are considered to be the most virtuous." She stood and turned up a hand, explaining. "Virtuous, and so the object of degrading fantasy, I know, but first of all, virtuous. Because studying is virtuous. It is of the mind." She collapsed in the chair. "I am so tired of the body."

I could not believe my ears. I was now sharing my life, this room, with a bold little professor in a skimpy chemise and lace drawers.

I thought about George, what he wore, how his back curved into his waist. I was thinking more about this man who had never been in my bed than about any of the regulars who had. I kept this from Susannah, and, as much as I could, from myself. It was important to pay attention to why we were studying so intently: to leave Vienna, and all its callous smugness. England was our destination. Everything depended on our being ready for English manners, assumptions, cuisine. But I found myself taking note of information about Canada. Our Lady of the Snows. Toboggans.

The topics for discussion of English life were wildly disparate: horse racing, radical politics, favourite desserts. Once, when George had forgotten his notebook, he took notes on an envelope while Susannah read. I admired the complicated stamp on the envelope: a lion standing with its legs braced on the world, its mouth roaring into the lines of a sunrise, and a side view of George V, his sweeping moustache and his arching eyebrow. George said the king was actually a nice old fellow who had been delighted to add these stamps to his personal collection.

"You mean a man could be a king, and still be likeable?" Susannah leaned forward. She had acquired her political views through the conversations with the Red Vienna supporters in the Moreno group.

"Well, yes. I could like the man and not like the job he did." George laughed. "And he has a very nice name."

I smiled at this. I agreed. I liked the *juh* of this name. You had to make a kiss with your lips when you said his name. At least, I did.

George told us about competing with the British Labour politician, Ramsay MacDonald—"Old Rambucket," he called him—to see who was faster at putting stamps on letters of solicitation. They had been volunteers on a mail campaign for the British Cycle Union.

So we are both bicycling enthusiasts. I turned this over in my mind often. I wanted to have things in common with someone other than my sister, someone who didn't have to be on my side, who wasn't an addict, who'd lived in the world. I told him about bicycling past the toe of Herodotus and failing to slap it, but I left out the circumstances. Neither Susannah nor I had ever talked to anyone about the death of our parents. No one at 13, Verstekstrasse talked about how she came arrive at the brothel.

But he asked about my childhood. No one else ever had. At first, I thought it would be a relief to talk about when we still had parents and a privileged life, how we had defeated several governesses when we were very little.

"So you didn't attend a school?"

"Our mother felt we were better suited to her own teaching."

Susannah interrupted. "But that was after we had been asked to leave several schools. All dedicated to learning submission and modesty. When I told a teacher at the last one that she smelled like shit, and to take her shitty hands off me, that I was only drawing pictures, that shit of a woman told our mother I must have learned to swear from servants, and that got the cook and the laundress and the maid sacked. From that point on, all our education took place beside our mother on the sofa, with her turning the pages of the newspaper and reading aloud."

That was the first time George heard my sister swear. He was so startled that he lurched back, nearly tipping his chair over. He soon became used to it. Like ugly wallpaper, eventually it didn't register. But that first time, I realized once again how shocking it was. It was hard to reconcile what Susannah looked like, so fair and fine-boned, with the vulgarities she so obviously enjoyed.

I wanted George to know Susannah wasn't always doing terrible things. "We had to remind Mama to read aloud, not silently. Sometimes what she read was so absorbing, she forgot us. Susannah would silently mouth, *"bla bla de bla,"* flipping her hand as if explaining something. And then when I laughed, Mama surfaced and would begin to read out loud again."

"Frankly, except for when you chose to swear, Susannah, your antics sound so mild."

I was astounded. She was the reason why we had no friends. I had loved being with my mother, with Papa, with their friends, and with her most of all, but it was also lonesome, and as it turned out, dangerous. No one had noticed when we disappeared.

Reviewing that old small world made it seem bigger when I told George about it. But it turned out that talking about the past doesn't let you re-experience it. There are not enough words for everything that comes at you from memory all at once. When you talk, you leave things out, and those things that you have left out return the favour, and leave you. Those memories are broken-hearted. They disappear and don't come back.

25.

ITOLD GEORGE HOW PAPA had taught us to hold our arms stiff and shove our fists into his hands so he could lift us up. Then he would flip us into sofas or into great, strong-smelling pools of water when we vacationed at spas. I told him how patient Papa was when he showed us hand tricks.

"That's why I'm good with money!" Susannah plucked a coin from behind George's ear. He applauded and held out his hand for the coin. I turned around, kicked off my leather slipper, and then slipped off my stocking and tossed it onto the back of the chair. I looked back at him as I extended my foot and picked up the stocking with my bare toes the way I used to on chilly Schottenring mornings when I was trying to delay leaving my warm bed. I could still do it, years later. What happy embarrassment when George said, "Quite Darwinian of you!"

He said nothing about his own father. His mother was still alive, tending to her rhododendrons and hydrangeas. I told him how we had been allowed to play, to dress up in our mother's prized coming-out gowns, while she napped. Susannah kept tripping because they were too long, so I found scissors and shortened the dresses. Our mother saw us standing ankle deep in scissored tulle and satin, and took to her bed for two days.

George had the most affecting, resonant, tenor laugh. It gave me time to think about what I wanted to say to him, to someone other than my sister. I wanted to explain *how it was* to someone who didn't know us, to hear myself talk to someone who was educated, to hear how he responded to someone who wasn't.

"We mostly had adults for company. Our parents were content with each other, and they were confident that we didn't need others, either." I left out the constant havoc Susannah caused, how it isolated us. "Their adult friends would croon over us, but often it was because they wanted to curry favour, especially with Mama—the beauty, the intellect."

"So you didn't know if any of them really liked you?" George leaned forward.

A frozen moment. *Mischlinger.*

Susannah freed herself first. "Fraulein Lowin liked us." She pointed to a photograph in her copy of the *Neue Frei Presse.* "There she is, still a *force majeure* in Vienna. People appreciate her ability to organize: parties, openings, railway station design."

"She's an architect?"

"No, just good at organizing the flow of things. Getting people to do things."

George stared at the photograph as though he were memorizing it. He folded up the page it was on and tucked it inside his jacket. He told us how, when he was fifteen, he had quit school to volunteer for the army. "To get away from my father. I was tall enough to lie about my age, but my very flat feet kept me out of the war. The recruiting sergeant said that with any luck they would keep me from dancing with all the girls while the rest of them were off fighting. I didn't learn to dance until the war was over, and not very well. Smile all you like, Fraulein Hedy."

George was already perceived as a regular at 13, Verstektstrasse, and no doubt some of the other whores thought he was a roué of no small financial means. But he was simply our English tutor every morning during the week. On Tuesdays, he was a guest of the house, as we didn't have callers, and as the old girl was accompanied by New Hans to do her rounds of banks and bribes. She didn't like us to open the windows, but as soon as she was gone, we all did it anyway. Songs from competing phonograph records filled the air in the street below.

Just after the war, when Bebe Raton left, she gave her phonograph to me, along with a packet of extra needles and four records in stiff brown paper sleeves. Before the war, she had taught everyone how to tango the way they did in Mar del Plata, where she was from. Her voice was very high—a squeak—but she had exquisite manners, beautiful soft brown skin, and white-blonde hair that she claimed was natural. We had learned her style of the tango, hanging off each other's necks and pressing close to each other's bosoms, taking little teasing steps in our high-heeled bedroom slippers.

I pulled out the heavy bakelite records and asked George to put "La Cumparsita" on the turntable. I reached up and put my arm around George's neck so that my left hand rested upon his left shoulder. My smaller height meant that if George deliberately held still, a pause necessitated by the music, I slipped down his body, suspended from his neck, my body held along his longer torso.

This music demanded unison. Unless we moved together, we'd both fall down. We let it tell us when to hesitate or trace a quick circle with a foot. We leaned in on each other, chest to chest, my balance depending upon him, his balance depending on me, especially when we were doing runs of quick steps. George knew to keep moving forward, to turn, to cross his feet, to try to insert his leg between mine. I mostly stepped backwards, crossing my feet and pausing, so that his leg was not between mine, but on the outside, so that he must try again. We played the same song, over and over:

Si supieras, "If you knew…"

Que aun dentro de mi alma, "Of the love in my soul…."

A soft knock on the door, *rappity-rap*. From the rhythm of the knock, we could tell that it was not Kreutzel but a sister whore at the door. When we opened it, we found a collection of types—"one of each," George said afterwards—of pretty, partly undressed women who begged us, please, to play something, anything, else.

"Just once more," I said, placing the needle in the groove to start the music again. While the others watched from the doorway, we moved around the large room, around the bed that we had moved to the middle. He held me close around the waist and imprisoned my other hand at his hip. The steps we took were small, intense, focused, like the whispers of lovers. We were dancing perfect questions and answers.

My right cheek was against his left. He had to bend his knees, and I had to walk on tiptoe, but that made it easier for me to do the *picado*, the backward kick that tossed a hint to anyone watching of how exciting it felt, to dance like that.

"In Argentina, that tango you do is the old way, the country way. 'Melting'—the way the blacks do." Lina was a thick-lashed brown-eyed Argentinian in lace drawers so low you could see the dimples above her light brown bottom. "The new tango is better; it is more upright." She straightened her back and clenched her bottom. "More white."

"But this is how the last girl from Mar del Plata taught us to do it," I said. "Little Mousie was also a natural blonde."

"I know nothing about that city. I only know Buenos Aires." She raised her voice. "I'm a *porteña*. And we laugh at this song. It's so old-fashioned. '*Oh, my lost love. Oh, even the little dog has left him.*'" She was getting angry.

"Perhaps so. It's possibly ironic. But it seems to me it's rueful, too. Sincere, in fact," argued George.

Just as I was bathing in how he stood up for me, how he defended my choice, just as I told myself I finally understood what "swoon" meant, Susannah walked in.

Susannah often slipped away, pretending to go out in the city. No one ever saw her slip back into Kreutzel's office with her key. She had been given one, but had been told it was for emergencies only, and to not let the others know. She honoured the last part of the instruction.

"Oh, please. It's just a song to dance to. Come in, ladies. And close the windows. The old girl is on her way to the front door." Susannah invited all of them into our room and closed the door.

She pointed to the bottom of the stairs. Then she mimed drinking from a flask, and made a *tlock, tlock tlock* noise with her tongue against the roof of her mouth. So many different women, all laughing—tall and thin, roly-poly, even one little Moravian whose eyes made her look like a Mongol princess. She played it up, keeping her fingernails long and her toes adorned with small bells. Susannah made a face like a drunk, her tongue hanging out, her eyes rolled up. "Palinkaaa," she croaked. Right on cue, they all laughed. It was New Hans's favourite drink.

From the bottom of the stairs, the usual threat, "Be quiet, you worthless women!"

"Yes, New Hans!" they chorused. He hated that we called him New Hans. We hated that he sat blocking the hallway with his big boots.

"The feet have spoken!" Susannah whispered.

Open laughter, louder. They all dispersed at her joke. She had also succeeded in converting New Hans's ire into a general complaint about worthless women, drawing the focus away from her, or George, or me. Comedy as strategy. She was as focused as I was on getting out of that place. After everyone had left, she turned to George.

"George. Don't be a source of trouble for Hedy and me with the other whores. Or with New Hans. He'd love to report an argument. Two things are important: the other whores don't get their drawers in a knot over Kreutzel favouring me, and Kreutzel continues to favour me. Old Crankycrotch has been happy since the war ended, as the British have money to spend in Vienna's brothels, and in hers especially. So she's happy that we're were learning English with you. But that could change if you start to get into arguments."

Kreutzel had replaced the Old Hans with another drunk, also named Hans. New Hans was not stupid like Old Hans, nor half as big. He may have also been a drunk, but he was surprisingly vigilant, talking like he was still on the police force, still able to make an arrest. After hours, his big feet were always sticking out into the hallway. Drunk, he would lie on the floor in order to look up at Kreutzel. We all had to crouch beside her chair now, and gaze upward. Her face had draped into itself, and her pain now was constant. When I wondered aloud if the pain from her spine was what made her so terrible to others, Susannah laughed. "No. Don't blame her being crippled for her being a shit. One thing has nothing to do with the other. She's just a terrible person who happens to have a spine that's collapsing."

The brothel was quiet for a Tuesday. It had finally stopped raining. By mid-day it was hot. George and Susannah sat in opposite chairs, and I lay on the bed. George went to the window and opened it a crack. He turned around to look at me, and just like that, grabbed my hand and pulled me to my feet. "Let's try dancing without an audience. The quick step. Shall we?"

Susannah stumbled over to the bed. I opened the door to the landing, George locked my hand in his, and we tripped down the stairs. "Just need a breath of fresh air!" I explained, as we skipped over New Hans's boots.

We slipped out the door on the other side of the vestibule from the madam's office and faced each other. It was not Vienna's May Ball, but it was my first invitation to a dance, in the courtyard of a brothel, among bleached and half-damp sheets. I was thrilled. George hummed in my ear and we were off, around the courtyard, very fast. Not only did we have to hang on to each other, but we also had to duck to the left or right, battling damp sheets, until George picked me up.

He carried me over the drunk and dozing New Hans, who muttered, "Be quiet!" as George ran up the stairs with me. He planted me on the floor outside our room. I was still in his arms. My face lifted toward his mouth. I didn't know how ordinary people did this.

Oh. I'm being kissed.

His mouth was soft but firm. It was my first kiss. I understood why people said "fall" in love.

Then we both laughed as if we hadn't meant it.

Later, to Susannah, who had seen the kiss, I claimed it was the kind of thing done in English society, that one had to know how to do it, how to kiss in someone's arms without letting bodies touch. Susannah smirked and raised an eyebrow, which was annoying, and put on her favourite phonograph record, *Hey Hey Charleston*. Everyone in the house liked it except for old Kreutzel, who said we were going to make her floors collapse, like that place in Chicago. Susannah opened our door all the way, and the other whores emerged out of their bedrooms and into the hallway, sleeves fluttering, like damselflies compelled by the sudden hot weather.

"I can't help it—I have to dance to this," said Lina, flinging her arms up at the elbows and pigeon-toeing her feet.

The story of how George arrived in Vienna might not have been admirable, but it was remarkable, and it had brought him here, to us. He told us that while he was at work at the Cycle Union, he had recognized an unusual stamp, switched it for an ordinary one, and sold it for a lot of money. By nightfall, he was on a ferry out of Southampton. "Out of bloody England and on to Red Vienna," he said, "the city after the war that was going to show the world how."

He had lived in cheap accommodations and sponged meals from others, but now his money had run out. He said everyone was in Paris. He had the names of contacts already working for the Paris-based journals. He kept up a heavy correspondence with a gossipy friend, and a careful correspondence with the ones he wished to cultivate.

I admired his perseverance. "He's so hard on himself, Su-sannah."

"Hedy, Vienna hardens all hearts except yours. And now it's even softer because George kissed you. I don't think he should have."

My sister, the love expert.

26.

GEORGE GRINNED AND WAGGLED the invitation he had just read to me. "It's because I've been working with you, Hedy, all these months, answering all your questions!" He'd been asked to write for one of the English political journals based in Paris. He sat up straighter. "I owe a debt of gratitude to you. I feel ready as a journalist to explain the world to itself, as much as it will let me."

I was surprised. He sounded old, like he was dedicating a bridge. Why was he talking to me so formally? I stood, my arm out so he could kiss my hand. "What do you mean, dear Mr. Andrew? Does the world want to be explained to itself?"

He laughed, and was himself again. "Oh, Hedy, I love how quickly you absorb what I say and then immediately, *immediately,* start to question it!"

I could listen to him begin any sentence with "'I love.'" He spoke so passionately, one topic leading surprisingly to another, wherever his mind took him, whatever connections he made; all, in the end, despite his belligerence, based on what was fair and fresh.

He would say, "Do you see?" And I did. I loved how he had started to put his stocking feet up on the bed when he talked. He shrugged and wagged his hands. Sometimes he squinted one eye and looked upwards, as if trying to remember something. I knew this meant he had toyed with what he was going to say to me, turned it over in his mind's ear.

For all his frankness and generosity, he was a complicated, ambitious man. His parents weren't wealthy, and he was from the colonies, so he didn't grow up, he said, among the people he wanted to make his mark with. He said Susannah and I were from a better class than him, but thanks to having to teach us, he had truly learned how to explain things. "If Oxbridge ever creates a Chair of English Cultural Studies," he said, "I will be a shoo-in for the job."

He had lined up the chance to stay in someone's flat in Paris for a month. He had learned how to charm people, small tricks absorbed from watching me and my sister, but he had also benefited from our direct instruction. If he wanted to be a top journalist, if he wanted to report on the powerful and famous, he would have to have a whore's wiles. The language of the body was useful anywhere, and we spoke it very well.

That room was our university. Our English-speaking callers gave their unwitting assistance to what we hoped would be their never being able to call on us again. We were thrilled when they said, 'How well you speak!' or 'Your enunciation is impeccable.' George was proud of us. He made us repeat phrases, and cared that we got the inflection right.

"Good afternoon. Now you. No, don't lower your eyes in that flirtatious way. English ladies lift their chins and look directly at men."

We kept our faces still. It wasn't just pronunciation, enunciation, or elocution.

"Again. Good afternoon, ladies."

We lifted our chins. We looked directly at him. We kept our faces immobile.

"Perfect!"

I loved being praised by this man. One afternoon, Susannah had left a syringe lying neatly across a glass on the bedside table. She usually hid what she had to do, even from me. There was no packet, no folded paper with morphine. When I said to her, "Do let's try again," Susannah tucked the syringe in a drawer. George's only comment was, "Yes, emphasis on the first word, well done."

My accent was getting better. Escape was getting closer.

New Hans told Susannah that he was sure old Kreutzel would get him to take over the business any day. He based this on her praise for his singing, and her sending him out for mandolin lessons. "She sees me as a kind of owner-artist," he had confided to Susannah on his way out one day. The truth was that she got rid of him so she could teach my sister how to run the brothel—what banks to go to, what bribes to offer, how to calculate the value of a sexual service.

She said Susannah was her protégé, just as she had been, little Hilde Kreutzel, for the madam who had taken her in when she was half-starved. "But I was a beauty, you know," she made sure to add. Then, as the madam had declined, little Hilde looked after her and the business. "She never wanted for anything. She had the best medical care. I made sure of that."

Susannah played along and took notes in a little book she kept in her desk for these meetings. What a good student. *Virtuous.* She also made sure she swiped all the banknotes she could from little Hilde Kreutzel every time she visited the office for one of her lessons. "Nothing like a wet thumb and flat chest," she said.

It was true: her dress bodices were not very well-filled, except when she returned from a visit with our madam. Then she had a bosom almost as large as mine.

Gold coins, we realized, would be too heavy to carry. We had to travel very lightly—using small suitcases to avoid suspicion—and given the devalued Austrian currency, large banknotes were necessary.

That fall, suspicion dominated 13, Verstektstrasse. Old Kreutzel could no longer lift her head to see the callers as they came in, so she demanded that New Hans describe their clothing to her. She monitored the shoes, since they were less likely to be chosen for disguise. She was determined that no one would cheat her. She had Hans construct an even higher platform for her chair, this time with steps. Her body was betraying her. Most of her whores were not, as they never felt any loyalty to her in the first place.

I didn't run with the others to the windows when Hermann drove up in his new Rompler taxi. In order for her to get in, he had to haul on her arms from inside the car, while New Hans had to have his shoulder under her ample bottom, boosting her from the street. The little Argentinian and Susannah provided a running commentary from our window of grunts and *oofs*, and "look out-look out-look-outs," whenever this operation happened. The other whores all gathered in our room so that even the ones who couldn't see out the window could imagine the scene and laugh. I despised Kreutzel, but neither Brigita nor I laughed at her. Her infirmity was a matter of chance— bad luck, as Billy had once said—and Brigita and I both knew about bad luck.

Kreutzel had to stop sending New Hans to listen at the doors. He would forget what he was supposed to be doing and start humming. "So you will have to be in charge," Kreutzel said, "of letting me know if anyone does something suspicious inside our house, Suzi." My sister nodded and ran upstairs to repeat the edict to me before shoving her face into a pillow to contain her guffaws, the way we used to laugh in the back of the Daimler.

One day on our way to the bank, we heard New Hans humming as he followed us. This was going too far. Susannah turned and deliberately waved at him. At first, he pretended not to see her, so she walked up to him and talked about the weather while I went into the bank and exchanged smaller banknotes for larger ones, as usual.

She complained to the Kreutzel about how inefficient it was to trail her instead of someone untrustworthy. After that, we didn't see or hear him when we were out. He decided, however, that since I hadn't been the one to complain, I must like him.

Every time he saw me, he rose from the floor with a particular expression—half-closed eyes and a one-sided smile. He gave me bottles of some awful home-made *palinka*, confiding every time, "This will rip the fence." I always thanked him. He nodded, proud and modest. He warbled, "Maybe some Tuesday, she will be mine," shooting quick glances at me if I came down the stairs ahead of my sister. She thought it was hilarious.

Kreutzel was convinced that she and Susannah had a great bond, so we knew that escape from the brothel would be an unforgiveable betrayal. We knew that we couldn't just leave the house; we had to leave the city at the same time. She was still capable of having us carted off to jail. New Hans mentioned regularly that his police friends would love a 'go' with one of the whores of the house.

"They're my friends," he said, as if that were a recommendation.

We had to know exactly where we were going and go there immediately. We had studied the railroad route maps George had brought us—Austrian, German, French, English. I thought about everything that could possibly go wrong.

My mind swung between the escape plan and George Andrew. His smile was so warm. He had kissed me. I had kissed him back. I was losing weight. I longed for him to touch me, to feel his hand on my breast, but not in that house where touching was commercial, regulated, written up.

I knew we'd all be leaving Vienna around the same time—him for Paris, us for England. I wasn't so stupid as to forget what we had been working toward for a year. My mind drifted into reverie. I had to remind myself—was it me or Susannah who thought love was disgusting?

I had decided that working with George was like an enquiry, an investigation. It was a small study in anthropology. I liked how he stood, feet apart, shoulders squared, resting one hand on his hip, the thumb turned back, the fingers splayed out. An elegant gesture. I commented on it, and he said, "All the Andrews men do that. I think it comes from being ready to grasp one's sword."

Susannah sat up straight. "So! You are like Rob Roy, only without a kilt. Oh! That would be embarrassing." She was wide-eyed, but the effect was not innocent. She was the pretty ingénue, always being surprised by a naughty thought. She was suited to the role, charming and slightly deviant.

His gaze always returned to me. He lingered, explaining things he needn't have, leaning over me, pointing things out. Did he imagine making love to me? Being at ease over breakfast, some big hotel? Reading books together?

I reminded myself that I was not stupid. How could he live, become famous, with a former whore? And I was going to England, a place he said he despised, even though all his explanations of English customs were so enthusiastic. He was like a rejected lover, eager to explain why he had loved the woman in the first place. He was a man for the continent, and France beckoned. Paris. All the writers.

What did we have in common? Bicycling, perhaps; tango, for sure. The ability to quickly pick up a new language. I couldn't think of anything else. I daydreamed about being together on the train to Paris. Walking on a bridge over the Seine. A pause in the pursuit of our lives and careers. His career. What career did I have? What was I going to do once my sister was better, other than marry a rich fellow? Art was the only thing I knew a lot about. That, and whoring.

George patted me on the hand. "I must be going." He stood up and shoved his feet into his shoes. I smiled at him. It seemed impossible that we would soon be parting. He smiled back, a little embarrassed. "You did mention, two weeks ago, about..."

"Being paid! Of course!" I reached my hand into my skirt

waistband and started fiddling with the loop on the button. It was caught, twisted.

He looked shocked. "I thought you intended to pay me in cash."

I stopped. I could feel my face going red. My hand went up to shield my face. Susannah hurried over and snaked out the little purse attached to my waistband. She handed over the banknotes.

"I'll be going then." His face was still red. I could feel mine burning.

"Goodbye, Miss Highstone. Miss Highstone." He grabbed his hat, slung his jacket over his arm, and was out the door without a backward glance. Susannah gave him a salute, and then flopped into a chair.

"Next time, make sure it's in the usual envelope. Where are your manners, Schottenring girl?"

I stared at the door. I sat. I could feel her staring at me. Then I heard the sounds of her preparing an injection. She did this with the precision and speed that came with practice. She went over to the small window and stared at the sky. I don't know how long we stayed like that: me looking at the door, her looking at the sky.

"There are so many," said Susannah.

I didn't move. I kept looking at the door. *She has her medication, and I have mine: staying still, like a statue.* "So many what?"

Susannah came over and put her arms around me. "So many who.... So many women." After a while, she said, "I'm used to hearing you talk, Hedy."

I leaned against her and sighed. Sometimes morphine meant she made no sense.

"All I can hear is your heart." She put on her best English accent. "I am Susannah Highstone, morphine addict and whore. And may I introduce my sister, Miss Hedy Highstone, also a whore, who loves the sex."

"Sex."

"That's what I said."

"No, it's not *the* sex—it's just 'sex.' I do love it because I understand it."

"And what else do you love, or, rather, who else do you love? Do you see yourself as the wife of a journalist who cannot earn a living?"

Yes. But keep this quick and light. "Susannah, dear. Isn't this a perfectly lovely day?"

"Perfectly lovely." Susannah got up and looked out the window. "I think the Englishmen who hire us are no better than the others, but they do have better manners."

"We cost too much money to attract those who would be rude."

"They do have money, like that English lord who keeps showing up. Nigel, Lord Something, but I forget what."

"Susannah, do you think our English callers prefer girls with manners?"

"If they do, they had better hurry. We're losing our fine manners—you, hauling money out of your damn dress." She saw my reaction. "Sorry." She turned away from the window for a moment. "It will all come back once we are out of here. We will find ourselves among our own again."

"I want out of here. I want my life back."

"You want George."

She has no idea how much. "Don't you like him?"

"He's too tall. As for Englishmen, I do like it when they understand what I'm saying."

"Or pretend to. How do you know? They aren't here for conversation."

Susannah's face was suddenly so sad.

It was the last Tuesday in September, a balmy day. I was sitting on the carpet counting banknotes and putting them in the small cotton pockets I had sewn. Susannah looked down at me, her head hanging over the bed. "We are lucky, you know. Our prophylactics have always worked. We have always stuck together. We don't fight, or hardly ever."

"Yes, as long as you get your morphine, we manage."

"Why are you sighing? You know I have cut back, little by little, for months!"

"I know you have. It's not that. It's money. Do we have enough?"

Susannah suddenly bounced off the bed, grabbed her purse and some scissors, and left the room, newspaper under her arm. "I'm going to see old Crooked Drawers before she goes out."

"My god. Why don't you move in with her? I could have this bed to myself."

Two hours later, Susannah returned and tossed a stack of banknotes into my lap and onto my head. "I found her secret stash."

"After all this time? This much? Where? No, don't tell me. Take it back. She'll find out. You have to take this back!" I was frantically separating my stack of banknotes from what Susannah had tossed down.

"No. She wasn't in. It was my perfect chance. Look how much is there." Susannah stood her ground.

"Where did she hide it?"

Susannah looked out the window. "Where?" She yawned and stretched. "In hollowed-out books. She's got dozens of them on that shelf. I thought they were meant to impress our callers."

"They do!"

"You know how she thinks I am the next Frau Kreutzel. She's always dropping disgusting hints about how I am just like her when she was young, and how I could take over the brothel and look after her. Why are you laughing?"

"She wouldn't hint that when New Hans is in the room."

"She might. She's been yelling at him for being drunk, for leaving *palinka* bottles everywhere. She lurches around downstairs and looks behind things, always searching for something."

"Wait, forget about her search for *palinka* bottles—what about the books?"

"That collection on the shelf above her desk. She asked me to hand her the first one, saying it was very valuable. I thought she meant because it was part of a set, all green leather and gilt. I thought she was hoping to make an even greater, glorious bond between us by having me read books she has read."

"I never see her reading a book. Just *The Tatler*."

"But Hedy, listen, she opened the book, and I thought, 'oh, no, she's going to read to me.' But instead, she plunged her hand into the book and took out a stack of banknotes."

"So literature is enriching."

"Ha, ha. She asked me to take down all the books one at a time so she could count the notes in all of them. Then I had to put them back. She laid her hand on mine and said she trusted me. Ha! She's so bent over she can't reach the shelf, let alone see it. So," she yawned again, "last week, I just took a few notes from the second book, *The Astrologer*, to put a deposit on that Italian scarf we saw, remember? And she didn't notice."

"Why not?"

Susannah flopped on the bed and stretched. "She only uses the first book for spending money. I filled the rest with fake banknotes cut from the newspaper."

"What's the first book called?"

"*Waverley*."

"So you pulled a switch!"

She smiled. "Like you used to do with Mama's ring and my shirtwaist."

I touched the ring on its ribbon around my neck. "You knew? You were asleep."

"Not all the time."

"Don't take any more until just before we go. And be careful."

Susannah looked at me as if she expected me to say something. I went back to counting. The door slammed. I should have thanked her, but she was gone.

27.

EARLY ON THE MONDAY, the day before we planned to
leave, George arrived just in time with the passports—hard
covers, dark blue, beautiful—with the photographs we had
given him firmly attached. Susannah and I had seen British
passports, and these looked completely genuine. I asked him
how he did it, and he was vague. "There are always clever
people, everywhere, who work in little jobs, and no one cares
about them, but they know the right thing to do, when they
are asked."

"And paid." I regretted saying something so cynical. I sounded
like Susannah. George was an idealist, which I admired.

"Actually, when fed. And listened to. But the right thing
matters."

I felt like I was at the bottom of a well, and no one would
ever come for me. "No one has ever asked me to do the right
thing. In fact, quite the opposite."

"Then it is a new start, Hedy. Miss Highstone." *He is so
kind. He understands.*

"Thank you so very much." I sat beside him and took his
hand. And a chance. "Why don't you accompany us? It would
be perfectly marvellous to have your companionship."

"I'd be in the way."

"At least to Paris. We could walk over the Seine together on
one of the bridges."

"You don't need me for that."

Susannah saw my reaction and moved to the other side of George. Now all three of us were sitting on the bed. "George." She cupped her hand. "Come all the way with us to England. We'll take care of the tickets." Hand on heart. "With you, George, we aren't as likely to get caught." *Say the fellow's name as often as possible. Look up at him. All the tricks.*

"Really, you will both be great successes. The English aristocracy won't have a chance, not against the wiles of young women of your calibre."

Continental whores, he means. "What if we don't want to be whores?" I looked at him directly. No tricks.

He was startled. "Oh. You have the potential to be the kind of wife any man would want to possess." He stood.

"Do you think so?" *He's thinking about marriage!* I got his hat. We were both standing.

"Of course." His lovely smile. "No one need know about your past, but they will be delighted to benefit from your experience. You're crushing the brim of my fedora, Miss Highstone."

"We'll write to you." I ran my thumb and forefinger along the brim. It was fine. It was a good hat.

Susannah stood up, her head tipped to one side. "Yes, I can report to you on the real English news, George! We can be your spies in London." She beamed at him. Anyone else, seeing her smile, would have started an entire espionage service immediately.

"Really, I don't think that's a good idea. I'm pushing off for Paris tonight, and I think we should all lie low." He got his coat. "I am sure our paths will cross." He smiled and moved to the door. He avoided looking directly at me, and when he did, you would have thought the room was full of a huge audience.

I cannot move.

"Don't put aside your Austrian papers. The world changes, and you may want to claim an Austrian passport at some point." He extended his hand to me for his hat. "Your clothing, by the way, is perfect."

We had invested in very expensive clothes, *coupe anglaise*.

I kept looking at him. He thought this jovial kindness was enough. Susannah gave me a shove and I walked to him and put his fedora on his head. On his beautiful head. I assessed how the hat looked and tilted it on a more severe angle. My arms were stiff. My fingers were the opposite of numb. I could feel the fine nap on the fedora. He finally looked at me. I could see from his eyes that he wanted me, but from his mouth, not a word. He held himself stiff when I kissed him. He didn't return the kiss. He opened the door and paused, looking at the floor. Then at me.

All of me, pouring from my eyes.

He took his hat off his head and jammed it onto mine. And then he was down the hall, down the carpeted stairs, gone from view, with no backward glance. The sound of the outer door opening, street noise for a moment. Then the door closed. Nothing. Silence.

I was on the bed wearing his hat. I didn't remember walking to the bed, nor sitting down. I didn't really see the room. "We have to leave first thing tomorrow," I croaked.

Susannah got up. "I still have to buy that Italian silk scarf. Want to come?"

I shook my head. My thoughts were a maze. How could Susannah think about shopping right now? Morphine lets its hostages focus on the next pleasurable thing, like an Italian silk scarf. George loved this hat. I leaned against the headboard. Susannah had all her saved-up ampoules. We had our small suitcases, monogrammed. Our hotel in Bath booked. We'd take the train, and then the ferry. George's face. We had our money. Too bad for old Kreutzel. It could easily be a full day before she realized we were gone. I would not see George tomorrow, nor on any other Tuesday in the near future. I heard myself sigh. What a loud sound.

28.

I WAS STILL SITTING on the bed, still wearing the fedora, when Susannah got back, the Italian scarf around her neck. She dumped her purse on her side of the bed. Bundles of banknotes. I must have been in such a daze that I hadn't noticed Susannah slipping down to Kreutzel's office.

"Was she sleeping? Did you stuff her books with the fake notes? Should you have let people see what you are going to wear tomorrow when we leave?"

Susannah stretched and yawned. "Yes, to everything. Did you sit here like that for the whole time I was gone? No one saw me take anything. The scarf shouldn't look brand new. Only yours has to look crisp. I need to sleep."

She climbed onto the bed beside me and took the fedora off my head. We both slept on top of the covers, in our clothes, just where we were, my arm over her. Or hers over me.

That old china swan flew from its pedestal across the room in the morning light and shattered against the door. "Oh, dear," Susannah said, as if she hadn't been the one to throw it. As if she were upset, and already in England. She looked to see if I got the joke.

I whisked the shards into a dustpan. "Did he love me?" I asked.

"Of course he did. The way cowards do. Not enough to risk any harm to himself."

"I think I liked that he depended on me, that he needed our money."

"Well, think about that, about how your mind works, instead of about how his does. You've got more of a chance of getting somewhere. Come on, we've got a real place to get to." Susannah's English was sometimes closer to the happy slang of her English caller, Nigel Lord Something, than to George's easy, polished tone.

On top of the one formal dress already in my suitcase, I put George's fedora, brim up, and filled it with banknotes. My sister had wrapped her banknotes in Mama's old striped scarf, and placed her chiffon frock on top. Then she plucked several pairs of ruffled step-ins from a shelf and dropped some in her bag and some in mine. "Really," she vamped, "what else does a girl need besides skimpy underwear and large banknotes?"

We had lots of both. Nigel Lord Something had said he never bothered changing his *kronen* until he was home, and that English banks gave a good rate of exchange. He had slouched against walls and draped himself over furniture, the way all our very rich English callers did. A man who stood up straight in England, according to George, might be mistaken for a butler or an Austrian aristocrat. It was true—we Austrians stand *properly*.

I heaved my suitcase onto the bed. "I'm truly glad we aren't carrying gold. My suitcase is almost too heavy, even with paper banknotes. Thank you, Tante." I wiggled my fingers towards the floor below us.

"You should thank the thief, Hairbrush." Susannah opened the arms on a pair of round dark glasses and put them on. I needed to hug her, or she needed to hug me. It was the same thing. We held each other. We were leaving. We had done it.

"This weather makes my hair frizzy, Hedy."

"Put your hat on." Over my own hair, I pinned the crisp white scarf with an appliquéd red cross, pulling it down low on my forehead. The secretary at the Albanian orphan relief fund had said it flattened the hair.

I had been careful to arrive just before the Red Cross office closed for the day. After making a very generous cash donation to the Albanian orphan relief fund and refusing a receipt, I had tried my very best approximation of shyness. "Could I get a souvenir for a niece who adores the Red Cross?" I had asked. "An old headscarf, if you have one?"

The secretary, anxious to lock up and go home, had taken a scarf from a drawer. "The way my hair springs up, I like wearing the scarf, personally. My best wishes to your niece."

"That scarf is not flattering." Susannah looked at me through her dark glasses.

"I agree. That's good. People will be less likely to look at me."

She took my hand. "Hedy. I promise. I promise to stop."

"When, Horsie? When will you stop?"

"Once we're safe, in England."

We continued to sit there in dreamy silence for several moments, or minutes—the ersatz Red Cross nurse and the not-so-blind girl. I was gentle when I pushed her away and stood up.

Look after her.

"Old Kreutzel has no idea we have her secret cache, right?"

"She doesn't have a clue." Susannah yawned and stretched.

"How do I look?"

"Nurse-like, Hedy. You look like a nurse."

"You were brave to steal that money so quickly."

"It's easier to do something than to imagine doing something. You're the planner."

I opened the door and stepped into hallway—and then quickly turned back and closed the door.

"What are you doing? We have to leave now!" hissed Susannah.

"New Hans is still here! Those big shoes are sticking out in the hallway!"

"Your prince."

"Why is he here, instead of out with old Kreutzel? He's been listening to us!"

"No. We would have heard him humming."

"But he might have heard us. How can we get her money back? We have to get it back fast, before she comes home and asks you to take it out of her books again."

"No. I worked for that money. Let go of my bag, Hedy."

She meant it, and she was right. I let go. I knew what we would have to do. "Bring sheets from the linen cupboard." She did. I looked out the door. "Now, Susannah. Go! I'll carry the bags."

We tiptoed down the hallway in our drab garb, everything grey and black but my white nurse's scarf and the green silk scarf around her neck. The sensuality of the blind. We made it to the empty bedroom at the end of the hall undetected. We closed the door. And froze. From one floor below, we could hear a slow, steady hammering.

"What is he doing?"

"He's keeping time to whatever he's singing. We're going to be late. Come on!" I whispered.

We carried the bed over to the window. It had no mattress, only springs. Outside, the street was empty. We tied four sheets together, pulling hard on the knots. We opened the window. The hammering continued.

Susannah stood on the bed and managed to thread the sheets through the ironwork of the attic balcony above the window. There is nothing like a tall sister. We didn't have to talk. I helped her pull the knot tight. We knew what the other was thinking. Four other sheets were tied together and attached to the suitcases. Now. *Now.*

It was cold. Anyone below would have seen a Red Cross nurse lean out an upper window. Two suitcases tied to sheets lowered by hand. They landed *thud, thud,* the sheets falling on top of them. Our luck held: the street remained empty.

I was shivering. A wind blew the curtains, and from the balcony above, the knotted rope of sheets swayed, its tail on the bed. "Time to climb out the window, Miss."

"Of course, Nurse." Susannah had that watery look in her eyes. "Morphine's sorrow", they called it. She tried a small bounce on the springs, her dark glasses sliding down her nose. I pushed them back up. She gazed primly over the top of them at me, and grabbed the rope of sheets.

"Right, blind girl. Down you go."

Susannah crouched, ape-like, and grabbed the knotted sheets. She pushed off the sill and swung out. And then back. A gust of wind pushed her into the frame of the window. She toed the sill.

"Slide down the sheets! Just let go and grab, let go and grab, until you are down."

"Down? Of course."

"Yes!" Susannah let go.

I clambered over the bed to the window and looked down. My heart was pounding.

Susannah had landed neatly, in a sitting position on her suitcase. "Your turn, darling nurse."

But there was one thing I had to do. I raced back to our bedroom, glancing quickly at New Hans's shoes, still in the same place. I wound up the phonograph. The turntable spun with the record on it. The song, I knew, was at least four minutes long. New Hans loved to sing along to "La Cumparsita," bellowing up from the hallway. Whenever the record stopped, he'd holler up for us to start it again.

Only this time, when he eventually stomped up the stairs to see why we didn't do what he commanded, he'd be away from the front door, and we'd be on our way, beyond his reach, away from the brothel.

I turned the *auf-aus* volume button as far as it would go. The louder the better. I lowered the needle and ran, on tiptoe.

At the bottom of the staircase, sticking out into the hall, were those big shoes I hoped to never see again.

The hissing at the start of the record began just as I grabbed the rope of sheets. The opening trumpets sounded, and immediately, besides the hammering, I could hear a boot tapping on the floor. A rhythm section to accompany our escape. I crouched at the window. A little orchestration and the singer moaned: "*Quien sabe si supieras que nunca te he olvidado.*"

With enough *palinka*, New Hans was confident in his Spanish, and he howled along with the record. The hammering adjusted to keep time to the music. I wound my legs around the sheet and pushed my feet against the sill to swing out.

"*...y aquellos ojos que fueron mi alegría...*"

Now, hand over hand, down, down. The whole street could hear him singing tearfully about the little dog, the *perrito*, leaving.

"*...y aquel perrito compañero...*"

Susannah pretended not to see me when I landed. She pawed at the air. What a comedienne. For her, there was always pleasure in pretense, even when we were in danger. "Brava," she said. "Brilliant, Hedy."

As we hurried with the suitcases towards the corner, Hans bawled his favourite part again.

"*...y aquellos ojos que fueron mi alegría...*"

It had started to rain. A newsboy appeared with an armload of unsold papers. "Fraulein, *Die Welt*?"

"Bugger off, can't you see I'm blind?" Susannah swung at him with her suitcase.

"You wasn't blind yesterday, Fraulein. *Die Welt*?"

Just as he was about to step closer to Susannah, an automobile roared up, making him jump back. Nigel, Susannah's enthusiastic caller was leaning out the driver's window and shouting, "Leave the lovely *fraulein* alone!" He jerked on the brake and flung open the door, smacking the newsboy. He lost his grip on his papers, which tumbled and blew about.

"Now look what you've done!"

"Yes, naughty Nigel. Look what you've done!" Another man leapt out of the white car and gave a handful of banknotes to the boy, who seized them and ran, leaving his newspapers to plaster themselves against hedges and wrought iron railings.

"See here, wait up, we were just coming to see you!" Nigel nabbed Susannah by the elbow, and then burst into laughter. "But I guess you can't see me! Come on, then!"

Susannah threw her arms around him. "Naughty Nigel."

He picked up the suitcases and they half-ran, me in pursuit, to the growling and purring automobile where his companion waited.

"Sister Hedy, this is Harold!"

"Well, Nurse, Sister Hedy, do get in my lovely dry automobile, it's raining. I'm Harold." He held open the door in an attempt to be gallant. He was not too drunk for this time of the evening, nor too loud for this neighbourhood, but the sooner he quieted down, the better. I climbed in.

He kept his balance gracefully by hanging onto the door, and leaned towards me in the back seat. "Nigel told me about your house. Respectable, Nigel said." He stepped away to let Nigel bundle my sister and our luggage in beside me. The blond fellow turned to look at me over the front seat. "But tonight, an intrigue! Do explain!"

"It's quite a story." I had to be sure our plan was not about to be side-tracked. "But whatever brings you here now, Nigel?" *If he will take us to the station, wonderful. I don't really care why he's here.*

"Ooh, Hedy! A gentleman isn't supposed to tell!" Susannah reached forward and put her finger on Nigel's lips, playfully. Then again, slowly.

She will own him now. If she doesn't already. This was not part of the plan.

"What brings me here? A desire to not be loitering alone, my darling night nurse, and to see your newly blinded companion."

"Whose car is it, yours or Harold's?"

"This, Sister Hedy, is my car," Harold answered, "but Nigel thought he would like to drive it."

"I'd like to have it, is what I would like. A Cottin & Desgouttes. Those front fenders. That star on the front. Say, what is that racket?" He turned off the engine. Loud hissing of a phonograph needle bouncing and repeating, hissing, hissing, at the end of the record's grooves. "Again, you worthless women!" New Hans's voice bellowed into the rainy night:

"*...y aquellos ojos que fueron mi alegría...*"

"Horrible!" Harold looked as though he'd tasted something rancid.

"That's the house musician, singing." I gave him my best smile.

"Reason enough to leave, then, I'd say."

"If you don't mind, could we? My charge here and I must make the next train. At eight o'clock. The Franz Josef Station."

"I wish that charge were in my care." Nigel looked back at Susannah. "A blind woman. It makes the mind boggle, doesn't it, Childe Harold? Beautiful and..." Nigel broke off, annoyed. "Is that foul bugger singing in Spanish?"

"He is, Nigel." Susannah pushed her dark glasses up on her nose. "He's singing, '*I look for your eyes, and I can't find them.*'"

Harold rolled down the window and shouted, "You can't find her eyes because she's got ears, you mad fool! She's hiding from your bloody, awful, singing!"

The others burst out laughing. I was beside myself, desperate to leave, but I couldn't help it—I laughed, too.

"Awful!" he shouted again. We were still laughing when a black-and-blue taxi drove towards us through the rain. Hermann's Rumpler. And, barely visible in the back seat, old Kreutzel, swaying as the taxi slowed to the curb in front of a house where we no longer lived.

I tapped Nigel's shoulder. "Sir, our train!"

Without another word, Nigel started the engine. We swung out wildly into the street and drove off. I looked back. From

an open upper window, a long white rope gestured in the wind.
On the street below, coiled sheets, like a snake's skin, shed.

29.

WE GOT OUR TICKETS EASILY. Harold kept stuffing banknotes, one at a time, through the wrought iron grill, laughing, and soon the prim desk clerk was laughing, too. I wasn't.

"Nigel's friend is drawing attention to us, Susannah! What if Hermann is driving Kreutzel here right now?"

"Did you not notice how fast Nigel drives? And you know how long it takes for her to get to the front door."

Nigel had bid us goodbye earlier. He was also leaving Austria, but in the Harold's car. "The motorways will be empty at this time of night, and I shall fly along!" he had declared. "Watch for me, will you? I will keep, as best I can, to a route that will allow you to see me from the train. Wave to me!" He had roared off, honking that terrible horn.

Porters in blue uniforms, with gold trim on their caps, helped us into our train compartment. A whistle. I held my sister's hand and kept my head down as platform attendants checked the carriage doors along the train. *Click. Click.* Only a minute before departure. The train lurched and then paused. Hissed.

"What's going on?"

"Just releasing the brakes, Nurse." Harold smiled sweetly at me. Susannah caught his look and tipped up her dark glasses to give me our half-wink.

Another whistle sounded, this one right outside our carriage.

Two young police officers appeared beside our window and then turned away to dash up the wrought iron stairs in front of them, two at a time, to roust a vagabond in rags who was using terrible language. The last thing I heard as the train lurched forward was, "I am a veteran! I was in the war. I killed Frenchmen better than you!"

The train left the station. Then it left Vienna, gathering glorious speed. Harold beamed and called out softly, "*Auf Weidersehen, Wein!*"

Susannah patted my arm. "You're smiling, Hedy."

"How do you know? You're blind."

"I can feel it."

We made our way to the dining car, settled into the green plush of the chairs, and ordered drinks. I removed the white scarf with its scarlet cross and replaced it with an asymmetrical grey hat. Susannah kept her dark glasses on. I thought every vertebra in my spine had been released. I shall be, I thought, at least two inches taller when I arrive in England. Susannah and I will be able to be happy, to make a life together, to do whatever we want.

We made a plan to watch the sun rising behind us as we headed west. Susannah ordered champagne and oysters, I ordered a cocktail, and Harold stuck to gin and lots of it. The train stopped briefly at Cologne, and another Englishman, Lorne, joined us. He had dark curling hair, smoky blue eyes, and only one arm.

"Harold, you splendid fellow," he said, "you're always turning up with wonderful women!" He lit a cigarette with one hand. He was more dexterous with one hand better than most people are with two. He offered it to Susannah. "Cigarette?"

She had never smoked a cigarette before, but she said, "Why not? Please put it in my mouth, darling." Lorne was instantly smitten.

In Vienna, we had decided very quickly to meet up in the

Hoek, in Holland. Nigel had everyone's luggage, which made me nervous, but Susannah whispered that if he were caught with that money, it wouldn't be us who were caught. I think I was giddy. This was like our old selves from long ago, planning, exuberant. As long as we stayed together, the world would be ours.

"This was the train Susannah and I had intended to take out of Vienna before the war."

"You must have been children!" Harold was stretched out, at ease. Blond and British.

"Yes. And..." I couldn't believe how loud my voice was.

"And?"

"And, this is fun!" I also couldn't believe how much I was smiling.

Harold said he would watch to see when my cocktail needed replenishing. Everyone forgot to watch for Nigel. Once we crossed the Austrian border, after years of drinking one of whatever was provided, I had four more cocktails. It had been years since I had been able to drink whatever I chose. I smiled benevolently. I even sang. In English. It was fun to emphasize all the *p*'s, pursing my mouth into kisses.

"I'm sitting on top-puh of the world.
Just like Hump-puh-ty Dump-puh-ty, I'm ready to fall."
And then I did.

I collapsed from where I had perched on Harold's knee to the floor between his legs.

Harold, to keep me company, sank to the floor beside me.

Someone pulled out a mandolin—not quite a ukelele, but good enough to launch into a version of "Hey, Hey, Charleston." The others in the car danced up and down the wide aisle between the lounge chairs, swiveling their feet. Even Lorne, whose sleeve was pinned into his jacket pocket, joined in. He tripped on Harold's feet and landed on the floor, but, using his one good hand, he immediately pushed himself altogether upright as if on a spring. And then, losing his balance, he tumbled into Susannah, who banged her head on the marquetry by the window.

I jumped up, but before I could reach my sister, Susannah stood up, wobbled, and then raised both hands like a Minoan goddess. "I can see. Darlings, I can see." She took off her little black glasses and batted her eyelashes as our fellow passengers cheered.

The mandolin attempted "I Wish I Could Shimmy Like My Sister Kate." Around three in the morning, the porter suggested that we all go to our compartments. Banknotes were stuffed in his hands and pockets with clumsy affection, and then we ricocheted off walnut veneer walls on our way to our compartments.

The porter tucked us in with blankets, and was about to pull down the canvas window blind when I asked him to leave it up a little. Susannah leaned on Lorne's shoulder.

"Shh, I'll watch her," said Harold. "You get some kip. This has all been a bit much of a muchness." My eyes filled with tears. That's what George said when he got frustrated with something.

"What is it?"

"You are so kind," I managed to say. "To volunteer so quickly to help us."

"Nigel explained your situation when he asked me to bring my car to your house last night."

"It was arranged?"

"My dear, did you think that the gods of rain had suddenly blessed you with our appearance?"

I had. I couldn't seem to either laugh or cry at myself, so I did a bit of both.

"Let's get some fresh air. Lorne will keep your sister safe." He led me to the back of the train, to a small platform outside the last car. We watched the dark world hurry away from us. The night air was chilly. I turned up the collar of my jacket and pulled my gloves from my pocket. Harold said nothing, but he kept one arm around me until I had stopped crying. On the way back to our carriage he spoke to the porter and by the time we were settled again, tea had arrived. When Harold asked me if I wanted lemon with my tea, I started to cry again.

"Miss Highstone, it is only tea."

"It is kindness. You are looking after me. No one has, not for years, not at all." I began to tug off my gloves.

"I say, would you mind doing that a little more slowly?"

I looked at him.

"I'm sorry. It's a weakness I have for the gesture. Nigel said that you and your sister were very discreet. Do you think me less masculine?"

"No." But I put my hands in my lap.

"Nigel had wanted me to join him at the Verstektstrasse place when he visited you, but I really don't care to expose my inclinations to others, not even to Nigel. So when he suggested this escapade, I thought, why not? On those rare occasions when a woman who understood such things would let me watch her tug off her gloves, I have felt so at home in desire, so simply myself. Are you offended?"

"Not at all. But perhaps I will delay for now. I'm very tired."

"You go to sleep then. I do want to say that I admire your dash. What you did tonight was the kind of thing that let men rise through the ranks in the war. You sleep, now. I'll keep watch."

But within minutes, his own exhaustion took over. I watched this kind man's chin drop to his chest, and his blond hair fall over his eyes. He was sound asleep, and I was now wide awake.

I watched my sister, and watched the sun rise on my own. A tong-bearing, white-gloved fellow came by with light sandwiches and coffee, and remarked that we were within half of an hour of Rotterdam. "And then," he winked, "you won't want to miss what you see when the morning sun hits the beaches of the Hoek."

Eight men, naked and shouting, "*Goeje morgen*!" ran in pairs through the grass of the flat beach into the water as we staggered off the train into the early morning mist. The sunlight glinted on the Channel and the wind blew about the Hoek. We discovered Nigel, asleep in the car, parked on the vehicle ramp for the ferry. I felt taller. I think I *was* taller.

Susannah climbed into the car despite my demands that she join us on the above deck. It wasn't because I was concerned that she would put us all at risk and make the ferry turn around. Or sink. Or that she might be in danger: captured and held for ransom by North Sea pirates, or lured into a scheme by a lurking stowaway. I certainly wasn't worried about Nigel.

I wanted my sister to be with me. It wasn't for the satisfaction of feeling that I had finally succeeded in protecting her, although that may have been a part of it. I wanted to experience all of this escape, and I couldn't unless she were by my side. This was to be a new beginning for the two of us, together. Surely that was true for her, too. But the horn sounded, and she turned away from me and kissed the sleeping Nigel.

Nigel woke up and wondered where her pretty glasses were. She put them on, just for him, she said, and off they drove onto the lower deck. Harold and I had to hurry up the gangplank, tickets in hand for Harwich.

"She's merely become more English than you realized," Harold said.

I hadn't said a thing, but Harold seemed to be keenly aware of the moods of others, or of women. Or of me. He smiled and buttoned up my jacket against the North Sea breeze. "The language itself will do that to you, you know, create independence in those who speak it. She's on her way to becoming an English eccentric, which is contrarily, a fine English tradition."

I tried to sense where she was below us as Harold and I stood at the forward deck rail and the boat pressed through the bright waves. I looked westward the whole way for my first glimpse of England, for the sparking lights that would tell me that my sister and I could begin again.

~

30.

NIGEL STOPPED AT THE WHITE HART INN as soon as I said I needed to use the loo. I slipped in and gave myself a quick jab of morphine. I only had a few ampoules left, but I wasn't worried. I was floating, and not just because of Madame Morphine. All of that long sunny day with Nigel belonged only to me. Not to me and Hedy. Just to me.

I had spent my whole life within minutes of her. We were inside each other's thoughts, moving in a rhythm of how the other washed, or bled, or laughed. There had only been one other day—not even a day, an afternoon—that belonged only to me: that time when Margarete and I rode bicycles and sold silverware in an alley.

That was the day Hedy lied to me for the first time. She knew Papa was dead, but she pretended he was still alive. Waving to us. She let me think Mama was sending us to Baden bei Wein. A second lie. The third was a lie by omission: when Kreutzel told her Mama was dead, Hedy tried to hide it from me. But there's a stop and go to breathing when someone is crying, and she was. I knew. I held still, and let myself cry later, not making a sound, once I was in the chair and that old sack of guts was in the bed with her.

My soft-hearted sister cried a few times after that, but I never did. My tears belong to me. I broke away from Hedy, little by little, year by year, like an iceberg separating underneath the water. Now I was in England, I was my own icy mass;

my needle-pricked ass and all the rest of me was below the surface, free from her.

And free from sex. After those first awful weeks, Hedy began to enjoy it, at least while it was happening. Not me. I didn't even really experience it. I watched what happened from a safe distance. If I stared long enough out the window at a section of the sky, I could deliver a feeling of hurtling upward; I could lodge myself near the ceiling to watch what happened in the bed below. Up there, looking out the window at the sky, I felt an odd presence, something safe. My sky women. I could get up there to them on my own, any time I needed to.

In one of Moreno's early sessions, one whore, younger than me, said she hovered in the air above herself the first time she was raped. "Like an angel," another whore had said, and the first one stopped talking.

I found her after the meeting. "Me, too," I said. "I go up to the ceiling."

She looked relieved. "I thought that it was something only I did."

"And neither one of us is an angel."

Everyone likes angels. Hat brooch angels, pageant angels. Stone angels with swords. Swords to cut off a head. Or several heads in one blow. I am not used to this much morphine and it is singing in me. *Wonderful and terrible, angels singing, with swords vibrating like time zones.*

I never told Hedy about going up to the ceiling, or about the sky women. She assumed that I was in morphine's embrace and that I didn't know what was going on. I was, but I did. Before we escaped, to wean myself off morphine, I began to dilute the usual dose with an increasing amount of a saline solution. Six months later, I had lots of extra ampoules in my suitcase. I could give Hedy the spectacular withdrawal she needed to justify her efforts. I could give her that, although I wasn't looking forward to it. I had never forgotten that first awful withdrawal after we tried to escape in the rain.

We stopped for a "bit of bother," which was Nigel's term for sex. I hardly knew I was doing it. Like walking up stairs. Who has to think about resting one's weight on the left foot at the same time as one raises the right? Not me.

"If your name were not Susannah, what would it be?"

"Mitzi."

Nigel wagged his foot and, at the same time, flattened the end hairs of his moustache with his thumb and index finger. He should have been in the circus. He could be given any number of things to do, and he would do them all at once. It meant that things got a little untidy. Some things didn't go where they should on the first try. *Like with dull swords.*

"And as Mitzi, what is your advice on the best course of action for me? And, what is most desired by Mitzi herself?" He poured a drink from his flask and started the engine.

"The best course of action for you and what Mitzi herself most desires are the same thing." It wasn't just having sex that was like walking up the stairs. I could talk this way without thinking, too. Sentence algorithms.

Our third stop. I stretched out on the seat that Nigel had dropped back. He used wrenches from a beige leather case with brown piping that matched the seats. While he put the tools back in the boot, I plunged a needle into my flesh. My own sword in hand. I could do this in seconds with my eyes closed.

Nigel threw himself down beside me. "This is the Purkinje shift, darling Mitzi—that time in the evening when the colours really mean it." He took a deep breath. "And can you smell that in the field beside us? The most natural aphrodisiac: new-mown hay. Second cut of the summer."

It smelled exactly like Hedy's perfume, Jicky.

He put his arm around me. "Mitzi! I love the name! Let me write it on your stocking."

I turned my head to answer, chin in hand. "I know. Mitzi is a good name." *Oh, morphine, your farewell tour. Anyone would like writing "Mitzi."' The swoops of the vertical* M. *And the horizontally horizontal* Z. Z *needs a little flattery, more words to describe it.* Z *is always at risk of collapsing. Like a wooden drying rack. You could get a* Z *up, like Izzy Reinhardt's penis, with a little cock-ring bar to support it. Brave, spunky* Z̵.

My foot was in Nigel's hand. "Make sure you write my new name correctly, Nigel."

He wrote it several times along the back seam of my stocking, dotting every *i*. He dragged the cross bar on the *t* so it sheltered the last *i*. This would be my fourth name. Susannah. Horsie. Suzi. Mitzi. The sky was beautiful. Great watercolour washes now, a wet sky.

Nigel shouted over the engine's French growl, "You are the most beautiful girl I have ever bothered with."

"Hmm?"

We were heading west, on a high road that allowed us to see the wide horizon. When the sun began his descent, I was glad I was pretending to be a blind girl. It allowed me to keep wearing tinted eyeglasses. No squinting. No need to hide my pursuit of *pensées morphines*. I surrendered and let myself go upward.

The sun had, only hours ago, rubbed himself up against the sky, right in front of us girls of the eastern sky. Who had loved him. How we made him light up! It is wonderful being within the safety of all of us, so many girls. We can approach the dangerous shine of a man when he wants us. Together, we were safe to sigh for him. How we sighed for him, even though he was the sun. And now the western sky women know what we know.

Nigel was smiling at me. I wondered for a moment who he was. He straightened his trouser buttons, started the car, and was once again wheeling around corners, the happy master of a French automobile. He had that British stamina for sex and drink and, apparently, driving. He tossed back brandy and, this time, passed the flask to me.

"Oh, this feels dangerous."

"I'm good at this. You're safe, you lovely girl," beamed Nigel.

I, the safe and lovely Mitzi, glowed back at him. The softness of the English evening, the speeding car, and its carefree driver made me feel as if I were thirteen again. Anything could happen, but this time I was bringing my sky women.

Sky women thoughts are like diagrams: true, implacable, empty.

We were driving into darkness.

It's terrible. It's like seeing your sisters from the bottom of their big dark skirts, looking up their skirts. I don't want him to see any of us when our backs are turned, when we bend over the sleeping world.

Like the bend in the mother's back, like Magdalena, from Moreno's sessions. She saw her little ones on Tuesdays. She had that pretty bending-over curve. Her bottom flexed outward, her full breasts swaying. Not like my breasts, which had remained smaller than Hedy's. Like little triangles, wider than they were deep. My mother's friend, Fraulein Lowin, had reassured me that a high bosom was ideal. "Like that of a goddess in the woods with her deer," she had said. I tried to think of the goddess, the one who could shoot as well as her brother.

"We are within an hour of Bath! One last stop before we see your lovely Hedy, and my good friend Harold."

"Hmm."

Nigel drove into The Dog and Bee and pulled up on the brake, bracing his other foot on the dashboard. Who but an Englishman would do that without pause? They are all individualists, the English. They prize the individual more than anything else. Only the English put a capital letter on the first person, *I*. And their personalities or psyches, as old Moreno would say, were always held in. Corsetted. Every quirk, held in. But not eliminated; every quirk was protected and allowed to flourish within. No wonder their upper class was so peculiar and their actors so good.

Like handsome Ivor Novello. Hedy and I saw him last year in *The Man Without Desire* at the Rotenturn Kino in Vienna. We almost didn't go in, but Novello was featured on the poster, and Hedy thought I'd like to see an Italian star.

I could tell right away he wasn't Italian. An English face, sad and mobile. Eyes almost looking up, and then looking away. The smallest turn of the torso, and there it was, another shade of meaning. That was why I wanted to be with Italians: I imagined that they were less complicated. But first I had to let Hedy help me.

All along those English high roads, free from Hedy's presence and sufficiently dosed with morphine, I was able to think without restriction about who I was. Someone who had escaped a brothel, and then Vienna. Someone who never looked back once the car tires touched English soil. I had kept who I was hidden from callers. They wanted so little, only what they desired. What I myself desired, I had kept hidden from them. And from my sister. And from myself. No one knew who I was, including myself.

I had been a good actress. Bedtime theatre. Dramas only an hour or so long, short runs. How would I manage marriage, the long run of a hit play? I did intend to marry. What else could I do? A rich, simple Italian. Easy to fool, I thought.

Nigel passed his little silver flask to me again. "I am inclined to think there's more going on in that pretty little head than you let on, you darling girl." He ruffled my hair.

I widened my eyes and made a face. If only Hedy were here to laugh. It was cold all of a sudden. I coaxed the sensation I needed, reached for the English sky women. Relatives of my sky women. Most beings in the world have relatives, except for my sister and me. It was late August when our parents died. *Maybe this is the time of year I am meant to experience departures.*

The name of the goddess, the one who escaped capture, came to me. *Diana.*

It was Hedy who had changed first. That session with Moreno freed her from a memory she hadn't truly acknowledged, and freed me from waking up every night to her sharp cry. She doesn't think about herself enough. My life would be easier if she did. That session let her be brave enough to ask a man for something. Such a little thing, a day in Paris. To ask was to already accept the risk of a "no." And that's what she got from George, the Canadian Scribbler. In a brothel, regular callers were not the unique characters they imagined themselves to be, and an identifying moniker was helpful. Like Dishpan Dick who washed his cock so well and so often that it suffered from chapping.

It's not just whores in Vienna who categorize and exaggerate. Anyone in Vienna with something to sell does it. Every middle class matron is Lady Whatever. Liars of Vienna, a big club I belong to. A charter member. I never told Hedy about the sky women: a lie by omission. I also told deliberate, flat-out lies. That money from the field marshals didn't get lost in the carriage. I took it. One of our callers had boasted about a stock that would do well after the war. He said it would take nerves of steel to wait until it truly peaked. I had nerves of steel. Hedy didn't. She just had nerves.

So I pouted one morning about not going out into the city, and tender old Kruetzel made Hedy stay back. I beetled with the money to the stock exchange, and told old Crankydrawers I had been caught in traffic. I told Hedy I'd lost the money. I knew she didn't believe me, but she didn't say anything. That suited me just fine.

It paid off, and I earned a very nice profit. Despite my terrible personal luck, I was always lucky when I gambled. I brought the money home in my purse just before we left. That was really where the money came from, not from Kreutzel and her Waverley novels. What a flat-out lie that was! Stacks of money in hollowed-out books? Please. I couldn't believe that Hedy had believed that. All I needed were a few details. They had to be physical because Hedy is all body, even the way she thinks. She shimmies when she gets an idea.

Old Kreutzel did have the whole set of novels. She wanted me to read them, but they had too much description. I only got part way through the first novel; the second one, *The Astrologer,* was impossible, dense and silly. I prefer newspapers. You can figure out what's true, and then use them for something. Like, start a fire.

I knew I had to keep quiet about gambling on the stock market. Better my sister thought me a thief than a girl who was good at managing money. Hedy was more manageable if she thought she was the one who was managing me.

"What is it like to wear sunglasses at night?"

I was being driven by a slightly drunk Englishman. Nigel. Lord Something. We sped around every curve, but the road broke empty. He was a good driver.

"Nigel, Lord Something, may I put my head on your shoulder?"

"Mitzi, you may put it on, take it off...."

See what I mean? Look at him beaming down at me, feeling clever. Sometimes I am really fond of human beings.

~

31.

WHEN I SAID I COULDN'T BELIEVE that Susannah arranged to have Nigel there in his car, Harold laughed. "Miss Highstone, no matter how much Nigel fancies my car, it isn't his! He also quite fancies your Susannah. A week ago, he told me that he knew of two hospitable young women who lived near the Kabarett Simpl. Discreet, he said, nice manners, spoke English. *Sophisticated*, he said, with that wink of his. Nigel had hoped to continue with *la belle aveugle* to Bath in the car. Going to Bath separately suited so many agendas."

"But how did you know we would be going to Bath?" *What does this man want?*

"You are not as alone in the world as you seem to think. Susannah confided in Nigel."

Who else did she tell? Was it the morphine? How could she? The train went around a curve and I had to shield my eyes from the sudden glare of the sun.

"Oh, my dear, don't look so shocked." Harold took my hand and patted it. He looked out the window. We were beyond London and its suburbs now, passing field after field of cabbages. Without looking at me, he rapped his knuckles on the window a couple of times, and then said, "Look, I've knocked about a bit—travel, the war—and I've seen my share." The harsh afternoon sunlight lit up his face. "May I tell you what I know? What I see? You, Miss Highstone, are a beautiful, well-bred girl, and I think you might be Jewish." He looked over at me. "Now. Don't be alarmed. I happen to think that the Jews are a magnificent lot. Somehow you have got yourself bound to that younger girl. Is she, in fact, your sister?"

"Yes!" *And she has all our money.*

Harold leaned forward. "She doesn't look particularly Jewish. I would have thought something Baltic." His voice was quiet, steady. "Another thing I wanted to mention. When I learned why you were going to Bath, it prompted a memory. My friend, Lorne, from the train? The veteran who got on at Cologne?"

"Yes. Please, do continue." *How tactful. Identified by where he got on, not by the lack of an arm*

The steward knocked, entered our compartment, and flipped down a folding table to accommodate a tray with cups, spoons, lemon, cream, sugar cubes, and an elegant aluminum teapot.

"Lorne was in my year at Cambridge. An Irish fellow—you can tell, can't you, with all that hair? Nevertheless, I quite liked him, and after the war, I visited him while he went through the cure at Bath. I could tell that your ... she's really your sister?"

"Yes, of course. My younger sister." *I need to plan what to do next.*

"Doesn't look like you. But then I don't look like my sister, either. Good thing, she's got thinning hair and a squint." Harold checked to see if I would smile.

I wasn't stupid, I did.

"I could tell your sister—lovely thing, by the way—was in the same shape as Lorne when he was coming round, finally getting off the morphine back then, in twenty-one." He picked up the teapot. "She's not got it very bad, has she? Lemon?"

I could hardly reply. I shook my head, and then nodded. How many of our secrets had Susannah told? Had we arrived in England at last only to find ourselves deported? Had Nigel driven off with our money and left my sister in some English ditch? But smiling was my professional default. I didn't have to worry about looking worried. I stirred my tea and watched the sunny circle of lemon run ahead of my spoon.

When we arrived in Bath, I was so anxious. Susannah had been sweetly logical about driving west from Harwich to Bath with Nigel. We would be less likely to be caught, she argued, if we split up. What two whores? Just a couple of wealthy Englishmen and their companions, all travelling first class with dark blue British passports.

A taxi took us to the Francis. *George's recommendation. George who loved me but didn't love me enough and went to Paris without me.* Harold approved of the choice of hotel, as it was respectable, on a quiet concourse, and had an excellent wine cellar. My arrival, however, was early. The hotel manager said my suite would be made ready as quickly as possible, and asked in the meantime, would I like to wait in the lounge with my companion, and would I care for some tea?

I was barely able to take in what he said, but Harold reassured the manager that his suggestions were acceptable. After an hour, I asked Harold if he would enquire of the hotel clerk if he had heard of any accidents on the road leading to Bath. There were none.

"Where are they? Susannah needs me." I asked again to look at Harold's regimental watch. Was the time on his watch correct?

"I think I should take umbrage on behalf of my regiment. I assure you, it keeps perfect time."

Did Nigel know for certain that he was to come to the Francis? Would he and my sister simply get drunk and forget where they were going? Harold persuaded me to walk with him towards the ha-ha, a terrible optical illusion ditch in the massive park near the Hotel Francis. It overlooked the road, and he said we would easily hear his Cottin & Desgouttes before we saw it. No one would see Susannah before we did.

~

216

32.

THERE SHE WAS, RACING towards me and Nigel. We barely managed to get the car under the *porte-cochère* before Hedy hauled the door open and snared me in a hug. I hurried up the stairs away from her so quickly that I found myself apologizing, very nicely, and in English, to an enormous potted palm. In my defence, I was exhilarated after my day of freedom. I was wearing my dark glasses. And I had taken quite a lot of morphine.

The next thing I remember was sitting on one of our suitcases that were somehow with us on the lift. The operator was holding the door. Harold was saying something about his own hotel address, so if Hedy needed to call, or would like to call, he would come to her aid, he said, 'instanter'. English was going to remain peculiar language, I could tell. Nigel beamed behind him, which reminded me: I needed to make sure Hedy understood that I had been apart from her for almost a whole day.

"Hedy. When we stopped for lunch today, Nigel had me pretend I couldn't see so he could feed me berries and some kind of lumpy cream."

"It's easy to see you've consumed more than that."

"I might as well go out," I aimed over my shoulder at Nigel, "with a bang! And don't worry, the English have prunes on every menu. Breakfast, luncheon, and tea."

"Darling Mitzi."

I pretended I couldn't see Nigel step forward and lean down

to plant a kiss. He waggled his fingers at me and spoke to Hedy. "Dear Miss Highstone, please tell Mitzi I'm waving goodbye."

The lift operator closed the door, and we rose.

"Why did he call you Mitzi? Does he not remember your name?"

"I can barely remember his. My medicine is gone. All gone."

I have images, not complete memories of what happened next. That night I shook and gagged and had trouble breathing. I shivered despite all the blankets in the room. My skin raised into bumps, like a cold, plucked goose. My feet flailed out. Hedy kept giving me lemonade. I moaned on the commode, saying there was no point in giving me anything. My body got rid of it immediately, and it was disgusting. I wailed with cramps. Hedy called me her baby sister, her Horsie, and bathed me. Twice, I think.

By noon of the following day, I was glassy-eyed and dehydrated. Still bending over, still cramping. But nearly sober. Hedy kept a poultice of ice, a few chips at a time, on my forehead and fed me black tea and dry toast. Withdrawal from this much morphine was astonishingly awful. Worse than I had expected.

Harold rang, asking if Hedy would perhaps be able to meet with him briefly in the winter room. She came back with several hands of bananas. They had apparently helped Harold's one-armed, lovely friend Lorne when he was in my situation.

"Harold says they stop the runs."

"How indelicate of him."

I told Hedy I only wanted her, no doctor. She agreed. I knew she would. And as soon as Hedy went out for just a few minutes of fresh air, I headed for the front desk.

"I need my own suite. Instanter."

"Of course, Ma'am. We have something on the same floor, two doors down."

"Nothing on another floor?"

"What are you doing?" Hedy, all fresh-faced from being outside, pulled me around to face her. "Come upstairs!"

"I'm getting my own room. Suite."

"With what money?" she hissed.

"Half of that money is mine, and I want it."

"Susannah, you don't know "

She was the one who didn't know. She didn't know the half of it. I am quite sure I raised my voice. "It's *Mitzi*. I do know. I stole most of that money, and half of it is mine."

"Pardon me, Ma'am, if you could lower your voice." The fool of a desk clerk looked alarmed.

Hedy pressed a banknote into his hand and tried to take my arm. "My sister is not well. I am so sorry, please excuse us."

I am not sure how I ended up in the lift. I was bent over the shoulder of a doorman. Hedy tipped him when he opened the door to our suite.

"Some of that tip is my money."

"Yes, Ma'am. Thank you, very much." He placed me on the bed as though he had done this many times before.

Hedy closed the door. "What are you doing? Are you trying to get us thrown out of here?"

"I want my own suite so I don't have to listen to you tell me what to do. There's enough money. It smells in here, anyway."

"Susannah, you are still feeling the effects of morphine. You don't know what you're saying."

I recall telling her we wouldn't even be in England if I hadn't had the nerve to manipulate old Kreutzel. That we would still be whoring in Vienna if I hadn't stolen money. She looked dumbstruck. Then I think I dragged her over to the window to show her how the view did not meet my standards. No stars.

Hedy was sitting in the chair beside the bed. I told her that Nigel had asked if she were Jewish and I had denied it, telling him that we pretended to be sisters to add piquancy to our bordello act.

"I don't care about that. But you shouldn't have told him about our plan to leave."

"Why not? It worked out really well. You should trust me."

"I can't. Look at all the crackpot lies you tell. Harold knows we're sisters."

"Harold doesn't know anything. Nigel's going to escort me about the town tomorrow. But tonight, I want my own suite. Now." I could feel myself alternating between belligerence and sulking. Hedy was taking off my shoes. I let her.

"Nigel and I talked on the telephone after you abandoned me earlier tonight. Where were you? He's coming over, so I want my own suite, under the name Mitzi." I lay down on the bed, wagging my foot. "Under the name Miss. Mitzi. Highstone."

"Mitzi is a ridiculous name. It doesn't sound English at all."

"A nickname. Mitzi-nitzy. Why not? Don't the English have Jews? From Spain, I think, according to what I've read."

"And you can't have male visitors in a place like this."

"You can if you slip a doorman a fiver. A *fiver*. Nigel said. And anyway, I'm not going to have sex with him, he's much too drunk to perform." I wobbled my baby finger at her, laughing. "I'm going to keep him that way, inebriated. I'm just going to have a little nap." It lasted until the next morning.

Hedy put her fork down. "What took you so long?" We were attempting an English breakfast in the dining room. The morning was chilly and it was raining. A light drizzle. "I was worried!" Hedy picked her fork up, as if it were a question. She was like a barker at a fair. At any moment I expected her to ask me to guess which cup the coin was under. Best thing to do is let her run on. So I did.

"You refused to get on the lift with me so you could take the lift by yourself. What were you doing? I had to order a second pot of tea."

"I'm here now, Hedy." I wasn't going to tell her what had kept me. My stomach was still upset, but my mind was clear.

Hedy was eating that terrible dry English toast.

"You know we survive by doing everything together."

"Yes, Hedy. *Zwei Dumme, ein Gedanke*—what Papa used to say."

"Two dummies, one thought." She crunched another piece of toast. "Not three dummies—that's what we would be with that Nigel." She was hissing at me through her toast crumbs. We both needed to have a big fight, but there we were, in a hotel dining room.

"Look. He was very courteous to us in the brothel. No, don't heave sighs at me. He took care of me."

"I take care of you. As I promised Mama."

I looked across the nearly empty dining room to the long windows. Rain was running down the long panes of glass. "I know. You have hung onto that thought to excuse anything you did. From that first night. And I let you. I thought it would break you if you thought you weren't protecting me."

"You let me! Susannah, I did protect you. I did everything I could!"

"Why didn't you yell or get out of the car, that first night then? Why didn't you wake me up? You knew I could fight. You just let it happen."

Hedy looked around the room until there was nowhere else to look but at me. "You're right. I did."

Her dark eyes, perfect for tears.

"I'm sorry, Susannah. I couldn't think. Seeing Papa's body coming down the stairs. I knew what I had seen, but I couldn't believe it. I was afraid you would make it worse with your temper. I tried to make the Old Dear turn around."

"The Old Dear. You can still call him that?"

"I don't mean he was! I told him lies about the train station, about Fraulein Lowin waiting to meet us. Susannah, I was trying to pretend to him that I wasn't afraid. And you were no help, you were sleeping. He hit me."

Her haunted dark eyes.

I steeled myself against feeling sympathy. Now that we were safely here, and no longer there, and the future was beckoning, I wanted answers. "But when we got to Verstektstrasse? Why didn't you yell for the police?"

"He had always been Mama's friend! And Papa's. I thought that Mama was angry with us. That she was sending us to some kind of house for young women instead of to Tante Freyda." Hedy had eaten all the toast. She stopped and looked at me. "And I didn't want to be rude."

We both considered the iron rule of manners in Vienna.

She smiled first.

Our howls of laughter caused the lone couple across the room to stiffen and to ignore us even more pointedly. The man flipped through the small notebooks piled by his plate. The lady adjusted a strap on her binoculars. Hilarious. I held up my fork towards them, as if it were a magnifying glass. Hedy and I began another round of laughing. And then, crying.

I never cry, but that surprising release of tears and laughter let me ask the most important question. While it was still possible. "You have to tell me this: how could you have liked him? It was so awful for me, to see how you looked forward to seeing him."

"I know. You let me know. Your scorn was frightening, but I was more afraid of him. If I did what he wanted, he talked to me. When he talked to me, I felt like the world outside the walls of that brothel still existed. And you had stopped talking to me, if you remember."

"You liked sex."

"Yes."

She's not ashamed. Just sad.

"What was worse than you not talking to me was the fear that they'd take you away. Kreutzel..."

"I don't want to hear her name ever again."

"After today, I promise you, you won't. Why did that make you smile? She threatened to take you away from me that first night, before she shoved me up the stairs into the house. And she made the same threat again after you threw the chair against the shutters."

I remembered. *What a great racket that had made.*

"The things that make you smile, Susannah! I had lost Papa, and I was almost sure, Mama, and I couldn't bear to lose you, to have no one."

I wiped her tears from her cheeks with my thumb. I couldn't bear to hear what she was saying.

She stopped crying and took a deep breath. "At least she has lost a great deal of money, thanks to you."

Let her think that. I patted her hand. "That will be worse for her than losing us." We sipped our tea. The rain stopped and everything glistened. A waiter padded up to a window and opened it a crack.

Hedy leaned back. "Remember George said that green in England is a smell as much as a colour? We can begin again here. We can make a life for ourselves."

She has no idea what I'm going to do.

"For a while, after that last session with Moreno, I often pictured Mischlinger dead. I didn't imagine killing him; I just imagined him dead, so he could do no more harm."

"I have thought about killing him. If I ever get a chance."

"How? And please, Susannah, whisper."

"For the sake of those nosey old buggers who are so obviously eavesdropping? I won't. With whatever is at hand. With luck, a gun."

The couple gasped in unison. They could go to hell.

Hedy's hand went up to her face, thumb on cheekbone, index finger on forehead. Her helmet visor. "Susannah, is this boldness because of the morphine, or the withdrawal?"

"Hedy, I've done it. I'm sober."

"I'm not so sure. It's supposed to take longer."

"I'm not stumbling. Do you want to see me walk along the railing of that balcony?" Through the French doors at the other end of the dining room was a balcony with tables for warmer, pleasanter weather. The air was now brilliant with sun.

"No! You were clumsy long before morphine."

"There's nothing in my system now."

"I'm not sure going through withdrawal is the same as being cured. We have money—quite a lot, thanks to you—but if it begins to run out before you are truly better, I promise to take care of you. I'm quite prepared to find callers. This hotel is like all hotels."

She has to stop thinking that my life is hers to manage. "Do you like being a whore that much?"

She slapped me.

It was a kind of relief. "You hit me."

"I can't believe you said that."

The older couple stood up as straight as possible and whispered something to the *maitre d'* on their way out.

"You hit me. No, don't try to hug me." I shrugged off Mama's old striped scarf. "Let go of me. I was on your side, you know, when you were in love with George." Salt tears in my mouth. I was apparently crying. Both of us, blubbering. Ridiculous.

"Yes, you were."

I gave her my handkerchief to dry her tears.

"Susannah, I'm not sure I know what else to be but a whore."

She looked down at my handkerchief. Still sobbing, she laughed and handed me her handkerchief to wipe my own tears.

"I'm sorry." One of us said it. Or both of us. We stared at the table, scattered with empty plates. We had eaten everything. Or Hedy had.

"Would the ladies enjoy a round of scones?" A waiter was talking to us. "With fresh strawberry jam? Some Devonshire cream? Bath buns, perhaps? Some tea?"

"Yes, please."

"All? Of course." The waiter moved off.

I looked around the room. No one. *The maître d'* responded to my gaze with military neutrality. It was his dining room.

We were his guests. He would protect us, from ourselves, if necessary. I had one more question. "Why didn't you sell Mama's ring?"

She put her hand to her throat. "I couldn't."

"We could have escaped long ago if you had."

"I know, but I just couldn't! Wearing it made me feel like she still loved me."

She took my hand. Or I took hers. "We didn't know very much, did we, Hairbrush?"

"No. Horsie, how could we? We had no friends. Just each other."

"No friends because of me. Mama hated my swearing. I miss German swear words in my mouth."

"Like what you called the headmistress at the last school? Remember Mama insisting that she be told what you said? The headmistress finally squeaked it out. And then Mama repeated it as if it were something in Sanskrit."

"*Scheissekopf!*" We both said it. We were laughing and crying. The *maître d'* continued to pretend to be deaf.

"Do I need a new name, too, Susannah? I mean, Mitzi?"

"Now you ask me for advice? No."

"Tomorrow we'll look at the Roman baths. You'll like them—they were made by ancient Italians."

The older sister, still in charge. She is never going to change.

"Thank you, Hedy." I leaned over and kissed her on the forehead. "Your hard Hedy forehead."

She kissed me back. "Your soft Susannah cheek." *Oh, my lovely sister.*

"Stay here. Hang onto this for me. I need a little air." I handed her my striped scarf, and then I walked out through the balcony doors into the sunshine.

~

33.

"MY SISTER IS GETTING a little fresh air on the balcony." The waiter had arrived with the second order and was almost able to hide his surprise that there was now only one lady at the table.

"Of course."

After a minute or two, he returned with a neatly folded receipt on a plate. I asked for a pen. He held one out immediately. I signed, thanked him, and went out onto the balcony.

Susannah was not there.

Nor was she below, sprawled on the grass. I grabbed my purse and Mama's old scarf and was reassured. Susannah would never leave that behind. But she wasn't in the lobby. Nor outside, at the hotel entrance.

"Have you seen a young woman, tall, blonde, in the last few minutes?"

"Ma'am?" The doorman inclined his torso.

"She's wearing a grey silk dress."

"No, Ma'am." He looked at me enquiringly. "Is she a guest here, Ma'am? Perhaps she has taken the lift?"

I pushed the ivory button. When the lift arrived, the day operator took me to the second floor. I ran down the hallway to our room. No one. The beds were freshly made and the windows were open. The telephone rang. The voice said, "Good morning, Miss Highstone. Front Desk, Hardcastle speaking. Lord Coleson...."

I couldn't hear for the sound of a Cottin & Desgouttes roaring away outside.

I knew.

"Lord Coleson, Ma'am. He wishes to speak to you. Will you accept his call?"

"Yes!"

Harold's voice came on the line. "Hello, Hedy. You'll never guess."

"Actually, I might."

"Nigel's buggered off with my car."

"Your car, and my sister."

Harold told me to wait for him. I sat down on the bed. The beds were still freshly made and the windows were still open. Two vases on the credenza. In one, lilies and roses with a card that read, "from H." The other vase also had a card that read, "For Mitzi, from Nigel." No flowers. Just water in the vase, and beside it, a pile of banknotes splattered with water. Anchored under the vase, a letter:

> *Hedy, my darling sister!*
> *I have taken only my share of the money. And Nigel's flowers. Take good care of yourself, Hairbrush, as you once did of your Horsie. Ciao, Bella!*
> *Mitzi*

~

34.

HAROLD REFUSED TO GET INVOLVED in trying to catch up to Nigel and Susannah. It was obvious: she intended to go to Italy, but I had no idea when, or what departure point she would choose. Harold assured me that Nigel would not let her come to any harm.

He hired a car, and we went directly to London from Bath. He said it wasn't the first time that Nigel had borrowed his car, and he was quite sure he would return it within days. Nigel had been with him at Reims, after all, picking blasted cathedral glass out of the mud.

"But what if Susannah is still suffering the after-effects of her addiction? What if she needs me?"

Harold held up his hand and closed his eyes. I stopped talking. "You cannot go to the authorities. You could put her at risk if her papers aren't in order, or if there's been a complaint to the Austrian police. If, upon close inspection, her passport is even a bit not *comme il faut*, the result could be worse than being apart for a few weeks. Your own papers might not survive careful scrutiny." He said to wait, to stay put until Nigel returned with the car and with news.

We stayed put—what a phrase!—not at Harold's own home in London, but in an apartment he maintained in Claridge's Hotel. I presumed that this was where he kept his mistress, when he had one.

"No! At thirty-four, I'm certainly old enough, and," he

laughed, "damned rich enough, but I have never had a mistress." He said he maintained the apartment for his business associates.

When Nigel returned two days later with Harold's car, he was quite contrite about having borrowed it. He also presumed, to my astonishment, that my questions were out of a concern for his emotional state. He said he saw Susannah leaving on the Calais-Méditerranée train, heading south. "She waved at me. That smile, you know? And then she put on those sunglasses." He sighed and fell silent.

"And?"

"And she looked so damnably fine! Oh. Excuse me, Miss Highstone. You shouldn't worry, really. She knows her cockles and shells. Finances, I mean."

He wandered over to the table where Harold had lined liquor bottles up on a tray. "She'll need those sunglasses for the glare off the water along the coast. Le Train Bleu has the most magnificent views," he said wistfully. "All the way along." He plucked a gin bottle from the tray. "I wanted to go with her, but she…. Well, I was somewhat at a disadvantage from a few drinks at the time. And I knew, Harold, that you'd want your nice French car back." He poured two fingers of gin into a crystal tumbler and added soda. "Say, would you have any limes?"

In those first two weeks, I was unwilling to go out in case Susannah should ring, or wire, or, maybe even, I sometimes thought, show up. I felt without ballast in the world, except when Harold was around, and then I stayed beside him. When he walked to the windows, I walked with him. When he spread out papers on the desk, I pulled up a chair. He let me. I was exhausted, and burst into tears.

How could she leave me? Where is she? No one wants me, not even my sister.

My eyelids were swollen, and, bizarrely, so was my mouth.

Harold was signing some papers when he suddenly put the cap on his pen and laid it down. "You need Nanny Harcourt's cure: warmed milk with nutmeg, no sugar. A fine soporific."

Nanny Harcourt was right. The next morning, I woke on the sofa by the telephone, under a light wool blanket. I had slept.

I needed to be distracted from the precise contours of the telephone on its own credenza in the entrance to the apartment, so I asked Harold to tell me about the shipping business.

"Am I good at what I do? Yes. I am very straightforward— take it or leave it—and I think that some of men I deal with are so thrilled by frankness that they have sometimes taken it when they might better have left it." He didn't look entirely rueful. His smile was crooked. He was spooning up porridge with raspberries and brown sugar.

"So, you're a hard man."

"Mmm. Are you sure you won't try this? Some of my confrères are older, and help out in soup kitchens or settlement houses, or raise money for earthquake victims in Greece. I'm too young to need to be seen as having a soft side."

"Ah. Then no charity cases. Except me."

"On the contrary. I'm not being charitable. It's a great relief to talk freely to someone. You can't will it to ring, my dear girl."

"What about romance?"

"You astound me! You so rarely make an error in English. Easiest language to learn a little, most difficult to get all the nuances. You must have had a very good teacher."

I could feel that upward movement of heat from my mouth to my eyes, but I pinched my nose and succeeded in keeping the tears at bay. I nodded. "And what was it you were saying about romance?"

"I wasn't. I'm afraid I'm considered a dud. Social negotiations, as required by the young women of my class, are not my strong suit. I think they don't mind how I look, but they do mind and are unwilling to overlook my other faults."

"Which are?"

"My lack of concern for the social calendar, for one. My apparent lack of masculine interest in them. And of course I cannot reveal my weakness. It would be all over the cast of Debrett's Peerage in a week."

He had been in the Great War, he had been to South America, South Africa, and he said all that had made him restless. He had no idea why his sexual proclivities were so specific. It seemed shameful to him. A joke. And yet. I remembered what he had said on the train, how he had felt when some kind whore had been willing to look at him while she pulled off her gloves, tugging at each leather finger before rolling down the tight calfskin.

He hadn't yet tried to initiate anything sexual with me. I couldn't muster the energy to foster his willingness to try, even though I knew it would make my situation more secure. Instead, we talked about business. "In negotiations," he said, "direct questions and then restating answers allow me to move forward. That and reading body language."

"I am completely fluent in that."

We were both surprised at our laughter.

"You see, you are direct, like me. And brave, to escape from the brothel the way you did. If you'd been a chap in my regiment, Hedy, you would have advanced in rank for that operation alone."

"I was desperate." Looking back, I could hardly believe that we had lowered ourselves out of an upper-storey window.

"And athletic! I don't know if I'm drawn to you because you're little or because you're Jewish."

"Neither, I hope."

"Well, I have always felt a sporting kind of sympathy for Jews. I like what I perceive as directness, in business and in the emotions."

All I could think was that I was a very indirect person. I stood and straightened a painting, but it was just a pretense so I could look at the telephone. And not be so little. I made myself as tall as I could.

"That painting is by Whitford—see how all the sheep have square bodies like shipping crates covered in fleece? I can assure you, looking at the telephone will not make it ring."

I dropped into the sofa as though someone had cut my strings. I put a hand up to my face.

"What long hands you have. You should have been a much taller woman."

"Like my sister."

"Hedy, I liked the look of you from the moment I saw you on that rainy street in Vienna. Your eyes. Look. I was willing, as a lark, to get you to England, and as a kindness, to get you to Bath. I half-hoped you would permit me to enjoy my peculiar inclinations in sex. Now I want to get you into my bed, my bed with me in it, as I am. Odd as I am. But willingly. Do you think that can happen?"

"Ask me tomorrow."

"I will. But first I must soften you up, literally. I've ordered a masseuse for you, so I'll leave and see you later tonight."

After the masseuse: those are wonderful words. Then bouquets of flowers arrived. I sat with Susannah's striped scarf around me, and sunk my head into French lilacs and lilies of the valley.

Please be safe.

He wanted me to go out that night, to walk along the Serpentine. He had a lot of faith in changing people's minds if he could get them to walk along while talking. I told him I was familiar with the idea of talking on the go, but perhaps we could walk about the apartment, given its size. I thought of Moreno telling us we could each be the monarch of our own life. But I had been a co-regent of a life shared. *Where is my sister?*

"I cannot understand you. You wanted to be out of the brothel, out in the world, but now you want to remain inside."

"There were two of us. We, my sister and I, the two of us, we wanted to be out in the world. I never expected that I would be on my own, that I would be left by myself."

"But you are not on your own, Hedy. I am inviting you to be with me. For the two of us to simply walk outdoors, wherever you like. Whenever you like."

I shrugged, and tucked my stocking feet in beneath me on the sofa. He had no idea how betrayed I felt. How terrified. I smiled. My smile was always ready, like a Scot's hand hovering above a sword handle. Like George's hand at his hip.

He took another tack. He refilled his cut glass tumbler with whiskey. "Whiskey-making and ship-building: by the gods, I like the Scots. And I like you, Hedy." It seemed that we shared an affection for things Scottish. How ironic to have lived on the *Schottenringstrasse*, the Scottish Ring Road.

Harold said he was tenacious in business. And apparently, not just in business. He sat down beside me. He made a sinuous movement with his hand. "There's a mist in the early morning that snakes in the air above the Serpentine, following the direction of the water below."

"Two serpents: one below, one above. I might like to see that some morning."

"Yes. Yes! Or if you like it less primeval, later in the day, there are more Londoners and foreign visitors out and about in the park, but not so many that you feel hemmed in. They are as amusing to watch as swans, and you don't have to feed them."

"A city of millions cannot feel primeval."

"You will have to see for yourself!"

A quick covert look at the telephone. Not covert enough. He stood up. The windows overlooking Brook Street gave him a green-hedged view of the liveliness and decorum of Claridge's guests coming and going. "You cannot, I will not let you make yourself a voluntary prisoner to a chance telephone call. How on earth would she track you to Claridge's, anyway?"

"My sister is not stupid. She's inventive. If she wants to find me, she will. She would have simply got Nigel to let her know how to get in touch, or..." I stopped. I could hear what I had just said. There was nowhere to look but straight into Harold's eyes. *If she wants to find me.* She hadn't.

"You see. You do see. Look, let's go out early, shall we? We can be back by eleven."

~

35.

WHEN I GOT OFF THE TRAIN, there were a dozen handsome porters, all speaking Italian. All willing to attend to my two small pieces of luggage, to escort me the very short distance to a car with "Hotel Speciale" on its doors, and, especially, to help me with the arduous task of climbing inside. *Mi scusi, signorina, Mi scusi.* It was like being in a musical.

At the hotel, the *addetto* asked me to sign the register. I signed "Miss Susannah Highstone." Earlier, Nigel had bought my ticket under that name. He had insisted gently that "Susannah" was a quite lovely English name, and I should stick with it, since that was the name on my passport. Also, he said that as I was fair, my hair blonde, and my nose, delicate, "Mitzi" would only confuse people, as it sounded like it was "of the Hebrew persuasion." The usual English unkind kindness.

He had wired notice ahead of the arrival of "Miss Susannah Highstone." So now the only person who would think I was "Mitzi" was my sister. *This suits me just fine.* An American had said that to Kreutzel once, when he realized he'd be charged more money for both me and Hedy in the same room. I thought the phrase was hilarious, but Nigel said not to use it. Not if I wished to be successful in passing myself off, at least in the beginning, as English. He said to avoid Americans in person, and in habits of speech. I loved how Americans talked, but I agreed with him. I was used to lying.

Nigel had been so happy to have a mission. To help a damsel

in distress, he had said. He had "borrowed" Harold's car, as I
had suggested, and he drove crouched down, wearing driving
goggles and a flat hat. For a disguise, he had said. Hilarious.
Then he had left the car at a garage and joined me on the ferry.
Once in Calais, he had helped me onto the train and supervised
the stowing of my luggage. He had re-wrapped his flowers and
adjusted the corridor blinds. He looked so woebegone when he
waved goodbye, his watchband sliding up and down his wrist.
He wore his watchband loose, like an African bangle. Nigel
had a busy brain, a busy body, and knew more than he let on.

The train sped south. We stopped at Gare du Nord for more
passengers, and didn't leave until the early evening. I couldn't
eat. The train attendant encouraged me to rest, and I went to
my tiny sleeping quarters. I think he suspected I was ill, as he
was meticulous about helping me without touching me.

The next morning, early, I woke up in Marseilles, and resumed my position by the window as we wound our way along
the coast. Nigel had told me which side to sit on if I wanted
to keep the sea in view all the way. Nigel. What a mixture of
protection and exploitation. The kind of man morphine helps
you to like. I looked out the window, immobile. I didn't think
of anything but this: no part of me belongs to anyone but me.
I watched the sky as much as the sea. I leaned my face against
the glass window, warm from the sun.

At the Hotel Speciale, the deep pink jackets of the staff uniforms flattered the complexions of the men who wore them.
Two men escorted me to my room with the courtesy reserved
for a young monarch before her coronation. They showed me
how to open the windows, and how to turn on the bath and
shower. After showing me where I could find the instructions
in inglese (by the telephone), they stood together and bowed. I
tipped both of them. *Grazie, signorina, grazie, é troppo gentile.*
Shy oblique glances, quick smiles, flashing white teeth.

As soon as they left, I locked the door to my room. *My
room.* Windows, *escritoire*, chair, chaise longue, a bed. I lay

down for a minute. *I am by myself*. Through the windows, I could see the sun setting on the Mediterranean. I had a bath, ordered a light supper, and opened the windows of my room to the warm evening breeze. *My room*.

The harbour was dark, and I ached. I had fallen asleep in my chair. I crawled into my bed. All through the night I kept waking. Each time, I was by myself, in my own room. I could hear the waves, their breath of relief every time they collapsed on the sand. The night was full of the scent of oranges and something else, something peppery, sweet.

I turned on a lamp with a pattern of amber dragonflies on its glass shade. I walked around the room in my underslip, dragging my hand along the walls. Soft shadows on cream-coloured plaster. I wanted to know, to feel, the boundaries of the space. I mapped the room in my mind, looking down on it from above. The way I used to look down on what happened to me with a caller. *But this bed, this room, is mine*. I lay back down on my bed, in the middle. I hadn't slept by myself ever before in my life. I turned out the light quickly and surrendered at last to sleep, my arms out on either side, across my bed to its edges.

The morning light expanded to fill the whole sky, and the cresting Mediterranean waves reflected the light back into the abundant air. It was so bright that it was easier to see what was inside the room than what was outside the window. I had slept in the bed alone. A pillow was lying beside me, like a body. I tossed it onto the thick carpet and turned over.

Ten o'clock. The water was bright turquoise, azure. Above it was the highest sky I had ever seen. I slipped my arms into a dressing gown and looked down on the street below: happy traffic, people promenading on the sidewalks, some under light-coloured parasols. The sweet complaining cadences of Italian, interrupted by the rasping of a tramcar along metal rails. What was next was up to me.

There was a hedge of deep pink wisteria cascading over the edge of the restaurant balcony, where I ate my very late breakfast of coffee, fruit, and *pasticceria*. The hotel was pale stucco, with curving vertical mouldings like the stems of flowers. Mama and her friends called this style Jugendstil. In San Remo, they called it *Liberty stile*. I couldn't imagine why they called it Liberty, instead of *liberta*, unless it was the influence of all the English tourists walking around in their Liberty cottons. I knew the Italians loved their textiles. The headline in *L'Epoca*, the newspaper I had been given, folded, with my breakfast cried: *Perche, per i Nostri Propri Tessuti?* I knew *tessuti* meant fabric, material.

I had thought to pick up an English-Italian dictionary when I arrived, to reinforce the image that I was an English foreigner. I had actually thought I would be through with everything English, but the Corso degli Inglesi was San Remo's main street. English money mattered. The English are like men who always want something different, as long as it's the same.

The waiter brought fresh coffee, not tea, and a fresh cup and saucer. Their coffee was strong and good, and served in very small cups. The outdoor furniture was black, with white-striped grey cushions on the chairs. Bowls of pink carnations on every table. I ate by myself, and I didn't hurry. I leaned on my elbows, my fists to my chin, and looked at the sky. I did not invoke the sky women. I was too interested in what I saw—the obedient waves, the saucy palm trees. Everything so available, so open. The waiter smiled, and put his head to one side. Apparently I had been smiling, too.

"*Dolce far niente*," he said.

I knew *dolce* meant sweet, and I was not sure of the rest, but it felt like a blessing, from a balding man in a pink vest and black pants.

Before I went back up to my room, I stopped at the desk to ask about luncheon, as I intended to spend the morning on the beach. The *addetto* begged me to forgive him, and told me that I could order a large umbrella at the front desk, and that cold drinks and a cold lunch could be brought down onto the beach. He apologized, and told me that, although it was warm during the off season, some people wore trousers or light lawn dresses over their beach shorts or sundresses. Or, pardon, their bathing costumes. They often changed in the hotel's black-and-white striped cabanas on the beach. The hotel had towels. And woven straw beach rugs. And sling chairs. And umbrellas. Oh, he had said that already. He was so sorry. I ordered everything, in order to forgive him. He was grateful. *Grazie, Signorina.*

On the beach, display was important. The hotel workers who set up for the guests rolled up their white shirt-sleeves to show off their forearms. When someone's beach ball rolled into the waves, they rolled up their trousers as much to show off their tanned calves as to keep them dry. There was no escaping from young men who were very anxious to show that they were virile. You were not a man unless everyone saw you acting like one.

The papers that morning featured Mussolini with his shirt off, discussing whatever new "Battle" he had begun. It might have been the Battle of Birth, or Earth, or Swamp. "*Battaglie,*" I said out loud, as I waited for the hotel beach attendant to finish fussing over the location of my umbrella and the flatness of a tightly woven grass carpet, its borders bound in soft cotton tape. Pink tape.

"Oh, the battles are never won. But it looks good to start a battle—especially if you are Mussolini's kind of handsome, yes?" A dark-haired woman on a linen-covered cot a few feet away waved her cigarette at me. She pointed at the newspaper. "You're *inglese,* yes?"

I looked at the photo on the front page again, and nodded. "Mmm." One of George's best gifts, the English acknowledgement of having heard, but not identifying whether one was in agreement or not. "His torso is admirable." What else could

I say? A ridiculous man, performing for the photographers.

Her cot was on a larger carpet of the same material as mine. She offered her hand without getting up, so I stepped closer to take it. She introduced herself. "*Buon giorno*. I am the Contessa Ragione." She held her cigarette out of the way.

"Miss Highstone. Susannah."

She did not tell me her first name. "You are much nicer than the Jewish couple who had that spot last week. From the Netherlands. On their honeymoon."

Another "Mmm" was called for, but I didn't have the stomach to acknowledge the comment. I busied myself with adjusting my straw hat. The *contessa's* location on the beach was fixed, apparently. Her rug was held down by her cot, by a wicker suitcase on one corner, and by two servants in rolled trousers and unbuttoned grey morning jackets. They sat, one on each of the two remaining corners, their arms folded over their knees, and looked out to sea, squinting under their neat straw hats.

"Oh, Miss Highstone." A flick of the cigarette, and a wide smile. "I must be clear: I didn't mind that they were Jews. I quite like Jews. It's that they were so affectionate." She rolled her dark eyes. They were long and narrow, like a Saracen's. "On their honeymoon, did I mention? Cheerful and frank, in that way the Dutch have." She put her sunglasses up on her hair. "I suppose it's all right if you insist on being affectionate." Then she indulged in the mischief of adding, "Or on being Dutch about it."

I placed my hand on my heart and looked up to indicate I was thinking over her oddly rude remark. Was this how people talked to each other on the beach? Or was it just this Italian with the gold earrings in her small ears? The beach attendant from the hotel centred my striped chair in the middle of my carpet with admirable geometric precision. He had already placed the striped umbrella so that the bottom of the chaise longue was in the sun, and the back was in the shade. I tipped him. When he turned to go, he undid his morning jacket and crouched down to whisper something to one of the fellows anchoring the corner of the *contessa's* carpet. She seemed to be asleep behind her sunglasses. I settled into my chair.

"Oskar and ... Edith." She was not asleep. "Their last name was ... something Dutch." She was wearing long tailored shorts, belted, and a sleeveless knit top. I took off my shoes, looked around, and quickly rolled down my stockings. I tugged up the hem of my dress, and within a few minutes, my legs belonged to the hot sun. Wonderful. Tomorrow, I would find a shop to buy beach clothing. At that moment, it was *dolce* to sit in the sun. And Oskar. The little blessing of hearing Papa's name. The *contessa* was silent. Her presence beside me was making me feel relaxed enough to go to sleep myself. I didn't know her, but I realized she had made fun of herself. And of common prejudices. I took that as a good sign.

When I woke up from my little doze, she continued her languid notion of a conversation. Contessa Ragione had been speaking English, not badly at all, at least as well as me. She seemed a little puzzled at my accent, and asked me if I had family in England.

I was startled. "Yes, of course. A sister." No one, not a doctor, a dentist, a caller, no one in my life had ever not known that I had a sister. She was always with me, nearly always in the same room. And I had not thought about her for two days. It didn't feel terrible. It felt wonderful, luxurious.

I would have to pay attention. I was making myself new, without anyone to consult. "I have always preferred the continent—for many years, I was in Vienna. This is my first time in San Remo."

"People come here and they never leave. Why would anyone leave? We have this *spiaggia*—this beach—the sea, lovely people. Plays at the casino, opera stars." She was interrupted by the arrival of waiters from the hotel carrying wicker boxes with our lunch and ice buckets for our soda water and limoncello.

It might not have been entirely necessary to learn Italian, but I wanted to know what was being said around me. So when I went back to my room, I looked up words in my dictionary. I couldn't help thinking, *it's my room. Mine.* I was aware that I was grinning like a madwoman. I looked at myself in my mirror, and there I was, Susannah the Delirious. They could have named a cathedral after me.

I opened my window shutters to see the sky. A habit, a way to summon the sky women. An old gesture, like that of an atheist who crosses himself before battle. When I was thirteen, I went high up and gazed down on what they did to the girl on the bed. Later on, I had sky women for company up there. It felt as though they came to me, not as though I made them up. I felt their presence. If I was with them, looking down, then what happened in that room was not real.

Hedy and I never looked at each other when there was a caller. Hedy sewed or mended, her head down. I read newspapers. We were alert for anything that could cause harm, but we avoided watching. There was enough watching in that room.

I locked the door. It made such a solid *click* that I did it again, pulling on the door. I was safe. The *escritoire* was tall, but I liked to sit when I wrote. I took my thick notebook and my dictionary to the dressing table. Earlier, when I had asked for a dictionary, the attendant in the hotel lobby had protested that there was no need—they all spoke English, and Russian, too, for that matter. My Italian would soon be perfect, according to her. She told me she spoke four languages and used to work in the translation department of Liguria Shipping, until the government said jobs like that should go to men. She scanned my face and then broke into a smile. She leaned forward. "You know, because men handle the stress so well!"

We both burst out laughing. She refused to take my money, saying no one had bought that book in at least two years. She also gave me newspapers, *Il Nuovo* and another one, saying that everyone already knew what was in them. Italian skepticism? *It suits me just fine.*

Back in my room, I removed the hand mirror from the dressing table and picked up my hairbrush. A dark strand of hair wound in the bristles. *Hedy.* I pulled the strand of hair free and let it float out the window.

I threw a scarf over the three-sectioned mirror and turned on the lamp. Then I picked up the first newspaper. Reading a newspaper always made me feel safer; it reminded me of leaning on my mother's arm while she read to us. I read one paragraph and then underlined a couple of words. Italian was easy; everything ended in a vowel. After a while, I put away my book and folded my newpaper, *mio giornale*, neatly. I placed my pen on top. I adjusted the pen so it was parallel to the edge of the notebook. Hedy managed quite well in a classroom. Not me. But I thought, *realmente,* I could study Italian at a desk all day. That night, however, I was going to the casino, the only one that Mussolini hadn't closed.

The building was lovely, with two square towers on either side. A grand wide staircase up to the doors. My six hundred pounds amounted to many thousand lira, but I knew they would not last long at the Hotel Speciale. I had to find a sponsor for my life in Italy. With any luck, it wouldn't only be foreigners who liked to gamble at the casino. I hoped to find a rich man, not a drunk, not English, and not Russian either. The Russians also liked something different, as long as it was the same. There was a Russian Orthodox Church nearby, crowned with splendid onion domes and gilt. If only there were serfs to free, and snow on the ground, it would be perfect for them.

No. I had my heart, whatever that was, set on an Italian. I lifted the scarf from the mirrors. I was going to wear my gold chiffon dress and my gilt shoes. I didn't have much time, so I had to work quickly. I had a little glow from the sun, and my bobbed hair had grown out into a blonde halo. What I had in mind was anything but angelic.

Straight strings of small white lightbulbs, all lit, followed the lines of the pale yellow Casino Municipale. It was after eight. At the entrance leading to the roulette tables, I paused to adjust my watch so that anyone who wanted to look at me would have a good opportunity. My own demonstration of *una bella figura*. "Cutting a figure," as the English say. I had just arrived at the casino, and luck was already with me. The *contessa* was there with a merry group around one of the tables. She introduced me to her friends—a sulky young man with macassar oil in his hair, an old man, and a middle-aged woman who introduced herself as Signora Della Costa. She was striking. A small chin, big eyes, a pretty bosom, and a diamanté headband.

The old man had thinning reddish hair and dark eyes. DiFelice, the young man, looked at me under his eyelashes and "accidentally" brushed into me. He didn't have a chance. I had already seen Della Costa palm him some money. The old man, Signore Cavalliere, had a firm body, an upright but calm posture. Italian men know how to stand. And unlike every other man I had encountered from the time I had stepped off the train, he was tall enough to look me straight in the eye. I had to look elsewhere. I hadn't been my own pimp before.

"Oh, Signorina Highstone, my appearance makes you look away. It is the fault of my birthplace. I am from Siena, where many have red hair. Unfortunate, no?"

I shook my head and smiled at him. "Do you miss Siena, Signore?"

"Alfonso, please. I haven't been to Siena for years. No one in my family there marries, so there are no weddings, and we all live forever, so there aren't any funerals either." He leaned back and smiled. "So I don't go to Siena. A cousin started a little business here in San Remo. I came to help him one spring, and," he spread his hands, "here I still am. Do you like the *roulette?*"

"It sounds much better in Italian!"

"Everything does."

The little ball skipped and bounced around the wheel. He watched me as I watched the game. No one was winning very much or losing very much. Champagne for everyone again, ordered by the old man with just a small nod. *He could be my Italian, or lead me to him.* Either way. I tossed my champagne back—just like that, a little *pennacchio*—and then managed a lady-like yawn and excused myself. I was not a gamine, but I could play that part, as he was so much older.

My hotel was only a short walk from the Casino Municipale, and, as I had thought he might, he immediately offered to escort me. I said *grazie,* but kept quiet otherwise, and hurried. His smile, his quick raise of his eyebrows told me that he liked my pace. He had no trouble matching it. Once we were at my hotel, he took my hand, and suddenly I was Viennese: knees locked, head to one side, arm extended. He was astonished for a half second. I was astonished myself. Schottenringstrasse lives.

"English ladies always surprise me. I like that very much." He bowed slightly and kissed my hand. *"Buona sera, Signorina."*

I closed the door to my room. "My room." I startled myself. I was talking out loud. I had wanted a fresh start, free of the brothel. Free of my sister. But she and I had always talked things over after a new caller left. One of us in the chair, one of us on the bed. What did he like, did his cock look healthy, the usual simple things of our business. What I needed to talk about now, feeling an attraction to someone, I hadn't talked about since my short-lived affair with Billy, who must be a grown man by now.

There was no one to talk to, except my own face in the mirror. "I like this Signore Cavalliere," I said out loud. "He is old, rich, and here in San Remo. Do I make myself available? Do I hide in my room for a day?"

I had to wait for my mind to answer. *Play this poco a poco. Contessa Ragione likes to gossip. Have the story organized, have details to trade—the way it worked in the brothel. What is your story?*

I watched my face closely in the mirror. "My mother fell ill in Vienna." I could see my eyes filling with tears. *Good.* "I didn't want to leave her." *And the countess, what would she say?*

"So, no society?"

I shook my head, as though I couldn't talk about it. *My explanation?* "I am afraid my most constant companion was a nurse."

Yes. Keep that, but without the grin. The best lies are the truth. My image looked back at me, completely on my side in everything. The *contessa* had told me she kept an apartment at the hotel. *I needed to stick to a schedule, one that she would notice and tell her companions about.* Breakfast, a walk along the beach, umbrella and sun, a light lunch, afternoon nap, the Casino Municipale. That way Signore Cavalliere could find me. Or someone could.

~

36.

LONDON IS OPEN TO THE SKY, and the air lofts easily over the old city in the morning. By eight o'clock we were walking towards Hyde Park. The city streets were, alive, bustling, and as in all big cities, crowded with people who walk at a fast clip. I thought about George's Canadian salmon, red with love, swimming upstream, and clung to Harold's arm. On the boundary of Hyde Park were stalls, where we bought some oranges, and Harold made me smile at his perfect peel. At the edge of the water, he made a little boat out of the orange coil, with a sail made from of a twig and one of the tissue paper wrappers the oranges came in. We followed its passage until it bumped into some taller grass on the verge. He fished the peels out, and remarked on how cold the water was.

"May your other shipping ventures be more successful," I joked, and then begged to go back.

There were no messages at the reception desk.

Once in the apartment, Harold made a fire on his own and ordered breakfast. We threw peels from the remaining oranges on the fire. Every time the telephone rang, I jolted upright.

"This," Harold said, "is like dealing with a veteran of shell shock. A new routine has to be laid down to take over in those moments when memory intrudes and creates chaos."

I knew he was right, but I felt that if I kept alive my desire to hear from Susannah, like a live wire, then I was just waiting for something that *would* happen. I didn't want to give up. I thought that if I gave up, I would be giving up on my sister. And who was I without her?

The next day, not quite as early, he took me to the British Museum to look at the Assyrian bas-reliefs, the Roman statues, and especially the Elgin marbles. Time was on a hiatus there. I strolled around the statues, seeking different points of view. I was moved by the sculptures, by the formality of their nakedness, these bodies of stone and marble. I talked to Harold for an hour, possibly longer, without once mentioning Susannah.

It was one of those chilly fall days in London. On our way back to Brook Street and the hotel, we saw a rabbit emerge from the stiffened ornamental grasses behind the black iron sidewalk railings. It darted out, zigged and zagged, and then sat upright on round hindquarters, shivering.

"'The hare limped trembling through the frozen grass,'" I said.

"'And silent was the flock in woolly fold.' You know 'The Eve of St. Agnes!' How splendid!" He beamed. "You are a rare creature. A jewel."

He was like every other wealthy Englishman, I thought, whom I had ever met in the brothel—he connected to other Englishmen by a shared affection for the same memorized lines. They would call out lines to each other, cheerfully, on the way up or down the stairs to the brothel bedrooms. "Alone, and palely loitering, old man?" or "The night was made for loving, eh? And the day returns too soon!" I had yet to see how English men connected to English women. I wasn't sure I wanted to know. Perhaps poetry connected all of them.

George had us memorize three poems. He had been a good teacher, choosing, he said, that which was "representative and lovely." Easy enough to discover that which is not lovely on your own, he'd said. I had asked for the culture, and for almost a year, he had provided. "The Eve of St Agnes." "Down by the Salley Gardens." And Tennyson's "Ulysses." George had been so delighted when I had said that "the lights begin to twinkle from the rocks" meant it was a rising evening tide, since only wet rocks could reflect the lights. I would have been happy to never have come to England, only have him teach me about it.

I missed him, his voice, the way he turned over his hand when he explained something. His stocking feet. Susannah had called him "the Canadian Scribbler" but in my head I called him *my love*. In fantasy, *my darling. Sweetheart*. In real life, I called him George, or Mr. Andrew. Never anything else.

That brothel bedroom had been like the desert isle in all the tales, where we had been given what was essential for survival—in England in this case, if only we could get there—three poems.

And three hymns. Susannah and I also learned to sing these, or rather, we both learned the words. It could never be said that Susannah learned to sing anything. I liked this English world, repressed in expression, deliriously attached to the natural world. *Pagans*, I thought. I wondered if all the sex I had with English callers had somehow influenced my responses to their language.

Harold brought some of his old Cambridge books over to the apartment for me. In the mornings, after Harold had left for his office, I pored over *Tess of the d'Urbervilles*. I tried to see what I would look like without eyebrows by covering them when I looked in the mirror. I didn't see much of a difference. *Goblin Market* was an oddly pretty book with its illustrations of languid and knotted creatures. The sisters within it were at the mercy of the lure of goblin men. It seemed that in English stories, women were tempted by men. In the old Austrian children's books, men were always tempted by women.

When I asked Harold about all the fruit mentioned in Rossetti's book, he brought another book, on botany, by Bowers, which Harold said was an eminently suitable name. He said that he would take me for walks at Twin Oaks, his country home, so I could see the fruit and flowers of the English countryside for myself.

I really liked him. Harold, kind and shy. I knew, even if he didn't, that eventually our relationship depended on me giving him sexual pleasure. I knew it wouldn't be difficult. I liked looking at him.

But he was not George, who was always in my thoughts. I stowed away what I was learning by having intense conversations with him in my mind. *Knowing the names of flowers matters a great deal to the English, George. Some of the most ordinary people, even downtrodden ones, use Latin names easily. "Erica" for heather. Funny to see, today at the stalls, a great thumping fellow referred to as "Pet" by a small woman in a flower-patterned kerchief. Funnier, George, to know she meant "Petal."*

One day when we got back from our walk, Harold made a fire and ran a bath for me as usual, but then remained in the steam-filled bathroom with me. He helped me take off my clothes, and he removed his own. He set his glass tumbler of whiskey on the flat edge of the sink, and helped me step into the tub and settle in the heat of the water. He sat on the edge of the steaming tub like the Dionysus in the British Museum, his legs splayed apart and his member exposed, flopped over to one side at first, then rising slowly, pink and glowing. Harold's face was solemn and puzzled, like the face of Dionysus, but unlike the god, he was not missing his hands. He picked up his glass and drank. He produced, wrapped in a small towel, a cup—a "hot toddy" he called it—and I drank, still immersed in the hot bath.

With loofah and sponge and washcloth, with finely milled French soap, he bathed me. I was as cooperative as a sleepy toddler. The back of my neck. The length of my arm. I bent forward so he could use the loofah on my back. I put a washcloth over my face and breathed in. I accepted his bathing me as if I were five, compliant, obedient, and silent. *Lift your hair up, Hedy. Good girl.*

Finally, he stood to lift the large towel from the heated rack above the radiator and asked me to stand. He wrapped me in the towel and rubbed it energetically against my skin. He was still naked himself, still firmly erect. He bundled me tightly in the towel and began walking me to the bedroom. I froze. It felt like that first night at the brothel, trapped in a blanket and being walked.

Harold paused. He released me and pulled a nightgown over my head. He tucked me in, tugging the counterpane up to my chin. Then he kissed my forehead and left.

Every day, we walked to the museum and drank the strong black tea. We bought asparagus and flowers fresh from the Jersey Islands. I bought a chandelier of onions from a French fellow—an "Onion Johnny," Harold said. I carried it, my prize, like a glockenspiel in a parade. After we walked back, Harold lit the fire and gave me a bath. He referred to me in public as Miss Highstone, and in private, as his "beautiful Boche" or sometimes, his "jewel of a Jewess." I was sleeping through the night, but every morning I woke to only myself in the room. There had been no word from my sister.

On the first of May—a shining, bright morning—I was ready when he arrived. He raised his eyebrows once, quickly, and said nothing. Later that day, the labour parades with their large cloth banners would fill streets, but this early, the city moved lightly, quickly. We had to wait for the museum to open.

There were always others who regularly climbed the worn steps to the museum, to gaze in silence: scholars and adolescents, curious for different reasons; foreign visitors; and artists, these last given away by hair that needed a cut, or the worn cuff on the well-tailored shirt. Harold knew how to be quiet. He knew how to look at stone and marble human beings who were perfectly, eternally still, but also alive in the small tuck of the cheek by the mouth, the tension when the weight was on the ball of one foot, the exquisite turn of the wrist made by a hand gesturing as if it were not made of dead and heavy stone, but light, made of muscle and movement.

The talk flowed between us as if we were catching and directing a stream of water. It was the kind of delighted talk that rose out of childhood for me, all about how a line could convey feeling. I was enamoured of necks and foreheads, and mesmerized by the tilt of marble hyacinth curls on the few statues that still had their heads.

When we returned and entered the lobby of Claridge's, we checked as usual for messages, a ritual that was beginning to be kept for its own sake. I greeted the lift operator like an old friend. When had I ever had an old friend? I had been friendly with Brigita the Romanian. Kislany the Hungarian. Susannah was a sister, bound to me without choice. At least up until a few weeks ago. A friend is not the same as a sister.

George, I thought. He was a friend. A kind of friend. I hadn't wanted him to be my friend. I had wanted him to want me. *This man with me, smiling at me in the elevator, he wants me and he is a friend. If a friend is someone you can count on to be good to you, he is the best friend I have ever had.* I smiled back at him, and he blushed.

"It's chilly out there," I said to the lift operator. "Nice to be home."

Once we were in the apartment, Harold placed his hat in the closet in his usual methodical fashion. I let him help me off with my coat, a courtesy performed with practised grace. He tucked his gloves into the left sleeve of his own coat, and stowed both coats away.

"Now for a fire." He glanced at me and stopped. I was standing in my underwear, my dress around my ankles. I stepped out of the pool of silk jersey, put both hands on his chest, and he knew to stand perfectly still. I took the gloves off.

~

37.

BEFORE THE SUN GOT VERY HIGH over San Remo, I walked to the eastern edge of the beach. Small commercial ships docked there, but there was also a strange building, old and made of stone. Its windows did not face the sea. They were all at the back, facing the city. I thought I could hear someone crying, a man. A policeman looked at me staring at the building and placed his hand on his belt, as if to say, "I am ready." I turned and walked back along the silky sand.

The *contessa* was already set up, legs out in the sun. She asked me to call her Marinella. "I watched you walk back along the sand, and I wondered why you had gone so far."

"I was curious about the odd-shaped building, the fort."

"Oh, Santa Tecla. It was built by the Genoese. A couple of hundred years ago."

"To defend the people of San Remo?"

"No." A mischievous smile. "To protect the Genoese from the people of San Remo. See those windows at the back of the fort? They are there so the soldiers could fire on us. If necessary. San Remo didn't like the Genoese occupying their paradise. Now it holds people, communists."

"Are there so many?"

"There are also Mafiosi, criminals. They are waiting for their sentences. Usually they get put off on an island, so it's easy to ship them from here." Marinella tipped her sunglasses back onto her head and smiled. "They are the only tourists who come to San Remo unwillingly." She turned over on her stomach, so I did as well.

Now I could see what rose behind the beach. The hills were steep: young mountains with tumbling gorges filled with cascading green, and then curious narrow horizontal trapezoids, terraces in red and pink. "Carnations," explained Marinella. *So that was what I smelled, peppery and sweet, the first night in the hotel.*

And along the streets, chinotto trees, some in fragrant white blossom, some with only glossy green leaves, and some with actual small, sour oranges. In the hills were overlapping patches of colour, buildings painted blue, red, pink, and turquoise. And yellow rectangles, partially exposed and partially hidden by mountain pines. Visual syncopation, one of the few things I remember my mother and Egon Schiele talking about. My sister paid more attention than I ever did to what they said.

"What is that spreading yellow?"

"Mimosa."

"And those buildings, all those colours?"

"La Pigna. The Pine Cone." She rested a tanned forearm over her eyes. The waves ran their tongues along the shore. Overhead, seagulls. A clanking of boats in the eastern end of the harbour. Marinella sat up and smiled again. "When we needed to hide from the Saracens, we could quickly race up the streets of La Pigna. The Saracens would become confused—you know how easily Arabs get confused." She looked to see if I got her joke. She liked to mock a prejudice by saying it as though she meant it, deadpan. If you shared the prejudice, you wouldn't get the joke. I liked her. This was a game of social logic: Arabs wouldn't really get confused.

"The streets," she made a spiralling motion with her hand, "twist all the way up. They're very narrow. And there is seldom anyone in the streets because there are small walkways, like arches, between the houses on either side. And at the one entrance, a big pinecone fountain to gaze at, and near it, a sluice pipe to pour boiling oil onto the invader. Or shit. Or piss." She looked to see if I had taken offence at her language.

Not me.

She nodded, once. "I'll show you the secret of La Pigna one day."

"Wonderful." She wasn't the only one who could be nonchalant. Inside, though, I was thrilled, sparking with energy. I was making a new friend. Someone who didn't have to talk to me, who wasn't my sister, who wasn't bound by obligations to a common brothel madam. Margarete had liked me, but she liked herself much more. Otherwise, no one had ever chosen me for a friend. Who would? I was a potty-mouth. A whore. Although Moreno seemed to really like us, he had a motive for talking to us. George needed money. And was ambitious. How do people make friends? Maybe I had to ask Marinella for advice, discuss a problem, perhaps, that she could advise on. That was how some whores bonded in the brothel. That, or laughing at men.

The next time I walked to the prison, I looked up. *"Unto the hills, around do I lift up / My longing eyes. O whence for me...."* I stopped singing. My singing is terrible, but George said it was important that we learn hymns, this one and a child's hymn, "When Mothers of Salem." The latter sounded like it should be played on huffing trumpets. He made us memorize the words exactly, perfectly. When I had said I liked "Bring me my bow of burning gold, Bring me my arrows of desire" in the Blake hymn, Hedy shook her head and commented, "Of course those are the lines you would like."

My longing eyes. What did I long for? To study, to be a student, modest in my smock, sitting in lecture halls, at the back near the doors, by myself, unnoticed, taking notes. I liked to take notes. I liked the presumed virtue of the student, like everyone else who knows they're bad. My notebook of Italian phrases was an object of adoration for me. I returned it to my suitcase for safe keeping every night. I wanted to read novels, histories, books to test my mind against the minds of those who knew their subject.

But what was my subject? I nearly bumped into a small woman with a good-natured face wheeling a bicycle. She handed me a notice, to come and see a race. She was apparently in the race.

I would have liked to ride a bicycle, but the roads here were so steep. And in town, there were carriages and cars and trams. In Vienna, Margarete had liked to crash over tramcar tracks. Margarete. A friend when I was a girl, the last day I was a girl. And then a friend, more or less, when we worked with Moreno. A friend and a thief.

I turned and headed back westward, towards Marinella. A man passed me, walking quickly on the sand. He wasn't wearing any shoes, despite his linen suit and straw boater. He had a blue canvas bag slung over his shoulder, and he was whistling "Va Pensiero." Such a lovely melody, full of longing. I used to sing it with Papa at top volume, both of us doing sweeping arm gestures. His voice made mine sound wonderful. Papa said I was right: Italian was the best language for singing. He never criticized me when I was off key, which was every time. *My misaligned fate, to love singing, and to do it badly. The opposite of fucking, which I do well but dislike enormously. The opposite of intimate relations, I mean. I have to remove the whore from my head, from my mouth.*

I didn't realize I was idly singing along with him until the fellow turned and walked backwards, talking to me first in Italian, then in German, and finally in English. I waited for the English. I remembered a morning in the Augarten, when Moreno had walked the same way.

"Do you know, Miss, how many loyal Italians wish to be home?"

"I thought the song was about Israel, beautiful and lost."

"Ahh," he shook his finger and squinted. "Verdi put the words in the mouth of Jewish slaves, so, yes, Israel, but he meant *Italia*!" He smiled triumphantly. "Do you think this country is not lost, when," he paused and lowered his voice, "so many are exiled to islands for the ridiculous crime of wanting the world to be for everyone, not just for the rich, *la mia donna inglese*?"

"How many?"

He stopped walking backwards. "I don't know. Exactly. But read this. You have a big soul, I can tell." He shoved a folded notice into my hand and doffed his hat, releasing many salt and pepper curls. His mouth was soft. We former whores know how to look. Yes, a big cock. *It isn't going to be easy to get rid of the whore.*

Two notices in one morning, before eleven o'clock. By the time I arrived at the part of the beach I now thought of as mine, Marinella was already set up. The fellow DeFelice was stretched out beside her, his hair perfectly oiled, a widow's peak on his forehead as if he had been painted. As soon as he saw me, he jumped up and sucked in his stomach. The sleeves were rolled up on his cream-coloured shirt. His forearms were tanned and lovely. He took off his round sunglasses.

"*Ciao, bella.*" He bowed, a small incline, and reminded me that his name was Carlo. He smiled at me with all his teeth. He wasn't trying to persuade me that he was glad to see me; he was trying to arouse himself into thinking he was glad to see me. I had seen this before: twinkling eyes when the man comes in, brusque and cold on the way out. Such a man says your name, over and over, or, "Oh, my darling," but it isn't you he means. He is merely trying to create the conditions he needs to finish with you.

"*Ciao.*" I didn't feel particularly *bella* but I didn't care. I could feel my trousers billowing against my legs. My straw hat blew off. He dashed after it as it skidded along the sand. Every time he reached for it, it eluded him. And every time, he turned to engage me in his drama. He shrugged. In the time it took to look back at me and turn on his glittering smile, the hat travelled further away. Eventually he had to go into the sea, and apparently couldn't swim, as the last I saw of that hat, it was bobbing on a wave headed for Corsica.

Marinella said that he had tried, and that I must comfort him. I pretended I was too shy to do such a thing. "*Grazie*," I murmured and looked down at the ground. Carlo flung himself on the carpet and sulked. He kept looking to see if I would say something to cheer him up. Not me.

I wanted to talk to Marinella, and I wanted to read the notice the fellow in the suit and boater with the bare feet had given me. I feigned sleep. When the other woman from the casino arrived, Carlo jumped up to help her with her basket and parasol. He helped her set up just far enough away to be out of earshot. He glanced over to see what effect this had. None.

The *contessa* took off her sunglasses and patted my hand. "He's not sure if you are rich enough for him, but he still thinks you should fall for him. He's more fun if he thinks you have fallen for him. Why not?"

"And the lady, Contessa?"

"Oh, Della Costa. She really wants him to want her, and he wants her to keep wanting him. For him, she's a way-station."

"But she's very pretty."

"It doesn't matter. They are both playing a game. She wants him to submit to her, to her prettiness, and to her gaze. He wants the same thing. They are both seducers. Do call me Marinella, please. Oh, look, lunch."

After lunch we returned to the hotel together. She told me she was a farmer. A sidelong look of mischief. She said she had a mimosa estate and her manager made sure the mimosa was the right quality for a soap manufacturer in Paris. "We have an exclusive. But you," she said, tapping my hand, "you mustn't be exclusive. Tomorrow, you have to come with me. The *passeggiata*. The promenade. Everyone here does it."

"Why?"

"They've always done it. You'll see. Only you'll have to walk more slowly than you usually do. Your walk is a canter—like a little horse." She clucked her tongue, mimicking the sound of hooves, and laughed. I returned to my room and talked to my image in the mirror, silently. *Horsie, this Contessa will be your newspaper. Tell her the right things, and she will tell everybody. She will be your pimp. Marinella, the Pimp Contessa.*

~

38.

AFTER YET ANOTHER MATINEE performance of *The Mikado*—for, according to Harold, it was impossible to see it too many times—he sat me down beside him on the pale grey brocade of the sofa. Then he looked away.

I was afraid. But I was not a child. I was twenty-four. I still had six hundred pounds, and even foreigners with dubious identification could find a place to live in London. Yesterday I had seen a shop for let, a former hat shop, when I was out with Harold. I could buy several hats, manipulate the brims, steam them, add wide grosgrain ribbon. My hats had always attracted attention. I could move quickly on a plan, if I had one. If I needed one. I looked at him. He said nothing. *Should I get up and leave?* I could feel my lip trembling. After a few long moments, I took a chance. "*On a tree by a willow, a little tom-tit,*" I sang softly. "Half the fun of that song, Harold, is how often you get to say 'tit,' don't you think?"

He said nothing.

I continued, "*With a shake of his poor little head, he replied, Oh Willow, Tit-willow, Tit-willow.*"

He sat, tapping out a beat with his knuckles on the enamelled wooden trim of the sofa. I snuggled up to him.

"My sister…"

"Hedy." He held up a hand.

Oh, no.

"I cannot bear to hear much more talk about Susannah. You

need to think about yourself. Not you with your sister. You with your mother. Your father. With anyone you have cared about. Who has cared about you."

George.

"What did they like about you? How are you like them?"

I was stunned. I couldn't think. My father thought I was a perfect older sister. Susannah did not agree. I looked like my mother, and I knew I shared a love of the arts with her. *If only I could hear what she thought about Van Gogh!* But I didn't know what she had liked about me. I was not sure what anyone liked about me, if they weren't paying for me. I threw my arms around Harold, and over the top of my head he said, "It's going to be a long winter, and we might well want a little sun, and you might well find yourself in Susannah's company somewhere on the Mediterranean, at a spa, or the like."

"She might not want to see us. Me."

"Just the same, we might run into her. And I want you to know who you are and what you want. Before you think about me," he said dismissively, "you have to think about yourself. People who don't know who they are, they're the ones in my business who make a cockup of things, and I have to spend weeks fixing the..."

"*Balagan.* Chaos. The chaos."

"Balagan. Is that more of your Hebrew talk? Perfect! That's exactly what it is. You, Hedy, now. What you have to do is go for walks—thinking is best done outside, on the move."

What part of his business am I? I kept my tone jocular. "On the move? Like a wandering minstrel? Shall I sing of threads and patches?"

"I think it's 'shreds.' And patches. But yes, maybe not sing, but wander out in the world. Talk to people. See who draws your interest, who is interested in you."

"No one does. Either of those things."

"Join the world, just a little, Hedy."

"Haven't I done that? Aren't you, more or less, the world?"

"Not quite. I'm older, but I am not the world. And I must leave, tomorrow morning, in fact. I'll be gone for six weeks, and I don't want you to spend your time sobbing into these nice pillows."

Oh. So he's only going away for a few weeks. Keep it jolly. "The body moves and the mind follows. That's what I told Susannah once, the first time the old madam allowed us out in the city on our own."

Harold ignored the comment about Susannah. "So, tonight, you'll meet Archie. I've invited him here for supper tonight."

"My hair!" I jumped up. "Who's Archie?"

"Dear girl, call down to the front desk. They'll send up a hairdresser."

I went to the telephone. "Who...?"

"Archie Stephens is my estate manager. He's been with me for years. I can't go up with you this time, of course, but Archie will take you to Twin Oaks with him tomorrow in the car."

"How much time do we have?"

He brushed his hair back from his forehead. "I will be boarding by the time you are ready to leave. Even though I own the ship, I shouldn't keep it waiting. Not a freighter, at any rate. Archie will bring you back in a car sometime Monday. He is, I suppose, the person I trust most in the world."

I dialled and spoke quickly, and within minutes the hairdresser knocked on the door. I let her in and led her to the dressing room. Harold went to join us, and the hairdresser looked shocked. He retreated. An hour later, my hair had acquired marcelled waves.

"Do you like it?"

"You look wonderful! Now, listen. I know you can talk to anyone, but I want you to feel at ease with Archie. He travelled with me when I was in the Argentine, arranging for cattle shipments. He likes cars as much as I do. Be nice to him."

"What do you mean?"

"I mean, be nice to him, let him get to know you."

"Do you mean get into bed with him?"

Harold put down his glass and picked me up, lifting my feet right off the floor, and sat down with me. He held me in his arms and looked me in the eye.

"No. That's not what I mean. In these modern times, I supposed I should say, 'if you want to,' but the truth is I would rather you didn't. I'm not a bright young thing, all permissive and living in London. Like in the bloody newspapers. I'm a veteran. I'm from the old school, and I like you being mine. As much mine as you like." He moved me from his lap onto the grey sofa beside him. He took a folded cheque from inside his jacket pocket and grabbed a pen. "Here. This is yours. They'll cash it downstairs. Listen, now. This apartment has been a *pied-à-terre* for me in London. I have my own place, as you know—my townhouse in Belgravia. Wilton Crescent. I've mostly used this apartment for people I do business with. I haven't stayed here myself in several—well, not since the war. About seven years. Hardly use it." He sat down again. "You have kind eyes, Hedy. A soul."

If this is how he does business, no wonder he is so successful. He proposes what he wants, clearly, but throws you off with a flattering insight. Am I kind? Is this what I want?

"When I get back, if you are willing, I will put this place in your name." He looked at me intently. "When I get back," he looked around the room, "you can decide if you want to see me."

"Of course I want to see you!" *I do. I couldn't stand it if he were to leave me, too. Maybe I am meant to be bought and paid for. Does he mean he will give me this apartment, whether I see him or not? I can't ask.*

"Hedy, I believe I am a good judge of people. You are one of those people who goes ahead, even though they are terrified. I saw it in the war. There is nothing more valuable."

He suddenly threw his arms up in the air. "I have to be both diplomatic and firm in business, and I like the combination;

it's stimulating intellectually. But I need to be loose, too. I need to be in a place where there are no weapons, no artillery, no shelling, where I can be my natural self. Which, as you know, is not entirely natural. It's why I have been alone, because I can't help being who I am. Liking what I like. I don't want to lose you, Hedy."

"I'm alone, too, because everyone goes away! I don't know who I am, and I am not as brave as you think." *I've said too much.*

"Look. Be my friend. My companion. I want you to meet my close friends, join my private life. I know everyone must have his own life. Her own life. You will either reconcile with your sister or you will become able to accept your grief over losing her. And that will be easier if you have something you really like to do."

"I don't know what I would like to do." My eyes were stinging. "I have had very little experience in choosing what I would like to do. I want my sister back. I can't think about what I would want to do unless I know she is safe. What if she has been attacked by some scoundrel? She has been out in the world even less than I have. When she was out in the world with me..." I broke off. I wasn't crying, not yet. I blew my nose. When I realized that I'd used a table napkin, I stared at it, horrified. I started to laugh. So did Harold. Then, half-laughing and half- crying, I said, "When she was with me, everything she saw, much of the time, had a dark blue frame around the edge."

"My Irish friend, Lorne, talked about that. My one-armed friend, from the train?"

"Yes, I remember. What if she's returned to morphine? If I could just talk to her!"

"You will. I'll help you. Look. I have contacts who ship out of the Cote D'Azur. And she's not stupid, Hedy. She's your mother's daughter too. And your father's."

He tipped his head to one side and looked at me. "Now, Hedy.

Do you want me to embrace you, or do you need me not to?"

I paused. "To. Not not to."

Inside his arms, I said, "I don't have to wait until you are back. I mean, I will have to wait until you are back, but I don't want to." *I actually am fond of him.* "I mean: yes."

"Yes, to...?"

"Such a businessman, such a closer of a deal! Yes, to everything."

Harold was very careful not to disturb my marcelled curls when he kissed my neck, my ear, and my mouth, too.

After a pleasant early supper with Archie in the dining room of the hotel, drinks and light-hearted goodbyes, we took the lift to the apartment. Harold, a little tipsy as usual, asked me if I could give him a hand.

I took off most of my clothes, but left on my step-in chemise, my small dinner hat and my gloves. I spread my fingers and waggled them by my hips. Harold pulled me into the bedroom, turned on the lights by the bed, and lay back, grinning. I unbuttoned the small button on the inside wrist of my left glove, then tugged helplessly at the fingers, gazing at Harold steadily. I rolled and rolled the sleeve of the glove down, and when I finally pulled it from my hand, Harold grabbed me and my glove and rolled me into bed with him.

I woke up naked the next morning, except for my hat with the net still tied over my forehead. Harold was dressing. He called his house and assured himself that his luggage—the calfskin shoes, the wide-brimmed hats—had been packed by his man. "Right, my darling, I'm off to East London, South Africa to buy a ship, Leith-built. I'll be back by Lammastide. First of August."

Everyone leaves me.

~

39.

T HE *CONTESSA* WAS FULL OF SURPRISES. "Look." She pulled out a grey notice identical to the one I had put in my trouser pocket and forgotten. "They are doing terrible things here to people. Look, they march and get killed. Many people walk out into the streets here. Unlike in your England." She stared angrily out to the sea. Then she sighed and her face changed, like clouds moving over the sky. Here was my chance.

"The weather's better here for marching into the streets. You look damned silly marching in the streets holding an umbrella."

She raised an eyebrow. "Oh, Miss Susannah, I do like your sharp tongue. These big men beating up women and children, and even our little bicycle touring heroes—look what they did to little Bottecchia." She held the notice out for me to see.

There was a blurred photo of a small man in a tight jersey leaning on the handlebars of a bicycle on the notice.

"He can hardly read, but he's been seen holding communist newspapers. So they attacked his tires to cause an accident, to force him out of the race." She stared at the photo, and made no effort to stop the tears welling in her eyes. She fished a handkerchief out of her straw purse and blew her nose. "We march, but we like the strong man. We think we can hide behind the skirts of a bully and be safe."

"The skirts?"

"Of course. These big men, they are fascinated with women; they are close to their mothers."

I thought of the sky women whose skirts I used to hide myself in, blue in colour like my mother's skirts.

"Don't frown. Have you never noticed that police officers always dress up like women when a costume is required? Or is that just in Italy?"

She signalled to one of the servants, who was anchoring the corner of the beach carpet, by wiggling her index and middle fingers as if they were glued together. The fellow retrieved her cigarettes and lighter from a small case. She blew cigarette smoke out of her nostrils like a pretty dragon. "Watch, the tide will turn, and then these big heroes will say they were duped by the fascists into doing terrible things." She sighed. "Men like to beat up other men." A big pause. "Some men like to."

I brushed the white sand out of my sandals and looked out at the azure sea as if I were talking to it, and not to Marinella. "Men want to beat up what they fear in themselves. They hurt what they resent being repressed within themselves."

"Oh. You really did spend time in Vienna! In Baden-Baden, you could tell if someone was from Vienna by how long it took for repression and desire to appear in conversation. Or desire and repression."

"What is Baden-Baden like lately?" *As if I have ever known it. I am sure we would have gone there if my parents hadn't fallen ill. And died. I would have contented myself with boring old Bad Ragaz forever if they could have lived.*

"Still lovely. Very few Hungarians now. What do you think about this pure *romanita* business?" She talked politics so freely. "It's ridiculous. Beautiful olive-skinned Italians, trying to figure out how we can be Aryan. Some of us have hair like Africans! And this palaver about how women and Jews have this mysterious power to pull strings to manipulate events." Marinella snorted. "If that is the case, why isn't the outcome better for women and Jews?"

Change the subject. "By the way, have you seen the big puppets they have on the eastern end of the beach? The ones that are ten feet tall? I couldn't follow the story."

"I saw them do it last week. But no, Susannah, I'm not familiar with the story either. It was something about 'Anna'—a queen of heaven, I think—rescued from the Kingdom of Death." Marinella leaned forward. "I like enormous puppets. They make you think about all the other fake things that are presented as enormous."

"I liked the rescue."

"Yes, so did the children. Big houseflies—so silly."

"Flies around death."

"Oh, of course! And the drums! Susannah, did you like the drums?"

"Yes!" We were leaning towards each other now, each eager to see the other's reaction.

"Great melodies, yes?" Marinella stretched. "That troupe is going to get in trouble yet. They made a comedy about housing that didn't go over well in San Lorenzo al Mare. So they are here, for now." The pace of conversation was quick now. "Susannah, what do you think, I mean, do you think men desire women, truly?"

"Some men desire themselves. They watch how the woman reacts and imagine what it would be like to make love to themselves."

"Ah!" Marinella sat up. "You've had a little more variety in your company than just a nurse."

"A little."

Around five o'clock, Marinella was waiting for me in the lobby. "*Bellissima*!" she pronounced, seeing my choice: a white dress printed with small black cat faces, and high-heeled black shoes.

"*Andiamo ... a fare una passeggiata*!" I said carefully.

"You are learning Italian so fast! Yes, let's do some laps, but put on these sunglasses."

"I asked the hotel maids how to say things. They call me *Signorina Come Si Dice*."

For the next two hours we joined everyone, every class of person, dressed in their finest, strolling, slowly, eating a gelato, slowly, moving along the beach promenade, slowly, walking up the wide steps, women pivoting the balls of their feet with each step, swinging the heel and the hip outwards until they launched themselves, slowly, into the plaza. And around again. Slowly. *La passeggiata.* When the guide lights began to appear on the ships in the harbour, we left for supper. So did all of San Remo. Some to their homes, the rest to the big restaurants.

"Who did you see looking at you?" Marinella demanded, over something with sardines and pesto.

"No one. Well, your friend, that Carlo, even though he was with the lady with the pretty bosom. And the buttoned-up Austrian with the daring green tie."

Marinella cocked an eyebrow and grinned. "DeFelice and Della Costa. Don't know the Austrian. Don't want to. Go on."

"The two radiant tall Swedes in naval uniforms. Those young Italians, four abreast, who each had to tie his shoe in sequence every time we passed."

Marinella laughed. "We Italians appreciate the obvious."

"Hiding in plain sight. Maybe some others."

"So, hardly no one."

"I wasn't sure what to do if one of them caught my eye."

"*Bella,* you smile and keep walking! Slowly!"

"Have you seen that fellow with red hair? Cavalliere?"

"Ohhhh, so. You like him!"

"No, just wondering..."

"You may like him! Why not? He's a widower, but you can see he's very supple, and he's rich from those silly leopard *pastiglie.*"

"Those are his? Those florettes? I've wondered how they make sure there is an even number of black and yellow in the box. And the box is charming! The leopard's paws reach over the top of the box where you open it. It looks like they are helping you to pull back the lid."

"They are better for you than those mint *pastiglie*. Lemon for a fresh palate, and licorice for the stomach. Digestive."

"Maybe it's you who likes him. You are defending his pastilles."

"Of course I like him. He's one of my dearest friends. He's out with his *primo*, his first cousin, on his boat. He will be back, don't worry. Tomorrow. He liked you."

"How do you know?"

"He asked about you, *cara ebrea*."

Dear Hebrew. I sat up very straight. There were some words I looked up in my dictionary ahead of hearing them.

Marinella opened her hands to the air. "Of course I knew you were Jewish. Every time I mentioned the word 'Jew' your face went blank. You don't look Jewish, but you act Jewish. It's not a problem here. We Italians are practical; we like people who can make things happen."

"You mean like how we Jews mysteriously manipulate events, like puppet masters?"

"If only you could. The old redhead would be here at your feet right now. His hair should have turned grey when he reached fifty last year, but redheads don't go grey until they are seventy. Never mind Cavalliere. I have another surprise for tonight, down in the eastern end of the harbour."

The working end. "Are you planning an insurrection?

Marinella looked at me.

"Don't worry, I don't think you're too smart to be Italian."

"So, you and I," she leaned back and grinned, her eyes dancing, "we both know how to hold back on what we notice until it is safe. I like that."

She would be good in a brothel, this Marinella.

She took my hand in hers for a moment, and then put it down gently. "So, yes, here it is. I don't want this world to be the same as it is." Her hand moved as if clearing the table. She lowered her voice. "I can't stand the fascisti, those stupid Arditi. I have a little money and nothing to do, so why not help people who struggle to change things?" She beckoned for the bill.

"But," I protested, "the struggle just sells newspapers. Revolutions make newspaper owners rich. Why not just find a gun?"

The waiter raised one eyebrow and brought us the bill on a plate.

We walked out into the warm night, feeling the breeze off the sea. "How much wine did you have, Susannah?" She smiled, but then she stopped and pushed me away a little. She leaned back, squinting. "You don't look like that madwoman who shot at Mussolini. Who are you going to shoot?"

"The powerful." I laughed, but I was astounded to realize that I meant every word. I stared ahead as we kept walking.

"Men and women?"

"I couldn't shoot a woman. The fascists make a cult of a hero, not a heroine."

"Yes, and they pretend liking Mussolini is the same as liking Italy."

We were two women in fine clothes and high heels moving along the promenade, intense in our conversation. I was beginning to speak with my arms, like a true Italian. "Why not simply find the powerful men when you have a gun in your hand and they don't? I don't believe in struggle, Marinella. I don't think it's noble or uplifting. It's just struggle."

"But that would mean you and I wouldn't have met on this lovely stretch of sunny sand."

"I am here to find someone to care for me. I cannot earn a living in any decent way. And you are here baring your body so you can be undercover for the anarchists, or the communists."

"The socialists, actually. And I don't bare very much."

"It's the quality of what's bared."

We grinned at each other.

"You are *una femminista*!"

"No, I told you. I am not interested in 'the struggle.' Struggle requires discipline. The feminists like disciplined people, too. At least, that's what I read. Meetings, passing motions—it's not for me. Screw discipline."

Now it was my turn to see if Marinella took offence at my language. We were nearing the working end of the harbour. Marinella took no notice, never mind offence.

"What is to be done, then? As…"

"I know, Tolstoy."

"He used to come to San Remo."

"I know."

Marinella raised both arms to the sky and looked up. She twisted her face into an expression of exaggerated anguish. "What is to be done, then, *Professoressa* Highstone?"

"Do nothing, *far niente*, and then kill them one by one with whatever comes to hand. Don't struggle. Throw a hammer into the factory machinery."

Our heels clicked in unison along the walkway.

"Well, I can see you have thrown off repression. Don't mention this hammer to the old redhead when he wants you to see his *pastiglie* factory."

"Marinella, I don't know what I think until you ask me and I hear my own response. And that is only what I think. What I have to do is different."

"Don't worry, I'm not turning you in, but there is something you must do with me. There is no moon tonight, and I want you to see something."

Marinella took my arm again, and we moved along the promenade, alternatively walking through pools of lamplight and then disappearing into tentative grey darkness, until the lamps were few, and then none, and we were absorbed into the soft grey night and its silence.

At the approach to the jetties of the eastern harbour, men in groups of four or five ran white painted boats out into deeper water, their rolled trousers getting wet. The waves sloshed, they jumped in, and two of them rowed. This happened five or six times, dappling the bay with barely distinguishable shapes and faint conversation.

"They are talking about women," murmured Marinella.

"How do you know? I can barely hear them."

"What else do men talk about?"

The boats disappeared from view in the dark, the stars too far away, and the moon asleep on the other side of the world. All we could hear was the sound of the oars.

"What are we looking at?"

"Shh. The fish have ears. The fish are waiting for the moon to rise, and then they will come to the surface in great moving silver balls to the surface."

"But," I whispered, "you said there is no moon tonight."

Just as she said this, a bright, full moon appeared, hovering by one of the boats out on the edge of the bay's horizon. It was a lantern, powerful, hanging on a sturdy pole over the boat's edge.

"Shh. Listen."

I heard nothing but the occasional oar creaking in its oarlock. Then a sound, somehow as close and intimate as from a pillow. "What is that groaning?"

"They're straining to pull in their nets. When they come back, their boats will be full of hundreds of small fish."

Another boat took its turn, and once again a bright moon hung just above the waves. The fish rose beside that small boat to bathe in moonlight and die in the nets.

~

40.

ON THE WAY TO TWIN OAKS, Archie was courteous, pointing out items of interest along the way, including Windsor Castle— and Ivor Novello, on his way to London.

Ivor Novello! Susannah's favourite actor, in sunglasses, tootling in the opposite direction in an open car. When we had seen him in that old movie at the Rotenturn kino, Susannah had forgiven me for thinking he was Italian. *What mistake do I need to be forgiven for now?*

"Often see him, Miss Highstone. He calls his place Red Roofs, if you can believe it." The light-hearted scorn in Archie's voice let me know that I was supposed to laugh, so I did, a fraction of a second too late. I must have also looked a little puzzled. Archie offered a clue. "Only a city person would come up with such a name. 'Twin Oaks,' 'The Meadows.' Those are proper names. From nature, you see."

I nodded, as if I did see. *But I'm a city person.* I had never been in the country in my life. "Please, do call me Hedy."

He looked over at me. "I think the man is Welsh, so that may explain it. They do speak the King's English rather well, the Welsh, I give them that." We drove along a ribbon of road, which wound up and over low rolling hills, away from London. Archie became more at ease, smiling over at me.

"All right, then?" He said this a few times.

We stopped by the Thames, and Archie opened an aqua blue Thermos bottle of steaming hot water, carefully placing the wide flat cork on the dashboard. "I wonder if I might trouble you to open the glove box."

I did. No trouble.

"Take out those two tin cups with the little metal straws. Tea's already in the *bombills*, those spoony things at the bottom of the straws. Did that last night. Drop the spoons in the cups. Steady." Archie poured the hot water into the two cups. "Stir a little." He plucked a small box of sugar cubes from the glove box.

I was enchanted. I held up two fingers, and he dropped two cubes into my cup. "What are these *bombills*, Mr. Stephens?"

"Got them in Argentina when I was with Lord Coleson. Please, call me Archie."

I thought of my gift from Argentina, the tango records. *George.*

"They drink something else in them, but I do like a cup of regular English tea. Let it cool, now."

We sat, sipping our tea, quiet, held companionably in that unchanging, unjudging, continuous present. Learning a language teaches you about time. The wind shifted the willows above us. The sunlight was dappled. Everything shimmered in the reflected light from the river.

"Father Thames," said Archie. Small skiffs appeared—two, three, five—each with scarlet flags. I opened my eyes at Archie enquiringly, unwilling to talk.

"Swan upping," explained Archie softly. "Some swans are counted for the king, and some are counted for the Dyers and Vintners."

"Why do they count them?"

"Well, at one point, the kings et them. Not now."

"So why do they count them?"

"They've always counted them."

By mid-afternoon we had arrived at Harold's country place, Twin Oaks, near Maidenhead. A long laneway, and there, two large oak trees in front of the house. It had begun to rain.

Archie put the car under cover and then shielded me with the umbrella so the only things wet from crossing the courtyard were my shoes. Once inside, they were placed on a wooden rack by a radiator, and I was given a pair of large woollen socks to wear across the slate floors.

I held onto Archie for balance as I put them on. This was the third, no, the fourth time in my life that I was touching a man who did not intend to sleep with me. My father. Moreno. *George.*

"Pauline!"

"I couldn't help but hear you arrive in that noisy French car. Here you are, Miss—lamb stew and some lemon squash." A fast-walking woman in a long apron flung a hand at a table where the stew steamed, and a pitcher sweated. She smiled as if she had told a joke.

I wondered what I was about to drink. George had told me that the English love their vegetables, but he had never mentioned that they drank squash.

When Archie saw the look on my face, he said, "Miss Highstone has lived mostly on the continent, and we are confusing her. Lemon squash is the nicest cold drink made from squashed lemons." I was astounded at how quickly he had read my face.

"That look, Miss! Oh, I can't wait to tell the mister!" Pauline went laughing back to the kitchen, happy. Archie and I ate unhurriedly, quietly. Stew, squashed lemons, and afterwards, brandy and a fire.

And apparently an afghan when I fell asleep. I moved it away when Archie said, "Miss Highstone. Miss Hedy. It's stopped raining. I've got some lady's brogues for you, and a treat, if you feel up to a walk. Keep those socks on." The brogues were a little big, so the socks were necessary. Archie pulled on his own boots.

Outside, a lively black dog waited. White legs, a ruff of white around the neck, and a white plume of a tail.

"What do you call it?"

"Ben." Archie looked directly at him and said, "Cast." The dog raced off, up and over the hill. "We're off to bring the sheep down for the night. You'll see something quite fine. I warn you, you might get the shoes all clarty."

I suspected "clarty" meant dirty, but I didn't care. It had been more than ten years since I last had dirty shoes, on that footpath by the Donaukanal.

We walked up a steep hill, the sky dramatic and close, the wind feathering the grass. Then, just as steeply, down the hill, digging our heels in to avoid falling on our faces, down to a small stream. The sheep turned towards us amiably, except for one that bounded up the other side of the small valley.

"By ta' me lad!"

Ben took off, low and fast, to the left, undulating black and white, until he was in front of the errant sheep. Archie whistled, then gave a single command: "Easy." Ben continued to move quickly, slinking low to the ground, never taking his gaze from the sheep, which stared back. "You see, Miss Hedy, a sheep has his eyes set in his head wide, so he can keep track of the others. It's the only protection sheep have, to move together."

I understood him perfectly. *What had Susannah and I been doing all those years, if not moving together for protection?*

"Way ta' me, lad!" Ben crept up to the lone sheep on an angle. The sheep stared, Ben made a small move, and the prodigal tucked in its round bottom and tail, trotting until it relaxed into a walking pace with the others.

"Here, use my stick." Archie ran to catch up. By the time I had made my way to join him, the sheep were penned in a large fenced pasture.

I was uneasy. This fellow was kind but obviously didn't want to undress me. He only looked directly in my face. I was going to have to learn to be among men like this. George had looked at me directly, but he was not calm like this. George was holding back.

Archie said he had to investigate a report that one of the

calves was having convulsions. "Lack of magnesium, more than likely." He said it had been a pleasant afternoon, and would say goodbye, and that I had been good company. "That is, you talk, but not too much." He grinned as he said that.

I was taken aback, but then I realized he was teasing me. I had heard others speak about this, those with older brothers. This was teasing—the thing a man who was your equal might do. Siblings have an innate understanding of democracy: *she's my mother, too.* He was teasing me! I was too taken with the surprise of this gift to respond. But from that moment on I would be ready. Oh, to look forward to doing something with a man who didn't intend to make use of you!

I was exhausted, not just from the exercise, but from having to speak so much. I was still running my English accent; it was mostly under control and obedient, like the dog Ben, but it was still new to me to be constantly speaking English.

Susannah and I had spent almost a year conversing in English. We had been disciplined. We had been making ourselves into something else, something other than what we were. Old Kreutzel had been delighted to send us Englishmen who were in turn delighted that they needn't shout to have their English understood. And while English is not so terribly different from German, we still murmured in German to each other in some small moments of life. *Bitte, die haarburste.*

I was also exhausted from trying not to act like a whore, from learning how to conduct myself outside of the brothel. I was used to following a man's inclination, and, without him knowing it, getting down to the business at hand relatively quickly. It was a matter of sequence and rhythm—undoing flies, removing collar stays. In this new life, I had to make sure I didn't look at men's trouser fronts, let alone calculate in my head how to get them undone. I had deliberately re-introduced that old gesture that Susannah had tried to correct: my hand beside my forehead, shading my gaze when out in public.

Harold seemed to think I feared meeting someone who had visited that house on Verstektstrasse. I did, but I told him, no, I merely needed sunglasses.

I went through the low doorway from the garden into the house, whose every window shone yellow in the country evening. When this house was built, I thought, the English must have all been my size. Short.

The next morning I looked over at Susannah, and experienced that daily moment of panic. *Where is she?* It had been two months, but in that moment when I woke and looked over to see my sister, I was whole, all of me engaged. And then I once again became someone who lived with missing someone. My mother and father, still too horrifying to think about for very long. George. I was willing to let myself moon about him, pretending to be the ingénue, looking into the mirror to see, in that moment when I thought about him, if I were attractive. But missing Susannah was like living with a disability, like those veterans at the train station. I was in the war. I had a sister.

~

41.

IT TOOK A FULL YEAR BEFORE Signore Cavalliere offered to take me up La Pigna. He had often been away, meeting his advertisers in Milan and wholesalers in Venice. Or Florence, or Rome. I had confessed to Marinella that I had some temporary financial concerns, some delays, and she had suggested that I stay in her apartment in the hotel. I didn't want her to know that my money had almost run out. I was surprised I had been able to make the wages of sin last as long as they had.

On impulse, I had sent a telegram to Hedy. And then wished I hadn't. Alfonso and I had gone to the telegraph counter in the hotel so he could send one himself. It had looked like fun.

I received a long, expensive telegram back, full of news, and even more, full of questions. I hardly needed the telegraph clerk knowing my business, even if he was as discreet and honourable as Alfonso said. I sent her another telegram asking her to stop.

Alfonso understood that I was estranged from my sister. He confessed to not being entirely fond of his late brother, and then changed the subject, asking me what I thought about politics, about music, about the little cat following us. We talked and listened, listened and talked. Everything seemed easier in Italian, not just because the language itself is very easy, but also because in that language, I was free from my old self.

We had gone out on his boat. He had kissed me, nothing more. He refused me no excursion, no sudden indulgence.

He knew all the little restaurants on this coast and how to get to them. We had even relaxed outside in the shade and read Deledda to each other.

But La Pigna. I could tell that even though he smiled when he invited me, La Pigna was different. He showed off his stamina as we climbed the steep winding streets, narrow and shadowed, narrow and sunlit. We walked under stucco arches that reached across the streets, their architectural gestures tense and delicate. Words my mother would have used rose within my thoughts. I wished she were walking with me. She was her best, most relaxed self when she was describing what she saw.

As we climbed, we heard fragments of conversation from the open windows high above us. We met two nuns in brown with white aprons and white conical hats walking in the opposite direction. As we walked steadily upwards, the nuns walked steadily downwards, until they paused abruptly on a corner and stood in silence, hands folded into their sleeves. I put my hand on Alfonso's sleeve. I wanted to watch. Within seconds, boys and girls arrived to stand behind an immobile nun, and then all moved off together. We could hear the chatter, and then the silent pause, more voices added, fading away as the children followed the nuns down the steep cobblestoned streets.

There were more windows in the tall narrow houses on the second and third floors than on the ground floors. At every walled corner we turned, Alfonso greeted someone, until finally we were at the top, looking at the sanctuary. The walkway leading up to the building had a serious, solemn feeling, with its heavy formal patterns and creeping thyme between the stones. Every footstep we took towards the sanctuary released a burst of scent, pungent and sweet. The building itself was very feminine, with little cupolas and turquoise-painted doors. I didn't want to go in. I might have learned a few Christian hymns, but I knew nothing about the protocols of going into a church. Alfonso was agreeable.

"Now, to go down," he announced. I wanted to rest on the stone bench in front of us, but he protested. "But you are young! You shouldn't be tired if I am not."

"I am not used to such climbs, and at such a pace. And it's pretty here, Alfonso—you can see the whole harbour."

"And when you are sailing and you see that top cupola, you know you are home in your own harbour. Your own harbour, Susannah—these are very sweet words. A sailor who prayed in a storm lived to build this." He nodded to a mother with two children crossing the small plaza in front of the sanctuary.

"Do you know everyone here?"

"Most. Do you want to go back down, Miss Highstone, without your feet touching the ground?"

"You are very fit, but even you couldn't carry me down the hill. And any wheeled transportation, Signore Cavalliere, would be dangerous."

"I promise not to carry you, in any way, ever. Come."

He led me to a doorway and knocked. After a few moments, an old woman opened the door, keeping her free hand on its edge. In the other hand, she held an apple and a paring knife with a very narrow blade. "Signore Cavalliere," she said and let us in, taking a fleeting look at me. I felt her glance. Had he brought others here?

I followed him up wide wooden stairs to an upper level where we walked through an aromatic room with storage bins, an old typewriter on a table, tied onions, stacks of grey paper in boxes, a baby cradle. Now through an arch and we were outside, above the street, walking along a small bridge, a walkway open to the sky, heading on an angle into another house.

We arrived at the next door and knocked twice. An adolescent with a new moustache opened it, saw Alfonso, and opened it wider. As we moved into the house, I sensed his gaze on my back.

We walked through a bedroom, nodded to an old man who was regarding himself intently in a mirror; then we passed through a sitting room, down three steps, and out onto another outdoor walkway which sloped downward, with ancient metal gutters for rain. The next door was held open by a fellow holding a baby goat. "This is Eduardo," he said, grinning at me.

Alfonso said something I didn't understand. It was Italian, but dialect. I was only able to catch *la donna*, which must have meant me. He patted the boy's arm, and I patted the goat. It nibbled at the young man's knuckles.

We headed through a kitchen. We passed a toddler wearing a cloth harness, the other end of which was attached to the leg of a sink. Alfonso nodded formally in her direction, and the child raised an eyebrow. In the next room, under a high ceiling, strings of laundry moved in the cross breeze created by open windows on either side of the room. Wooden shutters were folded back against the hard plaster walls. When Alfonso opened the door to the next walkway, the breeze picked up, making the hanging sheets applaud. The applause stopped when we closed the door behind us.

We stepped carefully over rainwater pots to the next walkway, the next house, the next walkway, and so on, until we were down the hill. And then, just like that, we were out into the shaded street entrance to La Pigna. It had been less that twenty minutes. I was speechless. He embraced me—a big, long, whirling hug—and then he bowed.

"As in matters of the heart, so it is in San Remo: it is sometimes easier to flee inside than outside. We of San Remo are the masters—oh, oh, Miss Inglese, and *the mistresses*—there, a smile, *brava*. We of San Remo are the *experts*—ah, now you are happy—at keeping ourselves hidden from invaders."

"This is what Marinella meant. The secret inside the secret."

Alfonso smiled. "Marinella knows secrets and keeps them. You will find I do, too. Only the very best person will be trusted. Tested, and trusted. Let's have something to eat at your hotel so that you can excuse yourself for your afternoon nap."

Alfonso took me out for long days on the Mediterranean, and later to the Italian Alps for a week of skiing. He skied, and I learned to, not well, but enough to escape over snow if I ever had to. We still did not sleep together. I had never liked sex anyway. Alfonso had let me know he was interested in sleeping with me, but he never pressed.

One day by the harbour, he asked me about romance. I could hardly draw upon my affair with Billy—that was more horseplay than *amour*. I thought about my sister with George, how she had been in love. That gave me the smile I needed to say that I'd once loved happily, shared a bed. I fell silent, letting my eyes look to the horizon. We were on his boat, rocking at anchor in the Mediterranean.

I shrugged. "The war," I said, looking at the sea, not at Alfonso. I stretched. I made my voice soft. "He's gone." Both things were true, and who could blame Alfonso if he thought one had caused the other? So many young men had been killed. Some of them had had the use of my body before they died. Alfonso could see I was upset, though he didn't know the real reason, and changed the subject.

Being a former whore was like being a whore. I didn't have to believe anything anyone said, and I didn't feel required to tell the truth either. I told lies composed of fragments of the truth, stories with exits. Hedy used to laugh at how I made sure I knew where the exits were in cinemas and cafés.

He told me that his wife had been a kind, pretty girl, very young, who had died suddenly. A high temperature, a bad headache for two days, and then she was gone. Their families had pushed them to marry, and the idea of being married, having their own house, was more enticing than knowing the other person, knowing what to demand from life. He shook his head. "I was too young to even grieve properly."

I told him I understood, and to my own surprise, asked him to dance, right there on the promenade. Although he stood in that formal Italian way, when he danced, he flowed. It made me calm, to dance with him. I wasn't calculating the effect of what I did. It was like riding a bicycle—you were only clumsy if you were too careful and went too slowly.

~

42.

WHEN HAROLD STAYED WITH ME, it was always a shock to see those composed features of his on the pillow. He was like a sleeping stone knight, his sword between his legs, his hands folded neatly on his chest, his toes pointing upwards. I basked in the safety of Harold's apartment, or his country house, and in the safety of him, himself. When he was away, I had trouble sleeping. In the middle of the night, half-asleep, need overcoming pride, I would move pillows and blankets, trying to imitate the way Susannah's arm used to be flung across me. On those nights when he stayed with me, both Harold and I slept soundly, as if a painting had been straightened on a wall or a cart righted that had tipped over. Like the restoration of a monarchy, if one were going to rule one's life.

In the frank light of a Berkshire morning, I often remembered Harold's instructions before he had left that first time. *How was I like my mother?* I had her dark hair and her full bosom, but not her height. I sat down on the fence stile and looked at my feet. The dew had soaked my shoes a darker brown. My stockings were wet too. *My mother always sat like this, with one foot tucked under the other. Her thumb tucked into her fist. Esther.* She was bold and withholding, I thought. She liked to do things herself, not delegate. The house always quiet, like a stage set ready for rehearsal, unless Papa was playing with us. Then it was a romp, a busker circus.

Ben bounded over the pasture towards me. Archie followed. "I think Ben wants to herd you back to the house." He gave me a hand to get up, and the three of us walked through a field to the house. Archie pulled an upper stem of grass to chew on, and I imitated him.

"Oh, it's sweet!"

"Timothy grass is sweet. Country knowledge." Archie tapped his forehead.

"I'd like some country knowledge. I wish I knew how to train a dog the way you do."

I was back in London, and I wanted to gaze at the Assyrians. I ventured out, a little afraid to be on my own, and bought some good walking shoes. I wanted to walk from Brook Street to the British Museum, and to be there when it opened. I was sure I wouldn't run into any of my former callers, not there, not at that time.

The Assyrians were stone friezes—mostly flat, but not quite. They bulged out of the wall a little, very stylized, but also very physical. A parade of men guided huge bulls with proportionately huge ballasts between their legs. The men were shown sideways, both feet taking an identical stride. Each man's arm held the same position. The men who held the massive heads of the bulls, however, had different arms. Their upper arms bulged with the strain of holding the bulls' heads, and their hands were fists holding the ropes. The arms of the men who followed—who carried shepherd's crooks—were smooth, perfect, indistinguishable. Men are marked by their work, by what they are good at.

The friezes were meant to awe, and they did, not only because of their immense size, but because of how true they were to the curve of a bullock's chine or the angle of a human arm. Even the amalgam beast-humans who flew, wore wigs, and had tails ready to lash were believable. If it's physical, I thought, it's real.

My father was a very physical fellow. He loved how quickly I could do back flips. *Is this how I am like my father?* He was the one who introduced all the new things to the house, like the telephone. I remember seeing a man in a bosun's chair right outside our third floor window stringing the wire. *How I wish I could talk on the telephone to Papa now. Or to someone who knows me.*

One late and windy London afternoon, in Hyde Park, over in the north corner, a big man wearing a cap and roomy trousers was pacing back and forth. The cap made him look like a navvy, but his manner was Olympian. He stretched out his arms. He took string from his pocket and tied it to a penknife, which he thrust into the earth by the fence. Then he walked the string out about twenty feet. A dog sat, watching him. It was a border collie, different markings and coat compared to Ben, but with the same intense look. The man was nearly beside me. I stood quite still so that I could continue to watch.

He stood, belly out, hands on his hips. He caught me looking at him, just as I was noticing his mouth. A lovely, fleshy mouth. He kept looking at me as he walked to the right and performed the same dance with the string, coming closer until once again he was beside me. He smiled. Gaps in his teeth, like those images of the sun, like Kaspar's grin. Surely that young thief would have survived the war.

The fellow was talking to me. "…And if you were interested in modelling, I have a studio."

"You have an American accent!" I was astounded.

"Pure Brooklyn, though I am English by commitment."

"Why England?" I surprised myself. I was talking to this fellow as if I knew him.

"They have the most exquisite manners, like virgins hoping to be wooed."

"So your own commitment doesn't extend past imitating their manners?"

He laughed. "Excuse me, art is no virgin. I have a studio, and excuse me again, you would make a wonderful subject. Your posture is, I would say, Sumerian."

"Do you mean like the Ishtar in the British Museum?"

"Yes!" he rocked back on his feet, beaming. "I *was* thinking of the Ishtar."

"I shall look at her more closely." *George said I looked Sumerian.*

"Are you an artist yourself?"

"No." Now it was my turn to be pleased. "But my mother collected art. What were you doing in that corner, committing yourself to British soldiering?"

"I served in the 38th Royal Fusiliers, Madam. I am a veteran of the British Army."

"My respects. Or condolences."

"The latter. When the War Office refused me as a war artist and called me up for regular duty, I had a breakdown. Complete. They found me wandering on the moors."

"And now you wander in the park?"

"Under the protection of the Commissioner. And my dog, Frisky. I know, please don't laugh. It's a terrible name, but it's the only one he'll answer to." He stopped and whistled, and the dog trotted over and sat beside him, ready, the way border collies are always ready. "When I'm out in public, I don't call him, I just whistle, so people like you don't laugh at me. Or worse, at him."

"Oh, I'm sorry. He's a fine dog." I reached out and patted the dog, who accepted my touch as his due. "What *are* you doing, then?"

"I'm making sure the site proportions for my work are correct."

I looked at him.

"Madam, I'm a sculptor. Jacob Epstein. A naturalized citizen. A veteran. The War Office, however, I will tell you, as a co-religionist..."

My face must have revealed how startled I was. I had no intention of revealing who I was. Or what.

"Sorry. England is not entirely perfect. They are nearly always polite when they express their distaste for Jews. I won't mention. But you look like my Aunt Ruth. Only much, much better. Here's my card. The studio is not far from here."

I tucked the card into my pocket, locked my knees, and extended my hand, loosening my arm at the last moment so he would shake my hand rather than kiss it. He could do with a little startling, himself. But it would apparently take more than that. Epstein shook my hand, once, twice.

"Good morning, Mr. Epstein."

He looked at me. "You are not easily frightened."

I worried all the way home: could I become an art collector? I would have to talk to people who liked art, and I didn't have my mother's gift for the clever nudging of a conversation in the right direction. Susannah had been right, I was not a good negotiator. And the sculptor fellow was right too. I did look Jewish, and while that meant, I knew, that I had to make more effort in seeking the approval of others, I didn't want to make the effort and I didn't care to have the approval.

Could I become a sculptor? When I was little, I used to model dogs out of *roma plastilina* so their paws hung over windowsills. Susannah made projectiles to throw out the windows onto passersby. But sculpture? No. I would not want to be judged on what I cared about: *how it looked.*

That year, when I visited the Elgin Marbles or the Roman statues, I often had Epstein's company. We were like slow dancers—moving, then still, then moving. The Ballets Russes had nothing on us. We both moved around to see from different angles; in my case, how, from the rise of the neck, the whole head emerged—if the statue had not been decapitated. Sometimes when I left, I felt as if I were being watched, followed by their blind and hollow gaze, as though I were leaving behind human beings I knew, who knew me.

In those long pauses we shared, Epstein usually sketched. I believed he liked my silent company, and his made me feel at ease. I had begun to bring my own drawing paper and pencils, and I had discovered that I could draw the heads and the necks rather well. I didn't stop there. I couldn't help it. Apollo looked wonderful in a cloche, but not in a fedora.

One fine spring day when I was about to leave, the sculptor flipped the stiff cover on his drawing pad closed and grinned at me like a satyr. "You know," he said, pointing to a head without a body, "I have one like this at home, in my hallway. Greek, from Turkey, if that makes sense. My wife decorates it with bands of myrtle. Don't ask. I pretend the dog ate it. Every time, I toss it out. The myrtle, not the dog. There's nothing like a dog for smooth social relations, Miss..."

I didn't reply. But I smiled. Like artists everywhere, he wore lovely clothes—supple wool shirts, beautifully cut wool trousers. No hat. *Some men shouldn't wear hats, and he's one.* Fine hand-sewn shoes.

"What I like to do, you see, is to fill those two concave eye sockets in the head with water, and in the evening, light candles. The face is alive, I'm telling you, Miss..."

"Hedy Highstone." Nothing like many weeks with the Elgin Marbles to make a girl lose her caution.

Almost immediately, he suppressed a laugh and looked at me skeptically. He could hardly keep a straight face as he took off his cap and said, "Miss Highstone. Allow me to introduce myself again: Jacob Epstone."

I couldn't help it—I burst out laughing. It was true, I hadn't met anyone with my last name, nor had I found it anywhere in any English directory. He laughed with me. A couple of Jews, neither of us English, laughing out loud in the British Museum.

We were asked to be quiet or kindly leave by a museum guard who, like the rest of the museum security staff, had fought in the war, and was not going to stand for anything as un-English as laughing in front of the Elgin Marbles. Nakedness in stony bodies was not funny, not at all.

Once we were outside, Epstein said, "There is going to be an unveiling next week of a piece I made to honour the fellow who wrote *Green Mansions*. About a bird woman."

"Oh, Rima! Such a sad, compelling story."

"Hudson deserves to be honoured, yes. A great book. He was born in Argentina, did you know? Do come. I'd like your opinion."

I promised I would. *Argentina and its gifts to me. Bombills and tango. George.*

It was in all the papers, a scandal. It was also beautiful. The girl's head bent back, so it looked as though she were falling (and so her head didn't stick out over the top of the flat stone.) Her breasts faced in slightly opposite directions, and the nipples stood up. Without a doubt, any mammal who gazed at the sculpture secretly longed to touch those small swelling breasts. Her lower torso was elongated like a medieval Madonna, awkward and vulnerable. And around her, birds, predators, also caught in the stone. *Oddly pretty.* Something my sister, who used to be known as Susannah, had called me on our way from Moreno's one afternoon. The best conversations, said Harold, happen outside. My best conversations were with people who were lost to me.

A telegram at the front desk, the paper very elaborate in style, from Italy, from San Remo.

ALL IS WELL STOP

It was from Susannah. Not "Mitzi." I sent a return telegram, long and expensive, full of eager questions and offers of help. I received another telegram:

ALL IS WELL STOP STOP STOP

So I did. I didn't feel like talking about it. I looked at it sometimes. It never said anything but its simple rebuke, masked in a joke. I felt like I was walking around with a sword stuck into my upper body. I held myself stiffly, against the pain. My walk lost its sway, which had always been an odd sort of comfort to me. With Epstein, however, I could talk about art. He presumed sorrow to be normal, and didn't comment on my evident physical distress.

But I couldn't talk to Harold. I couldn't. He finally had his own doctor look at me. I didn't talk to him either, except to answer his questions. I ate, I slept, I smiled with my mouth when I waggled my gloved hands at Harold. He finally told me the sex was still wonderful, but he felt terrible that he was unable to make me happy. He said I acted as if my heart were broken.

"It hurts to talk," I said.

"I can't make her talk to you, Hedy, but I can tell you she is safe. She is seen regularly in San Remo, walking on the promenade, and she has been seen in the company of some very respectable people. She'll be in touch again."

He had news and hadn't told me? I plied him with questions: when was she seen, who saw her, can I talk to who saw her, was she steady on her feet, what was she wearing?

Eventually, Harold handed me two pages of single-spaced typed notes on onionskin from whomever he had hired. There were some misspellings, Susannah without the *h* on the end, which threw me. Did this fellow know what he was doing? But it was her. It was my sister. I carried the two pages with me everywhere, and read them in the British Museum whenever I went for a cup of tea. Their tea was as strong as coffee, and almost as good. Almost. And good coffee was not available in the few neighbourhoods I was familiar with. Maybe it wasn't available in London at all, any more than the sound of a sister's voice, or the clumsy racket when she stumbled over her shoes. I wished Susannah would call me. I wished George wanted me. No one wanted me. Not even Harold. He was charming, always courteous, and so well organized, so able to put things in categories. If I were to disappear, he would have minded. But his heart would not have been broken. If I had liked alcohol, I would have joined Harold in drinking until I was more drunk than he had ever been.

He returned in August as usual, and we went directly to Twin Oaks. He was his kind and tolerant self. He moved Ben from his spot on the day bed and sat down beside me. "I like how you speak Scots to the dog and English to me."

"Harold. Do you know what I would like to do?"

"Does it have anything to do with gloves?"

"Tangentially." I smiled up at him. "I would like to make hats. I will have to find a small place—on one of the side streets off Oxford, I think—and see if I can hire some girls to help me. What do you think?"

"Go into trade? My hostess? Well, why not? It's the twenties, and *nice girls do*. Or so they say. And a Scottish Jew should be able to handle the money." He winked at me. "Time for a drink."

It was always time for a drink with him. Harold meant well. His insults were always intended as compliments. I had come to realize that businessmen like Harold were always acting in plays, for very small audiences, for very small runs. They were always improvising their lines, and they had individual ideas about how the plays should end. Some of the stimulus went beyond balance sheets. They were actors, and the bigger the bankroll, the bigger the dramatic role.

Harold liked his work and his whiskey. And sex with me, as long as there were lovely gloves. My background meant that he felt he didn't have to hide anything from me. I was fond of him, and he was sure he had won me.

George had made no effort to win me. Some of what he did seemed shadowy. The ease with which he secured the perfect fake passports, not to mention that old story about the rare stamp funding his arrival in Vienna was, in retrospect, more than a little suspect. But with me, and with my sister, he seemed frank and open, not trying to be anything but himself. He didn't have wealth; he didn't have a family name. We were disreputable, deniable, and used to people practising the effectiveness of their lies on us before they presented them to the world. But it seemed to me that George was, in anything that mattered, transparently honest. He cared that what he said revealed what he thought was true. All he wanted was someone to publish what he wrote. And pay him.

My efforts to win George had been rudimentary. I was too shy to approach him physically. Me, a whore. I had no idea how to make someone love me. I had only been, always, paid for. But when George danced with me, he was with me, moment to moment. In England, he was my default thought, always in my mind. Like a ghost, like a phantom limb. Harold's soldier friend Lorne had said the doctors told him the pain he felt in a non-existent arm was simply a matter of nerve buds struggling to grow. Lorne talked about bumping the elbow of an arm he no longer had. And how it hurt.

Am I in George's thoughts? When he is alone, if he were to say his thoughts aloud, would he be saying my name? Would it hurt?

~

43.

BIG WHITE TABLECLOTHS FLOATED, suspended in the air for moment before they settled on the tables. Alfonso had directed that all the chairs were to be carried outside, and two of Marinella's fellows were posted on the perimeter of the terrace to wave smoldering torches, their smoke keeping at bay the little insects who liked to arrive at parties fashionably late.

By evening, a crescent moon hung over the bay below, and we could see, in the hills above us, the glowing yellow windows of La Pigna. We had already eaten and filled our glasses with local wine, and we had already laughed. Alfonso stood up.

I whispered to Marinella, "He could give classes on standing." I sounded like my sister when she used to talk about George. She appreciated what was physical. Moreno was so intuitive when he presented her with her own hand and called it "the mind."

I missed her.

I could hear Alfonso going on about his beloved San Remo, the pleasure of friends. And then he proposed. In front of the guests, who were already happy with the long sunny day outside, the *porchetta*, the wine.

I didn't hesitate. I was shocked, but I knew how to play this. I stood and kissed him. "*Sicuro*," I said, with my best Italian shrug. Laughter and applause.

"And now," he put his arm around me, claiming me, "it's an engagement party!"

Marinella beckoned with her cigarette behind her head. Three young musicians, in open-necked shirts and black vests, and one grizzled old fellow in a battered fedora stepped forward and started to play guitars and sing "Torna a Surriento," full force, full heart, from the beginning to the end. I was used to hearing songs with big finishes, but this, according to Marinella, was the Neapolitan style—big beginnings, big middles, and big finishes. "Everything from Napoli is big, you know. Or so the men say."

They sang several others in the same fashion. But when they played the opening chords of "Santa Lucia," the same passion was there, but gentler. We all sang. Even me. *Soft over the water, moon's argent crescent.* I looked up at the crescent moon in the dark sky. *Time,* we sang, *laughs with pleasure.* I belonged, and that made me uneasy.

~

44.

M Y FATHER WOULD HAVE BEEN PROUD. There they were, Cambridge old boys and captains of industry trying to pluck coins from each other's ears. Thanks to my mother, I also knew exactly who should sit where, and the sequence of forks, spoons, and service. Thanks to Cambridge customs, I wasn't worried that some Englishman I had entertained with my sister would show up for dinner. Harold had persuaded a Cambridge official that he needed copies of the graduating years' photographs. He claimed that so many of them applied to work for him that he needed the photos to keep them all straight.

I pored over each year's rows of small oval portraits. While there were many specialty brothels in Vienna, it seemed that none of Harold's friends had patronized 13, Verstektstrasse except one fellow who had the good manners to die in Australia, and Nigel who had decided to race cars in America. I was free to plan the evening.

Harold's friends were delighted when he informed them that I had agreed to act as his hostess. We all pretended that was all I was, someone to preside over the dinner table and be gracious to guests. Others among them had relationships that were similar, and I never put a word, or a foot, wrong. "You're a treasure," one murmured as he departed. "Harold's a lucky man."

Other than the splendid apartment in Claridge's, my treasures were few: my mother's topaz ring, now on an 18K red-gold chain around my neck. That striped scarf. Susannah's letter on the Francis Hotel stationary and her two telegrams. And hidden in an old small suitcase, the hat that had been jammed on my head that last night in Vienna, My life was full of comfort, and I was restless.

I found myself buying several papers, not just *The Times*, hoping to read the by-line "George Andrew." Political reporting juxtaposed a kind of flatness of description with an urgency of sequence. I wondered what it would have been like to talk to Susannah about the affairs of the world. I might have understood my own sister better. Or, maybe, the Balkans.

Threats of a general strike meant second and third editions of newspapers sold out, and the street news hawkers were hoarse with delight. George's favourite monarch, his namesake, apparently disapproved of what was proposed by the government for the miners and said, "Try living on their wages before you judge them." George had fine instincts about goodness when it existed in powerful people. He would have disapproved of Harold, I think. And maybe of the apartment he had given me.

But he didn't want me, and Harold did. I wondered what it would be like to be part of a couple that was equal in their desire for each other. That would be a democracy whose politics I would be interested in.

The politics of the shouting crowds on the street were easy to understand, and there was something thrilling about their shared physical energy—thrilling and frightening, especially when you suddenly heard shouting and singing from above you, from fanatics in the top section of the open air buses.

Adjustments had to be made, The police began to wear long white sleeves over their uniforms in order to be seen more clearly as they tried to control traffic, and I realized I could arrive faster if I walked back from the museum to Claridge's by a circuitous route: Tottenham Court Road, Goodge Street, and along Mortimer until I got closer to Brook Street and could turn down.

That route brought me past several art galleries. On my way home, I stopped in to look at paintings. All the Van Gogh's in London were yellow, flowers or houses. Only people who don't get enough of the sun could love it so much. To love what you miss: England was perfect for me.

Long after the general strike was over, this detour remained my route. Sometimes I saw artists, young men, and some women walking along Goodge Street with telltale paint on their shoes. I adjusted my pace so I could listen as they discussed Gauguin, the London Group, who was getting commissions right from the Slade's teaching studios.

Following these conversations, literally, reminded me of the talk around my mother's table—the intensity, the need to find a way to say what they saw. Harold encouraged me to go to galleries, to buy what I liked, as long as he could first see the painting in the company of its fellows hanging on the wall. He said he wanted to understand the context that it had sprung from. He avoided openings attended by the near or new aristocrats, saying that he didn't much care for their company.

I suspected that this was to protect me from saucy enquiries, or the possible embarrassment of being recognized by former callers. The dealers and their young employees were cautious in the conversations I initiated, and I fantasized about having a friend like Fraulein Lowin with whom I could compare frank notes on the paintings. I felt like I was on an ice floe. Or the ice floe itself. Funny to think that, and to think that Harold's business was shipping.

On my way back to Claridge's one chilly Tuesday, I stole a dog. Earlier in the day, I had seen it as I walked past it, and it was still there, tied up, outside the pub in the evening. In the morning, it was alert, ready. By nightfall, it was still alert, but shivering. When I walked over to it, it whimpered and licked my hand.

I had never been in an English pub, not even with Harold. The bartender came over to me and raised his eyebrows in enquiry. "Is the owner of the dog on the premises, sir?"

"Dog, Ma'am?" said the bartender. He called to the two lone dart players. "Did he leave Mist again?"

"Hugh were in a hurry. Ran out back door," said the taller one. He looked at me, threw his dart. And then confided to the bartender, "Said filf were after him."

I wasn't sure I had heard correctly. "Who was after him?"

The dart player turned away.

"Sorry, Ma'am," said the bartender. "He means the police. She's a good dog, good at warning barks. So Hugh says."

The other dart player, not fat, but wide as a door, threw his dart and smiled at the first fellow. "Lady Luck is with me today, son."

I turned back to the bartender. "I'm taking her. Mist. She's been tied there since this morning. It won't do. If this Hugh wishes to claim her, he can contact me at my address." I tapped my card on the smooth counter. I wanted that dog. The bartender took the card and looked at it.

I didn't hear what else he might have said. I was back out on the street, untying the dog. When I said, "Come, lass," the collie, all business, was perfectly content to trot along beside me.

When we arrived at the hotel, the doorman gave us a quick look and then held the door for us. "Miss Highstone."

"George." Every other Englishman is named George.

A small dog was nothing at Claridge's Hotel. The manager nodded in approval. "Your companion matches the black-and-white tile of the lobby."

I took a chance and tried a shepherd's call. "Way fra me, lass!" Mist bounded up the curving staircase and waited for me on the mezzanine, her head tilted to one side. I leaned back over the balustrade and waved at the lift operator. In response, he shook his head, only a little, just enough to acknowledge, not enough to comment, and waved one gloved hand.

Mist and I found a storefront to let. The little place was painted that greyish turquoise-green preferred by every English man and woman for fences, boxes, and frames. I rang the telephone number on the sign, and negotiated the terms. Harold pretended to be light-hearted about it all, but set me up with a good bookkeeper and plied me with questions—good questions, not as amusing as he pretended, which helped me move forward steadily to the opening.

"Why, my jewel, do hat stores have full length mirrors?"

"Proportion. You have to see the whole body. Since women's hips are universally wider than the shoulders above them, my mother's generation wore wide-brimmed hats. They let women have the delicacy, the vulnerability of the seemingly un-upholstered shoulder."

"But hats are so small now. Have hips changed?"

"How they are imagined has."

"Will we see your creations in photographs of the Ascot?"

"No. I am not interested in confectionary headwear, nor the flimsiness of a market limited to one day."

"Why do we bother with a hat, we gentlefolk?"

"A good hat is something you can walk out under. It defines your space. The way curtains on a stage do for an actor."

He was quiet then, and raised his glass to me.

In the north end of the city, I bought oak mannequin hat forms made from limewood, and then hatpins from the supplier next door. The next day, Mist and I looked at the window of the shop with a shared attentiveness. Hats need to be displayed. Most millinery windows displayed hats on hat blocks or stands. Some had mannequin heads, but those looked to me like they belonged in museums dedicated to the pagan English head: noses like bricks.

I rang Jacob Epstein, who was enthusiastic when I told him that I needed some sculpted heads. When I told him what I wanted them for, he said that if I thought he would do anything so ridiculous, I had better think again. I was insulted that he was insulted. I said I simply wanted to know where to buy good clay, so that I could make the heads myself.

He invited me to come by his studio, which was some distance away. It was not quite walkable, and I was leery of the underground. I took a taxi. And the dog. When we ducked in under the canvas hanging in the entrance to the studio, Epstein made more of a fuss over Mist than he did over me. His dog approached, tail wagging, and then the two dogs chased each other around, running up and down the sturdy ramps that Epstein used to work on his huge sculptures until we both said "Stay." Our dogs lay down then, panting, eyes darting over to each other and to their respective human beings.

Epstein showed me how to slam the clay so that there were no air bubbles. After a few tries, the effort to throw the clay down on the table meant I had to take off my jacket. This clay was heavier than the *roma plastilina* I had played with as a girl. I plucked a knife from the choice of carving tools he proffered from his big hand, leaned over the damp clay, and made an S. Then I peeled and sliced curls and ribbons of clay until I had formed the beginning of a snake. "Portrait of a Madam," I said.

Epstein had been watching, breathing through his nose like a bull. I paused and stood back to see what I had done, to see what I needed to do. In two movements, Epstein squashed what I had done, picked it up, and slammed it on the counter, again, again, until he was satisfied. He pointed to the tools, knives, a small flexible paddle, pieces of burlap.

"My head," he said. He sat down on a box.

I went to a sink and washed my hands with soap. He looked at me, disapproving. I ran water over my hands and wiped them on a towel. I rubbed them together to warm them, as I did in the brothel before touching a caller. Then I rested my hands lightly on Epstein's big crown, dropping them to feel the bones, the cock of the nose, the tilt of the upper lip. I placed my hands on either side of his lips and let them fall back over his cheeks to his ears. I placed my hands flat on his nape, twice. I rocked my hand over his chin.

At first, Epstein's eyes, his big wide eyes, opened, shocked at my boldness, but he stayed as still as the twenty-foot-tall statue half-carved behind him. I pressed two fingers of each hand, index and middle, together and laid them over his closed eyelids.

I turned to the clay on the counter. I grabbed the clay with both hands, pressed it, and shoved it, staying within what my hands remembered when I had touched his face. He sat on the box, watching. How long was it? An hour, an hour and a half? I stood back several times, and then finally sat on the box with him, exhausted, drying splatters of small clay bits all over my blouse, my hair, my shoes. I felt sated.

Epstein laid his head on his arm on the counter and looked at his head in clay. The surface was too smooth, he said; it would never catch the light and be alive. His nose was surely much smaller, but the mouth was right. The eyes. I had scooped them out, hollows. It was him, and it wasn't. He pulled open a shallow drawer on the side of the counter, a terrible screeching sound. A candle. A quick dash of water in each eye socket. He struck a match on a block of stone by extending his hand back without looking. He lit the candle and turned out the overhead lights.

He sat back on the box with me, and we sat there, Hedy and two Jacobs, two of us looking at the one with the flickering eyes. After a while, the spell was broken and I stood up. I went to blow out the candle, but he held his hand up to stop me.

"Let him be alive here for a while yet."

I brushed the dried clay from my hair, my blouse, from Susannah's striped scarf. I don't know why I had taken to wearing it, but I found a way to, as often as I could.

Jacob grabbed a huge breadbox-sized hunk of fresh clay and slung it onto the work counter. He tore off a length of butcher's paper from a roll, and slopped a large muslin rag through a bucket of slurried water. He wrapped the clay in the rag, packaged it in the paper, and tied it with some coarse string. He wanted me to go. "Come back for more if you need to. *Zol zayn mit mazl!*"

"Thanks. I'll need it." I couldn't lift the package off the counter.

No one batted an eye when the doorman staggered in after me with the parcel. I bought two lengths of oilcloth and used one to cover the dining table in the apartment. Two of the hotel porters lifted the table onto the other oilcloth, which I had spread on the floor. One of the maids who liked me lent me a hotel smock and a bucket. I tied up my hair, poured water into the bucket, and began to slam chunks of clay on the table, adding to the heap as it got soft. Eventually I began to model the head. It looked like Susannah. Then I made another head, which also looked like Susannah. The next one looked a little androgynous, which was advantageous, given the inclination of fashion. Then a wet and muddy George smiled sweetly at me until he dried to a pale grey. And one of Harold, who looked even more noble in clay than in real life.

I found a supplier of boiled felted wool in one of the east end markets. Another for ribbon, another for feathers. I experimented at home, steaming the felt in the bathroom so that I could shape the fabric around the wooden forms. To get a custom fit, I would have to find a way to pad the forms. My skin became dewy, and my hair renewed its inclination to curl.

Harold walked in and embraced me. Then he looked around. He was quiet for a moment. "It's a good thing that you are here at Claridge's instead of at the Dorchester." He told me to let him know when I would be able to close up the atelier, and left for his home on Wilton Crescent.

The next day when Harold came in, all was restored: hydrangeas tumbled from a low vase on the dining room table and the bathroom was airy. After a lovely meal downstairs in the hotel dining room, and upon our return to the apartment, I kept my gloves on. However, the clay heads lined up on the bureau in the bedroom caused Harold to complain about the element of voyeurism I was introducing into our sex life.

The following morning, Harold suggested that when starting a new project, it was smart to hire someone with experience. "I look at my competition, and I try to gather information. Then I steal their best man who is not yet their best man, the one on the way up."

The not-yet-best-man making hats would be someone not yet in the Mayfair shops. I went to Selfridges, bought their two best hats, and then asked to compliment the buyer. The buyer wasn't in, but the floor manager admired my own hat, and I was able to charm her into giving me the address of the supplier.

I hired a cab immediately to take me to the north end, where an ambitious woman took my interest to be that of a potential investor. I watched twelve young women at work, bent over, needles flying in and out— pleats, tucks, feathers. Some were working with stiff buckram, and others with shaped felt. A young fair-haired girl in a red smock brought in a stack of hats. "From the shaping room," said the owner, Lucille. I asked to see the shaping room.

The next day the same young woman was bent over hats on the crude assembly line. "One of my most versatile workers," said Lucille. *Not for long,* I thought.

The girls burst out into the free air for lunch. The blonde, still in her work apron, lit a cigarette when I rolled down the window of the hired car and asked her if she would come to work for me, for double the wages she was getting now.

Our Daise, her mother called her. The girl brought her mother up from Birmingham for the interview. After the first day on the job, my new assistant asked to be called "Kay," and said she had signed up for elocution lessons. Kay was quick, pretty, and hard-nosed. She could have run a brothel, but all I had was a hat shop. I decided to call my shop "Hats, From Esther" and had the storefront painted dark grey with black lettering, not so different from the front of that *Die Zeit* telegraph office, where I had once ruined my life. And that of my sister.

45.

HAROLD WAS AWAY AGAIN. I skimmed *The Times*, which the hall maid brought ironed and refolded, or *The Evening Standard* from the hotel lobby. I wanted to surprise him upon his return with an intelligent comment on the shipping news from a fellow entrepreneur. Our lives were going well together. Or so I told myself.

An article in *The Evening Standard* about the missing French airmen, Nungesser and Coli, changed my reading habits. The news of their disappearance had been reported elsewhere, but here it had appeared with the byline "George Andrew." Any dateline Paris became what I read, in any newspaper at all. From street vendors, I picked up the *Daily Chronicle*, which Harold winced at, so I thumbed through it in cafés when he was in town. Doing that reminded me of Vienna, but the coffee soon ensured I had no difficulty remembering where I was.

For the last four years, I had thought about George every day on the way to my shop. Not the one who might on occasion be in London, but the one in my memory, intently seeking my response when he talked, and listening intently as I had taught him to, as a whore must learn to do—paying attention to the phrases that are repeated, keeping silent until the speaker reveals more information than they intended.

As I walked, I thought about the fun George and I had mocking social customs, the gossip about political figures. His fantasizing about desserts—none of them Viennese pastries, but apple or rhubarb pies and something called Junket. He could be bought for a good bread pudding, he had said.

In the last five minutes before I arrived at the shop, I always thought about dancing with him. When I entered the shop I would be beaming, and then I would stop thinking about him for another day. Clients and shop assistants commented on my morning cheeriness.

On the way back from work, I thought about my sister. I often found myself losing my rhythm, and once I caught my foot in a small upward rising piece of concrete when I crossed sunny Goodge Street. I had been thinking about her so purely that an "*Oh, schiesse*" escaped my mouth. When I knew I couldn't prevent myself from falling, I surrendered and did my best not to break anything. I bruised both knees. After that, Mist became solicitous and herded me a little when it was time to cross that street.

Another article with George Andrew's byline. This time about a riot in Vienna, close to where I once lived, minutes away on a bicycle. A crowd of thousands had stormed the Palace of Justice and set it on fire when the murderers of two Social Democrats were set free. George waited for the opening of the next paragraph to say the two Social Democrats were an eight-year-old boy and a veteran of the war.

The story was shocking. The police had fired into the crowd, killing almost one hundred, sending six hundred to hospital. Five police officers were killed. The old Justizpalast broken into, furniture smashed and files set on fire. But it was George's last paragraph that had me transfixed. The fire burned for over a day because the crowd had cut the hoses of the firemen.

I remembered riding my bicycle over one of those hoses. They were thick and tough. That detail forced you to understand that crowd. Not wild. Deliberate and determined. It was July, and no doubt the Donaukanal was stinking, but who would have guessed the city of the beautiful lie would be inhabited by people capable of that kind of anger? And why was George back in Vienna?

I was reading several papers every day like my Susannah used to, looking for his name. In *The Guardian*, his name was attached to something more than reportage. A featured opinion. I read it and felt a surge of humiliation. I had forgotten what he had done, once, and here in the paper, he was doing it again. I rolled up the newspaper as if I could somehow use it as weapon to strike him.

Years ago, in Vienna, when a session at Moreno's had suddenly been cancelled, Susannah had gone to the bank while George took me to a café, Bruckers. Perhaps as there was only one Edelstein whore with him that day, he felt he could afford to pay for the coffee. We had plucked the same newspapers from the rack in the café so that we could easily share what caught our eye. He pointed to a photo of a miserable Ramsay MacDonald in a crowd, wearing a top hat. "He looks like he needs someone's arms around him."

I was moved by what I thought of as his kindness. Here was a man capable of tenderness, I thought, a man who trusts me enough to reveal a softness, an almost parental empathy for someone stuck in a role. As we hurried through his neighbourhood to meet Susannah, two friends of his approached, one with his wife. I knew I looked pretty in my new spring clothes, my pink hat, my high heels.

He introduced me as Miss Highstone. My first outing as her. They asked him if he were going down to watch the parade of diplomats and he said no. Then he mentioned that the last time he had seen MacDonald, he looked like he needed someone to give him a hug, if they were so inclined.

They laughed. Were they delighted with the idea of that stiff fellow being embraced, or did they understand he was making a little theatre of words and insight, and were being polite? I was shocked to hear him repeat himself. I had believed, only moments before, that he had been talking to me, to my mind, to engage a response from me.

MacDonald's plight hadn't touched him, or not very much. Humour requires aloofness. His joke required distance enough to see the humour in anyone attempting to hug that severe fellow. How many of our conversations had been trial runs for what he intended to write? His real audience was a grand, imagined one. What he said was a performance.

The Guardian opinion piece had begun, "On this recent day of failed diplomacy, MacDonald looked as though he needed to be folded into the safe protection of someone's arms." A repeat performance.

He had embraced me once in the controlled intimacy of Moreno's studio when I was barely aware of my own presence, having just returned to myself from being Mischlinger, from being assaulted. I was in the midst of the fresh discovery that it had been my own cry waking me so many nights, not Susannah's. Was that why I wanted him so? Because I had felt his arms about me when I was raw? And his arms had been around me during a tango lesson when there had been a kiss—it had meant something, before we both quickly denied its having any meaning. All that looking into my eyes. To assess the appeal of what he was saying?

Only an unwanted, abandoned, and ruined young woman could have imagined that he had genuinely wanted her, I thought. A foolish whore. People think that whores are worldly. How could they be? They are isolated from the world, naïve about many things. I had wanted him to want me. I had wanted him, and instead he'd given me his prized Paris fedora, just before he left, down the stairs, out the door, and gone.

The dog came over and stood beside me. She leaned her head on my knee and looked up. I was still clutching my rolled up *Guardian*, my weapon. The only person I had ever struck was Susannah. How could I have done that? No wonder no one wanted me.

I dug into the wardrobe in the guest bedroom. We rarely had guests, but it was good to have the extra room if Harold had a cold and I needed to sleep. That old small leather suitcase was intact still, at the back, hidden in its flannel bag under a never-used camping quilt.

Inside the bag, his hat. I pressed my nose into it, and allowed myself to imagine George's arms around me. I closed my eyes, my head tipped back. "La Cumparsita." The little parade of sorrows. The *picado* of the tango, the kick as you turn.

I pitched the hat to the dog. She was not playful, but willing to play fetch if I asked, if it made me happy. I threw the newspaper in the dustbin. I would tell the upstairs hall maid in the morning not bother with newspapers while Lord Coleson was away. I could turn on the radio if I needed to not be the last person to know the world was ending. I patted the bed, and Mist jumped up, placing a paw on my arm. The upstairs hall maid came in. I apologized for the dog's happy bark, and she responded, "A dog in the bed or a gun to the head, Ma'am."

In 1928, I had a ring, a dog, and a box with Susannah's letter and her two telegrams. An old hat and an apartment in Claridge's Hotel. A striped scarf. My shop. Harold. But I had been abandoned by the two people I truly loved. This thought was so unbearable that I sheltered two hopes that didn't bear close scrutiny: that George might have loved me and might love me again, and that Susannah might return.

~

46.

M Y CREAM-COLOURED WEDDING DRESS was a marvel
of simplicity. The woman wearing the dress was a little
more complex. Susannah, the Bride. I was not sure I had the
courage to let myself love Alfonso. *Maybe if you play a role
long enough, it becomes true.* The advantage was mine. Or
so I thought. What would it be like to give up that advantage,
to be honest?

Hedy came to my wedding. Alfonso said he was inviting
all of his family, even the ones he didn't like, and if my sister
and I were estranged, it was time to reconcile. I didn't want
to talk on the telephone. I wrote a letter instead. I said that I
was happy, and I hoped that she was happy too. I asked her if
she thought she and her companion might attend the wedding.
I kept it formal until the end. Then I wrote that I missed her.
Then I crossed that out and started again. Finally, I kept it
formal, but signed it "Horsie." She replied with a telegram, a
letter, a telephone call. Another telephone call. I was surprised:
she made no suggestions, no bossy pronouncements.

She stayed with Harold in the Hotel Royale San Remo,
where they hosted the rehearsal supper. They gave us beautiful
English bicycles, cream-coloured Stanleys, custom ordered
with beige canvas panniers piped in the same brown leather
as the handle grips and seats. She prompted Alfonso to look
in the panniers.

There was a bottle of the best whiskey in one pannier, and

inside the other, a dog, a small Italian greyhound. "Oh, how handsome! A *piccolo levriero italiano*! My favourite dog!" Alfonso was delighted. "And the dog likes the same whiskey I do. He'll share, I'm sure!"

"Now, you, Susannah!" Hedy's voice was excited.

I held up the whiskey I pulled from one of the panniers. And from the other pannier, I held up another little greyhound. It kissed me, and then everyone else did.

Hedy still wore Mama's ring on the gold chain around her neck. For the ceremony, she wore a grey silk dress from Worth. "Worth every franc," Harold joked happily. We embraced warmly, but we had both been whores and knew how to fake warmth.

I was glad to see that her lovely swaying walk had returned. Any man would want Hedy to leave him, as long as she returned and he could watch her leave again. Her complexion was alive, lovely; British weather was good for something.

Even though Mussolini had been making noises about the Church being officially required in every aspect of life in Italy, we chose a civil ceremony and held it at the Casino Municipale. The required and signed documents still added to my legitimacy. Alfonso had a remnant family in Siena, and a pair of ancient unmarried uncles and aunts, siblings, two of each, came to the small wedding. The *primo*, the cousin who was Alfonso's business partner, was the best man. He was cool to me, but then he was cool to everyone who wasn't a part of the production of pastilles. Alfonso was the human part of the business. He was the reason their business was successful, or so everyone said. Business in the summer of 1929 was good. The wedding was quiet, pleasant, and thanks to Marinella's contacts, well executed.

My husband had no children, no siblings, and the pastille business would become his cousin's when he died. Alfonso told me not to worry, that he had Swiss bank accounts. I led him to believe that I was unable to have children. I was already a former whore as a daughter. I didn't want to be a former whore as a mother.

I told Alfonso that I wanted to manage my finances, to be enterprising. His reaction surprised me: he found ambition endearing. His wedding present to me was a small carnation farm. That and, surrounded by yellow diamonds, what I had requested: a dark topaz ring.

With Hedy's help, I had a hundred English rosebushes imported for my gift to him. It was necessary in San Remo to keep up the fiction of English roots. And, in sly memory of our childhood, I planted a dozen seven-year-old copper beech trees for a hedge. It reminded me of the one close to our old home on the Schottenring, but I kept that fact to myself. Horticulture was the key industry in San Remo, and I intended to take my place among the wealthy flower growers of Liguria.

This suits me just fine, I told myself.

Before the wedding, Harold went to see the harbour with Alfonso. Marinella was very discreet, and made herself a feature of the background, a character with no scenes in this part of the play. In the hotel bedroom, I sat with my sister as we had long ago—one in the armchair, one on the bed. We could have talked in the suite's drawing room, but this was where we found ourselves, without thinking. We talked lightly, without any real emotion, about our homes, our servants. We praised our respective partners, and chatted about what we read of the world in newspapers. After an hour, silence.

"Your carnation business is going well?

"Yes, I will pack some properly for you to take home. Your hats are popular. I saw one of your hats here in San Remo last week. I should get one from you."

Hedy leapt up. She called the front desk and demanded a measuring tape. She took a pair of manicure scissors from the dresser, lifted her skirt, and, just like that, cut off her slip at the waist. She retrieved some straight pins from her suitcase. "I'm so happy to do this, Susannah." She smiled, all of her hope and hurt in those dark eyes. But I was not going to apologize for abandoning her. I needed my own life, and now I had it, in San Remo, in that holiday city.

A discreet knock on the door, and before I knew it, my head was in her hands, being measured. She pinned strips of cloth to each other in a rapid sequence on my head until it was covered, and then numbered the strips with a pen. She said that the light that reflected off the sea was too harsh, and closed the shutters. She was trying not to cry, and that suited me just fine. She measured the strips and made a note on hotel stationery. "There! All the latitudes and longitudes. Now, Susannah, sign this."

"Why?"

"All my clients do." *How cheerful she can make herself!* "No one ever gets a From Esther hat that doesn't fit perfectly."

After I signed, she turned away from me to fold the paper very carefully, tears welling up. I felt sorry for her, and angry, too. *I had to leave her. I had to find out what my own life could be.*

She hugged me, and I consciously made my body limp, relaxed. She put the cloth pattern pieces in her purse. I put my arms around her, on impulse. "Let me be nice to you, Hairbrush. Ask me for something."

"I never ask for what I want. And if I do," she shrugged, "I don't get it anyway." Hedy looked out the window. "All this sun."

"It does rain here. In the winter. But we have our greenhouses, and we sometimes go to Tripoli on Alfonso's boat."

"I see your photo sometimes in the fashion magazines. You decided against the name Mitzi after all."

"Our secret."

"We have a few."

"George is writing for the English papers."

"And Billy is writing for the kino people in Berlin."

"Writers. You'd think we'd have fallen for artists."

That was as close as we came to mentioning our shared past in a Vienna brothel.

"I saw the Lempicka show in Milan—she's taken Jugendstil and made it erotic."

"Art Deco with sex, yes. You wouldn't believe the trouble my friend Epstein got into for putting nipples on a sculpture. Someone in the House of Lords suggested ivy as a solution to the offence to English eyes." How lightly talk about art lets you slide over the past.

After the wedding, we spent time on each other's yachts. Both men pretended that they were skiffs, little and inconsequential. "Messing about in boats," Hedy said.

Harold beamed at her and called her "Ratty." The English talk in code, affectionate and precious, and impregnable. We hugged and kissed. We shook hands, and promised each other soon, soon, soon. But it wouldn't be soon at all.

~

47.

BACK IN LONDON, I couldn't focus. I asked Pauline to run the store for me. Many visits to Twin Oaks had made us allies, and she still delighted in a story about my alarm at having to drink squash. She proved to be as brilliantly intimidating as was needed with our clientele. Little Kay and Pauline: Birmingham and Berkshire. Kay was capable of running everything herself, but there needed to be someone to take my role, that of a boss to be deferred to, and Pauline was willing. I stayed home and read, and everything I read made me think of what I had lost: my home, my parents, my sister, my life. George.

Harold asked if I would like to go with him down to the gold coast and back on his latest freighter, but I felt too off-kilter to be someplace where I couldn't hide. I designed hats, but didn't go to the shop during business hours. I read and, when Harold wasn't there, I let myself cry. I felt like a child, and it frightened me. Mist padded over, her tail wagging. Her gaze never left me.

The weather changed, a cool and lovely April. Pauline insisted that she needed to get back to the farm. I returned to the shop and resumed cradling heads in my hands. I worked with Kay, whose elocution lessons had paid off: the Brummie never appeared. I marvelled at this control to Harold.

"Well, she would have that, wouldn't she? In the trenches, one

soon realized the strength of the men one had. The self-control
of the British working class."

Kay did all the hand steaming of the felted material on the
limewood hat forms, which were padded to the precise measurements of the client's head. Hats "From Esther" were always
a perfect fit, so they never flew off. I found I could make them
with brims astonishing enough for Ascot after all, or brimless
and feckless as the wearer wished to be. My clients found it
amusing to say they got their hats "from From."

In the shop window, as if rising out of the waves, a pale grey
clay head leaned on a pale grey hand. Two pale grey hands
were raised behind another clay head as if putting the hat on,
like the Greek winner of the race tying on his victory garland.
I had made good use of my time in the British Museum. The
arms and hands had been taken from mannequins and had
been painted the same pale grey as the dried clay heads. The
heads themselves were a rather feminine George and what I
remembered of my mother, Esther. Harold had grown to like
the head of clay I had made of him, and he always put his hat
on it when he entered the apartment.

One morning, as I was working my way through my order
list, I arrived at the Ss and opened the paper with Susannah's
measurements and signature. She had been kind but adamant
about not coming to England. Her signature was long: "Signora Horsie Mitzi Susannah Cavalliere Highstone Edelstein."
I thought about the hat I had made for my mother, with its
green stems bobbing. I wrote to Susannah and asked if a pale
grey hat with fine gold-wired ribbon would work for spring.
Whenever I put a stamp on an envelope, I thought of that first
British stamp I had seen, the one with George V and the lion
roaring at the sunrise. *George*, I said, without making a sound.

Susannah wrote back "Of course!" Her letter arrived inside
a waxed paper envelope, which she had stuck on top of a box
filled with carnations from San Remo, ready to bloom. "The
only thing I am able to make," she said, "is the occasional

friend. I can't make things like you can."

Harold was the closest I had to a friend, and we were mostly very careful with each other's feelings, and about our pasts, especially my past. Archie was a good fellow, anticipating what I might like, always with some teasing compliment, but he maintained a necessary, practical distance. I had no friends of my own. Pauline was completely loyal, but did not like to speculate about others. My thoughts would have shocked her. Kay would not have been shocked, but she might well have been disappointed. She needed this occupation to feel like she had moved up a rung on the ladder. A woman needs a woman to talk to. Or a sister.

Why do people do what they do? My mind released this arrow constantly. As for the answers it sped to, George was the only one I had ever met who was equally interested. I had devoured everything he wrote for a while, everything that I could find, like someone with a dietary deficiency. I remained very alert when I went out. I made every effort to avoid running into him, and every effort to look as wonderful as possible if I did.

~

48.

OUR HOME WAS HALFWAY UP the steep hills of San Remo. Alfonso liked to see the ships coming in with Arabic gum; the best, *kordofan*, was shipped from Port Sudan. We often watched as the crews unloaded baskets of fresh lemons from the groves in Eritrea. Licorice roots from Calabria arrived under our windows in carts headed for the factory. Alfonso's cousin was meticulous about maintenance and repair, and Alfonso, for his part, was always looking for new clients, for places to advertise. He was happy in his life; he was a vigorous lover, an attentive man who loved to be outdoors—swimming, skiing, sailing. In the back garden there was a square swimming pool installed for me, an anniversary present. He preferred the sea.

He didn't bicycle. "Not after what happened to Bottecchia. He got his start here, in San Remo, and they killed him. And then they told such a stupid lie about his death. They can't be bothered to make up a good lie, even about our champion." So our wedding presents were dusted, oiled, greased, and not used by either of us. I should have been happy. He loved me, openly. That might have been the problem.

On our honeymoon in Rome, we had stood in front of Caravaggio's *Maddalena Penitente* and the *Conversione della Maddalena* for a long time. Alfonso said it was the same prostitute in each one, Anna Bianchini. He said that Caravaggio was sympathetic to the street people he fell in with. I commented only on the clothing and on the lack of footwear in any of his paintings. I was thinking about Moreno, though, and about how no one cares what happens to young girls. We are hidden, except in art, and those who depict us get in trouble.

I don't know why I was morose when we returned to San Remo. My little carnation farm staggered through a cold winter. I learned how to talk about manure, about straw, irrigation, shipping methods. But the business managers of the carnation estate, two sisters, knew what they were doing and didn't need me. What Alfonso called my *nuvola nera*, my black cloud, returned, and made me so bleak that when he suddenly lost an account to a French rival, I told him dismissively that he'd had a good run with that client. He was offended. He deserved that client; he had been good to that client. That client was dishonourable.

I said, "Sometimes you have to let people go." I understood this very well.

"I want you to be honest when you talk to me, but a little warmth or sympathy is not deception, Susannah."

Finally, when he was about to go on a trip to ports shipping lemons that he had to make, he said, and "only once a year," I argued with him over the dogs, Romulus and Remus. I said they should stay with me.

"But I like taking them; they are so quick and pretty. Obedient. I like to show them off."

I shrugged and looked out the window. The shrug was in Italian.

"I'm careful with them, Susannah. I will always use the leashes."

"They will smell bad when they come back. Where they sleep on the boat is disgusting. They will come back smelling like they have been to a dog brothel." I was shocked at what I had said.

He was also shocked. "Where is my Susannah?"

"Would you have me on a leash?"

He turned away. I said I needed a holiday from my life, a little one, a week, ten days. He said this was a good idea, as that was the time he would be away. With the dogs. He kissed me very formally, and said, "They'll have more fun with me on the boat than in a strange place with you."

I kissed him just as formally, and he left, walking down the hill towards the west end of the harbour where the yachts anchored. He never turned around, even though he must have heard my footsteps following him as I tramped down the hill after him, along the promenade. Into the Hotel Royale San Remo. I asked for and got the same room I stayed in when I first arrived in San Remo. Then I called Marinella. I told her everything. It took three days.

49.

MARINELLA HAD HER SECRETS, too. When she was sixteen, her parents had sent her to relatives in Rio de Janeiro. They adopted the boy she gave birth to.

"Do you wish you had him here, with you?"

"No. Where he is, he is loved, and he *belongs*. No one questions who he is. A real *Carioca*. Truthfully, he is a little abstract to me. I can't imagine being a mother. I can't imagine being a wife, unless I want to spur myself to anger. I like my life, how it's turned out."

"The father?"

She shook her head. So we talked about everything else: Freud, the fad for tanning, motion pictures, and most of all, sex. What if an orgasm was not the release of tension? What if, instead, it was the creation of a presence, a heightening? Release suggested that the process was not pleasurable, which, Marinella assured me, it was. I had not experienced an orgasm, though I knew how to fake one impeccably. Marinella urged me to trust Alfonso, to let go, to surrender. His first wife had adored making love with him, everyone knew that.

"I'm afraid."

"Of what? Of being compared to her? She was a little mouse, not really suited to him. A family arrangement, when they were both too young. He was good to her. But you, you *have* him. What are you afraid of?"

"Of liking it."

"Liking an orgasm? Without a doubt, you will."

"And of wanting the person who could deliver it."

"Mmm ... you know, in truth, we deliver our own orgasms, really. And besides! You like being married! Alfonso loves you. Everything you have told me, you could tell him. In fact, after my problem, he was the one who encouraged me to be myself, to find what I liked. It turned out that I liked politics and arguing with men."

"But you have sex with them."

"Oh, yes. I'm not very gentle with them, but I like it."

We sat, Marinella in the chair, me on the bed. "If I tell Alfonso, Marinella, I will be the ruined daughter of Esther and Oskar. A victim. He thinks I've had one affair. *One.*"

Marinella climbed up to sit beside me. She talked to the ceiling. "As a girl you expect that as a grown up, you will be an older, taller version of yourself. That there will be a continuity. But if someone seduces you—or worse—you lose whatever your natural future might have been. It is gone. Taken from you."

Silence. The ceiling fan. The soft waves collapsing on the beach. I was not sure if I was talking to her, or to myself. "Even as a child, I hated doing what I was supposed to do."

"But that got you out of the brothel."

"It also got me in."

"You can't blame yourself. You were kidnapped—you said so. And like me, raped."

I leapt up. I did not want to hear what she said. "I don't blame myself, Marinella. I simply don't want to be a victim. Victims are repellent."

She followed me to the open doors of the balcony and hugged me. From the safety of her arms, I looked over her shoulder and talked to the view, the sea and its clear horizon. To the sky. "Even though I was only thirteen, as soon as you say 'rape,' a curtain of doubt falls. Everyone has an opinion." I pulled back and looked Marinella in the face. "Let me try one of your cigarettes."

She lit a cigarette for me. I wanted to gesture with it more than I wanted to smoke it.

"Marinella, if you were to say 'he terrorized me painfully, in my most tender regions,' then anyone would assume the man is a sadist."

"You argue like a lawyer."

"Oh, I would have liked to have been a lawyer!" I borrowed the silver lighter from Marinella and lit my cigarette again.

"It wasn't your fault." Marinella paced about the room. "Sex that is coerced—by fear, by force, even by seduction—it isn't really sex. Here, have my handkerchief."

But my tears were not going to fall. Not if I could help it. "No matter what else I ever do, there will always be that 'but.' 'A lawyer, *but* she used to be a whore. Or, an art historian, *but*. How can I tell Alfonso about this?"

We were both exhausted. Quiet. Marinella began to talk without looking at me, as if she had come some long distance and was making a report. "It was my cousin who hurt me. I watched his face. He looked satisfied when I said it hurt."

"The madam screened callers who were inclined that way. She steered them to Katerina, from Martinique. She could fake agony instead of orgasm."

Marinella pressed her hands to her midriff. "Ah, that makes my stomach hurt."

"We can stop."

"No. Tell me about Katerina."

"The madam was one of the first to take photographs and use them as currency for protection from the law. She never sold them. 'That will get the brothel closed down,' she said. 'The photographs stay in the house. They are leverage.' She thought I was her protégé. She thought I would run the house and take care of her in her old age."

"So no one saw them?"

"She let men see the positives of themselves with Katerina."

"Oh. So, to look at themselves."

"Yes! You understand! When they looked at the photographs, they stared at themselves."

"Let's sit outside. There's room for our chairs on the balcony."

We dragged the white wicker-backed chairs out into the sunshine. For a while we sat, our eyes closed, the sun on our faces. It was *agrodolce*, bittersweet, this time, *far niente*, to do nothing. Marinella went back into the room to get her cigarettes, and an ashtray.

"How many women stayed with her, the madam?"

"About twelve. It was well managed, discreet, and expensive. She made sure that we were properly fed, and had the best medical attention. The place was clean, the linens impeccable."

"It sounds like a spa."

"Except for holding onto our identity papers, our documents, and the threat of violence. And we were at work, not on holiday."

"Spas always have lots of whores. Hotels will hold onto your passport for you—they say it's for safety, but it's really so you don't skip out on your bill. But I haven't seen any violence."

"No one wants to be beaten up. For a whore, it means no business until the bruises go away. If it is only bruises. Every now and then, the madam would choose badly, and the new whore would be rebellious. She would become cooperative or be dumped in the Spittelberg."

"A river?"

"A rough neighbourhood, flooded with criminals."

Silence.

The afternoon offshore breeze began, lifting the curtains. Marinella walked around the room, picking up and putting down the newspaper, picking at the leftovers on the plates from lunch. She arranged herself on the chaise longue. "I had a little baby boy, Susannah, and I gave him away. They gave me something to stop my milk, but it doesn't stop right away. When my aunts were out of the room, I grabbed him from his cradle and held his mouth to my breast. I was a little crazy, too, for a few minutes, maybe longer. I was so afraid of them seeing me do it. I knew I couldn't keep him. I knew we were parting. I knew there was a loving couple aching to love him. I knew I wasn't supposed to nurse him. He suckled. I wanted him to know from the beginning that what he needed would be there for him." Marinella stared. "A week later, I was on an ocean liner."

"To Italy."

"No, to London, the London School of Economics." She shrugged. "With gorgeous clothes. And bigger breasts—well, of course they aren't now, that was years ago. Stop looking! I had excellent marks in school, and my father knew the Czarina. I know, that shouldn't be a qualification, but it helped!"

"The bigger breasts, did they help?"

"*Zitta!* Shut up! They helped me learn English." Marinella's naughty smile. She yawned.

"Now you have made me yawn. Come here. Lie down beside me, Marinella, I'm tired and I need someone to lie beside me."

"I can't stand to sleep with someone beside me. I'll stay until you fall asleep."

The next morning, I was in the bed by myself, and Marinella was on the chaise longue. Over breakfast, she said that the shock of her cousin's attack had never gone away. After it happened, she felt she had disappeared. "That's why I like mirrors." Marinella stood up and looked at herself. "It's not because I'm vain. I'm Italian. I know I look good. I look in the mirror to see that I'm still there."

I peeled an orange, and said, between mouthfuls, "We whores—don't wince, that's what I was—we whores struggle to get through each day. We pluck, we shave, we curl, we wax—anything that means you have to pay attention to what you are doing and not what you are thinking. Why don't you smoke inside?"

"Wipe your chin. It's disgusting to smoke inside. On the

beach, on balconies, why not? But it makes everything smell if you smoke inside."

"So you understand why I didn't want the dogs to come back smelling! They get up on our bed; they like to nestle in our arms."

"Mmm. I understand why you were concerned about the smell, but why did you fight about it? You, *mia cara ebrea,* have been on edge ever since your sister went back to London. And whenever you get a letter from her, you snap at me. At me! And at poor Alfonso. There are things you don't know about him."

"You mean the Swiss bank accounts? I do know. See this ring? The numbers are engraved on the inside. I know he's not enthusiastic about Mussolini, and I know he gives money to your socialist friends."

"You are so sure it is about money."

"Like a whore, you mean. Or a Jew. And you can't blame Hedy for my—whatever this is—this sorrow."

"No, no, and I'm not blaming her. I like her! Look, your Alfonso helped me. You have no idea how we walked up and down La Pigna, talking. I could have sprinted for Italy in the Olympics. I had calves of steel. He listened and talked. He didn't judge me. He didn't try to take advantage of me. I thought that was what he wanted and sort of offered myself, and he told me how beautiful I was, and how he was not the right man for me. He said that the right man would come, and that he would stand by me and be my friend. And he has."

"The right man has come?" Susannah asked, now curious.

"You met him that first day. On the beach. Bare feet and a boater."

"Oh, that fellow! I see you arguing with him, but that's what you do with most men. He's attractive. Sincere. I can see how you could like him. Why he would like you."

"It's more than 'like.' I have to see him. He has to see me. But I cannot live with anyone. I need to have my own bed."

"But you could have that. Many people who are married have their own beds, their own bedrooms."

"I could plan a beautiful wedding, but I don't want one. As long as we do not marry, we can fight. And I like to be able to fight!"

"We aren't going to say his name."

"No."

"I never told Hedy everything. When we were doing those sessions with Moreno, I saw how she had suffered,"

"Oh, the therapy fellow. The Viennese should spend more time on beaches and less time..."

"No, he really helped. Hedy especially. As for me, I wasn't ready, and then he moved his work to the outskirts of the city. I think he's gone to New York now."

"New York is the new Vienna. Here's lunch." A small cart, a tip at the door. Something with sardines and pesto. Some mineral water.

"I realized that Hedy had suffered, but I still didn't want my life to belong to my sister."

"This is about *now*, you and Alfonso. In some ways, you are both ruthless when you have to be. Let me tell you what he did. Half a lifetime ago. When I came back to San Remo, I had to see that cousin every weekend, at family suppers. He would stare at me and smirk. It made me sick. Alfonso made a plan. So Italian."

She cut another portion from the platter. "Do you want another piece? You are like me—I eat like a pig and stay skinny. So. First, Alfonso hired him, at a great salary. He was actually paying him some of his own salary. My cousin bought a car, a boat. He was always going to Rome and coming back, boasting of his conquests. After nine months, Alfonso promoted him to supervisor, only the job was in Eritrea, in the lemon orchards.

"And he went?"

"Of course. It's not that far. And the money would go farther there. The company villa there is free. It has a pool. It's only a few days away, really. Alfonso knew my cousin would not behave himself there. Eritreans are smart and inventive. Quick. It wasn't long before my cousin insulted a young woman. Then my uncle got a telegram. My cousin had had an accident. The young supervisor had been on a ladder with a scythe for trimming lemon branches. My uncle flew in a doctor. Imagine the cost. He stayed there."

"The doctor."

"No, my cousin. He didn't come back, not until my uncle's funeral, a year later. Limping and with part of his nose gone. I laughed. Right in the room with my uncle's corpse. It is very helpful to have a history, however false, of a mental breakdown at sixteen. That was the story my family told when I went to Rio. People make allowances afterward. My 'breakdown' worked like your use of morphine. I hope he dies there. He's marked—everyone in that community knows him."

"But that means he will sleep with whores."

"No, he will have no inclination. Another part of him was damaged in the accident." Marinella stood up and went to the window. "He's become religious."

"I used to think that all Italians were religious. My family always acknowledged being Jewish. They never converted like some others, but they weren't observant. Just the holidays, and not always those. My mother was innovative: she used to have Purim parties, full of costumes and villains. I have to tell you, from the time I was ten, I loved everything Italian."

"Are you going to continue to keep up the story of being English?"

"One raised on the continent. Why not? I will never go back to Vienna. It's a city repulsive to me. It would corrupt my mind with thoughts of revenge, and it would waste my time. I would have to think about him, Mischlinger. I want my thoughts to fly freely, not have revenge as a home my thoughts fly to."

"Like those pigeons that always go back to the same place.

Don't think about him, then—you're right. Tell me, how did you get off the morphine?"

"I made myself take a little less, a little less."

"And how did you know when to leave?"

"I was always good with numbers, so I invested. The Paris bourse was much better than the Vienna bourse where my father worked when he was alive. And when I was ready in my body, and Hedy was ready in mind, we left."

"And you say you don't like discipline."

"Not anymore. I know I must have a different culture to belong to. One that doesn't make demands on me."

"You don't want demands made on you? What if Alfonso needed to make demands on you?"

"But he won't. Not for a long time, I hope. In the meantime, little by little, I can become someone who is strong enough to handle demands. San Remo is perfect."

Marinella looked at me without saying anything, and then, as if she had made a decision, said, "I agree. *Con tutto il mio cuore*. With all my heart. And now, it's time to get ready for the *passeggiata*. It's almost five o'clock."

We walked arm in arm for the full two hours, smiling at everyone. Then we ate, something with sardines and pesto. Wine, this time. We sat on the beach while a crescent moon rose, and Miranella smoked an entire pack of cigarettes. In the morning, I went back to my house and waited for my husband.

50.

I TOLD ALFONSO. He sat with his head in his hands, crying. Then he took me to bed, and sometime later, we made love. This time, I felt myself disappear into pleasure—no ego, nothing, just a drop in body temperature and then, waves of pleasure, over and over. "I'm new," I whispered into my husband's ear.

On some winter days in San Remo, it can be quite chilly. Someone took a photo of me walking along the promenade in a leopard skin coat. When it was published in the society section of the San Remo paper, Alfonso said he loved the boldness in my step.

"Look," he slapped the paper, "how relaxed the float of the arm!"

He bought the photograph and used it to advertise *Leopard Baci*. Leopard Kisses, it said at the top of the advertisement, floating over my head. *Leopard Pastiglie* was in a very small font at the bottom, under my boots.

~

51.

HAROLD ALWAYS SAID that he survived the war because he had a sense of what was coming up behind him, or what was soon to be in front of him. It was why he still held the record for the fastest time running the Sutherland maze. It was why he survived when a shell hit his platoon near Reims. He carried a piece of red stained glass, in his pocket, always. Handkerchief, pocket knife, piece of the Reims cathedral: ready to go.

Those intuitions came from minute but unacknowledged observations. A necessary alertness occurs when a person knows he is peculiar in matters sexual. He had access to the same information as everyone else, but his instincts meant that he spent the early part of 1929 discreetly selling much of what he owned.

"I'll miss the enormous fun of working with the Scots. Yes, Hedy, *fun*. They know how to build ships better than anyone on earth." He had made good guesses, he said, on draughts for ships in the shallow Suez, had avoided passenger trade, and had stuck strictly to cargo.

His relationship with me was accepted by his closest associates and by his old friends. But my origins were mysterious, and Harold did what he could do shut down any gossip before it began. That meant a scrupulous avoidance of newspaper articles or photographs. He invited others, like the woman he referred to in private as "Lady Berserkshire, " to sponsor his ships, despite the fact that her family owned a rival business. It made him look sporting, most of all, and provided a layer of sly amusement as, he said, Lady Beserkshire was wildly enthusiastic about smashing many things, not just champagne bottles, and everyone knew it. She was an awkward young woman, who fluttered her skirts in artless displays of flirtation in front of the photographers at the ship launch. When she slipped on her eyeglasses, I suddenly thought of Brigita, who left the brothel after the war to become, she said, the newest whore in old Romania. With luck, the most successful one, too.

When we joined Harold for dinner, he apologized for exploiting the young woman. "You," he said, "are my most smashing success." Rich men and their predilection for puns, I thought.

The acceleration in the number of business successes troubled him. Some others in the "here-to-there" business, as he sometimes called it, were taking risks; among them were those who cast big shadows on the sea of finance, gambling with borrowed money on foreign markets. It made him very uneasy. Just before Susannah's wedding, he sold everything but his own yacht.

When the crash happened, he bought farms adjacent to his from newcomers to Berkshire, who were grateful for the cash and for his discretion. He allowed them to continue to use what they used to own, and Archie nudged their farm managers to his way of thinking, gracefully. This was no surprise. Archie had once joined Harold on a cattle-buying spree in Argentina, and one of their hosts had called him "*Archibaldo el diplomatico.*"

Harold had invested in Canadian airplane manufacture and Argentinian cattle farms. A lovely house in Bermuda. The purchase of two penthouses in New York was accomplished in less than two days.

"How is the distant empire?" I sometimes talked to Harold by telephone when he was away. He was often away, sometimes for several months at a time. He never wavered in his affection, and every now and then it seemed he missed me. I made jokes about his attentiveness to his properties, urban and rural, but in truth, I was lonesome.

I felt the anxiety in the air: so many thousands were out of work. Those in lodgings walked the streets all day, or became patrons of the library, until they could go back in the evening. Some men had now been out of work for years. In Italy, Mussolini was banning women from work in order that men might have employment. Susannah wrote to say that superficial obedience is very Italian. Her accounts said that she was paying the money to the man in the woman's life—father, husband, underage son—but the women continued to work for her and got the *lire* in their own hands.

In England, some women had worked at men's jobs during the Great War, and then kept on working when, as many of the those who had once held those jobs—and those women—hadn't come home. Now, there was a political organization for every single idea on how to fix the world. The speakers haranguing in Hyde Park were gathering larger and larger crowds, no matter the topic. I wondered if they would hoist some wooden statue of the workingman, and hammer nails into it. I hated the sound of people shouting speeches. Harold was sitting across from me, nodding sympathetically from his armchair.

"Why don't you come to Bermuda with me, if the *balagan* here bothers you so?" He loved to use Yiddish words with me in private. "You'd like the little colony. I have met some sculptors there who are good with their hands. Like you."

I realized he was waiting for me to acknowledge his joke, and obliged. "Surely, Harold, you've not experienced their work first hand."

Harold was delighted. "Absolutely not. They are a highly respected family, first rate."

"I'm sure they are wonderful, but I would have to get there. You know I feel claustrophobic on the yacht."

"There you go with that marvellous Viennese ability to label your feelings with Greek names as if that makes them scientific instead of amorphous. How can a feeling be something objective when it is experienced so individually? I ask you."

"Amorphous is also Greek."

"It takes a good half hour to walk the deck of *The Handsome,* and that's if you go at a good clip. I don't know how you can feel hemmed in. Dear Hedy, do come." He had never pressed me with such tenacity.

I began to pace. "I need to run my business. You of all people should understand. It engages me and needs my attention. You said that you're happy that it's such a success. And what if, finally…"

"I know. You are going to say, 'what if Susannah wants to visit.'"

I looked out the window.

"Are you going to tell her it's stopped raining in England? She won't believe you, you know. Your sister has never visited us. She just keeps sending boxes of carnations and those blasted Italian lozenges. I'm sick of carnations." He had never spoken so bluntly. "And I think it's obvious that I am not first in your affections."

"Susannah…"

"I am not talking about Susannah. Here, Mist." The dog padded up to him and sat. "She brought me this today." It was George's old fedora, a little worse for wear. He tossed it onto the sofa. Mist glanced back and forth between it and him.

"Oh, I can explain! The man who…"

"I don't think I could bear to hear your explanation. I am not going to pry into why another man's hat would be in your apartment. One with a Paris label." He poured another whiskey for himself, and set it down.

"That hat has been here for years. I was foolish to keep it. It belonged to a friend, a man I never…"

"And yet you kept his hat." He had never cut me off like this in conversation before.

"I used it to play fetch with the dog! I told you about him.

The fellow who gave English lessons to me and my sister."

He held up his hand. "But you never said you kept his hat. You kept it to play fetch with your feelings." He poured another drink. He tipped his head and smiled. "My jewel of a Jewess. Please let's not talk about this."

"You brought it up!"

"Well, then. You said he was a journalist."

"He left Vienna before we did. I haven't seen him since."

"Yet I have noticed lately, every time I am here, how many papers you read. I thought you were turning into your sister. And then I discover a man's hat in your apartment."

"Our apartment."

"No, Hedy, it's yours—you have known this for years. And it will remain yours. But I think I am right: for years, all this time you have been with me, you have kept a hat that belongs to a man, a journalist with whom you once spent a great deal of time. Who wears hats with Paris labels." He stood up. "I'm off to Bermuda. Perhaps my absence will make the heart grow fonder."

"Harold, I couldn't be more fond."

"Perhaps that's true." A measuring look. "Archie will help you any time, in any way that he can. You know how to reach me if you need me." He kissed my forehead. "My lovely Hedy." He got his coat from the vestibule closet, folded it over his arm, and left. It was as if he had never been there.

Now no one wanted me, not even in the mild and peculiar way that Harold had. I knew he wouldn't be back. And he was right. I liked him. I relied on him. I looked forward to talking to him. But I had never wanted him. Not the way that I wanted George. *Even now.*

Over the last year, Harold had stayed up late, drinking, and had come to bed long after I was asleep. Sometimes he had nudged Mist off the bed and climbed in beside me, but more often I would briefly awaken to him gazing at us before he took himself off to his place on Wilton Crescent. At first I asked him why he didn't stay, and he said he didn't want to disturb me. Then I stopped asking.

It seemed to me that he had finally settled on what he wanted to do most, and that was to drink steadily. He had become furtive about it, having a drink going in several rooms, so that he appeared to be nursing one drink, when in fact he had four or five on the go at once. I was about to become one of those strange unescorted businesswomen whom nobody invites to dinner. Mist brought me that damned fedora, and I put it on Harold's clay head. And then I felt guilty and took it off.

I still went to my shop four days a week, but I couldn't bear to go to Twin Oaks for long weekends. I attended afternoon concerts at the Royal Albert. I went to art galleries, though not to the openings of shows. I went to the British Museum. I donated to the RSPCA. I felt more moved by the fate of the pit ponies than by the abuse of citizens in Spain, but on the spur of the moment, I donated a rather large sum to the Spanish cause. Soon afterwards, one morning when I entered the shop, a client, imperious despite a head covered in a fluttering helmet of muslin strips, greeted me with a wave of her hand, as though she thought she were a Bedouin stopping a caravan.

"Oh, there you are. Good morning, Miss Highstone."

I returned the greeting, said good morning to Kay, who continued to pin the strips of muslin. I headed for the elevator for the office I kept on the second floor. The only way to handle some clients was to treat them as if they were not quite worthy of attention. It made them over-value me and, perhaps, think my hats were better than they were.

"Miss Highstone, if I might interrupt your labours." *Oh, one who is not going to be ignored.* I turned and raised my eyebrows. I kept my face calm, my mouth closed.

"If I may venture, you have more to offer the women of London than the very best hats." Kay was pinning another strip of muslin above the lady's left ear, and she widened her eyes. She kept her face down, her smile held in and hidden.

"I am not so sure, Lady Bertram, but I do thank you. If you will excuse me. You need to check the right temple strip, Kay. Good morning to you." Kay put another pleat in the muslin.

Just as I opened the folding gate to the elevator, Lady Bertram spoke again. "I think you need not be sure, but nevertheless, you must come to this event. We are going to entirely improve the Jewish Maternity Hospital. My husband is donating much of the cost, but it is important that women of every kind support other women. You, my dear, are an example of generosity to others."

Kay made a face, and I wasn't sure if the woman noticed her rolling her eyes. I also wasn't sure what was coming next. Was I going to be asked to make hats for the indigent? I had allowed Kay to remodel the hats we had made for a customer who died before she could pick them up. Kay had young friends desperate for suitable interview attire.

"Kay, would you mind very much getting my maroon binder from my desk?"

The maroon binder was the agreed-upon signal to leave me alone with a client. Lady Bertram was tall and slender, with a long face, a long upper lip, and narrow grey eyes. This meant that an asymmetrical and wider brim was necessary to balance the head on the body below it. She was a viscountess, a very wealthy wife of one of Harold's rivals in shipping. I had never met her socially, but then, I hardly met anyone socially.

"I am not sure that my presence would add anything at all, but thank you."

"Might you consider a contribution, then, a small donation, to our fund in support of Jews in Germany then? What is going on in Germany is terrible!"

"Yes, of course."

Although she was wearing a tight cap of strips of muslin on her head, the woman gazed at my reflection in the mirror steadily. "I have no problem at all with your arrangement with Lord Coleson."

I could feel my face get hot. "I see," I managed, anger coursing through me.

"I think that respectable women and—others—can be friends. Allies, if you will. Please think about it. Do come." She turned to look into my face as she handed me a small envelope with a card in it. She even had the nerve to lay her hand on my forearm.

I knew my face didn't betray how many had laid a hand on me, or not touched me at all. Susannah once said that if I were in a foul mood, my gaze had the same metal quality as bullets, and almost the same intention. The viscountess, who was rather proud of how she put her egalitarian principles into active practice, chose to ignore the barrage heading in her direction. Kay emerged from the elevator, tentative and alert.

I took the maroon binder. "Kay, if you will carry on. Good day, Lady Bertram."

Once inside the elevator, I thought about a joking remark my mother made after my sister and I had been away at Tante Freyda's—how peaceful the house had been without my constant arguing. How astounded I had been, first, and then how hurt. This is how we learn to accept the world's rejection—our mothers do it first. I tore the envelope and the card into small pieces. I had no intention of joining anything that put me in the category of "others." Then I bent to pick up the pieces and put them in my pocket.

"You surely don't want to join in with that Mosley fellow. You look better in red than black, if I may so say, Miss Hedy." Archie's banter never crossed any boundaries.

"No, no. I want to join in with the others, the ones who are against the Jew-baiters. Who want to raise money for Spain."

"Who says?"

"This flyer."

Archie took the folded notice and stared at it, not reading it.

He was no doubt thinking about what he would have to say, what he would have to do. He told me once that he thought it was always better to 'take a moment.'

"Mr. Stephens, what a face. It can't be worse than whatever happened to you in that casino in Mar del Plata."

"You shall never know, Miss Hedy." This was a long-standing joke between us.

"I want to go. My shopgirl, Kay, says she's going to go and punch a fascist in the face. Her father is an amateur boxer in Birmingham, and I'd like to see her try."

"In Birmingham, everyone's father is an amateur boxer. Look, the police are already booking in extra men. No one is allowed to be off duty."

"Then it will be safe."

Archie looked at me. "And I also have it on very good authority that no one has thrown out any vegetables in the bins on Cable Street for a week."

"Who is this good authority?"

"My dustman."

"What has that got to do with seeing Mosley?"

"You may not see him for tomatoes." He ventured one of his tidy smiles.

"Then I really must go."

"You might be laughing now, but you have always disliked crowds."

"Just the same."

"What if I arrange for you to see it, but not be actually in the street? I know a fellow who films for those newsreel theatres, and he told me he's going to be on a roof at the corner of Christian and Cable."

"But..."

He held out a flat leather case. I knew it well. The case held dozens of keys, all attached to small clasps. It locked and unlocked all that Harold owned in England

"Here. Pass on my resignation to Lord Coleson."

"I only want…"

"Miss Hedy, I can't allow it. Londoners are going to give that man in his little black costume a welcome he won't soon forget."

"Which is why I want to see what will happen."

"A bloody riot, that's what will happen."

And happen it did. When thousands who weren't Jews in East London, who were fed up with no work, who were socialists or communists, who were on the side of Spain, and who simply felt that Nazis had nothing to teach good British men and women joined ranks with the thousands who were Jews, only a few minutes of insults, tomatoes, and hurled chamber pots made Mosely turn tail and hurry to Hyde Park where he could be, the police urged, more easily protected. Cable Street was choked with many thousands of people who took umbrage at that attempt at protection.

The crowd battled the police wholeheartedly up and down Cable Street, mostly avoiding injury and arrest. The newsreel of the event played for weeks, and newspapers went into fourth editions for days. A month later, a law was passed banning the wearing of military costume to public protests. Without the fun of dressing up, fewer bothered to come out, and overt support for Mosley petered out.

On the evening of the riot, once Cable Street was quiet, Archie escorted me back to my apartment. My hands trembled so much that he had to take my key to let me in. I sat, still shaking, and put my head on my dog's head. "That's it. I want nothing more to do with politics."

"Well said, Miss Hedy. Cup of tea?"

~

52.

ALFONSO WAS HORRIFIED. Marinella's cousin was back from Eritrea briefly, and in our house, uninvited. He was laughing about a dog that kept trying to crawl out of a fire barrel as he kept shoving her back in. "You should have heard that dog howl! But she wasn't going to steal any more from Italians!"

Alfonso excused himself, and was sick, vomiting. I was speechless and stared. The man lacked most of his nose and his damaged face stared back at me, contemptuous, and then he left without a word. Alfonso said never to mention it. He was shouting, which was so unlike him. He was not only ashamed of his family business, he said, he was ashamed of Italians in general. Especially those going to help Franco. "Idiots! Imagine following a man who says, 'Down with thinking, long live death.'" He said he was thinking of selling, of letting his cousin buy him out. He was sixty-three, and he had lost his smile.

Sometimes, though, he smiled at me. One late January morning he said, "You canter up to me like an Arabian on those long legs. An Arabian horse, that is." So Italian in his humour: impulsiveness followed by a qualification. And the dogs, Romulus and Remus—old now, and getting thin—always got a smile from him. But his business made him unhappy. When the advertising fellows presented new designs for Leopard Baci, I sat in. Alfonso looked at the mock-ups and batted them away with the back of his hand, tipping them over the edge of the table. "I don't care," he said and walked out, leaving the kisses on the floor. And me with two stunned young men.

They had thought their idea was funny. They had redesigned the leopard so that only one paw opened the box, giving the fascist salute. They didn't know that Alfonso was interested in politics, so they thought that he might find it funny, too. Alfonso was certainly circumspect about his politics. But when he saw the banner draped over the Casino Municipale with the image of Mussolini, he stood on the steps and, as loudly as if he were announcing a race, called out, "*Porco mondo!*"

One day in early February, he walked out of the house with thousands of *lire* in his billfold. He said not to worry. It was the only way, he said, to buy a lemon orchard without alerting the stupid *fascisti,* who would want a cut. Above all, I was not to worry. When he came back, he had nothing to say about what he did, except that it seemed the best lemon orchards were not for sale, only old or poorly run ones.

A week later, when I asked him to do a few laps of the *passeggiata*, he said that he wanted to stay in and listen to the wireless, that he couldn't bear to listen to the racket of stupid talk in the streets. Later that same evening, he said he was going for a drive. When I complained that we'd see nothing but roads, like white ribbons in the dark, he said calmly that he would ask Marinella to join him instead, as if he had anticipated my protest. My husband was somehow becoming an irritable old Italian. After a few days of this, Marinella went on these excursions with him as a matter of course. Why drive around, I thought, when there is nothing to see, when no one can see you?

A few weeks later, I wanted to go out, to look pretty, to see others notice that I looked pretty. Alfonso was dozing on the balcony with the dogs beside him, one on each side. I decided I would go to the Casino Municipale on my own. I kissed the top of his balding head and stuck a tiny note, "*un po' di roulette,*" to the kiss. He had laughed the last time I had done this, and I hoped that I would find him in a good mood when I came back.

The ball bounced and rattled around the spinning wheel, and I won a little. Drank a little. Laughed. Enjoyed a little flattery. At thirty-nine years old, it was nice. When I announced I was going to take my winnings home, there were several offers to escort me, even though it was only a few minutes walk away.

"*Grazie*, but it's perfectly safe, my San Remo."

Several people also made sure to kiss me goodbye, and one pointed out the full moon. It was silver and still climbing in the sky when I returned home. Alfonso was gone, and so was his car. He was still out at four in the morning. I called Marinella. No answer.

Their bodies were found, by the side of the road, some several miles from the car, their lovely heads caved in. The two little dogs, the reporting officer said, were pawing at the bodies. "It was disgusting," said the officer. He shook his head. "They shot them."

My Alfonso. Marinella.

"They shot my husband? My friend? Who did this?"

"The dogs. They shot the dogs. Signore Cavalliere and the *contessa*, they were thrown from the car. An accident. The brakes failed."

"On a Hispano-Suiza?"

"Yes."

"And the car was found three miles from the bodies."

"Animals may have dragged the bodies. That explains the head injuries."

I looked up at the sky. It was empty, empty.

I had to identify the bodies, they said. My husband and the *contessa* together—it was nothing, they said, maybe a little flirtation, they said, enjoying my immediate denial, and seemed disappointed that they couldn't provoke more of a reaction from me.

It was morning, and servants were hurrying to work. I caught the arm of a servant on his way to Marinella's villa. The boy who once sat looking out to sea, with his morning coat undone. He was older now, married, living in his own home. He wanted to go back and tell his wife what had happened, but I had an iron grip on his arm. His bruise would last the week.

The closer I got to the building, the more slowly I walked. I still had on my pretty black sequined dress, with the silver-and-black sequined triangle scarf. When the officer brought us into the room to see the bodies, mauled and broken, the boy who once sat on the beach and lit Marinella's cigarettes, gagged and ran.

It was cold in the room. I shivered. "How did this happen?"

The duty officer yawned. "There are a lot of communists on the roads these days. Driving around, organizing their stupid followers." He yawned again. "No doubt your husband ran into them."

Alfonso's first cousin arrived, and after a quick look at Alfonso, his gaze travelled up and down my dress, up and down my sequins. He drew back his small chin in disapproval and told me to go home. I argued, but I was tired. Tired. He would handle the arrangements.

"Communist Bandits Murder Prominent Businessman." This was the headline, not just in the San Remo newspaper, but in the ones from Rome as well. This was what was bruited about in public, on balconies. Privately? No one discussed what people said privately. No mention of Marinella was made in the papers. Privately, they may have retold how she had once turned Mussolini down after he had sent an invitation for her to attend a reception at the Casino Municipale. The car he sent to pick her up waited for half an hour before a servant confessed that the *contessa* had gone to Baden-Baden two weeks earlier. She had only gone the day before, but this way she could pretend she had not received the invitation. She acted a little crazy once she got home. Just enough.

Marinella's funeral was first. The servants, her cousins, and her aunts all sat together, an orchestra of sorrow, quickly summoned. The clicking of beads. I spoke to an old whiskered aunt softly and then sat down. The casket was open, and Marinella's head was turned away, as though she were holding a cigarette behind her. Barely enough of a cheek to kiss, but I followed the others and did so anyway. I kissed the cold cheek of my friend, whose own greenhouses had supplied the flowers in wicker buckets, drooping yellow banners of mimosa. We waited for the priest.

The clicking of beads.

Marinella's servant, the one who had once weighed down a corner of he beach rug, arrived, and leaned towards me. His eyes were swollen. "Signora, please. There is someone outside," he whispered, the rhythm of his words interrupted by the tightness in his throat when he swallowed. "He is waiting for you by the sacristy door. Outside."

I wondered if that someone was waiting to kill me, too, but I went, remembering to turn and cross myself at the last moment.

"I don't believe them. What they say happened." That was what I immediately told Marinella's friend. Under his boater hat he was wearing a head piece, a pink bandage that went under his chin, and around his face, and covered most of the back of his head as well. He took off his sunglasses. His eyes were circled in purple and red. He moved very slowly, like an animate statue. "Come around the corner," he begged in a whisper. He put his hat, a trilby, on over his headgear. "I would like to smoke, but my face may fall off if I do."

"What happened?"

"Plastic surgery."

I stared at him.

"I was in the car too. There were lights, lanterns swinging. I would have driven on, but they fired a gun into the air. They were all waving guns." His mouth barely moved as he whispered. "They were so happy to wave guns. I stopped the car, but kept the motor running.

"One of them held a lantern above his head and asked what we were doing. Your husband pulled money out of his pocket that was meant for Spain. I kept my hands on the wheel, as if I were a chauffeur, not someone they were looking for. Then Alfonso made a sound, a shout. I think he had a heart attack, Susannah."

I looked up at the polished blue sky.

Marinella's friend continued, staring into memory. "Marinella pulled out a gun. She killed one, but there were half a dozen of them and they jumped in the car and dragged her and Alfonso out. Your Alfonso, I think he was already gone, but my darling was screaming. Swearing. You know how she could swear. My last memory of her is not her beautiful face but her beautiful voice, her voice, saying, '*Voi figli di puttana!*' *You sons of bitches!* Like an anthem. Ah! I can't cry, and I half want to laugh—what kind of beings are we? When we have no more hope, everything is possibly funny. Ah! I can't smile. It hurts, and my mouth will collapse if I do."

His voice was coming out of a mouth that barely moving, unrelenting, talking. He was gesturing with a non-existent cigarette. In the past, he had always been talking—talking to Marinella, mostly, but also to anyone who might need the truth. Why stop now?

"Me, they were going to slit my throat, but I gunned the car, an automatic impulse, and it threw the guy behind me right out of the Hispano-Suiza. They only got a small slice of me."

"The brakes didn't fail."

"On a Hispano-Suiza? That's why Alfonso liked it; it was perfect for these hills and these roads. No. Can you move over here? I have to stay out of the sun, in the shadows, so I heal properly."

We went underneath a series of thick open arches extending out from the church, and stood in their shade.

"I don't remember driving. I don't remember hiding in the ditch. When I woke up, it was almost morning, and I staggered out of the ditch and crawled to a farmhouse. They called a priest. He gave me the last rites first, and then put me in a cart and took me to the hospital. A friend to our cause, a surgeon, saw me and repaired me. And did a little extra around the eyes, so I can appear in public as a vain man. Vanity will explain my disappearance: I had to go into hiding because I'm vain. Not because I wanted to live." He put his sunglasses back on, looked around the corner of the wall jutting out beside us, and, just like that, he was gone.

I continued to watch the accumulating clouds, sooty grey laundry piling up for giant sky women. *Will they come? Do I need them, my old allies from my brothel days?* No. I was stunned with anger. I was angry with my husband, with my friend. With the friend of my friend. They hadn't trusted me—to be strong enough? To keep a secret? Did they think I would have refused aid, refused money to the Republicans? *If I had been there. If I had known.* I stumbled on the steps leading to the sacristy, just as the priest opened the door.

"Signora, please." The priest could barely contain his contempt. The Church alone ran all personal formalities now, including marriages and funerals. Mussolini had a new arrangement with the Vatican. The priest knew that we Alfonso and I had only had a civil ceremony. We were sinners. Socialists, or worse. He snapped his cassock skirt out of the way as he pushed the heavy door.

I followed the black swinging gown of the priest back into the church and sat down again with the others. I didn't feel anything, I didn't look at anyone, or anything, including the coffin that was now closed around my friend. Her broken head.

My friend's feet pointed at the altar. The end began. "*Requiem aeternam dona eis...*"

Alfonso's funeral followed that evening. His first cousin had taken over the arrangements. He had rung Hedy. She rang back and insisted she talk to me. There was no flight arriving in time for her to attend the funeral. I couldn't talk to her.

I had to get away. *If they have done this to my Marinella, to my Alfonso. To poor Romulus and Remus.* I was afraid. I was more alone in San Remo than when I had first stepped off the train so many years ago. Then, there had been men in pink vests eager to help me. Now there was no one.

The funeral was small. Abundant flowers, abundant Arditi uniforms. They hustled Alfonso to his grave and buried him in quick shovelfuls of dry soil. I asked if the dogs could be buried with him, but his first cousin just looked at me. My insistence that my husband be buried and not interred was already considered crazy.

I wanted my darling to be outside, where he liked to be, in hot weather or cold. I thought about snowy Bardonecchia, how quickly he had glided down the slopes.

And then Marinella's question glided down from the past and stopped me cold: *What if Alfonso needed to make demands on you?*

People gave me quick glances, and looked away. Fearful. If this could happen to Signore Cavalliere... Someone drove me back to my home. No one came to the house except the first cousin. He told me I could continue to live there, but for tax purposes the house belonged to the business. When I asked if he was moving in, he said no, but he told me that Marinella's cousin who had been supervising the lemon orchards would be moving in, instead. He enjoyed smiling at me.

I knew what I had to do.

~

53.

"COME AND LIVE WITH ME." I woke up saying those words into the telephone, still half in a dream. I turned on the lamp by the bed. Outside it was dark with sleet. "Wait, where are you?"

"Baden bei Wein. The casino."

"What time is it?"

"Four o'clock."

I had been napping. "Three o'clock here."

"I emptied Alfonso's accounts. I had to sit on my suitcase to close it."

I was fully awake. I understood. "So that's why the casino."

"Yes. I can say I won the money at baccarat. The casino gave me one krone for ten *lire*, so now I can open my suitcase without an explosion of Italian banknotes."

I had rung Susannah immediately after Alfonso's cousin told me the terrible news. In a flat voice, she had said she was afraid to stay in San Remo without her husband, without her dogs. Without her friend, the *contessa*. When I had suggested then that she come and stay with me, or that I go and stay with her, she had refused. She said she was going to Switzerland, that she needed to think, and for that she needed the cold.

"There has always been a train from Baden bei Wein into Switzerland. Or you could fly."

"Hedy, I can't do either. You know Austria—two bureaucrats for every citizen. The hotel manager said that in these times, their policy is to keep passports secure in their safe. I handed over my old Austrian one. He called me Fraulein Edelstein. I'm still recognizable from that old photograph. He advised me to get my passport updated or I would have trouble leaving Austria."

"What about the British passport that George arranged for us when we escaped?"

"I threw it out after I married Alfonso. Hedy, my Alfonso."

Silence.

"Susannah? Are you there?"

"They killed him. I travelled with him all over Italy. But not outside the country. So, no Italian passport. No Italian husband."

"Go to the passport office, get a new passport, and get out."

"I tried! The line went around the block twice, and there were four guards keeping everyone in order. My suitcase was heavy, but I was afraid to put it down. Someone said, "What have you got in there, money?" They were laughing until an official came out and said they were out of passports and to come back tomorrow. Then the yelling started up. It was awful. I took a taxi back to the casino."

"Sew the money into your coat."

"I'm not like you, I don't know how. And it's still so cold, I'm wearing my leopard skin coat."

"And the hat I made to match?"

"Hedy. Yes. But I'm attracting way too much attention in this outfit."

"In Baden bei Wein?"

"I know. Even here, where everyone shows off. I'm frightened."

"I can barely hear you. Buy another coat. Leave that one behind in the changing room."

"It wouldn't do any good. There he is again."

"Who?"

"I don't know. He got on the train at San Remo, and he

was sitting in my hotel lobby this morning when I left to go to the casino. He got up and followed me, and now he's sitting in the casino lobby. He isn't even bothering to hide behind a newspaper."

"Too bad there's no Nigel waiting outside in a stolen car. Sorry, not funny. Look, get in a taxi and get on a train. Go to Vienna, first class."

"Right into the wolf's mouth. No. I swore I would never go back."

"Me too, but that's where the British Embassy is. Listen to me. Susannah, are you still there? Buy a ticket for the first train that leaves for Vienna in the morning, so you can go directly to the British Embassy. Don't talk to anyone while you wait, or if you have to, speak Italian. Be Italian, until you are inside the Embassy. Then speak English. Don't leave the building until I get there. I don't care if you have to screw the janitor. I'll wire Harold right now. I'm sure he can arrange for you to have British travel papers as my sister, especially if I am there to vouch for you. And I will be, I promise. I will leave tomorrow for Vienna myself."

"I guess I am going to see your home after all."

"British weather hasn't changed. In fact, it's sleeting right now. Just so you know."

"I'm hoping that guy will get up. He must have the bladder of a camel. Hedy, you'll never guess. I saw Fraulein Lowin in the Baden bei Wein train station. She still wears that violet coat, remember? She was still smoking, just like she used to. It was that husky deep voice that made me look. She didn't see me. Harold knows people, doesn't he, Hairbrush?"

"He can get a diplomatic voucher, whatever papers are needed to get you out, Horsie. Put as much money as you can in your underwear, and forget the suitcase. We don't want anyone to think you're leaving until you're already gone."

I called Harold in Bermuda. He called a friend who had the

Vienna desk, who said of course it could be arranged as a favour from one Cambridge old boy to another. He said he was glad to hear from me. He never called me, but on occasion—his birthday, Christmas—I called him. He always got off the telephone quickly, and this time I was glad he did. I packed a suitcase with my most impressive clothes and sewed all the money from my hotel account into the suitcase lining. I called Archie and asked him to look in on Mist.

All the diplomatic activity meant that hotels in Vienna were full, but that did not deter Claridge's front desk from finding me accommodation in a good, if not the best, hotel.

Early Tuesday morning, the papers I needed were waiting for me at London's British Passport Office and I caught the train for Dover just in time. By dusk I had crossed the channel and was in Calais, and then on the Orient Express, rolling past Normandy fields anaesthetized with snow, through sleepy Reims. I thought of Harold's cathedral glass, and touched the topaz ring on its gold chain. *Get Susannah*, I thought. *Get her out of Vienna.*

Again, was the caustic thought which followed. The train passed through Stuttgart, and then climbed up the Jura hills. Trapezoids of light flickered along the snow banked against dark still pines, their long branches briefly articulate, and then gone into shared darkness again. Strasbourg, its cathedral tower lit in the night, and then the border of Alsace-Lorraine.

Passport matters were taken care of, official to official, one speaking French and the other, the mismatched music of a French accent speaking German. I felt a rush of energy as we left France, a readiness that over rode any exhaustion. I didn't think I would sleep for days.

In the train compartment, two elderly women knit without stopping, without looking at their work. They gaze steadily into the increasing darkness. I feel chilly and tuck my chin into my coat's collar. They're alert; their bodies carry immense

*tension—a trembling leg, a low sound in the throat. They
encourage each other with quick pats on the knee to look
there! Or there! I can see nothing. Without a word, as the
light fails, they put their knitting away and hold hands in
comfortable silence. They smile at me, nodding, not speaking.
I admire the jaunty angle of their grey wool hats, trimmed
with grey-and-white fur. The hats curve up higher on the
sides, an older style. One of the women bends over her thick
middle to adjust the foot rest for the other. They place their
paws neatly on the armrests. They sigh and tip their heads
back onto their headrests, turn their faces towards each other,
and collapse into sleep, thin black lips smiling, sharp teeth
barely showing.*

I woke up. The conductor announced breakfast and instructed
us to adjust our watches to the new time. We had lost an hour.
A change in the sound of the train as it crossed the bridge
over the Danube. We passed through Ulm, then Munich, too
overcast to catch a glimpse of the Alps. I sat up with a jolt.
The train was going back, westward.

"Everything is in order," said the conductor when I enquired.
In a few minutes the train had moved through a double
switchback, and was heading east again. The old conductor
raised his eyebrows as if to say, "See?" The train climbed
through the mountain passes, and although the heat in the
car was steady, the vital cold of the Alps was present just
outside the window. By mid-morning, we were in Strasbourg.
Austrian border agents walked through the cars, quickly
matching their list to the passengers and their papers. My
heart leapt, thrilled to hand over my British passport and
get it back so quickly.

A pause in Linz to connect a car from Hungary. There were
dozens of people at work shovelling and sweeping the platform, and men on ladders with torches and paraffin heaters
painting the lettering on the sign. Typical Austrian fussiness.

The conductor adjusted his cap and opened the door to the corridor. He looked back over his shoulder. "Be careful on trains," he said, his mouth barely moving. Another brief stop, and then Vienna.

54.

IT WAS FREEZING COLD. There was no snow on the ground. Young men loitered about the platform and in the station. They looked as though they were still out from the night before. They were hoarse from singing, unwilling to give up the defiance of singing German nationalist songs in Austria. "*Uber alles*," they bawled. One rushed at me.

"Carry your luggage, Miss?"

I ignored him. He grabbed the handle, and I pulled it back. "Do you mind?" I said this in my most plummy English, looking about for a station attendant. I sounded like Harold's friends, manners impeccable, lineage the same.

"Ohhh, an Englishwoman." He was performing for his friends, who laughed at his boldness. He blocked my path and tried out his English. "Did you know your king is like me, an Austrian? You and I should get better acquainted."

I hooked the back of his right ankle with my foot while I pushed on his right shoulder. He was down, to even more laughter. Some of my skills were not those of an English aristocrat. The fellow in the bright green uniform rushing to my aid stopped to help the fallen man instead. Snow began to fall. I slid into the first taxi I saw and said, "British Embassy."

On the balconies above the arched entrance to the Embassy, snow was beginning to settle. The pale yellow building was architecturally tame compared to the more extravagant buildings in Vienna. I pressed an ivory button by the double doors. They released immediately and I hurried in. *Oh, Harold, you sweet drunkard.* I was here. I had a chair, a cup of tea, and the papers I needed for Susannah. Now all I needed was Susannah. She wasn't here, but she might have had to catch a later train. I had already bought the return tickets. I knew I was smiling. I had won at every step so far. I listened for the sound of a woman's shoes coming up the open metal stairs. There were solitary quick footsteps in the corridor, occasionally a sudden flow of cold air, and tumultuous pounding of many feet up the stairs, but all voices were low and urgent, and none of them Susannah's.

The balcony windows were closed against the chilly March air outside. Inside, below them, radiators hissed. I waited in my chair for an hour, and then asked the uniformed fellow outside the door where I might wash my hands. He asked me to wait, and a young woman, assistant to an attaché, arrived to escort me to the washroom. On the way back, she was quite chatty.

"It is a bit of a maze here, I'm afraid, Miss Highstone. We keep adding offices and officers to go in 'em. It's something of a church jumble sale. But that's politics, isn't it, Miss Highstone? Oh, turn down this aisle. That's it."

She waited for me and then took my arm lightly. She was a bosomy young woman with large blue eyes. "Things are changing so quickly," she said. "Every hour." We were somehow back at the doors to the room where I had waited earlier. "Sorry I can't keep you company. *The Times* is there, and if you aren't too fussy, someone's left *The Guardian*. Would you like me to bring you a cup of tea?"

I declined; she smiled. I could hear the sound of her sturdy heels hurrying away. My suitcase was not beside my chair.

"Miss!" I ran to the door. "Miss!"

No answer.

I hurried down the corridor in the direction, I hoped, of those heels. I opened a door on my right, and there were two men standing over a table, examining the contents of my suitcase.

"What are you doing with my things?"

"We do apologize, Madam. I'm Adjunct Officer Wynn-Jones. Since that incident in Paris, I am afraid this has become necessary. People have carried bombs into buildings inside suitcases full of frilly underwear."

He didn't look Welsh at all. "I have not."

"No, Ma'am, apparently not. Our apologies. You do understand."

I turned the suitcase around and snapped the latches shut. *Good thing they didn't get to the lining where the banknotes are.*

"I will continue to wait in there." I pointed to the waiting room. "Unless the deputy ambassador needs to speak to me."

"Yes, Miss Highstone, of course. And, if I may ask, why are you waiting in there?"

"I came to get some papers, necessary travel documents for my sister."

"And you have them?"

"Yes."

"Then, I do apologize, but I must ask again, why are you waiting in there?"

"For my sister!" I realized I had raised my voice. "I beg your pardon. I have been travelling, and I'm a little fatigued. And a little anxious about my sister."

"Perhaps we can arrange a ride to your hotel, and as soon as your sister…"

"She is meeting me here. Today. She's arriving on the train."

"Very well, Miss Highstone. Would you like a cup of tea?"

I waited. Apparently everyone here knew my name. And apparently it was true that the Empire ran on tea. I checked my watch. I realized that I was in that zone of time that happens inside every hospital and courthouse, every brothel and jail, a time zone self-referential and implacable.

The afternoon lumbered on. I went over to the windows.

I remembered those skies, Vienna grey. On the street below, people were bundled up, but they walked smartly, keeping the pace that Vienna demands. *Where is my sister?*

The muffled sound of telephones ringing somewhere in the building was constant. Every few minutes, a brief blast of cold air wafted up the stairs, but Susannah didn't appear. The strawberry blonde with the stacked heels was back. Miss Piers. "Would you like a cup of tea?"

"Thank you."

"I think we can find a biscuit or two."

I thought that if I accepted a cup of tea, they would let me continue to sit there. The first embassy officer had welcomed me briskly, handed me the papers, already prepared, and then said he was so sorry, but he had an appointment out of the office, and asked if I would mind waiting on my own. That was at mid-day, hours ago. It was now five o'clock. I picked up my purse and my suitcase. I headed to the door to find someone, anyone. Voices in the corridor, hurrying footsteps. They would never have allowed such noisy men's shoes in the last place I stayed in Vienna.

The streetlamps were lit; the office day staff had gone home. There was no sign of Susannah, no telephone call, no telegram. Miss Piers rather firmly, but just as cheerfully encouraged me to go to my hotel and rest. She assured me that they knew the number of my hotel, and that if Signora appeared that night, I would be called. That it was understood that she was formerly Susannah Highstone, and that she was related to Lord Coleson. That if my sister appeared, she, personally, would call since she, Miss Piers, was pulling night shift again, with some other officers. Miss Piers was obviously looking forward to the night shift, as well might those other officers. She was a good-looking woman, despite, or maybe because of the severity of the cut of her suit.

"We've called a taxi for you." Miss Piers picked up my suitcase and had me take her arm as we descended the wide stairs to the entrance. "The snow didn't last, but people do slip here sometimes, quite drastically, even in drier weather. The driver will ring the buzzer."

Within a minute, he did. He was a silent, skull-faced fellow. Miss Piers called to me as the driver opened the taxi's rear door. "Don't worry!"

I did, though. I was beside myself with worry. *Where is Susannah?* I got to my hotel and walked into the lobby. I was greeted by Mischlinger.

55.

I WENT INWARD, into myself, as I moved towards the counter with its beautiful tall lamps. *He is dressed in the kind of suit a floor manager might wear in Selfridges.* I made my face go blank, as if this were a play, and I had performed in it a hundred times. *He is still tall, with the same bulky body. Dark circles under his eyes. The skin of his neck wobbles above his collar.* I remembered Harold saying that wounded men claimed time slows down, so they saw everything, every detail. Mischlinger squinted at me and waved a directing hand at the youngster in a pillbox hat who was carrying my suitcase.

"Lovely, lovely, yes, Madam, the front desk is right this way." Mischlinger's hand hovered in position about a foot from my back, and he walked with me as I approached the front desk.

"You have been here before, Madam? I seem to recognize you."

"Miss Highstone," I said in my coolest tone, turning away to the well-dressed clerk who rotated the ledger towards me.

"Yes, Your Ladyship. Ah, yes, here it is. Claridge's said you would be arriving today. And here you are!"

An advantage. Vienna always inflates the title. I signed. Then I turned away again and tipped the bellboy.

"Of course. Lady Highstone," said Mischlinger, after squinting at the register over the counter. "How is Lord Highstone?"

"I wouldn't know," I said mildly. "He's been dead for ever so long."

Mischlinger shrank. *We whores know how to provoke a re-action. Another advantage provided to me by this dreadful city.*

The blond clerk behind the counter smirked, and leaned forward. "Never mind Herr Mischlinger, Madam. He's been here too long, haven't you, old fellow?"

Mischlinger raised his chin.

"And he never remembers his eyeglasses," continued the desk clerk. "Your key, Milady. Franz will escort you to your room. Elevator to the left, and welcome to the Hotel Vienna."

I locked the door. I sat on the bed. Then I leaped up, checked the door, locked it again. I hung up my coat and then sat on the bed again, looking at the telephone. I was cold. I pulled the white monogrammed bed quilt around me. Mischlinger. That solicitous voice. *He used to own hotels. Now he's a night manager, here, at this hotel. He's alive, and in this hotel.* Claridge's had made the reservation for me. They had apologized, at the time, saying the diplomatic crisis meant that all the usual hotels were full, but this one, they had assured me, still had a good reputation.

I had all along presumed he was dead. My life in this city was dead; my parents were dead. Vienna was in the past. I thought of it only when I chose to remember, which was seldom, or if an odd thing reminded me. And whenever I thought of my old city, it was from the safe purchase of my life in London. Even when the train pulled into the Westbahnhof station, I hadn't been thinking about being a girl here, or about living as a whore in a brothel.

I had been thinking of the next thing, how quickly I could get to the Embassy, whether I should go to the Embassy or the hotel first. If I got what I needed from the Embassy right away, and Susannah arrived on time, I had thought that we would go directly to the train station. So the Embassy first. Calais, Dover, London. Twin Oaks. I had been thinking about how the sitting room near the west wing bedroom on the second floor at Twin Oaks could be made over for Susannah. About selling the shop. Or maybe, expanding it, if Susannah were interested in working with me. Fast trains are good for unhindered thinking.

He didn't recognize me. The clerk had said "eyeglasses." *Why isn't there enough heat in this room?* I didn't dare call down.

The way he shrank. I laughed out loud. *He's not so big.* Not as big as he had been in memory. *Mischlinger.* I relaxed a little, took off my hat.

The bathroom, fast. I almost blacked out when I vomited. I had always had this reaction, blacking out when vomiting, and it frightened me. I felt dizzy and out of breath. I bathed my face in cold water and held onto the doorframe until I could put a hand out to the bedside table, and then the bed. I lay perfectly still, waiting for the nausea to pass. *I can't stay here. I must get a room in another hotel. But it's too late at night to do that now. And what if Susannah were to call?*

My sister. I had run my life for the last several years with that question at the forefront of my mind: what if Susannah were to call? I had been held captive by a fear that I would miss her call, by the hope that there would be a call at all. Resentment held me captive, too. Guilt. And now, from Baden bei Wein, Susannah had called. Like cards flipping together in a hand trick—arrangements, travelling, my mind hurtling faster than the train. I looked at the telephone. The clock said nine. I was surprised how alive my hatred was for Mischlinger, how fully I felt it all. Another wave of revulsion.

In the bathroom, cold water dripping from my face. In the brightly lit mirror, I looked baleful, felt terrible, and appeared completely healthy. No one looking at me would have ever suspected the churning turmoil within. I sat on the bed, pulled the bedcover around my shoulders. Again, I looked at the telephone.

Cold, bright sunlight streamed through the windows. I was

lying on the bed in my travelling clothes. Some urgent sound, repeated. I reached for the noise.

"Good morning, Lady Highstone. May I put a call through?"

"Yes!"

Some fellow from the British Embassy who claimed his name was Dauntless was speaking to me. "I'm calling to let you know we have a Signora," the man paused, "Cavalcade here, who also claims she is Susannah Highstone."

"Cavalliere. That's my sister. Miss Highstone. May I speak with her?"

"One moment."

There was an interminable pause.

"Madam, I'm sorry. The lady is agitated. She speaks Italian, then German, and then English. Her language is colourful—that is, we have had to..."

"That lady is my sister. You must forgive how she speaks. She's a recent widow and she's very tired. I have her travel documents. I'll come and get her immediately. Please, do put her on the line."

"I'm afraid that won't be possible. This is a security problem for us. We are receiving a delegation from Italy within the half hour. No nationals will be allowed for the duration of their visit. Right now, we are arranging for a taxi to take her to your hotel."

"No! Do not send her in a taxi here! Tell her I will meet her—at the Café Arundel. Please arrange for the taxi to take her..."

"To the Café Arundel, the Augarten. I know the place."

"Why wasn't I called as soon as she arrived? Lord Coleson will hear about this."

"Madam, you are welcome to lodge a complaint, of course, and I am so sorry, but now I must ring off. Current affairs are keeping our lines rather busy."

I grabbed my coat, my hat, and my purse, and ran back for my suitcase. Then I rushed down the stairs rather than wait for the lift. I spun out of the revolving door in the front lobby and stepped directly into a cab. I gave instructions to the driver and took out my compact to apply my lipstick.

I took a table just inside the door of the Café Arundel and ordered a coffee. There was a giddy, anxious feeling in the café. It felt like anything could happen. People sipped their coffee and drank their chocolate, but their sugar spoons rattled the cups, and they snapped their newspapers when they turned the pages.

I plucked a newspaper at random from what seemed to be the same rattan rack that had been there when we met Moreno, but there was no *Neue Freie Presse*. A *Wiener Neuste Nachricthen*. *The Tagespost*. The one I picked up was full of scandals and exclamation marks—diplomacy in disarray; "Juden" this and "Juden" that; rapists, robbers, swindling bankers, all Jews, all corrupt. I put it back and rifled through the rack for something less harrowing. They were all the same, so I took one at random and sat down again.

My hand went up to my brow, shielding my face in that old way. Half an hour went by. I turned the pages, but I couldn't read what was in front of me. I had read about the changes in Austria in *The Times*, and I had donated a few hundred pounds to the plight of German Jews, but this was a flood of reveling in Jew-hating.

I asked to use the telephone, and one was brought to the table. The embassy line was engaged. My waiter was solicitous, and brought me another cup of coffee. Then he brought lunch, something garnished with cucumbers.

What has happened to my sister? I asked to make a call, and once again the waiter obliged. The line was engaged. *Where is Susannah?* I asked to be moved to a table immediately by the window where I could see and be seen. I scanned the sidewalk crowds for a tall blonde. The café filled up with people ordering their mid-day meal. It was past noon. Someone shouted.

Outside the mullioned windows of the café, people were bunched up, pushing and shouting. A space cleared. A man with a white beard pressed his face up against a pane of glass, his nose flattened and his mouth squashed, not six inches from my face. He disappeared. The others in the café stood to see where he went, looking at each other and laughing at the suddenness of it all. I stood, too.

There on the sidewalk, hauled along by his beard, was the same man, moving in a half-crouch. He was led by a fellow who walked insolently along, not looking at the man, as if he were walking a dog. No one intervened. The young fellow pulling him along was assisted by another, who kicked the old fellow every time he tried to stand up or grab a lamppost. When he finally succeeded, and patted the air in front of him, he smiled at his tormentors. The two young men laughed and walked along past him, looking for other amusement.

"The old Jew looks like he enjoyed that," said a young woman in a smart tweed coat and matching hat.

"All in fun." Her companion smiled., "And it teaches the Jew a lesson." He pulled out her chair.

"What lesson?"

"To respect our Austrian youth." He smiled at the waiter. "Two coffees, please, and some torte."

Some customers noticed the time and left. Others, like me, sat down again. I picked up a paper and put it down quickly, as it gave away how much my hands were trembling.

The staff had a shift change. One of the new waiters came over to my table, and I ordered a hot chocolate *mit schlag*. The waiter, who was broad-shouldered with a neatly trimmed beard, brought it with a flourish. "Your accent is wonderful, Madam. You live abroad?"

"Yes, in England."

"And yet you come here. To read our newspapers."

"They seem to be full of the same news."

"They do, don't they." He flicked the table with a napkin, tucked in a chair, and raised his eyebrow a fraction. I smiled. He leaned forward and straightened the carnations on the table. "What brings you to the Arundel, Madam?"

"Today? I am meeting my sister."

"Yes. But why in Vienna? Soon it will no longer be all waltzes and Lippizaners." He pointed to the newspaper, extolling the virtues of a leader homegrown in Austria, Hitler.

"Please, I am not seeking any attention. My sister…"

"But you have been here all day, and switching tables is not going to make anyone forget a woman in such a beautifully tailored suit. And your hat!"

I could barely manage to remain sitting. I pointed to an item on the menu. "Have you seen her? She's blonde and slender. She's wearing a leopard skin coat."

"I'm sorry, I haven't seen her, Madam. The supper hour will soon be over."

"I have to wait for her. Might I use your telephone?"

"Again? They are going to think you are a spy if you keep calling the British Embassy."

"How do you know who I've been calling?"

"This is Vienna. Known for chocolate and intrigue. And we close within the hour. Sorry."

I rang one more time, and this time I got through. Miss Piers answered. She said that she understood that my sister had rung my hotel, and when the clerk said I wasn't there, she had tried the café but each time, the line was busy. Miss Piers suggested I go back to my hotel, since my sister had that address, and wait for her to contact me. To let them know when she had. And if she could be of any further assistance?

At the hotel, I slipped in unnoticed through a crowd of Italians registering at the front desk. Susannah wasn't among them. I went directly to the lift and to my room. I called down to ask if there were any messages for me, or any visitors. No. The room seemed very warm. I took off my suit and climbed into bed in my slip, and slept the perfect sleep of the guilty.

56.

THE NEXT DAY, outside the window where I sat, small
groups of happy, defiant young men—and a few young
women too—were walking along the chilly street with their
arms linked around each other's waists, singing "*Deutschland,
Uber Alles.*" In the café, I could hear the gossip around me:
there are Germans at the border. The Nazis have taken over
small towns already. The Italians are at the border. The leader
of the moderate party has committed suicide. The Jews have
smuggled in relatives with contagious diseases. Hitler is on his
way to visit his mother's grave in Linz.

The same waiter was there, working the morning shift. He
leaned over the table and pointed to a newspaper. "Shall I get
rid of this rubbish, Madam?" I gave a slight shrug, a roll of
my eyes to the left. The waiter swooped it away. "You look
refreshed. You looked splendid yesterday, but a little tired.
May I compliment you on your hat, Madam?"

"Thank you. You look well yourself for someone who is
working around the clock."

"A few years back, in Berlin, they used to call me the wake-
up boy." He blushed.

So. He's a homosexual. An ally. He would know how to
keep it discreet.

"I haven't seen your sister, but I have—hold on."

A loud commotion outside. People rushed towards us to look
out the windows. A woman on her knees, holding a toothbrush.

"Clean the street, you Jewish whore, right where you walked on it!" A big fellow in his twenties with a double-breasted coat stretched tight across his belly was barking orders. The coat was not new. A small crowd watched without much enthusiasm. The woman brushed the sidewalk in wide swoops and then concentrated on a spot immediately in front of her, her head down.

"Your kind has been making our city filthy for years, with your constant building of huge homes! With your swinish relatives who haven't heard of a bath! With..." He seemed unable to think of anything else. She was sobbing and moving her hand.

"You kill babies for your *matzoh*." This was an old accusation, tired old stuff that the tormenter's parents or grandparents might have said. Trying to hold his audience, the fellow put his boot on her hand. There was no change in the woman's movements. She moved her hand more slowly with his boot on top of it. He was jostled off balance and fell on his leather elbow. Behind the crowd, someone began to beat a drum, someone else shouted, and a larger, more excited crowd appeared, swallowing up those in front of the café.

"She's a filthy Jewess!" the fellow shouted at their backs. The woman seized her opportunity and fled, fear and anger fighting for dominance on her face.

I realized that a man at the next table was staring at me. My waiter was talking to me. He had brought chicken paprikash, some hot vinegar and celery seed on sugar cabbage, and a small plate of *rösti*. I picked up my spoon, and saw, sticking out from under the bowl, a folded piece of paper. I picked up my purse and opened it on my lap, as if I were looking for something. I slid the note out from under the bowl and opened it inside my open purse.

Don't leave the Café Arundel without paying compliments to the chef.

I closed my purse and ate. When my fork was upside down beside my knife on the plate, the waiter came over to my table.

"My compliments to the chef."

"Would you like to pay them yourself?"

I picked up my small suitcase and purse and followed the waiter, who opened the door to the kitchen. Gleaming silver, steam, sizzling grills, and several waiters lounging against the aluminum counters. They stepped aside for me. The waiter smirked at his colleagues suggestively.

"Oh, a score."

"Oh, oh, oh!" A jolly slap with a towel by my waiter on the sous chef's back, past the dishwasher's elbows deep in suds, and we were around a corner. We stopped at the bottom of a short flight of stairs by an open door. The waiter leaned around the corner, opened his mouth in a big grin like someone in a vaudeville production and shook his head at his coworkers. As soon as he slammed the door, he said in a loud voice, "Oh, you *Englische* baby!"

Guffaws from the kitchen.

"That comment will hardly help my reputation."

"No, but it will help mine."

"Stop. Where is she?"

He opened a door. "Go in there."

There was no one, just shelves and boxes and an industrial lamp, its metal shade creating a cone of light. The waiter slid open a heavy door on a track. My eyes adjusted to the gloom. A small girl sat, drumming her heels on a box in a desultory fashion. She was dumpy and pouty, with a short chin and a turned-up nose. Behind her, in a beautiful long camel coat, tailored trousers, and fine shoes, with a fedora in his hand—I had my arms around him before the thought finished—George.

George.

He grinned. A big, open grin. He embraced me back. I had apparently already embraced him. I took a step back and then another.

"Hedy. You look wonderful!"

Hearing him speak English was like shedding a carapace. *Come, thou tortoise.* "George, what is going on? Where is Susannah?"

"Hedy, let me explain."

"Is that noise necessary?" I glared at the child, whose feet froze in mid-air and then continued. An uncombed, badly cut mane of hair fell over her forehead.

"I want to eat in the restaurant."

"She speaks English!"

"A little." He smiled at the little girl. "How about another sweet?" George handed candies in a long paper cone to the girl. He nodded to the waiter, who left, sliding the heavy door on its track until it closed with a *clank* behind him.

"Susannah was being watched from the moment she left Italy. Some relative of her late husband notified the Austrian authorities that she was entering the country, that she was a Jew, and that she had made a questionable withdrawal of money. Apparently her husband was active in supporting the Republicans..."

"Yes, yes. Where is she?"

"She's safe. We have our own eyes and ears. She's with the sister of a cab driver who works with us."

"I don't know who this 'we' is, but I have papers, British transit documents, everything needed to get her out of Austria. Take me to her."

"Hedy, I can't. She's at risk. But we can get some people out of the city, Susannah among them, and into Switzerland, in a few days. We have done this several times in the last month." The little girl who had been furiously chewing on a caramel now sawed its cellophane wrapper back and forth, creating a crackling racket.

"Can you make her stop doing that? You are talking so softly I can hardly hear you. You and your 'we' can do whatever you like. I want my sister."

"Hedy. You have to trust me. We don't have much time. The

transit documents you have for Susannah weren't going to stop the British from interrogating her. Never mind the Austrians. Fortunately, we have a contact at the Embassy, and she told Susannah to make a fuss to get her out of there."

"You have a contact! I have been reassured by the deputy to the Ambassador…"

"They want to ask her some questions. They think that she may have information."

"You sound like you think it's reasonable to detain her!"

"No, I don't! I'm asking you to see it from their point of view. Damn it, Hedy, there isn't time for this! Tomorrow morning, this city is going to be really dangerous for Jews. There are forty-foot-long banners, swastikas on red flag silk, ready to unfurl all along the Ringstrasse. This city is ripe, and wants to be plucked. And two days from now, Hitler is going to enter the city. If the British don't hold you, you don't want to see what the new police chief of Vienna might do. And either side might hold you to see if they can flush out Susannah."

"But Susannah is only interested in politics in print, not in real life. She's not an activist. She grows carnations! And I have lived a perfectly respectable life in London, England. They wouldn't dare detain me."

"Listen to me, Hedy. She was seen with a suitcase, a literal *suitcase* full of money. Her husband was involved with the communists."

"Susannah said socialists."

"Do you think they really care to make a distinction?"

"And for that matter, I have a lot of money in my suitcase. A lot of people do now. She didn't know what Alfonso was doing. They had been leading somewhat separate lives. She was growing flowers and swanning around on a seaside promenade!"

"We will keep her safe, I promise, and get her out to Switzerland first and then to England, I promise. As for you, let us accompany you this time."

"This time, as opposed to last time. And who would like to go with me, who is this 'us'?"

"I am one, and I would like you to meet my friend, Ruth." He gestured towards the girl. She had loaded more candy into her mouth and was trying to suck some sugary drool back into it.

"No. George. I am here for my sister, not for some illegal half-baked underground spy games. I have the right papers for her. I have our tickets for the train tonight."

"And they will have officers waiting for you to pick up your passport at your hotel."

"I have transit papers." I pulled them out of my purse and flapped them at him.

George nodded. "Well done. But they will be at the station if you try to board a train. Please, Hedy. You and I, with our child, here, little Ruth. A different identity. Not two noticeably beautiful sisters. Thank God you still dress so well. I have had to learn. For what I do, it's important to look respectable.

What I do. Not journalism entirely, then. I looked at the child. "No one would believe I would dress a child like that. Look at her."

The child scratched at her stomach ferociously, and then her head. "We will have her cleaned up. Top to bottom."

"No."

"Hedy, they might well believe that you and I would have a child like this." He smiled at the urchin, who gave him a wobbly smile back. "I got the Edelstein girls out before and I am going to get both of you out again. Trust me."

"Why?"

"Damn it, you would have left with me fifteen years ago."

How dare he? "As you say, fifteen years ago when I met a wonderful fellow who has made my life safe and supported me in every way. Who has connections, and those connections will get my sister and me out of this awful city. Why would I risk that to go with you?"

"Because, Hedy, I am here, and he is in Bermuda."

"How do you know where he is? What else are you, besides a scribbler?"

The latch on the sliding door clanked, and George froze. The small girl ducked under a canvas tarpaulin. The waiter entered alone. "Not yet?"

"No, Diederich, we're still talking."

"Look, the lady is going to have to go with me. I can't fake a romance if you're in here with her. You take Ruth, and we'll exchange partners later in the Augarten."

Diederich had long legs, but he adjusted his pace to walk with me. The Augarten and its familiar paths. My mother. Moreno. Susannah. New Hans, who had helped me find Susannah that awful night after she and I had quarrelled and I had let her walk away from me.

"How long have you known that little girl?"

"A few days. Her mother is helping us. Her father was arrested two days ago. That's when Ruth was attacked. I rescued her. I have her travelling clothes here. There's George."

But who is us? George was hauling the little girl along, forcing her to walk. She had locked her knees and leaned back so that he had to drag her by her stiff arm as if it were a wagon handle. We could hear them arguing.

"I don't want to go to that stupid lady's hotel. I want to stay with Diederich." She ran and grabbed the waiter's hand.

"Ruthie, I'm not safe enough for you to stay with me."

"Because you kiss boys."

"George." I had hold of his lapel. "My hotel isn't safe. We can't go there. Mischlinger is the night manager."

George took this in. After a few seconds, he said, "Diederich. Hang onto Ruthie one day more. Clean her up, and bring her to my hotel before eight o'clock tomorrow morning."

Diederich took Ruthie's hand and they tottered away through the Augarten's alternating pools of streetlamps and darkness.

"So, you've been spying on me."

A pair of young men emerged into the pool of light that spilled from a nearby street lamp. They pulled an Austrian flag back and forth between them, squawking in turn as if they were the double eagle on the cloth, all for the amusement of their followers. "Heil!" they shouted, laughing and stumbling towards us.

George pulled me off the path, his arm around me. "Stay still. I'm supposed to be kissing you and you are supposed to be liking it."

I was sure I gave the right impression.

When the little pack left, George lead me down a cross path. "I did keep track of you. I cannot tell you the alarm I felt when we found out that Susannah was to meet you. Did Mischlinger recognize you?"

"He hasn't figured out who I am. He will."

George grimaced. "I've never forgotten that session at Moreno's. Hedy, you can't go back there. I won't let him harm you ever again. You cannot go back to that hotel."

"I know. That's why I'm lugging this suitcase around, despite there being a manly fellow walking me along the canal. Why can't I talk to Susannah tonight?"

George blushed and took the suitcase. "They don't have a telephone in the house where she is. We do everything by messages, runners. Like Hitler supposedly did across the German trenches in the last damn war. He just carried messages between generals; he never ran a damn trench in his sorry life." We were about to cross the Augartenbroke. "She's safe, Hedy."

"So you think there will be another war?"

"Before the year is out, yes. So, here's my hotel. I'm afraid I'll have to sneak you in the service entrance."

57.

A S SOON AS THE DOOR to his hotel room closed, George convinced me. He told me a little about the Canadians, the British, the French, and even some Austrians who were in on this semi-unofficial scheme to get a few more people out before it was too late. His newspaper contacts made him valuable, a source of reliable information, a person with a plausible reason to move around. "They approached me," he said, with something like pride.

George's room was tidy, notebooks open, stacked on each other. The bed made. He brought a blanket from the closet and put it around me. He took off my shoes. When he took off his own, I felt safe for the first time that day.

"I'd forgotten—you have really flat feet! Just like Susannah."

George shrugged and stretched. *This was where I came in. This was where our story had left off.* He poured us each a whisky. I gulped mine.

"Hedy, are you sleepy?"

"No. I'm wide awake."

"Me too. When news start to break like this, I'm my most alive."

"You like this."

"Yes."

He told me what he had seen in Paris, and in Addis Ababa. How he liked being a journalist, the strange combination of lying and truth, lying to get at the truth. How to get people to confide in him, the need to make constant decisions about information, to argue with editors and then go for a drink with them afterward, to meet deadlines, and most of all, to be readable.

"Tell me something personal, George."

He took my hand. "Right then. One time, I was chasing after what was going on in Ethiopia, and I got suddenly sick and had to hide in a sand dune from the Italians until my friends found me and carried me back to safety along old routes run by the stars. Apparently I kept talking about 'tumbling constellations.' I don't know what those Ethiopian fellows gave me to drink, but by god, they can..." he broke off. "You don't like the story." He let go of my hand.

"It's a good story, but you've told it so often that it tells itself. You won't remember if you told it to me because you've told it so often. What do you need to tell me, in particular?"

George was silent. He stood up. "Good lord, what paper hired you? You could do my job. Fair enough, Hedy. You're right, I've told these stories often. All I am are those stories. I'm telling you who I am, what has happened to me. I have no one except the people I sometimes can help. A surgeon who operated on the battlefield, who saved Republican lives, he's a friend. He comes and stays with me when I'm in my digs in London, and talks my head off and sleeps on my couch, avoiding his parents in Rosario and his wife and kids in Reading.

"He walked around with me one day in the British Museum, when I was following you. You were looking at the heads of the statues, one after the other. You moved your hands, just a little, like this, as if you were touching their heads. Nothing obvious. He said you were the most attentive person he had seen that day. Actually, he said for years. That is surely personal enough for you."

I took this in. *He had seen me and had said nothing.* "You followed me? And you have investigated Harold. Did I make a hat for one of your sweethearts? How many brats do you have? What is the name of your virgin queen, your chaste bride?"

I didn't really think that there was a wife, or children. I was thinking about all those times I had longed to talk to him! I was drinking in seeing him again. I was angry, not because he had followed me, but because he hadn't talked to me. Had I been looking my best, or had I been under the weather, wading through sorrow? He was clearly unfair, selfish. I had been scrupulous in avoiding him, even though seeing him was what I deeply desired. I was angry because I knew I should be. *But would he please hurry up and hold me as he had on the street?* I narrowed my eyes. "Who do you think you are, a character from Puccini? Gianni Scicchi?"

His face broke into laughter.

"I have observed you too."

"When?" He stopped laughing, astonished.

"Your dispatches. You haven't got a spontaneous bone in your body." *Except when you dance. Or laugh at my jokes. Why am I so combative?* I reminded him of the oft-repeated comment about old Ramsay needing to be held tight. How he had been careful about taking me into his neighbourhood.

He blushed and tried to divert. "Poor old Ramsay. His principles as fair as his hair and his fate as dark as his moustache."

"How soon before I read that in one of Beaverbrook's rags? When I knew you were in London, I'd avoid you by going to Twin Oaks or to Bournemouth." A lie, especially going to Bournemouth, but I wanted to win. *What was it I wanted to win?*

"Bournemouth! You were serious!" He started to walk around. He turned out all but one table lamp. I said nothing. I was the one who had taught him how to wait someone out, after all. The lessons of 13 Verstektstrasse.

"I never took you anywhere." He looked full of regret. "Did you ever walk over the bridges of the Seine?" He brightened. "Did you go into the old part, into the Marais? There's a bakery..."

This was too painful. "You didn't want me. You made me ashamed of wanting you."

George was silent. He stopped pacing.

"After all these years, you still can't say what you feel."

He sat on the bed. His voice was ragged. "I will. I'm not used to anyone caring. I ignore how I feel most of the time. And I think anyone who wants me must be crazy. I did think I had found someone once, someone wretched like me."

"Was she pretty?"

His face lit up. "She was." Then his face clouded, his gaze turned inward. "Drinking was a problem. There was a child, a boy, who died. Not mine."

Arrows plunged into me, pulled out, lodged sideways. "What happened?"

"I don't know. I don't think she could stand the implications of being loved, the knowledge that she would have to do right by someone."

I was asking about the child. He was thinking about himself, how he had been mistreated. My mind flew great distances away from this man. *He has loved, but not me.* Speeding back to this man. *But if he has loved before, then he can love again. I want him to love me.*

"What happened to the child?"

"Influenza, apparently. Before I met her."

"Why didn't she stay?"

"I was sick with pleurisy after I nearly drowned in the Black Sea, and I couldn't help her. I think she saw me as a leg up and I let her down. When I wasn't able to introduce her to the people she wanted to meet, she accused me of being selfish. She stayed with me until my money ran out. She was like Russia to my Spain. She emptied my bank account and left me stranded in Copenhagen. Wonderful Copenhagen. Queen of the Sea."

His glass was empty. He turned it around in his hands. "I need to talk about something else, please, for a few minutes.

It was a great shock that you were coming to Vienna, this week of all weeks. We have scrambled to get what was needed for you and your sister and have had to adjust our plans for little Ruth. And right now, I must work. I have to file a report tonight and take it to the telegraph office. I should be typing it right now."

"Fine. Type away."

"No, Hedy, it's not that simple. I have to think about what I am going to say, usually before I write it." He laughed. "Some of my colleagues think I just wait until the last moment to bash out a story. The truth is, I do most of my writing first of all in my head, looking out a window."

He's losing his British accent. The a's are flatter, there is a declamatory tone. Not quite American, but not British, either.

"A truce, Hedy, for a few minutes."

Canadian. I picked up a notepad, a pencil, and began to draw. I made one sketch after another of a hat that could only work if it were red. He was startled and watched me for a few moments before lighting a cigarette and walking over to the window. He opened it briefly, and I could hear the ardent noise of people still in the streets, some city blocks away. His cigarette burned down, and he put it out at the last moment. After a while, he lit another. He was silent, still, staring out the window at nothing, at his own thoughts.

He pulled out a typewriter on a metal table with squeaking wheels, lit another cigarette, and put it in the glass ashtray beside him. The smoke curled up, and the cigarette went out. He lit it again, took a drag, and began to pound out his dispatch. He got his notes out from his jacket pocket to check something, took a drag on the cigarette, and then clattered away, the skitching sound of the cartridge returning, his body not there, only his mind and his fingers, bashing out the story on the keys.

A rolling rip of the paper from the platen. A look over to me. I looked back, steady as a mirror. "I have to get this down to the dispatch courier. There are lots of journalists in this hotel, so they've got a runner for us."

He was back in minutes, locking the door. "Let me tell you about Spain."

He went on to talking, things he knew but wasn't allowed to report, and things he and others could easily predict: that the atrocities that were already happening in Germany would be worse in Austria. "The reverse side of *Gemutlichkeit*, of sentimentality, is brutality."

I stood up. "I expect to read that phrase in *The Evening Standard* within the week. Now, George. *Now*. The world is going to hell, I know. If you won't talk to me now about how you feel about me, if you won't take that risk, why should I take all the risks you are asking of me? Why shouldn't I walk out that door and go to the British Embassy tonight and tell them my sister has been kidnapped by socialists? Or communists. Or whatever you are."

He faced me. There was a nerve jumping over his left eye. "I've told you, Susannah is safe. I have called in every favour to keep her safe. Because she's your sister, Hedy."

"I'm glad I am not alone in caring about my sister's safety." I walked to the closet and got my coat.

"All right. Here. Not a week has gone by without at least a fleeting thought of you. And there you were, safe, with your titled fellow, and there was I, still scribbling out a living, no savings. I'm not a warm and cheerful fellow. I argue with people, and I boast, and I sometimes talk about things when I really don't know very much about them. More than one person has called me callous, and more than a few have said I'm pompous. People in the news are important people. Being known to them, to have their acquaintance, gave me a sense I belonged. I could plant them like famous fence posts around me, be protected by their fame from attacks by people who would like to see me gone. People who think the colonial boy doesn't belong. Well, now, I do."

"And that is what you feel about me?" I put on my coat. "That was all about you. I am not famous, George, and no one should look too closely at my circumstances. I don't like it if they do, and they don't like me if they do."

"You are the only one who knows me from when I was just beginning."

I put on my hat.

He stopped me at the door. "When I see your face, when you look at me like that, with all of you pouring from your eyes…"

"What?"

"I'm afraid."

"Of what?"

"Your scorn. It has always mattered that you cared about me. I could think of you, imagine you really liking me. Until I caught my breath and could be ruthless again."

"Do you have to be ruthless?"

"I'm afraid not to be. Yes."

I said nothing. *Am I also afraid?*

"Hedy, talk to me. You were so strong, like you were made of adamantine."

"So I am hardened, like every whore."

"No, I think you are soft beyond measure. Kind."

"So's your great Aunt Tilda." *Thank you, Pauline.*

"I love how you walk, so purposeful. You move forward, but you sway, like you are swimming upstream."

This was exhausting. Whenever I had thought about him in the past, the thoughts never developed very far. It was like a list of lovely things. Running down the list, I would be adrift remembering his voice, his hands, everything so dear to me. I had not thought I would be trying to convince him to tell me what I meant to him. We were both quiet.

It was well after midnight, and, below on the street, city sanitation workers were singing and throwing garbage from bins into trucks on the street below. Free to be noisy. Things were about to change. He closed the window.

"Tell me about your life."

I told him first about my hat shop, how I liked making people look good, but didn't actually like being around people. I told him about walking, in Berkshire and in London, and about the steadiness of animals. My dog Mist. About Harold, eventually, and how he had disappeared first into alcoholism, then to Bermuda. About the wound of Susannah's absence. I said nothing about his fedora, and what it had cost me.

George said he went back to Canada when his mother died, but he hadn't been back since. He said there was little affection and lots of disapproval of his altered accent and of his opinions. Perhaps of his opinions because of his accent. And yes, there had been women. A Spanish woman, in particular, who was married to a professor of linguistics. A person he couldn't marry.

"Or wouldn't, like me."

"I was ambitious, and I didn't know what I know now."

"I wasn't likely to advance your career."

"Hedy, I loved you as much as I could have loved anyone at the time."

"And now?"

He shrugged. "Words fail."

"No, not this time. You don't get to do that. You are not a man without words."

"I'm a man who has trouble trusting."

"I don't care. I need to hear someone tell me some words, someone who isn't saying them from a place of safety. Who is taking a risk to say them."

"Then listen," he said, and I did. Eventually I was listening in his arms, and after that, we made love, my mother's ring bouncing on its gold chain, glinting in the light.

It was early morning when I awoke. He was fully dressed, with his typewriter, a Royal, tucked under his arm. *O my love.* That's what he had said. *O my love.*

"I have to get my pick ups from the dispatch office, and then I'll take you to see Susannah, and then, my love, we will leave this town—you, me, and our darling daughter, little Ruthie."

He returned late from the dispatch office. The wire services had been flooded with news. He had had to bribe them, finally, for an earlier turn at the telegraph machines, and barely had time to make his meeting with Diederich. When he walked into the hotel room with a transformed Ruth—bouncing curls, a bow, her hands inside a square muff of rabbit fur, I was astounded. Diederich was a talented man. She chewed on her hat ties and glowered at me.

"Are we taking her with us to go and see Susannah?"

"Susannah has already gone. I'm sorry, Hedy."

I had his lapels in my hands. "What have you done with her!"

"Hedy, I'm sorry. It was felt that things had to move more quickly."

"By whom was this felt? Who felt this? What does that mean?"

"If I don't tell you, you can't tell anyone else, and you are at less risk."

"You mean your 'whom' is less at risk."

"Hedy, everything is in play. The Germans are advancing into Austria. Flowers for them, in this weather! The wooden barrier crossings are being lifted by Germans and Austrians in love with each other, for at least as long as it takes for a photo. Hedy, stop." He took my wrists in his hands. "Hedy. My love. I know you love your sister. We have done the best, safest thing for everybody. She'll be in Switzerland within a few days."

I pulled away from him. Susannah had been counting on me.

"Hedy, wait. Have you seen the street outside?"

I had. Scarlet banners bleeding down the front of all the buildings. The stabbing black gear of the swastika.

"She sent this."

I grabbed the paper bag he held out. Inside was the wedge cap in leopard skin I had made for Susannah five years ago, a jaunty version of a military cap. And a note, in English: "DON'T WORRY, HAIRBRUSH, THIS IS THE SAFEST THING TO DO, UNDER THE CIRCUMSTANCES. ONCE I'M IN GENEVA, I'LL CALL YOU AND COME TO YOU. HORSIE."

It was printed in fast block letters, but only Susannah could have written it. I felt a sudden pain, a small axe, in my left eye. I tucked the note into my brassiere and the hat, folded flat, into my purse.

A deep breath.

George pulled out our new passports. Ruthie was travelling on my passport as my child. Ruth, Mrs. George Andrew's child. I put the passport beside the hat in my purse and took one of Ruth's hands. George straightened the lapels on my coat and picked up my suitcase. I let go of Ruth's hand to adjust the tilt of his fedora.

O my love.

We grasped Ruth's small, warm hands for the second time, and walked down the stairs and out into the noisy streets. Bellowing and shouting, marching and singing, Vienna had finally let its basement creature loose, and it careened about the city, unrestrained. The street swarmed with hundreds of people, wild and chaotic. And then, just like that, it was empty—they were gone like locusts on the wind, to feed on something else that freed them to shout, to scorn, or to mock.

The cab driver was someone George knew, and they exchanged a few uneasy words. And then back alley, back alley, double back, horn blaring as we drove on a wide path in the Augarten, entirely illegal. But what was illegal today?

Into the Westbahnhof Station, down the metal steps—*bang bang bang*—and into the right train compartment, out of breath. The station was full of people, a hullabaloo of shouting and excitement. It was also strangely full of dark grey pigeons, lining up on the wide steps in gurgling rows. They had to fly up to the rafters or all the way outside whenever passengers trooped down to the train platform. Each time, after a few minutes, the birds returned, waddling on pink feet to the seats they had left, cooing and settling in for the show. And then up and away again. A terrier, tied to a station cart piled high with suitcases, barked every time the pigeons took flight.

On the mezzanine above, the sound of young people calling to each other, following the anxious instructions of a woman with a smoker's voice. I couldn't pay attention to what they were saying. Red banners began to unfurl from the railing around the mezzanine. Some got caught or tangled. There were more instructions, and gradually, a scarlet waterfall fluttered down towards the entrance floor. More voices, then, but I had not slept, or slept very little—*o my love*—and the whole station was drowned in noise. George patted the back of my hand and showed me the tickets.

Ruth dashed to the compartment door that opened to the platform. I was just as quick to pull her back, but as I did, I saw a woman in a leopard skin coat, too long for her, walking along, casually smoking. Her hair was grey, brushed back into wings. She carried a large violet-coloured valise. She glanced at me calmly as she turned to step up into the next train compartment. She nodded. *She knew who I was.*

"George! I just saw Fraulein Lowin, and I swear she's wearing Susannah's coat! She just nodded to me. What...?"

"Shh, Hedy." George pulled me back from the door. "Her own coat identified her too easily.

Susannah's coat will be the conductor's bribe, once we are across the border. Fraulein Lowin has been a great help to us."

"She's part of the 'us'?"

"Yes. She has to leave today, too. Be still, Ruth."

"But what does Susannah have to wear? It's freezing."

"Something warm and less conspicuous."

Ruth burst out laughing. "Look at that stupid lady!"

Others were laughing, too. At the bottom of the stairs, some guards were trying to restrain a stout woman who was brandishing a toothbrush at them, lunging at them as if she held a rapier. She was dishevelled; a huge stain on her coat rose from the hem in a circle up the back. It was the same woman I had seen yesterday outside the Café Arundel. Yesterday seemed months ago. The woman flung herself free and ran to the edge of the platform. She peered into the compartments, dashing from one to another, shouting, "I know you!"

"I know you! You took my money!" Everyone watched her. She was saying every awful thing that had happened to someone in the station: a mad, perfect litany. The guards crept around behind the watching crowd so that she would walk right into their arms. She pursed her cupid's bow mouth before every outburst.

"I know you! Did you fancy my Albert?" she called into the compartment next to ours. George cautioned us to be still. When she appeared at our door, she looked directly at me. "I know you! You were a bad little girl!" I shrunk back into the compartment, to the delight of Ruth. The woman swooped on to the next compartment, but we could still hear her, magnificent in holy accusation.

"I know you. Bribes don't help forever! Ha!"

"Stay away from the windows. Both of you." With the skill of every journalist of his generation, he got a cigarette out of a pack, stuck it in his mouth and lit it, all with one hand. He took a drag, making sure to keep the cigarette clear of his beautiful coat. He had one shoulder back, torqueing as if to deliver a blow.

Ruth gazed at George's back. Her little chest lifted and subsided. "You always know what to do, George. When do I start talking English to people?"

"Not just yet."

Ruth put her head down. She reached into the rabbit fur muff and pulled out a caramel. Once it was in her mouth, she concentrated on removing every bit of moisture and sweetness. She knew better than I how to wait. She looked like a hundred-year-old child.

More shouting. I leaned forward to look out the window again. The woman was gone. There were only well-wishers seeing people off, waving hankies, blowing kisses. The train brakes were released. Uniformed station guards marched by, their gloves tucked into their belts. George turned around. I was already looking at him. He smiled steadily at me. *O my love.* In one movement, George tossed his cigarette, sat down, and kissed me on the mouth.

"Eww," said Ruth. George reached out his hand to Ruth. She put a caramel in his palm.

"Thank you, Ruth. Everyone be still." Outside, Wagon Lit conductors in dark blue uniforms, silver-trimmed hats set correctly on their heads, moved in pairs to the front of the train. They began to close and secure the compartment doors that opened onto the platform.

Shouting. A man running. It was the waiter, Diederich. He was being chased by green uniformed Westbahnhof station guards. In his arms was a small boy. *What has he done?* The terrier, beside himself with alarm and joy, barked and bounced stiffly on all four legs. George looked at me, a fixed moment, then jammed on his fedora and leaped out onto the platform.

George ran towards the melee. He blocked the path of a guard who had almost caught up with Diederich. After some jostling and pushing, the fellow was on the ground, grabbing for his cap. George handed it to him and helped him to his feet. Then he hung onto the guard's arm, as if to help him, preventing him from moving easily, and gestured extravagantly as he talked to him.

From the ground where he had been tossed, the boy leapt up like a circus acrobat. He ran, zigzagging around pillars, and ricocheted off the stack of suitcases on the cart. The terrier strained at his leash, letting out great gulping barks as a guard punched Diederich, one blow after another, until the waiter collapsed on the ground. Other guards ran to join in, blowing their shrill whistles, as if they couldn't get them to make a loud enough sound. I wondered, in the way you do when you are in shock, about something odd: if, that morning, the sound was absorbed by the huge crowd and their thick winter clothing.

George tried to block the guards, talking rapidly, walking backwards. The crowd hampered them, too, by not getting out of the way, slowing them down. Who knows how many not-quite-legal trips were being made from that station that morning? Vienna loves to collaborate, as Moreno had said on a much nicer morning than this.

The guards were red-faced and sweating now, angry. Everyone was watching them be made fools of. They finally pushed George aside. They kicked him and then they used their truncheons on Diederich—in the face, hard, in the groin, harder. Diederich rolled himself back up to a crouch and then sprung up, both fists hammering at the guards. The boy ran back, his fists up and his face knotted in fury. He, too, was having trouble getting through the crowd that now milled around the wrestling match, putting their suitcases down inconveniently, bunching up together in cooperative awkwardness.

"John!" A sharp cry, from Ruth, standing in the open door. The boy halted.

"*John!*"

The boy saw her, and slipped between a dark wool coat and a large buckled suitcase. He flew across the platform and dove into our compartment, balling himself up under the overhang of the seat, hidden behind my long coat.

I shoved my feet forward and spread my coat out. The boy huddled, trembling. *Like a hare through frozen grass*. More guards arrived on the scene—shouts, commands rang out, and all remaining open compartment doors were slammed shut. More whistles. George was still on the platform, still talking to the guards. The train began to move. I got up and tried the handle. Ruth jumped up and shoved me so hard that I fell back into my seat, my feet outstretched. The waiter was being hauled off, the toes of his lovely shoes dragging on the platform. I couldn't see George.

The train cleared the station, gathering speed. The locomotive horn sounded twice. I had to think about what would be the next thing.

O my love. Leaving Vienna on a train again. *This time with Fraulein Lowin in the next compartment, wearing my sister's coat.* Without George. Without Susannah. I didn't look at Ruth, and I didn't dare move my long coat away from the small boy underneath it. The train found its rhythm, and I could feel the soporific effects of its movement. *Alle, alle zusammen.* All together now. Except my sister. Except my sister. *Alle, alle zusammen. Last time, George, you at least left me your hat. This time, in my purse, I have a hat that matches the coat in the next compartment.* I started to laugh, but it hurt my throat. The western suburbs of Vienna disappeared.

I took a deep, ragged breath. The boy's arm reached up. In his hand was a dark blue British passport. In it, three transit permits, perfect papers, listing "John" and "Ruth" as children on a passport apparently belonging to a Hedy Highstone, wife of George Highstone. From Bournemouth.

The day brightened, and the train was moving smoothly through snowy fields. The axe in my eye had disappeared. It was warm in the compartment. I took my gloves off. How many passports had George prepared? I tried to follow my usual train of thought, to stir up my old memories of George. Those old thoughts always calmed me. Now I had an additional, extraordinary memory. George. Last night. With his arms around me, making love to me. All I could think was this: if he and the others he works with are thinking this far ahead, and had this many passports ready, Susannah is certainly safe.

O my love! I smiled. *Be safe.* I felt he would be. He would land on his feet like this small boy under my coat. Ruth pulled him up onto the seat beside her. How old was he supposed to be? However old he was, he was tiny. He reminded me of another boy I had once known, also small for his age: Kaspar. I looked at the passport. John Highstone, eight years old, a lively-looking boy. Nicely dressed. He got down and stood at the window on tiptoe to look out.

He looked at me and then he bellowed, "I want my Diederich!"

Ruth pulled him away from the window, and in an instant stuffed one of my gloves in his mouth. "Do you want to live? Are you going to stop with the yelling?" Ruth kept her hand over the glove in his mouth. He nodded. Ruth eased the glove away.

~

58.

IT WAS EASY TO CLIMB OUT the bathroom window. I left it open. The room wasn't heated, and the pipes could freeze. It would serve them right. Whatever they were doing, they weren't telling me the truth.

The cab driver who had arrived at the Embassy had been very courteous. Once I was in the car, he said Hedy Highstone had arranged for him to pick me up. Just as Miss Piers had said.

"Where is she?"

"She's not at the Hotel Vienna. It's full of Italian fascists right now—disgusting. My name's Emil, by the way. I've been ferrying your sister all over the city since she got here. Here's the thing: it's not safe to go to the hotel right now, so the plan is for you to stay at my sister's house. When I get off shift, I will take you to Hedy. Oh. I'm to say "Horsie" to you, whatever that means."

I relaxed, a little. I was exhausted from my experience in the Embassy—far too many people, far too solicitous, asking far too many questions. I knew something was wrong. When that strawberry blonde looked at me with that look that all women know which says, *you and I, we know what's really true*, when she said, "Make a fuss, *now*," I did. Rather well.

I figured we were somewhere in the north-western suburbs of the city. Emil glided to a stop, headlamps off. "Stay in the house until I come back for you. It's just a precaution, so don't worry."

I did. The time to worry is always when someone says, "don't." He was very gentlemanly, quickly helping me out of the car and into the house. He hung my coat in the closet and brought me a knitted blanket. "The old divan here is great for naps. The bathroom is down the hall. Don't turn on the lights."

"What if someone comes to the door?"

"Don't answer."

"Will you ring me, just before you come back, so I know it's you at the door?"

"Sorry, no telephone. I have to go. Just rest, and you will soon be on your way out of Vienna."

I woke up in the dark to hear a telephone ringing. Someone, a woman talking fast. *Sorry, no telephone.* Sorry, won't wait. I went to the closet. My coat was gone. So was my hat. I grabbed another coat and went down the dingy hallway to the bathroom.

Under the first street light, I got a chance to look at the coat. It was loden green, very Austrian: epaulettes and brass buttons. Ridiculous, but warm. Short in the sleeve. I headed towards the inner city. The snow had not stayed on the ground, and my high heels rang on the cold pavement. My underwear was itchy, top and bottom, with all the money I'd hidden there, and my arms and hands were cold. I pushed my hands down into the pockets of the coat and kept going. I joined a bunch of people walking towards the Ringstrasse.

"Vienna belongs to us! This is our city now!"

I moved with the crowd, mostly young people, mostly men, but also a few women who had been waiting for a chance to yell in the street. Sometimes they all ran, banging on the wrought iron railings in front of the houses. This was an affluent district, full of nice homes. I walked fast enough to keep up with the ones at the back of the swarm. We had been walking for nearly an hour. I wasn't cold any more, and I genuinely liked being out on the street at night. Up ahead, some police stopped the people at the front of the lurching parade, asking for papers.

"Let us walk! This is our city! We are walking in our city!"

I slipped down a cross street and turned up my collar. It was wool, and it smelled like the coat had hung in a kitchen. I walked automatically, as if I knew where I was going. I didn't, but my feet apparently did. I found myself in front of our apartment on the Schottenring. I walked into the lobby and rang the bell.

~

59.

THE CHILDREN WERE SLEEPING. I took the passport and the papers back from the conductor, who looked at me coldly and caressed his blond moustache. He checked off something in his book, zipped up its leather case with a flourish, and tucked it under his arm. He continued along the corridor.

Within moments, he was walking back, with a leopard skin coat folded over his arm. He gave me a knowing look and kept going. I slipped the ring from around my neck into my glove, nodding to Ruth who watched, yawning. Hours to the French border. Ruth started kicking the base of the padded bench. I told her to stop. She kept kicking, sullen and defiant. "It wasn't my idea that we travel together."

"Too bad for you. Now be quiet."

"Talk nice to me, or I'll wake up John. I'll call him by his real name. Izzy."

"Go ahead. I'm the one who has a proper passport. You don't. Shut up."

"Maybe I should tell the conductor you did this to me." She pulled up her blouse and undershirt. There, on her stomach, a red J. Scabby, healing. I jumped up, and shoved the blouse back into the skirt. "Diederich stopped the bad boys," Ruth whispered, and then pressed her lips inward, her mouth a line above her chin.

The conductor was back. "I'm sorry, our train is held up a little. The motorcade crossing the tracks at Linz is larger than we were told. Only a few minutes. Any problem here, Miss?"

"My nice old mother is just helping me," volunteered Ruth.

"Your old mother is very nice. Where is Papa Old and Nice?"

"He missed the train. He's always late, my Papa. He's English."

The conductor nodded, and checked his register. "Aren't you also English, little ... Ruth, isn't it?

"Yes, but we've been living in Vienna."

"Don't lose your accent. It's perfect. As for you, Mrs. Highstone, I know what you're doing." I knew he knew. I placed some banknotes from my pocket on the seat. He picked them up and left.

"I saw what you did." John apparently could feign sleep. "I want George."

"So do I."

~

60.

B EFORE I COULD RING THE BELL again, the door was jerked open by a woman in a well-tailored coat, a purse under her arm. She had a ghastly rhinestone angel pinned to her hat. She was smoking. "What do you want?"

"*Gruss Gott.*" A bad dye job on the woman's hair. Black hair didn't suit her—it made her look like a thousand other people—but something prickled, a sense of something familiar.

The woman just stared.

"Excuse me, dear Frau, my car, my Hispano-Suiza, has broken down and I wonder if I might use your telephone." I had kept the keys to the car in my purse. I pulled them out. *Alfonso, you loved me, and it's my fault you didn't trust me to drive the car. Or to know what you were doing. Me, who espoused Red Vienna. And said I didn't want demands made upon me. My fault, my fault.*

The woman looked at the keys and didn't move. Makeup to cover a bruise over the right eye. A green eye.

"There have been so many hooligans in the street these last two days."

"Where is your car?"

"Three city blocks south from here. May I use your telephone?" Oh, not a thousand other people. *Margarete, from Schiele's studio. And Moreno's.*

Margarete walked into the lobby and opened the door. There was no one on the street, nothing but a horse standing with its head down, ice on its mane. Steam out of its nostrils. Light blue lettering on the wagon, "Die Milchwagen von Viktor." Margarete stubbed out the cigarette on the door frame. The door to our old apartment. *She doesn't recognize me.*

"Come in." She waved me forward. "The telephone is there."

And it was, still on the same cherrywood table Papa had bought for it. The wide bottom, its exaggerated receiver. Margarete dug around in her purse. I bounced the receiver buttons until an operator came on the line. I asked to be connected to a cab company. One of Margarete's hands pushed the buttons down and took the receiver out of my hand. Her other hand held a gun.

"I know who you are. Where's your sister?"

"What? Oh, It's Margarete! I didn't recognize you. You look wonderful! The black hair is so dramatic!"

"If you're here to get your apartment back, forget it. That old pig Mischlinger can barely hang onto it himself."

Mischlinger is living in our home. "Oh, you look lovely! Not a day older. So *elegante.*"

Margarete smiled at the compliment. "Susannah, right? Why the Italian accent?"

"That's where I live. In San Remo, Italy." *Think quick, keep saying her name.* "As for Hedy, Margarete, my sister lives in England. With some peer of the realm."

A footstool, good. "Oh, shit." I tripped over the footstool and staggered in the direction of the door. "Well, it looks like we've all done well, Margarete! How long have you been living here?"

"Mischlinger brought me here." Margarete had moved around so that she was blocking the door.

I tried to keep a neutral face, as if this were just the news I had read while I had waited in the embassy: *Warm weather in Capri this March. Margarete lives in my Papa's house with Mischlinger.* "Do you like the place?"

Margarete looked around the ransacked room. "I didn't have

much of a choice. It was here or a prison for degenerates. I have to dress up like a schoolgirl for him. It's ridiculous. He's the degenerate."

Think about the news. *King Carol has returned to Romania. Margarete has a gun.*

Margarete plucked a cigarette from a leather cup on a side table and put it in her mouth. She had a gun in one hand, but the table lighter was meant for two hands. She couldn't light the cigarette without putting down the gun. I took a step forward, pasted an inquiring look on my face and held my hands forward, a gesture of supplication, like a martyred saint in an Italian fresco. Art has it uses. Margarete nodded, and I stood close. Think about the news. *Balenciaga's hat, like that of a Spanish nun ravished and dressed in a hurry.* When I had read that, I thought about Hedy, how she would laugh. I smiled as I lit the cigarette.

Margarete waved me over to a chair with silver cutlery all over the seat. She indicated her open purse, and I gathered it up and dumped it all in.

"Just like old times, no?" My German flowed, and so did my movements. This was my old home. The windows, there, the space between them where the painting of me and my sister used to hang.

"So you're not here for the apartment?"

"I just ended up here, Margarete, after my car broke down. I was on my way out of Vienna. Can you put the gun away?"

"Not yet. I have to think. I'm supposed to call the old creep when I finish packing. He packed most of this last night."

"When are you calling him?"

"I'm not. That old sack of guts thinks I'm going to leave with him and all this junk in that old Daimler of his. He drove off in it to the hotel this morning, waving his stubby old hand at me. I'm leaving, but not with him."

"Where are you going?"

"To Switzerland. *Yodel-eh–hee-hoo.* With an old friend who's got a car and some contacts to get rid of this garbage." She waved her gun at the large boxes by the door.

"Myself, I have to get to my husband's bank. Might there be room in the car for me?"

"A Swiss bank. Sure. Say, do you remember riding bicycles at Schiele's? You were so nice to me. You know, you were my first rich friend. Remember Moreno's?"

Margarete's eyes welled up and she jumped up to hug me. I was surrounded by the fumes. *Palinka.* Hungarian brandy. I could feel the side of the gun on my back. But this was Margarete. She liked me. Or my bicycle. Or the sound of a Swiss bank account.

~

61.

THE CONDUCTOR HAD TURNED ON the overhead lighting. It was night, and once again, we were moving west, then east, then west again. The confusion of Munich. We stopped only long enough to take on a few passengers, and for the Munich custom officials to check the manifest.

When the conductor came back, the children were asleep again. The little caramels had an extra ingredient, it seemed. I handed him the passport with money tucked inside, and he slipped it easily into his pocket. I wondered how many people on the train were bribing this man. He took the money like a pimp, like it was natural, his due. He leaned on the doorframe. "Shall I pull down the little boy's trousers and check his pecker?"

"I would complain."

"I will take this with me." He left with the passport.

"We should hide in another compartment." Ruth was not asleep, after all.

"No. The train is moving closer to our destination every minute. Let me read this book." I pulled out a dog-eared copy of *Hansel und Gretel* from Ruth's satchel. "Once there was a poor woodsman." I could see another conductor with metal glasses and an extra badge on his cap pause to look at me reading. He knocked on the door. Ruth got up to open it.

"Such a heartwarming little scene. These are yours, Madam?"

"Yes."

"Did you see the motorcade at Linz? Something the children

will remember. There must have been a hundred cars in the motorcade."

"There weren't a hundred." John was awake, too.

I shrugged and smiled. "I thought you were asleep, John." I patted his leg. "His mathematics are not so accurate."

"Like the passport you handed over, Madam. Not so accurate." He smiled at the children, who were very still. "Come into the corridor for a minute, if you will."

I closed the door behind myself.

"So you're a Jewess."

"I beg your pardon. I am English. What suggests…"

"Madam, your eyes suggest. Your nose. And those brats you have with you. Obvious."

"Excuse me, but the British Embassy…"

"Yes, yes. But right now you are on my train." The conductor with the blond moustache was now standing behind me.

I pulled out a wad of banknotes from my purse. "But gentlemen, how hard you work for the state."

"You can help us with our work. This way."

~

62.

A CAR HORN HONKED. Margarete, still holding the gun, said, "Just a minute." She went to the door and, within a minute, there on the threshold was Kaspar, smiling, handsome, gold crowns glinting on his front teeth. I stood up.

"Susannah! You are still so beautiful! Oh, I knew you right away!" He was exuberant. Happy. Kissing Margarete. He hugged me. He apparently loved *palinka*, too. "Where is Hedy? We are going on a bicycle tour, and you are just in time."

"Bicycling? In this weather?"

"It's about to change. A *fohn* is blowing and is going to warm everything up. Is Hedy here?"

"Hedy? She lives in England."

"Susannah, come upstairs with me." Margarete was bubbling with enthusiasm, still waving the gun.

"Why should I go upstairs?"

"You need to look sportier. Like someone who might ride a bicycle. I have some trousers you can belt, and some light sweaters. I am not sure what we can do about your shoes. Your feet are very long."

"And narrow," volunteered Kaspar, who was staring at my feet. "Get a pair of the old boy's leather tennis shoes. She can wear extra socks. Give me the gun, Margarete. I'll put it in the car."

"Are we really going to bicycle in March, Kaspar?"

"No. We're only going to take bicycles for show. Mine, and

that old one in the driveshed. But you know, you'll be surprised. The snow is already gone in some of the Swiss valleys. The goats will be up on the higher meadows any day now. And Margarete said you have keys to a Hispano-Suiza?"

I handed them over.

Kaspar tossed the keys up in the air and caught them. "*Yo-del-ay-hee-hoo!*"

If I have any particular skill, it is to instantly adapt to the agenda of the moment. I looked at myself in the hall mirror. *Time to shine, little glow-worm. My sister and I had once waited here with trapped fireflies in our dresses.* I followed Margarete into my parents' old bedroom. She threw some clothes on the bed and went downstairs.

She yelled, "*Oh-dee-lady-o*! Susannah! There's a cape in the closet that will make you look like a sporty girl on a sporty holiday!" She was happy and frantic.

The cape had a saddle-stitched pocket in the front. I put it on inside out, which made it marginally less ugly. I pulled a toque with snowflakes down over my hair and shifted into the trousers, thankful she had gone downstairs. She didn't need to know about all the banknotes in my underwear. I was glad about the extra pairs of socks. The idea of putting my foot where Mischlinger had put his made me gag. I shoved my feet in gingerly and tied the laces tight. I carried my Italian shoes, black with pale grey snakeskin, and flapped down the stairs. No one was there.

I looked around our old dining room before going out to the kitchen. No. At the door to the service entrance, the air was so cold. No one. Around the side, to the front. *Two men.*

I ducked back. Mischlinger got out of his Daimler. I knew it was him; I recognized his prim manner. He had shrunk, but he still had his bulk. *Pig. Piece of pig shit.* He approached them quickly, his head up, the old hotelier smile in place, a box in one hand. I felt sick and shrunk back behind the multiple bare branches of the copper beeches.

"Shall we step into the lobby, gentlemen?"

"You degenerates can't take the cold."

He held out the box. They ignored it.

"I've always admired this building, Herr Henker. The apartments are so large."

"Not so fast, Herr Parrech. I remind you: I'm senior to you." Without warning, Henker bellowed. "Mischlinger! This is your last chance to keep your miserable job!"

Mischlinger flushed and scanned the street. A milk wagon. A horse. "I will bring her to you, the English spy, before the day is out. I have my..."

"Your famous contacts? We are the only contacts who matter, old man."

"Here. The *Punschkrapfen*." He handed the pastry box to Henker. "And I have another present for you. Don't you need an all-purpose criminal? Someone no one will vouch for? What about a Hungarian, a thief who's been stealing from me, and from," he waved a hand in a vague semi-circle, "everyone around here."

"The one who was here yesterday? Dark hair? Bulgy frog eyes? Doesn't speak German?"

"You could make her into something."

"Give us the Hungarian, yes, a good idea, but you must deliver the Englishwoman. We can hold off the big shots from giving you the boot for another day. But only one. And we take the credit, or the deal is off. By tomorrow, you understand? We don't have much time. A possible spy like her will not be noticed in the middle of what's going to happen to Vienna in two days."

I shifted. Crouching like that made my legs ache.

"Let me bring the Hungarian out to you."

"We can't wait. Bring them both in, Mr. Hotel. It shouldn't take you very long. They can't be of interest to you. They're not little girls with no tits."

They got in their car and left, and Mischlinger held up his

hand to wave. As soon as they were out of sight, he dropped the smile. He opened the door to the lobby and disappeared. I was freezing. I could hear him call sweetly for Margarete. I plastered myself against the building, still hidden behind the stiff branches. *Where had Margarete and Kaspar gone?* Mischlinger ran back out. The milkman emerged from a side lane, two buildings away.

"Have you seen the lady of this house?" He pointed to our old building.

"Are you making a milkman joke?"

It's Viktor, our milkman! Mischlinger's-a-shithouse-rat, Viktor! I wanted to run out and hug him. *Viktor, still grinning and delivering milk along the Schottenring. Our housekeeper's dreamboat.*

"You idiot! No!"

"Guess this idiot didn't see her then." He snapped the reins, and the horse moved.

"Wait, wait, I'm sorry. She's missing and there are so many hooligans on the street."

"Look, old cock, I saw them get into a Mercedes."

They have left without me. And I'm wearing these ridiculous clothes.

"Them? Who is them?"

"Your wife and the fancy boy with the gold teeth. And the Mercedes."

"Did you see which way they went?"

"Along the Schottenring. That way. But I have an idea where they were really going. If you could take this milk off my hands..."

"Yes, yes." Banknotes exchanged for a wire crate of milk bottles, each with a frozen cap of milk above the rim.

"They were both yelling '*Yodeli-oh-oh-ohh.*' And laughing."

Mischlinger got in his Daimler and roared away. The milk wagon headed in the same direction, but in no hurry. I wondered if I should chase after it. Ride along the streets, help him deliver the milk. And the jokes. *What am I going to do?*

I emerged from behind the thick branches and stepped out onto the sidewalk just as Kaspar drove up. When he saw me, he guffawed. "How Bavarian! Never mind. The Swiss don't care about fashion. Get in the back with Margarete."

He hurried into the drive shed. Within a minute he had brought out two bicycles, an old one and a new one, and secured them to a rack on the rear of the car. He hopped back in and grinned at us over the front seat, his gold teeth glinting.

"So, do you recognize your old Stern? I oiled the chain, and it's operational. The new one on top camouflages your old clunker. Anyway, they're just for show. You have to look like you're crazy sports fanatics." He patted his chauffeur's hat. "And I have to look like a chauffeur." He turned on the engine.

I turned to Margarete. "How did you end up here with Mischlinger?"

"He caught me in the apartment a couple of years ago. I was helping Kaspar. The old piece of shit came home early and grabbed me. Kaspar had been stealing stuff from here for a while, and he knew the way out the back entrance, from before, when we first met you and your sister. I let myself get caught because Kaspar had a lot of jewellery on him, and the profits were going to be great. But then Mischlinger had me. I'd known him from before—I'm not sure if you remember. I had to do what he said, or he'd call the police."

"That I understand."

"Kaspar said the old bugger would die soon, and that I should stay. It was better than fucking who knows who every day." Margarete lit another cigarette and wound down the window. Kaspar pulled a cork out of a bottle with his teeth. He took a slug, and backed the car out of the driveway.

"I'm the one who ratted about the little girls he dragged into his car. They don't care, but they use what they know to make him do stuff. They don't really care about him being a Jew, either, but it's been a good excuse to get what he owns."

Margarete snorted. "He worked like a dog last night, wrapping things up, tying towels over his precious paintings. They've got him over something stupid. Some English aristocrat walked out without paying her bill at his hotel. Well, it used to be his. The Hotel Vienna?"

"I've heard of it, sure." *Very recently, too.*

"They're pinning it on him because he's the night manager, right? As if it's his fault. Her passport turned out to be fake as hell. What a surprise. Vienna is full of fakes."

"Always was." *She's talking about Hedy. Margarete is so pleased with herself. She's talking so fast. What has happened to Hedy?*

"And yesterday, you wouldn't believe. I opened the door to a couple of big shots. They walked like their pants were full of shit—you know the way those government guys do. A government car running its motor outside. Frightened the crap out of me. I pretended I was the maid and spoke Hungarian to them. All I said, over and over, was '*meleg turos bukta.*'"

Kaspar looked at her in the rear-view mirror. "You said warm cheese bun?"

"I know! But they didn't know!" Margarete rocked with laughter. She turned to me. "They thought I couldn't speak German, so they spilled the beans. They were discussing which one of them would get the apartment." She lifted a lid on a hamper. "I almost forgot this when you rang the bell, Susannah. What a shock to see you! Look, schnapps and ham sandwiches."

"You thought of everything. And what a car, Kaspar!" *My whore's ability to instantly flatter.*

"Do you like my Mercedes? I know all the back roads from here to Hoek. And I know where to find every found-goods dealer along the way. The chauffeur's hat is a nice touch, no? Besides, I look good in it." He looked at himself in the rear-view mirror. "There's a buyer for the paintings on the border, and I understand that once we get you over the border, you will make a donation to the cost of travel. Oh, we looked for the

Hispano-Suiza. I was thinking we'd use it, but it was nowhere to be seen. Where did you say you left it, again?"

"Three blocks north. I locked it."

"Oh, I thought you said south. Good. Let's have a drink. To art!" He glugged a couple of swallows and then handed the schnapps bottle over the seat to me and Margarete. He draped his arm out his window. We passed the bottle all the way around, twice. I hadn't had anything to eat since yesterday morning on the train. But who knew what was next? I glugged as much as I could. I rolled down my window to clear my head. "This car is like an oven!"

Margarete and Kaspar wound down their windows. Kaspar leaned out and sang out, "*Yodeli-oh-oh-ohhh!*" Hilarious. We all yodelled over the noise of the car accelerating. What a nation the Swiss are—secretive banking and yodelling. There was so much noise in the city anyway. Everyone was yelling something.

~

63.

THEY PULLED A CURTAIN across the conductor's rest area. Coffee urn, magazines, clean pairs of socks, each in a paper band. An iron, a clothes brush. A man with his trousers around his ankles. I braced my hand against the bench and knelt.

~

64.

THE MERCEDES FLOATED ALONG the roads. There were more cars heading towards Vienna than away from it. The old roads climbed and curved through one sleepy town after another—Traun, Weiss, Ebensee, someplace outside of Innsbruck. The weather was getting milder. Ischgl. Gravel flew from the wheels, and then a gate was lifted, a little money donated, and we were travelling at high speeds along a well-kept road, up and around hills, through a tunnel. Kaspar turned off the road, throwing me against Margarete, and Margarete against the door. Then he jumped out and stood pissing, his back to us.

Margarete yelled out the window. "I'm not dropping my bum into this snowbank."

Kaspar hopped back in and said, "Next stop, a winter picnic in Fiss." He put the car in gear and we roared off.

The schnapps kept us all going—talking, laughing. What is better than schnapps, and a cold ham sandwich with good mustard? Stories from hell—beatings, men with purple dicks—and stories about money: how Kaspar got the old hens to talk about their homes, helped carry things in for them. The old cocks, too. Then he went back when they were out. He only stole things that would fit in the Mercedes, but that was a lot; it was a big car, with a big trunk.

"And the driver has a big something too."

I revelled in the vulgarity. A third of my life had been this kind of talk, and I was not sure how much more life I would have. They were drunk, and, at this point, so was I. Hedy was in trouble with the law, Mischlinger was crafty, and the Swiss border was hours away. Anything could go wrong.

Another bottle of schnapps. The soft *fohn* was melting the snow as we sat with the car doors open. Margarete and Kaspar wrestled in the front seat. The wrestling slowed down, but didn't stop. It turned gentle. Margarete put his hat on and climbed into the back seat. I got out and let Kaspar in. From the front seat, I could see that the road was bare and dry, and that there were spring flowers, snowdrops, there by the side of the road where we had stopped. A dead bird. Death is vulgar. Nature is elegant and vulgar.

What is the difference between an icebox and a woman? One doesn't fart when you take the meat out. Oh, terrible, and wonderful. I ignored the business in the back seat and waited with the car door open, my eyes closed, my pant legs rolled up to the Alpine sun. *If only I had a newspaper.* I looked in the glove box and saw the gun.

~

65.

T HE SLEEVE ON MY JACKET was torn away from the shoulder. I was lying on my stomach. The second conductor, unable to perform, grabbed my left breast and turned me over. I was amazed at the pain. Something, a muscle, was torn. He slapped me. It was black and then there were stars.

The first conductor laughed. "Maybe you need something smaller. Look, a little Jewess. Maybe you won't fall out of this one."

Ruth had stuck her head around the curtain. Then the rest of the curtain was wrenched open. A fireman entered the room, over six feet tall and half that wide, his face blackened with soot. Goggles on his head, white skin around his eyes. His huge hands were dark with soot, but his left hand sported a topaz ring on the little finger. *Dark, brilliant.* He brushed his hands on his denim uniform. "My turn, boys."

I grabbed the note from Susannah from the floor and pulled up my brassiere.

The fireman said, "You pussies get back to work, or I'll fuel up this train with your guts. You won't be the first pieces of garbage I've shoved in the fire box. Get."

The one with the moustache tried to snatch his hat from the floor as he left, but it was kicked out of reach. A blackened hand raised to belt him all the way back to Vienna made him scamper to join the other two, long gone. The fireman turned to me. "Don't worry. Get yourself decent. *Heile, heile.*"

He held Ruth's hand, and I followed them, past our compartment to stop at the next one. He knocked gently. Ruth darted in and back out within a minute with a tiny paper packet. He beamed, more spaces than teeth, and left, thumping on any wall or door he chose.

Back in our compartment, John was still asleep. Ruth lay down. She was wearing my gloves.

"I'm tired, really tired, Our Mum Hedy. George told me to call you that, no matter what, and to look after you. And to get Fraulein Lowin in case of an emergency." She put her hat ribbon and her thumb in her mouth and went to sleep. I opened my door to a corridor full of cigarette smoke. Fraulein Lowin, one hand in the air behind her, gazed in my direction. She nodded. Her tucked-in smile. Neither of us said a word.

I sat down. *Josef Singer*, it said on the cover of the packet. *The sharpest and the best.* Inside, a needle with thread wound around it many times. I floated the thread out and wet the thread on my tongue. The thread was bloody, but I knotted it and mended my jacket. We were almost at the border.

~

66.

THE MERCEDES WAS THE ONLY CAR on the road, and it easily climbed the rising hills. It was so warm that we rolled the windows down. When we reached the Hotel Alpenstern, Kaspar left us in the car on the other side of a rise in the road, out of sight, while he made arrangements to take a few things across the border for a friend. While we waited, Margarete and I passed a bottle of *palinka* back and forth until it was finished. The temperature was dropping. This was not at all like the ski hotel vacations I had taken with Alfonso in the Italian Alps.

It was dark when a happy Kaspar got back into the car. "The border sneaks up on you fast here. Margarete, come and sit up front with me." As he drove, he rested his arm on the back of the seat to fondle her ear. "Get the vignette out of the glove box, Margarete. No, the other one. That one looks fake. I don't want to pay a fine."

"Aren't they all fake?"

"Yes, but that one looks fake."

She found a better one and stuck it against the window. I turned around to look out the rear window, to get a final view of the sinking sun, the dark hills. Then, rising over the top of the hill below us, the headlamps of a car. For one long second, everything I was went still.

"Kaspar! Down there! It's the Daimler. Mischlinger is following us!"

Margarete wound down her window and stuck her head out. "Kaspar! It's him!"

Kaspar grabbed the wheel with both hands and swung off the road onto a wide dirt lane. "Hang on." He turned off the headlamps and floored the gas pedal. Margarete and I were thrown about as we rumbled over the deep ruts in the back road. "Don't worry!" Kaspar laughed. "I did this before when some crook didn't count his money when he should have." He doubled back, then turned up a steep side road, and then we were alone on the main road again.

Relief was short-lived. From the deep valley below us, the headlamps of the Daimler rose steadily upwards.

"Kaspar, he's going to catch us!" Margarete was shrieking. "What are we going to do?"

"Waltz," said Kaspar. He stopped the car, the motor idling. "Get out. Get your things." We leapt out into the meadow grass, wet with evening dew and icy cold. Kaspar pulled the bicycles off the hitch. "I wasn't going to get much for the paintings anyway. Susannah, can you ride?"

"Of course, don't you remember?"

"Yes. You crashed all the time." He inhaled deeply and started looking around on the ground.

I shoved the straps of my small bag over the handlebars. Kaspar picked up two rocks and placed one on the brake pedal and the larger one on the gas pedal. The Mercedes very slowly, in widening arcs, began to roll, two beams of light reaching into the high darkness, swooping over the meadow. Waltzing. Within seconds, the sound of the Daimler's engine accelerating on the road below.

~

67.

"WILL WE LIVE?" Ruth was holding my hand. There had been no trouble getting on the ferry.

"Yes, I know some people who are very high up."

"Everyone is very high up if you are on your knees."

I had no reply.

"I'm sorry about your ring."

"That's what rings are for, Ruthie."

"I could have stuck it up my tush. My papa said that's where I was to put something, if it got dangerous, but I never got a chance to take anything from our house when they came to get him." She scratched her stomach. "They tried to make me tell them where he was, but Diederich saved me. I didn't know where Papa was, anyway."

Stars hung over the North Sea, which was relatively calm. Ruthie and John wanted to be outside, so we leaned against the railing and watched for the harbour lights of Harwich. The children let me take their hands. After a while, John took a step back onto the deck and bowed. In an astoundingly loud voice, he sang, "*You'll find me at Maxim's where I feel quite at home.*"

He knew the whole song. The hand gestures. We clapped for him. Ruthie demonstrated what she said was the Charleston. John joined her until he hurt his knee trying to cross-kick. Ruthie laughed at him. "How in the world can you kick yourself?"

"It's a skill," he said, and launched into "*Mein Schtetele*

Belz." Another passenger asked us to please stop singing German songs.

"Never again, sir! You can call me John." What a great smile this clumsy little one had. He flung out his hand. "This is Our Mum Hedy."

Be safe, Susannah. I looked up at the moon and willed my sister to be safe. *And you too, George. O my love.*

When the ferry docked, a woman in a terrible hat and a trench coat—tied, not belted—called out to us, and we got into a waiting Land Rover. The children settled on quilts on the metal benches, and we were off.

"How was George when you left him?" she asked.

"I think he's well." I knew instantly that she was in love with George, and that she knew that I knew.

"The journey was a piece of cake, after all, like George said?"

From the back seat, Ruth said, "Don't ask."

"You don't mind coming along, do you, Hedy?"

Americans really shouldn't try to wear British clothes. Or drive British cars. After a few near misses, she asked me if I could please take the wheel. "You have already done so much, but it's this wrong side of the road thing. I'm afraid I go where I shouldn't."

"That's obvious, Betty." It was satisfying to say that, cheerfully, as if I were the best pal in the world. "Are you taking John and Ruth to America yourself?"

"Yes, I'm going with Ruth and Izzy. It's all arranged."

"Good." *George Andrew belongs to me.*

"Look. Our Mum Hedy." John leaned his head as far as he could into the front seat. He flapped a small hand, palm up, to help with his explanation. "George said my name was John. He changed it. Special ceremony. Girls not allowed."

Betty started in on why Izzy was a perfectly good name, and I finally told her to leave him alone, that it had been not entirely a piece of cake, getting the children out.

"Okay, Izzy-John." Betty twisted around to smile at him. "I'll cut you some slack."

I pulled the car over to the side of the road and wrenched the brake. I thought about pushing her out of the car. I looked at her until she said, "Fine. John."

I had never driven so far, on a strange road, and at night, but I was glad to do it. I needed to not think about what had happened to me. I hurt everywhere. I was exhausted. I concentrated on the road.

I thought about Susannah. She wasn't stupid. She could think on her feet. George obviously belonged to a good network of whatever-they-were. But Susannah was without papers, and she was in Austria. Hitler was in Austria. And the last time I saw him, so was George. *Had he slept with this one? Is she trying to look like him, like a journalist in that trench coat?*

"How are you feeling, Hedy?"

Ingénues ask questions like that. I didn't know how I felt, and if I did, I would never tell anyone like her. I wanted to get home, so Susannah could call me. I had to get my arms around my dog, so I could figure out what I felt. I had driven around Twin Oaks pasture roads, but I didn't have a licence and these roads weren't lit. I was tired, and there were many miles ahead of driving with this Betty person. I asked her if she would mind if we didn't talk for a while. I wanted to hit her. The children were both snoring in the back, and I was going to have to share the front seat all the way to Southampton with a smug amateur.

I don't have my sister. I don't have George. I don't have my mother's ring. Four days ago, I had been a respected, long-time resident of Claridge's Hotel. A small, successful business was mine. A safe life. And once again, I had tried and failed to look after my sister. Once again, I was an abandoned Jewess, who could be used at will for sex. I pressed down on the accelerator.

There were tickets waiting for Ruth and John. And, after a

while, for Betty. A couple of female officials, Taylor and Roach, were waiting for them on the quay. They shook our hands, looked at all our papers, and had a word with the purser, who went away stiffly and came back all smiles. He waved them towards the gangplank. I made a note of the ship: the *Loudolph*. I bent down and hugged Ruthie and then John. My legs were trembling from exhaustion.

"Be safe!" I called out to them as they walked up the gangplank, just as my left and right forearms were grabbed.

John stopped. "Ruthie, look, they are arresting Our Mum Hedy!"

Ruth looked back and froze. John bellowed, "Take your hands off Our Mum Hedy, Taylor and Roach!" He bolted back down the ramp towards me. Ruth ran after him. Betty reappeared. She collared Ruth but John wriggled free and kicked her, yelling over his shoulder, "Let Our Mum Hedy go!"

Ruth joined in. "*Schiessekopfe*! Get your hands off her!" Ruth and John took turns kicking their heels at Betty, who hung onto them while they hung onto the railing.

Taylor and Roach let go, but stepped behind me like chorines.

"Wave, Ma'am," Roach said, "or they may not leave on the *Loudolph* tonight."

I smiled and waved, blowing kisses. *Kazeet choke alohma*, I thought, I kiss your hands, as Margarete once said to my sister. *Be safe, Susannah. O my love, George.* Be alive, be safe. I waved until I could see nothing but the huge bulk of the ship and its lights moving beyond the harbour and into the open sea.

"You can stop waving now, Ma'am."

"Right, then. What *are*," I continued, in my best upper-class intonation, "you doing? I have told you who I am, and you have seen my passport. Why are you holding onto me? If it has anything to do with that young lady with those children, I can tell you that she is reliable." And on her way, away from here, from me, from George. *George.*

"She has been so far."

"Whatever is going on?"

"Ma'am, you have to come with us."

"I would be happy to, once I know who you are, and I have contacted Lord Coleson."

"We serve His Majesty, and his government, Madam. As I mentioned earlier, I am Special Officer Taylor. This is Special Officer Roach. You will come to no harm, and it won't take long. We need to talk to you. Here, I'll take that bag."

"Kindly do not. My passport is perfectly in order. Well, one of them is. The one you have. This one I have was a bit of a last-minute botch, to get those children out, which I think you know something about, given how solicitous you were to that Betty person. Now, if you don't mind, I need to catch the next train back to London. Someone is waiting for me."

"Who would that be, Ma'am?" Special Officer Roach was tall, wore a tie with her uniform, and had a very kindly, rumbling sort of voice. Kindness always does me in. My face felt hot.

"My dog. She has been waiting for me for days. She is being cared for by our maid, but even Claridge's maids can't do that forever."

"Claridge's, is it? And what kind of dog is it?" Her voice was gentle.

"A border collie." My eyes were stinging.

"Oh, now those are the best." She offered her handkerchief. "Have you been to the sheep trials in Berkshire?"

"I have!" Tears were running freely down my face. We had been walking steadily, up two flights of swaying dockside stairs, and now we were outside.

"Here's the car, Ma'am."

"Please." I couldn't control my tears. But I could control what I said, and how I said it. "I simply want to go home. To my dog."

"Ma'am. We understand. Truly. But there's a fear, you see, that Nazi sympathizers will slip into England, or try to, given what's happening over there. You understand. You qualify for the net the government is casting. You are patently not Mrs. Andrew. The passport left in the hotel in Vienna was, I'm sorry to say, judged to be a forgery. You see how you might seem suspicious. On the other hand, you might simply be a friendly enemy alien. They'll sort it out, and there'll be no mistreatment, I assure you."

"I have lived in London, in Claridge's Hotel, for over sixteen years. I have a little millinery shop. I pay taxes. I have a border collie! Kindly allow me to leave."

"If you don't mind, Ma'am, either get in the car now, on your own steam, instanter, or we will have to place the cuffs on you."

I got in the back seat, and the two women got in the front. I was crying. I couldn't stop.

"'Instanter.' What public school did you go to, Anne?"

"I didn't. Comfortable back there?"

On the other side of the back seat, handcuffed to the door, stiff with fury, sat another passenger. He raised his chin. He had stumps for teeth and his breath reeked. "In Germany, we are not forced to sit with wailing Jewish whores!"

"Shut up, Fritz."

"That is not my name!"

"It will do until we find out what it really is."

"Once the Fuhrer takes charge of this place, England will be better for it. He'll rid you of these Jews. They control all the banking. Who do you think caused the Depression? The Jews! Once Hitler..."

"Oh, do shut up."

"Women like you two *lesben* will not be..." And that was as far as he got before Special Officer Roach shoved a fist in the man's neck and held it there. The handcuffed man gagged, and his arm flew up.

"So we're all quiet now. Good." Special Officer Roach wiped her fist on the back of her seat before turning around. The car continued to roll along in the night.

"Thank you, Nicky. I do think we need a little air in this car."

"You're welcome, Anne." They rolled down their windows in unison.

Enough. This was simply too much. To have done all this, to have gone through all this. My breasts were bruised. My mouth hurt. Everything hurt. Fraulein Lowin in Susannah's coat. My mother's ring. What will they do to Diederich? *Susannah. Be safe. George. O my love.*

"If you please, Special Officers Taylor and Roach—Anne, and Nicky, is it? You do seem to be heading north, not to London. My dog will be so upset." And then from somewhere within me, all my anger. "And I do not think that we British women should have to listen to such nonsense from such a man!"

The two women in the front turned to each other, and smiled. They turned back to the view in front of them for a few moments, and then turned to each other again. Nodded.

"You're right, Ma'am. Anne, don't you think we need to stop for a breath of fresh air?"

"I think we do, Nicky, I think we do."

They pulled the car over and got out. Anne opened the door for me. I stood beside them as they lit cigarettes. They offered one to me, and I took it. There was a furious, indistinct noise from the back seat of the car.

"Are all those Nazis such pricks, Nicky? I could kick him."

I joined in. "I could kick him." Nothing stood between the world and my anger.

Special Officers Roach and Taylor turned to each other. Nodded. They could take this act on the stage. "I'm sure, Madam, that we wouldn't notice. Look at the moon, Anne, still out in the sky."

"Almost morning, Nicky." They turned their backs to look at the moon. I understood. I walked over to the other side of the car, and jerked the door open, dragging the man attached to it by his arm half out of the car. He yelped. I kicked him, for me, hard, and again, for Susannah, for Diederich, and once more for everything. Maybe more than once more. I was shaking and out of breath when I walked back to Special Officers Taylor and Roach.

They were still companionably smoking and looking at the moon. I felt paper thin, but alive. *Alive*. I wiped the toes of my shoes on the wet grass. "Would you notice if I went home to my dog then?"

"Not sure we would, Ma'am. You might simply get lost in the dark while we try to restrain Fritz back there, who is obviously trying to escape. You might be frightened and confused. We know where you live in London. Shall we bring your bag, or will you be taking it with you, in your confusion?"

The moon was now on the right, rising higher, getting paler. So was the sky, brightening along the rim of the horizon. I walked along the road like a vagabond, my bag slung over my shoulder. It was so nice to see a milestone. I did like this England. Small birds singing. The sun rising. No wonder in a place where it rained so often that there would be so many gates, their slats radiating out from the centre. The sun was everywhere in England, just not always above.

I arrived back in London, looking very much the worse for wear. I had hitchhiked a ride with a lumber dealer, who had stacks of neatly piled and tied boards in the back of the truck.

"London's windows are going to need protection, Miss," was the driver's prescient explanation. He pulled up with a great squeaking of brakes to Brook Street.

I climbed down, and walked to the front desk. I asked if the porter would mind opening up the apartment as I seemed to have forgotten my keys. He didn't mind at all, and of course said nothing to suggest that he had noticed how dishevelled I looked. There was a message that Mist had gone to stay with Mr. Stephens. As soon as I was let into my apartment, I rang Archie, and ran a bath.

I was drying my hair when I heard Mist whimpering in the lobby. She knew I was home. I opened the door, and could hear her hurrying up the stairs, all business, all urgent business. I knelt down and was greeted with small barks of anguish and joy. She was whimpering, shaking, and licking my hands and my face. When I moved, she moved, always at my side.

My own doctor saw me, and I was relieved. I was sore, a fading yellow star of a bruise on my breast but no other serious physical harm done. I slept, and bathed, and repeated in my mind, over and over again: *Susannah, be alive, be safe. George, be alive, be safe. O my love.*

Four months later, I came downstairs to find Special Officers Roach and Taylor waiting in the lobby, sitting very erect, caps in hand. They had dressed up for the occasion, it would seem. They stood when I went to greet them, and then escorted me calmly out to their car. Archie followed us in the car with Mist, all the way to the camp.

I hugged Mist until Archie cleared his throat and handed me my bag. Roach and Taylor nodded to Archie and lead me through the camp gates. I watched a couple of young women in uniform sort through the small suitcase with the initials, HH. The dog whimpered, and I heard her bark over the sound of Archie driving away.

68.

IT WAS A FORMER HOLIDAY CAMP, with silly sayings over the toilet: 'We aim to please. You aim, too, please.' The beds were changed once a week, the air was fresh, and there were only three others waiting to find out if they were to be interned, or merely watched closely: a couple of Hungarians, mother and daughter, who spoke no English. No one, of course, could speak Hungarian. This didn't matter as they had each other to argue with. They always made up, kisses and hugs. *Kazeet choke alohma.* But I didn't say it aloud.

There was a little German woman, Ursula, who never raised her eyes from the ground. Her mouth was pulled to one side, a grimace of embarrassment. She wore trousers and smoked. I didn't smoke, but cigarettes were part of our rations, so I gave her my cigarettes. "*Danke,*" was all she said.

There were more guards than prisoners. The guards were all local girls, fresh-faced and new to lipstick. They all tried to take themselves seriously, but they ended up laughing and joking with each other, the happy intimacy of women confiding their secrets and those of everyone they knew. They stopped calling me Miss Edelstein. It was easier to call me Hedy. No one was paying any attention to those who might yet be in charge of Enemy Aliens, Female. It wasn't clear if this camp would be designated for Enemy Aliens, Male, after all.

In a letter carefully addressed to Archie but meant for my eyes,

Harold said he was going to remain in Bermuda "as someone has to keep an eye on the former king." Archie said, looking away, "Kidneys are shot. He can't travel." It was his first and only betrayal of Harold's confidence. Harold had been in touch with old chums in government, who agreed to allow Archie's visits and to speed up the resolution of my file.

While I waited, I willed Susannah to be alive, to be safe. I willed George to be alive, to be safe. *O my love.* I went through the motions of washing my face, combing my hair, making sure my stocking seams were straight. I joined in on the calisthenics hour led by two freckled young guards, and I folded sheets. But these were my only thoughts: *Susannah be alive, be safe, George, be alive, be safe. O my love.* I was afraid to think anything else. I couldn't talk any more than the others.

Archie once again arrived with Mist, this time bringing with him a pamphlet on the upcoming sheep dog trials. He had slit open the thick paper and slipped inside, via the incision, a tissue-thin telegram:

"I AM SAFE STOP FLEW INTO SWITZERLAND STOP HORSIE."

I answered to every name on the roll call, not just Miss Edelstein. I was giddy and hugged my guards, who hugged me back. Archie had also brought a lantern full of flowers, "From Pauline," he said. The camp guards decided they had to do this right. They hadn't had anything to report since they got there. Nothing interesting. They were going to have to write up a report, so they removed the flowers, one by one, and made a list of what they were, in case their names were code. They thought for a while about what other investigations they could conduct, and finally one ran a hose into the lantern for a full minute until she was satisfied. She put the flowers back in the lantern, not really the worse for wear. "There you go. It's a cute wee lantern, so it is."

Rolled inside the handle was another telegram:

"I'M SAFE STOP SEE YOU SOON MY LOVE STOP GEORGE."

When I was released, Archie and Pauline drove up in the car with Mist in the back seat, and took us back to London. I closed up From Esther, for the duration. Kay had already left to take pilot training at Marshall's in Cambridge. Harold had helped her with a recommendation. They were going to need women to ferry planes between factories. This war and these maidens were going to be very different than the last time.

Harold wrote a letter; it was a little maudlin. The Claridge's apartment would be mine beyond his passing, all taken care of by his solicitors. I was welcome to come and join him if I wished, but if I didn't, he would always treasure the gift I had handed him. I wrote back, of course, but that sly joke was the last note to me before he died.

Archie came to tell me the news. For a moment, his calm face crumpled. For a moment. He said he was going to sign up again. At his age. He said he was confident of his return, as Harold's piece of stained glass from the Reims cathedral had been delivered to him by diplomatic courier. We hugged, for the first and last time.

69.

ONE EARLY WINTER NIGHT, I had come home from my volunteer turn at the Red Cross, and it was already dark enough to turn on the lamps, light the fire, and tune the wireless to the BBC. I ordered dinner up from the hotel's restaurant, and I had no sooner hung up than there was a telephone call from the front desk saying that a visitor was on the way up. I didn't want to miss any of the broadcast so I rang off quickly, as I presumed it was Kay again. She had taken to dropping in when she was on a break from her training. I loved hearing her explain how to fly a Tiger Moth. George hadn't arrived in England yet, but it would be any day. Or night.

When I heard the knock, I stayed where I was on the sofa and called out, "Come in! And hush, the news is on." There was a BBC reporter speaking from Prague about refugees in the train stations and de-mobbed soldiers going home after the German invasion.

For a full eight and a half minutes, an amazing length of time, I continued to listen to the broadcast as my visitor came in and sat down. Only when the announcer signed off did I turn to look. For another long three seconds.

Susannah tipped her head to one side and looked back at me. Layers and shards slid free. I took a deep breath inside an embrace, in Susannah's arms.

"Oh, Hedy! You smell so good!"

"Mimosa-scented soap, sent to me by some Italian. Oh, you're alive, and safe!"

"Of course I am." Susannah pulled away. "Your awful British weather has turned my hair into frizz."

Susannah stood up to look at her hair in the mirror over the mantel. I stood and looked in the mirror at Susannah's hair, and at Susannah, and at the two of us reflected in the mirror. I kept my arm around her. It was like going from two dimensions to three.

"I can send for a hairdresser to come up." *I will give you everything I have, only stay with me a little longer.*

"No, I only want your company, thanks."

My company. I hid my smile by looking down at Susannah's luggage. "You still have that little suitcase. SH." *I must have absorbed Harold's sangfroid. Look how calmly I am talking to her.*

"Yes. I told Alfonso the initials meant 'Sweet Horsie.'"

"If you would like to wash your hair, I know a trick to make your curls behave. Claudette Colbert's method, supposedly. A Hungarian with curls like yours showed me." *Don't go away just yet. Stay.*

"Where?"

"In a holiday camp."

I washed Susannah's hair for her in the large white marble sink in the bathroom. I had given her a blue kimono, with a pattern of pointy white bamboo leaves, flat silk, not shiny.

"Now, quickly, bend over and let your wet hair fall straight down." I combed Susannah's hair as she stood, bent like a stork, and then, like that, pulled our mother's old striped scarf taut against the top and sides of her head.

"You can stand up now, Horsie. Come and dry your hair by the fire and tell me what happened. No, leave it in the scarf. Your hair will be perfect." I pulled the two armchairs closer to the fire, closer to each other.

"What happened? When do you mean, Hedy?"

"What happened in Vienna, how you arrived in Switzerland. The whole story."

"I will, but you go first, Hedy. First tell me how you got out."

So I did.

"Oh, Hedy. I am so sorry." She hugged me again. "Wait. Shit. My coat. I wonder who's wearing it now? Oh, Hairbrush, you got out. You rescued those children."

"I can't talk about that, according to George."

"He should have stayed with you."

"It might not have made any difference. Mama's ring saved me—and a little girl who didn't like me at first any more than I liked her."

"The thought of Fraulein Lowin and the fireman being on the same side." Susannah got up and then sank into a chair. "Speaking of which, there's something I have to tell you without delay. I have been invited to join the First Aid Nursing Yeomanry. Tomorrow."

"What? Are you going to shoot arrows of burning gold at the enemy?"

"Not real ones. Supposedly we are to be ambulance drivers. I think we've been recruited by Special Operations."

"A spy? You can't even drive."

"I can learn. But I think it's a cover. I think I'm going to listen to Germans. Radio messages. And to the Italians, once they take up arms. Hedy, I watched their reactions to how I answered their questions. Brothel skills are almost universally applicable. No one can know what I'm telling you."

"What else have I done, most of my life, but keep secrets? Where will you be sent?"

She shrugged.

"You aren't going to stay in England."

"I don't know. But if there's a warmer place than this…"

I looked at her. "You have to let me know when you're leaving. You have to see me before you go. You have to let…"

"I will tell you, I promise. Hedy, I know I'm going to be good at this. Like you, what else have I done, most of my life, but lie and keep secrets? I imagine the training will be several months. I won't be able to talk about it."

I hadn't said "lie." Just "keep secrets." But then I'm not very good at lying.

It struck me that George didn't talk about his work, either. The two people I loved the most. Both of them, spies, probably. More or less. Almost certainly. Sometimes I felt like the straight man who hadn't been told he was in a comedy.

"Hedy, I'm exhausted. Can I tell you about my escape tomorrow or the next day? I have had to tell so many people today about how I got out, and it wears me out. And it brings back what they did to my Alfonso. To my Marinella."

She climbed into bed with me, and we slept the sleep of lions.

The next morning, an urgent call came from the supposed First Aid people, and she had to leave. It turned out that we didn't have much time at all. She left for training. Then four weeks later, to the day, she stayed with me, an overnight pass, and said she was ready to tell her story: all of it, what had happened right up until that last moment in Austria. After the Claridge's restaurant waiter had come for the supper cart, I made a pot of proper Viennese coffee, poured a brandy, and sat in the chair opposite her by the fire. She tossed back her coffee and then the brandy.

"Let's go outside and walk, Hedy."

"But it's so dark now!"

"Even better for what I have to tell you." So we put on our coats, hats, and gloves, and slipped down the curving staircase to walk out into one of London's soft winter evenings. She put her arm in mine, but she talked to the air in front of her. Her story, what she had to do. What she had done.

"I was pedalling as fast as I could on your old Stern. Kaspar had put a new battery in the front light, but the bulb was old and it went out. There was a moon over on my left but I could only glimpse it now and then. I really couldn't see anything but the road right in front of me. There were so many small hills, and I wasn't sure how far it was to the border. My little suitcase was secure, but the toes of Mischlinger's tennis shoes kept catching on the pavement. When I got to the top of the last hill, I don't know how it happened. I wobbled onto the gravel shoulder and was thrown into the ditch. It was so cold! I had trouble catching my breath.

"I could see Kaspar pedalling up the hill towards me. He was like a machine, lurching from side to the side, the way he always did, remember? The moon had risen above the treeline by then, really bright. Margarete was on the seat behind him."

Susannah was quiet for a moment, walking on Brook Street with me, but apparently transported into a very real and recent past.

"Those gold teeth in that terrified face. Margarete wearing the chauffeur's hat. The wheels of their bicycle flashed right by my head where I lay in the grass. The red light on their back fender disappeared over the hill. I could hear Margarete shouting, 'Open the gate! Open the gate!' I scrambled to get up. I was going to run down after them, so I could get in too, but the grass was slippery, and I fell."

She looked at me, as if gauging my response. "I fell twice, and just as I was scrambling up through the grass, I saw that old Daimler heading up the hill towards me. I stayed down. Mischlinger didn't see me.

"That old car of his mounted the hill and headed right towards the border gate. Margarete and Kaspar were on the flat approach to the gate, almost there. Mischlinger was leaning on the horn, flashing his lights, bellowing out the window. 'Stop them! Thieves! Thieves! Stop them!'

"I could make out a couple of Swiss border guards swinging lanterns at the barrier. Margarete was screaming. 'Open the gate!' *Screaming*. And Kaspar was shouting. 'It's Kaspar! It's me! Kaspar!'

"They flung up the bar at the last moment, and the bicycle whizzed through just before the bar clanked down again. I would have driven the car right through the gate, but not Mischlinger. He loved that old car. They wouldn't raise the bar for him. He shouted at them. Flung his arms around. I could tell he was threatening them. I stayed in the shadows. I was tempted to sneak over the border while he was making his big fuss, but there were cement walls on both sides of the gate, and thorny bushes in front of the walls. The Swiss think of everything. By the time I got close enough to hear, it was hilarious."

"You think the most awful things are funny, Susannah."

"They are, and it was! The guards were so polite. They said they couldn't let him in if he didn't have a vignette. He offered them money, and they said they couldn't take his money.

"'All you have to do, sir,' the guard said, 'is show us a vignette. Or you could go back to the nearest police station, about five kilometers—not far, sir—and they will issue you a permit. Then we could let you in. Or you could wait until the vignette office opens in a couple of hours. Then we could...'

"Mischlinger got back into his car and just sat there. Then he jerked the car around and began to drive it up the hill, going slow, babying it. I knew what I had to do."

"Susannah, what we have to do is go back to the hotel. It's getting too cold out here on these streets. I want my fire."

We took the elevator, and, once inside the apartment, I stirred the embers and poked a twist of *The Evening Standard*, encouraging it to flare. I used the tongs to put a fresh log on the grate and settled into a chair.

"Now, come and sit beside me on the sofa, Hairbrush."

I did. She took my hand.

"When the car was nearly beside me, I stepped into the road so he could see me. I waved. He stopped and wound down his window. He asked if I wanted a ride. That solicitous voice, remember?

"I said, 'Lovely.' I walked around to the passenger side and got in. It was so cold. I tucked my feet up on the seat. We hadn't gone very far when he asked me my name. I told him 'Esther.' He asked me where I was going and I said, 'With you.' He looked over and smiled, and went to pat my leg.

"And then he recognized his shoes. He looked up at me. I was holding his gun. I shot him in the head with his own gun." Susannah looked into the fire. "Twice, to be sure. It was terrible and perfect. Disgusting. There's a lot of blood in the head."

70.

I MIGHT HAVE SAID, out loud, "Thank you." If I didn't, Susannah heard me anyway. We sat there, it seemed, for a long time, floating in dark shared memory, side by side on a grey silk sofa in Claridge's Hotel.

"The car rolled slowly into the ditch..."

"He's dead."

"Yes."

Mischlinger is dead. He can never do any harm to any girl, ever again. We looked at the fire. I was calm. Relief flowed out, surrounding me. *Mischlinger is dead.* It felt as if I were being launched, set afloat. "But finish the story. How did you get into Switzerland?"

Susannah stretched her arms up and looked past me. Through the window, the lights of London's streets glittered and mapped how truly dark it was outside in the city on that early winter night.

"I walked all the way back to the Mercedes. Its headlamps were still sending two beams down into the meadow below. I wiped my hands on the wet grass and then I wiped my face. The dew was so cold. The moon..." She stopped talking, and then suddenly began again. "I don't remember taking off those bloody shoes. Or the cape. I must have. I remember putting on my Perugias, black and grey snakeskin, did I mention? I sat down on the backseat with my legs out in the moonlight. I left the door open. I didn't want anyone to hear the door slam. I don't know why I thought I still had to be quiet. I walked back to the bicycle. Your old Stern, Hedy.

"The moon was high in the sky now. On my right. I got on the bicycle and rode all the way down the hill. Past the Daimler and Mischlinger in the ditch. The motor was still gnashing away—remember how he couldn't hear what we were saying when Mama sat up front with him and we were in the back seat?" She looked over at me.

"But how did you get into Switzerland?"

A look, swift, not even a second long. And in that moment, a thought, as if a cliff of ice had sheared off, and the sea was rising, propelling me forward: *she doesn't need my protection.*

"I was gripping the handbrakes so hard my hands hurt. I was going really fast by the time I hit the barrier. I was thrown, a full somersault, into Switzerland."

"That's how you flew into Switzerland." I smiled. "Your telegram said you flew into Switzerland."

"I knew it would make you smile, once you knew. Oh, Hedy you don't know how much I have missed making you smile!"

She might not need my protection, but she might need me to love her.

"I couldn't believe how far I was thrown. Once I knew what was happening, I just let myself go loose. I surrendered. I was not responsible and it was thrilling." She paused and stretched. "I was lucky. One of the border guards saw me heading towards the barrier. He was already running when I hit it and flew up in the air. He dipped down when I landed in his arms. He set me down on the ground. In Switzerland. I said, as if we were at a party, as if nothing unusual had happened, '*Buona notte!*' And he said, 'You're Italian!'"

Susannah turned to me. "I've wanted people to say that to me all my life. I couldn't believe what I said to him." She tipped her head over on one side and looked up at me. She put one hand on my knee. "I said, 'I'm Jewish.'"

I laughed, quickly, and just as quickly, stopped. I looked

at her and nodded. And then—I couldn't help it—I laughed until I sighed.

"It's not that funny, Hedy."

"It's not that true, either. But it's a wonderful story."

"That's exactly what happened."

"Fine. You will be good at your new job. Tell me about that note from Horsie when we were last in Vienna."

"What do you mean?" She was smiling, but her eyes were assessing me.

"What if I were to ask George about the note you wrote?"

"Oh, that note?" She stretched, buying time. "He'll say…"

I had my answer. *That stretching. Has she always done that?* "Never mind. He'll say something. You're here, and he will be today or tomorrow. Or soon."

And there she was, with me, wanting my company, at least for that moment. I didn't have to know everything, which was good because, with my sister, I never would.

I could ask George about the note. I imagined him blushing, confessing—or else I would get to see what he looked like when he was lying. Or I could let it lie, like Mist asleep between me and my sister on that grey silk sofa. I could just say, "*O my love.*"

I laughed again and hugged Susannah, who pulled back to give me a wary look, and then a smile and a shrug that only life in Italy can produce. She apparently didn't have to know everything, either.

Acknowledgements

With the fourth word I spoke, I demanded that my mother "Read!" She picked up *Black Beauty* and I listened to all of it. I listened to the radio, and to the "verses" my grandmothers told me, and asked me to recite to company. My grade three teacher let me write my spelling list as poetry, and when Susan Stancer, my high school English teacher, read my short story aloud to her colleagues, I began to think that writing was something I could do.

It turned out screenwriting was something I could do. Pat Watson championed me, as did the head of the National Film Board's Studio D, Kathleen Shannon, and the head of CBC television drama, Stan Colbert.

I began writing a novel after hearing a person's story of a great aunt and grandmother suddenly orphaned and taken, not to relatives, but to a brothel. That person does not want to be acknowledged, as this story, to them, is more of the imagination than of memory.

The first reader was Sheilah Crichton, whose aesthetic sensibility I trusted. If she liked it, I could go ahead. One of my last readers was the late film critic, Peter Harcourt whose failing eyesight meant he read it in thirty-six point font. I am grateful for his support for this book as I am for the support of Michael Redhill, my mentor from the Humber Creative Writing program, whose attentive and positive remarks gave me confidence. Christine Pountney showed me how the past tense, a novelty for a screen writer, could be engaging, and Martha Webb's suggestion that the two sisters speak in the first person was freeing.

The turning point for the manuscript was Amy Jo Cooper's question. Amy is an accomplished novelist and screenwriter, and currently an appellate court lawyer in Los Angeles. "Why are you withholding?" she asked. As a screenwriter, I was used to creating the lines that allowed the actors to emote. In this novel, I had a challenge: to inhabit the emotions of the sisters and let them reveal how they felt.

The responses of readers like Barb Speirs, for whom writing has to dance, or Gail Florence who needs clarity, or Nan Marie Wismer, wise in all things, or my sister, Margaret Ankiewicz who knows something about the comfort of animals, helped me stay true to the story.

Susan Feldman whose kindness and honesty have never failed anyone was an early reader. Terri Favro, who knows a thing or two about pacing, Jess Taylor, who understands something of the complexities of sexuality, and Canisia Lubrin, who has a stellar sense of all things literary, all read the manuscript. Their responses reassured me and appear on the back cover of the book.

Former literary editor Aldona Ledochowski let no error of taste or grammar miss her gaze, and thankfully knows when, exactly, linden trees bloom. Professora titular Lucia Cavalcanti de Albuquerque Williams shared her perspective from her studies of sexual exploitation of minors, and Wilma Wallis shared her familiarity with Italian culture. The director of

Galerie St. Etienne in New York, Jane Kallir, who knows the art of Vienna well, and also avers the value of giving those you love some room, was very encouraging of this work, and poet and novelist Susan Glickman gave good navigational advice.

The designer of the book's cover, Val Fullard has surprising instincts which led me to the fresh realization that this is a book with many escapes, physical and emotional. I am grateful for the legendary energy and good humour of Renée Knapp, Inanna's publicist and marketing manager. Editor and publisher Luciana Ricciutelli's good will and commitment to feminist literature are exemplary, and the singular delight in saying her name aloud should cause all to want lessons in Italian.

I also salute my old WAVAW *compañeras*, from whom I learned lived feminism, and I raise a glass to the other graduates of Emerging Writers (Duffy's Tavern campus) and to the Pivot Reading series: I am thankful for your companionship and your inspiring work.

Finally, my late husband, Jim Brown, who always supported my writing, my beautiful and astute daughter-in-law Tammi Taylor, my son Adé Hollins, who told me I should put some card tricks in the book, and my son David Brown, whose judgement on plots and people in real life, and in art, I treasure: their love keeps me moored here, writing in this world.

Photo: Daniel Williams

Hannah Brown is a prize-winning screenwriter who happily taught film and English at the college and collegiate levels. A return to writing full-time resulted in poems, short stories, blogs, and essays appearing in many North American literary magazines, and a short story "The Happiness" (*parenthetical magazine*) was nominated for the 2016 Journey prize. She lives near the lake in the Beaches neighbourhood of Toronto. *Look After Her* is Hannah's debut novel.